The Musketeer's Seamstress

Sarah D'Almeida

GOLDPORT
PRESS
MYSTERY

Goldport Press

Contents

The Impossibility of Murder; Where Aramis Questions His Sanity; A Naked Fugitive

The Chevalier Rene D'Herblay, known for some time now as the musketeer Aramis, was sure that no one could have murdered his mistress.

A tall, slim man whose long blond hair and normally elaborate attire made people underestimate his strength, Aramis stood naked in the inner doorway of her room. His numb hands gripped the wooden frame for support, because his knees had gone unaccountably lax. He looked out, unbelieving, at the huge bed that took up a quarter of the bedroom.

The bed was high and heavy and massive—a solid construction of Spanish oak that had probably come in Violette's dowry when she'd married a French duke. Upon the oak, soft draperies had been heaped, to make the bed suitable for someone of Violette's soft skin and softer habits— there was lace and velvet and a profusion of pillows of all shapes and sizes.

Aramis knew that bed better than he knew his own. He had been Violette's lover for two years and he'd spent considerably more time awake in her bed than his.

He grasped the doorway hard, for support, and blinked dumbly at the bed. Because on the bed, Violette lay -- dead. Violette who, only minutes ago had been lively, full of fire, eager for his embraces and inventive with her own.

Now she lay . . . He felt sweat start at his hairline, a cold sweat of fear and disbelief. And blinking didn't seem to change the scene his eyes showed him.

Violette could not be dead. And yet she lay on the bed, motionless, her normally pink body gone the color of cheap candle tallow, her mouth open and her eyes staring fixedly at the canopy of pink satin over her.

Between her perfect, rounded breasts that his hands and lips knew as well as his eyes did, an intrusion—an ivory handle—protruded. And around her breasts, there was blood, dripping into the lace and pillows, soaking into the satin and frills.

Aramis swallowed hard, fighting back nausea and a primal scream of grief that wanted to tear through his lips.

His mind, still in control, feverishly went over and over the reasons why this was impossible.

First, he'd left her alive when he'd gone into the small room next to her room where—out of modesty or high breeding—she kept the chaise percée used for calls of nature. Second, he'd taken no more than a moment there. He was sure of it. And he'd heard no doors close or open anywhere. Third, the door to the room was locked— as it had been locked when they first lay down together. He'd turned the large key himself, heard it click home. Fourth, they were three floors up in the royal palace, with sentinels and guards all around and thick walls encircling the whole structure. And there was only one small window in the room—too small to admit anyone—and a door to a narrow balcony well away from other walls and trees. The balcony was large enough, only, for two people to stand close together. The structure of the bed was built too low to the floor to conceal anyone beneath it.

No one could have come into the room. And Violette was not the sort to commit suicide. Or to commit it with a knife to the heart. No woman was. This Aramis—who knew many women—knew. They were more inclined to the poison that would pluck them from life while they slept. Not that he'd ever had any of his mistresses die this way. But he'd heard about it. He'd . . . read.

He struggled to stand on his own, pulling his hands away from the doorway. Violette couldn't be dead, ergo, she must be alive. And if she was alive this must all be a tasteless joke.

Trying to stand steadily, he took a deep breath and inhaled the sharp, metallic smell of blood. But Violette would be thorough in her jokes as she was in everything else. It would be real blood. Animal blood. Yes, that must be it.

He charged forward, to the bed, and put out a hand to shake her hand resting, half-closed, on the frilly coverlet near a pool of blood that seemed more abundant and darker than he'd have imagined possible. It was soaking into the fabric and probably into the mattress beneath.

"Violette," he said. This close he could see the blade of a dagger disappearing into the flesh, and the wound into which it plunged, and the blood . . . Blood was only trickling out now, but it already looked like there was more blood on her than there should be in any human being. "Violette," he said. "I am offended. This is in extremely poor taste. You must know—"

His hand touched her arm. Before he could control himself, he jumped back, his hands covering his mouth, but not in time to hold back his shocked scream. She felt . . . not exactly cold, but not as warm as living flesh should feel. Blindly, he reached forward, grasped the handle of the knife, pulled it. It came away in his hand, stained red and dripping. It had truly been buried in her flesh. And her skin felt dead.

Aramis knew dead. He'd killed men enough in duel and in combat ever since that day, when he—still known as Chevalier D'Herblay—was barely more than nineteen and a young man had caught him reading the lives of saints to the young man's sister. Well, at least that was what Aramis still told everyone he had been doing. The truth was somewhere closer to his having demonstrated to the young lady the biblical intricacies of the word know.

The young woman's brother had objected and challenged D'Herblay for a duel. And D'Herblay, knowing instinctively that his fashionable looks, his command of Latin grammar or even his wielding of sharp rhetoric would not get him out of this situation, had looked for the best fencing master in Paris, Monsieur Pierre Du Vallon. So good had Du Vallon's lessons proved that D'Herblay had killed the prudish young man. Which, since dueling was forbidden by royal edict and punishable at the end of the executioner's blade, had led to D'Herblay's and Du Vallon's going into hiding under the assumed names of Aramis and Porthos in the uniform of his majesty's musketeers.

Since then Aramis had fought more duels than he cared to think about. His and Porthos's acquaintance with a disgraced nobleman who called himself Athos and with a young Gascon hothead called d'Artagnan had done nothing to make his life more peaceful. Among the four of them, one or the other was forever challenging someone to a duel and calling on all his friends to serve as seconds.

He'd killed men, he'd seen corpses—Aramis heard his lips, loudly, mutter a string of Ave Marias over his past sins—but he`d never been near anyone murdered like this, in the safety of her room, in the privacy of her boudoir. And not while only Aramis was present. Not while only Aramis could have done it.

His hand over his mouth, the other hand gripping the bloody knife, he'd backed up until his behind fetched up against one of Violette's innumerable, amusing little tables, covered in more lace, velvet, satin, and stacked high with books she never read, her command of written French being shaky and her interest in the written word being far secondary to her interest in other pastimes.

Through the roaring in his ears, he was dimly aware that people were knocking at the door and at least one, female voice, was shouting a string of Spanish names, followed by other, equally Spanish words. The names were Violette's. Her real name was a string of proper names—starting with Ysabella—followed by a string of surnames, all connected by y and de which Aramis could not hope to understand or remember. Ever since—on a cold night, when he stood guard at the royal palace—she'd approached him and told him her name was Violette, he'd called her that and nothing else.

But the knocking on the door seemed like a distant worry. Closer at hand, Aramis was grappling with his soul. Ever since his father had died, when Aramis was no more than two, Aramis's pious and noble

mother had decided her young son was bound for the church. So, wher-
ever his path took him, he dragged with him the excellent, thorough
and insistent religious education his mother had given him.

Even now, in uniform for many years, Aramis considered himself a
priest in training. As soon as he cleared his name enough for some
monastery to take him, he would take orders.

He was aware of the serious and grave sins he committed with Violette who was, after all, married to some French nobleman living in the
far provinces. True, her marriage had been one arranged to match the
marriage of the Queen, Anne of Austria, her childhood companion and
friend. Violette, to hear her talk, barely knew her husband, with whom
she had not spent more than the two weeks of the wedding festivities.
He enjoyed rural pleasures, and she'd lingered at court with her friend
the Queen. And she'd found Aramis.

And there, Aramis thought, lay the crux of the sin, for they'd sinned
often and in very imaginative ways. And had not, perhaps, some angel
reached from heaven to smite with ivory dagger the cleft between Violette's perfect breasts?

But the banging on the door grew more insistent and Aramis's
knowledge of Latin allowed him to guess that the Spanish-speaking
woman wished to know who had screamed and why. She would not
be appeased by anything but Violette's voice. A voice that would not be
heard, again, till the angel of the apocalypse sounded the final trumpet.

Naked, scared, shocked, Aramis stood and stared at the door which
shook under the impact of many hands, many fists.

Cold sweat ran down his face. He felt his hand tremble. He'd never
trembled in battlefield or field of honor, but this . . . This supernatural
retribution, he could not endure.

And yet, if an angel had struck, would he not have killed both of them
while they were abandoned to their pleasure? And why would an angel
wait until Aramis went to the little room to attend a call of nature?

Despite his education—or perhaps because of it, for, after all, it had
included logic—Aramis had an analytical mind which shouted over the
vapors of his fear and the madness of his religious guilt to tell him that
a human hand had killed Violette. A human hand not Aramis's.

Perhaps, he thought, there was a tunnel into this room? After all, any
palace of any age at all had more tunnels, secret passages and hidden
rooms than a rabbit warren had exits.

But, looking around the room, he could not imagine where the tunnel would open. Every available palm length of wall had one of Violette's cabinets, tables, chaises leaning against it. And all of it was solid,
heavy Spanish furniture which would not be moved by a simple door
springing open behind it.

And now a man pounded on the door and called out in French,
"Madame, Madame, if you do not open we'll be forced to break down
the door."

Aramis, well versed in the art of ordering palace staff knew that it would only be a matter of minutes before some sturdy lads were brought forth and their shoulders applied to the door. The lock was solid, but not that solid. It would open. And they would catch him here. Alone. With Violette's corpse.

How long before the gibbet was built and he was hanged? Or would he be lucky enough to be beheaded? One of his long, pale hands went, unmeant, to his long, elegant neck.

It would kill his mother.

He edged towards the balcony door. It was the only way out. But it was not a true way out. All he could hope for was to fall to the hard ground and die. But at least he wouldn't die on the gallows or the block. He would not bring that shame onto his mother.

Filled with a decision he could only half muster, his hands tore at the door, forcing it open.

The warm air of spring rushed in on him, a scent of trees and grass and, beyond that, the scent of manure and cooking fires that was the essence of the great, bustling city of Paris.

His ears unnaturally sharpened by his fear, he could hear somewhere on the grounds of the palace the rough laughter of musketeers on guard and the sound of dice being tumbled. Was Athos or Porthos on guard tonight? He could not remember. Truth was he could not remember what day it was anymore and his normally perfect knowledge of his friends' guard schedules had slipped wholly from his mind.

It was a punishment that in the end, his wit, which had always been his defense, would desert him. The sound of the knocks on the door changed. Ah. Sturdy shoulders applied with a will.

Aramis stepped out onto the balcony, which was semicircular, built of stone and surrounded with little cylindrical columns of stone topped by a carved parapet.

The polished stone felt rough against his nakedness, as he leaned over to look three stories below, to the paving of an ornamental patio surrounded by flowerbeds. On one of the flowerbeds, in front of the balcony, a lone tree stood, filled with the kind of tender green leaves that spring fostered, leaves still small enough that one could see the tree branches thrust skyward like the hands of beseeching sinners beneath their sparkling green livery.

If Aramis flung himself out . . . If he threw himself out towards it . . .

He narrowed his eyes, calculating the distance, which was more than that of his outstretched body were he laid in the air between it and the balcony. And worse, the thickest part of the tree was a good story below.

His body had been honed through years of duels and sword practice. He knew his muscles could perform amazing leaps in the heat of combat. But here, in midair, with nothing to push against, how was he to reach for the saving branch of the distant tree?

And even if he managed to get down there, how could he save himself, naked and—he looked down—somehow smeared with Violette's
blood? How could he escape the palace and its well-guarded entrances?
Everyone knew he was in here with Violette. Or, if not, everyone would
guess when they found his uniform tossed casually over one of her
chaises.

He took a step in the room, not so much intending to retrieve the
uniform, but thinking of the uniform, the image of his blue tunic in his
mind and a vague idea that he should collect it.

And he heard the crack of the door, as it gave under the assault of
young men's shoulders.

If he jumped, it would be suicide. But if he stayed here, they would
kill him. Suicide was a sin.

Without thinking, with no time to plan, he scrambled up onto the
little stone parapet. He put the handle of the knife between his teeth.
He could always use it on himself if it looked like he'd be captured alive.

He would shame neither his mother nor his friends.

He crossed himself. And then he jumped, somersaulting, his body
twisting midair, his arms reaching hopelessly towards the impossible
hold of the distant tree branches.

A Hierarchy of Branches; Running from Fate; Where Fear Gives Not Only Wings, but Ears

Aramis's fingers closed on twigs and an abundance of leaves, mere tips of branches and no stronger than a toothpick.

Half disbelieving, he grabbed them, hard. But he'd barely got a hold on them, when he felt them give under his weight, snapping, as he fell. He scrabbled madly with sweaty fingertips, waving them around, till his left hand closed on another branch, scarcely thicker. Which in turn gave way letting him grasp a yet thicker branch, which also gave under his weight, letting him drop again, tilted and kicking out with his legs, waving his arms, trying to find—

He fell hard, straddling a branch, bark and leaves and sharp twigs introducing themselves to his notice with a bump so sharp that his eyes teared and he managed a scream around the handle of the knife in his mouth.

A scream which, his half-conscious brain realized, would only bring pursuers to him.

Blinking the tears away from his eyes, he took stock of the tree, which was, fortunately, verdant and, this low, had dense enough foliage to hide him. Or at least, it would be if he weren't straddling one of the lower branches, his naked legs, covered in fine blond hair, hanging on either side of it and his naked feet dangling freely below.

Quickly, scraping both legs on the bark, he jumped up, and stood on the branch. He was aware that scratches covered his legs, and that his muscles hurt. But he had no time to think about it. He scurried along the branch, towards the center of the tree, trying not to disturb the foliage.

Remembering his view from the balcony he judged that the outer wall of the palace should lay against the branch directly opposed to this one. He ran along the branch to the other.

From beneath came a confused babble of sounds, a noise of voices raised in that tone people use when asking each other what to do next.

Aramis reached the farthest point of the branch where he could safely stand. The wall of stone, which rose beyond that, was only visible as a glimmer of gray between the leaves. Too far away to reach even with extended arm.

The voices on the ground became audible enough that he could understand what they were saying.

"He must have gone this way," said a shrill voice, clearly a woman's or a young man's.

"He can't," countered the deeper voice of a male. "How could he jump from the balcony and survive?"

Aramis, his blood pounding in his ears, his vision dim, and all of his body hurting as if he had been flogged, wondered how he could have survived too. He only half believed it.

"Well," the shriller voice said. "Then where could he be? For he's not in the room. Phillip yelled down he wasn't. So he must have jumped. And you see that tree yonder? Look at all the broken twigs and leaves at the base."

Aramis bit harder into the handle of the knife that had killed his mistress. He stifled a moan of despair. They would find him. They would—

"Ah, here comes Pierre, with the dogs," said the man, over a low, vicious snarling.

Aramis jumped. He jumped, hands extended, forward and up, towards the garden wall. And met a surface that some mason had taken great pride in making as smooth as possible.

His fingers slid off the stone and he managed to muffle a whimper as he scrabbled with hands and feet and felt skin tear and nails rip. He found a foothold and one handhold, and scrabbled madly with his other hand, till he found another hold, higher up. His other foot found a place to lodge, a bare crack between two stones. More by force of will than by the strength of his hands and feet, he scrambled up the wall.

Balancing atop of it, drawing a trembling breath, he heard the snuffles and whines of dogs. And jumped over.

On the other side, all was dark and still. The evening had deepened and the road that ringed the palace was deserted. Save for the sounds of voices and dogs, now muffled by the wall, all was quiet.

Aramis took a deep breath and wiped the sweat from his forehead to the back of his arm. He trembled and told himself it was with cold, despite the warmth of the balmy air.

Leaning against the wall, he tried to think what to do next. He could not run through Paris naked without being noticed. And besides, very soon they would send someone to his lodgings. They would be there, ready to arrest him before he could get clothes.

He took another deep breath and faced the prospect of going into the night, naked and alone. And where could he go? Any half-wit would also take the precaution of sending guards to wait at his friends' homes. The four of them were known as the four inseparables. And the Cardinal, who would soon enough make this his business, was no half-wit.

And then he heard, from the left side, as he stood, the sound of dice rolled in a leather cup and a curt, low imprecation, "Damn."

It could have come from many mouths. But the choice of the single word and the tone in which it was said—as though the gambler had lost a great deal, but didn't deem it important enough to allow for more than a word—made Aramis think of Athos. Athos always lost at games of chance. And yet he always played.

The voice had been too distant and too faint in reaching his ears to be easily identified. To be sure, it could be almost anyone who had sworn so quietly into the evening air.

But Aramis wanted it to be Athos. Willed it to be Athos.

From the other side of the wall came the barking of dogs, and someone saying, "There's blood here. He climbed the wall here."

Aramis ran towards the sound of dice. He would risk it. Knitting himself with the shadow, he ran, hoping that one thing in this disastrous evening would go right. Hoping to find sanctuary.

Rounding the corner of the wall, he emerged into the shadow of the palace, where the bulk of the walls hid the scant light of the stars in the evening sky.

In the dark, he saw three men, sitting in front of one of the palace gates, playing dice. He hesitated. With them sitting, like that, it was hard to tell what the men looked like, save that they were musketeers, wrapped in cloaks and wearing their hats. Three musketeers. But d'Artagnan wasn't a musketeer.

The one facing Aramis stood and said, "Holla, who goes there?"

Athos' voice. Weak with relief, Aramis surged forward. He removed the dagger from his mouth, held it tip down in his trembling hand. "Athos," he said.

Athos, tall, ivory skinned and blue eyed, graced with an incongruous cascade of dark curls down his back, normally looked like nobility incarnate. Less like a man than like a statue whom time and events could not touch. Now his eyes widened in shock; his face went paler yet; his dark blue eyes opened wide. "Aramis," he said.

The other two men stood and turned, swords in hand. One of them, the smaller one with the dark hair, wore not the musketeer's uniform, but the similar uniform of the guards of Monsieur des Essarts, in a paler blue than the Musketeer's clothes. He was very young, not yet twenty, dark haired and dark eyed, with the olive complexion of Gascony which was close to the border with Spain. He turned with the feline grace that was his characteristic.

The larger one—a giant with red hair and beard—stood and turned with the gracefulness of a dancer or a fencing master. His handsome face was undeniably that of Aramis's oldest friend, Porthos.

"Please," Aramis said, his strength almost gone, his heart beating at his throat from the sound of dogs approaching from behind. It was all he could do not to run and try to hide behind his friends. "Please. You have to help me."

A Fugitive in Need; Where Four Show They Think Like One; A Fine Predicament

Athos heard the sound of approaching feet and, farther off, the sound of dogs and pursuit. He stood.

Out of the gathering dark, gloomier here where the shadow of the wall hid the moon than in most places around the palace, a strange apparition came running. He was tall and blond and had, in general, the form and shape of Aramis.

Athos's mind told him it was Aramis, but his senses denied it. He'd never seen Aramis like this. It was not like his gallant friend to be running around naked, covered in blood, with a dagger between his teeth and an expression of pure panic on his regular features. And were those twigs entwined in the long blond hair that Aramis normally brushed till it glimmered?

"Holla, who goes there?" that part of Athos that refused to admit this could be one of his oldest and closest friends asked.

The man took the dagger from between his teeth, and held it in his hand, tip down, in such a way it was clear he had no intention of attacking. "Athos," he rasped.

There was such a tone of relief in the voice, such a tone of having found just the sanctuary he'd been looking for that Athos could no longer deny who this was. "Aramis," he said.

And on the name, his two other friends stood up, d'Artagnan quickly scooping the dice into his leather cup as he went.

"Help me," Aramis said. "You have to help me. They're after me. They will catch me. They think I murdered—"

"Silence," Athos said. There was the sound of dogs and the sound of pursuit from behind, and surely Aramis didn't mean to speak that loudly. There was only one thing to do, but Athos was afraid of saying anything, of calling any attention. At any rate, he was a man of quick mind but few words. The natural garrulousness of youth had been quelled in him for over ten years, since the day he'd hanged his wife from a low branch in his park and left his ancestral home and his title of count to join the musketeers under an assumed name.

Instead of talking, he unlaced his cloak, threw it over Aramis's shoulders. He looked at d'Artagnan and in the dark, quick eyes of their youngest friend, he caught comprehension. D"Artagnan removed his hat and shoved the mass of Aramis's hair under it, before pushing the hat on Aramis's head. It was a plumed hat and blue. True the blue was somewhat different than the one the musketeers wore, but in this dark place, only those who had reason to suspect it would look for the color difference.

To Athos's surprise, Porthos, a man who thought with his huge hands, his sharp, overdeveloped senses, didn't need an explanation. By the time d'Artagnan stepped away— having pulled Aramis' hat down over his face to hide his blood-stained features—Porthos was there, holding out what seemed like a pair of breeches.

A casual glance revealed that he had not indeed exposed himself. The breeches he had on were embroidered velvet. The ones he held out to Aramis were over-breeches, slashed, to allow the embroidery to shine through.

Count on Porthos to wear twice as many clothes as needed. However, the plain dark breeches, when on Aramis, were loose enough not to display the slashes.

Athos nodded his approval, and nothing remained but to fish in his sleeve for his own, silken handkerchief and use it to clean Aramis's face of blood enough to pass in the gloom.

The whole had taken very little time, but the voices of Aramis's pursuers sounded near now. Without speaking, with hasty gestures, Athos directed the rest of them to sit or kneel on the ground. He, himself, pushed on Aramis's shoulders, forcing the younger musketeer to kneel down in the boneless manner of a man in shock. He adjusted the fold of the cloak he'd loaned Aramis over Aramis's bare feet.

At the last moment, noticing the ivory dagger in Aramis's hand, Athos took it and slipped it into his own belt, in a place where the folds of the hem of his old-fashioned, Spanish style doublet hid it.

Athos ran back to roughly where Aramis's footsteps left off, took his own shoes off and then ran past them to a place near the road. He put his boots back on, and scuffed the sand, kicking and running around a bit, like a mad man. Then he jumped well away from the scuffled area, and ran back to them.

His friends were looking at him as if afraid he might have gone mad. All except Aramis who looked down at the ground as if it contained the grave of all his hopes.

What was Aramis doing, running around with a bloodied dagger? Whose dagger was it? Athos did not remember ever seeing his friend with an ivory dagger. What had Aramis done with it? Why were servants and dogs pursuing him?

But the questions would have to wait, because the pursuers were on them. Just before they reached them, d'Artagnan somehow flourished the dice cup and threw the dice, a distinctive and non-frantic noise. The noise of friends relaxing together.

Athos managed a smile at the young man, before the pursuers arrived.

Then he turned, away from the men seemingly engaged in a game of dice, and faced the pursuers' sword in hand. They were, as he expected, the sort of rabble that can be roused in the middle of the night and sent on any pursuit at all for the sake of being able to scare another human being, evildoer or not.

There were five men, one of them almost as tall as Athos, all of them unkempt and clad in what appeared to be servant uniforms much the worse for the wear. Two of them held dogs straining at the leash, sniffing around disconsolately.

They wouldn't be used to tracking humans, Athos thought. They were primarily hunting dogs, who followed various animals through fields and meadows.

Chasing Aramis must have been easy. There was just the scent of a human, a bloodied human, at that. But here, they would be confused by new smells. Aramis was wearing borrowed clothing with their smells upon it.

Before the men handling the dogs could give a command, Athos said, "Who goes there?"

The taller of the men, holding a large brown and black dog on the leash examined Athos from head to toe with a look Athos was not used to receiving from anyone, much less a peasant. "What business is it of yours?" he asked.

"I guard the entrance to the King's palace," Athos said, straightening himself, and only managing to hold his temper in check because it wouldn't do to call their closer attention to them or to Aramis.

"A fine job you've done," one of the pursuers said. "Considering that murder was done within."

"Murder?" Athos said. "Within the palace? Then why hasn't the alarm been given?" He gave the servant a glare that implied that the man was a bit worse for the drink.

The man stopped at that. Clearly, he'd never thought to give the alarm to the palace at large and was now wondering why he hadn't.

A small person pushed from the back of the crowd. A woman, Athos realized, as she came forward to stand before him. She was very short, barely coming up to his chest, she was also very round, not so much fat as spherical, with the sort of coloration that betrayed she was either Spanish or from somewhere very close to Spain. Her hair was tucked up into a bun and her clothes were the genteel but not too fashionable attire of a maid of honor to a noblewoman.

"It is my lady," she said, wringing her hands together in front of her. "My lady Ysabella de Ybarra y . . ."

"What happened to your lady?" Athos asked.

"We heard a scream from her room," the woman said. She looked up with sad black eyes. "We heard a scream and went to look, but the door was closed. Locked. She was—She'd been—"

Athos raised his eyebrows. If the Lady Ysabella was the woman whom Aramis called Violette, and if Aramis had been present in her room, Athos could very well imagine what she'd been.

The woman clearly could not bring herself to say that her mistress had been disporting herself with a musketeer. Instead she shrugged, an elaborate and very Latin gesture, and said, "Well, she was with a friend whom she trusted. But no one answered when we called, and when we knocked the door down..." She took a deep breath with a hint of sob to it, as though she were just holding hysteria at bay. "When we broke down the door, there she was, my lady, on her bed, with a wound between her breasts."

"Did she tell you what happened?" Athos asked.

Again the elaborate shrug. "She was dead. But from her balcony there came a sound and we went to look. We think the miscreant who was with her, jumped from her window."

"On what floor was your mistress?" Athos asked. "And did you see him jump?"

"Third floor, and no," she said. "In fact . . ." She shrugged again. "It is hard to believe he could have jumped. But he must have, because he left behind his musketeer's uniform. So he was there with her. And the door was locked. Who else could have done it?"

"He was the musketeer who goes by Aramis," one of the men said.

"That's his friend," another of them said. "Where is he, Monsieur?"

"Sangre Dieu," Athos said. "My friend Aramis is there." Aramis had enough presence of mind to look over his shoulder at the sound of his name, showing just his chin, a bit of his face, not enough for them to examine for blood, but enough that his reaction of turning to look seemed natural and proper. "He's been with us all night, playing dice."

"Are you sure?" the man who led the searchers asked. "Because he—"

"Would I not know who my friend is?"

"And he's been with us all the night," Porthos said. "Wish he hadn't been, in fact. He's won quite a few pistols off me."

"May I help you?" Aramis asked.

The man looked confused. He turned to the woman, "I thought you said—"

The woman shrugged again, theatrically. "He was blond and handsome and dressed in a musketeer's uniform. How am I to know if it was the same? My mistress seemed to be very fond of him, but—"

Unspoken, in the air, was the fickleness of women in general and noblewomen in particular, and if none of them would say it, then neither would Athos that most women at court had the mind and manners of a cat in heat. It had so long been an article of faith with him, at any rate, that it would come as no surprise to anyone who knew him.

The maid of honor was giving Aramis's back a suspicious look. "Someone," she said, "ran through the garden. And scrabbled up the wall, leaving a trail of blood. Someone who left a uniform behind in my lady's room. Surely you're not going to tell us a man could run naked through the palace and out here without anyone noticing."

"Except, perhaps, he stole a uniform?" Athos asked. "A servant's uniform, perhaps? The better to disguise himself?"

The men with the dogs looked at each other, while their companions traded equally suspicion-laden glares.

"But," one at the back that looked to be the brightest, or at least the most alert of them, said. "Someone ran ahead of us. Someone the dogs were following."

"Well," Athos said. "As to that, there was a man who came running out of the palace. Blond and scared looking." For just a moment he was afraid that Aramis, in the state he was, would assume Athos was giving him away and would try to run. But Athos didn't dare to turn and look at Aramis, so he continued. "He ran past us and over there." He pointed to the place where he had, carefully, scuffled the sand.

"Look," one of them said. "He's right. The footprints lead this way."

They followed to the place where sand met road. Athos didn't go with them, not wanting to look overeager. His friends were displaying cool heads and self-control even better than what he'd come to expect of them. Aramis and Porthos remained sitting, looking at the cup d'Artagnan was shaking with the motion and expression of the man who can barely wait for a pointless interruption to be over so he can resume his all-important game of dice.

"There are no horse hoof prints," one of the men said.

"Oh, don't be an idiot," the other answered. "Can't you tell the horses would be on the paved road?"

"Hey you," one of them yelled turning towards Athos. And, doubtless, seeing the expression on Athos's face hastily changed it to, "Monsieur Musketeer, would you please tell us if this man had horses?"

"There were horses and a group of people by the road," Athos said. He pointed down the road. "They rode away towards Paris."

A discussion followed among the men and the one woman, about which of them would go on, which ones would stay and who would go tell the captain of the musketeers as well as their majesties themselves, that there had been murder done within the royal precinct.

Horses were brought forth. Two of the men mounted, to follow the imaginary fugitives.

The other ones melted into the night but, before doing it, one of them looked at Athos and said, "Why did you not stop this fugitive, then?"

Athos shrugged. "My purpose," he said. "Is to prevent people from coming into the palace, not to stop people from leaving. I couldn't desert my post to go haggle with people disposed to leaving."

They had no defense against those words which were— even if in-sane—undeniably, true.

When they had vanished into the night and even the whining and scuffling of the dogs on the leash could no longer be heard, he turned to see how Aramis was holding up.

Aramis had slumped forward onto the sand and lay immobile.

Where Strength Is Tested; The Sad Lot of the Musketeer's Servant; The Inevitability of Drunken Musketeers

Porthos rounded on Aramis. He knew there had been some great harm done. Not that he quite understood it. From what he had heard of the servants' talk, a woman had been killed.

Porthos had known Aramis for many years—since the young man, then barely more than a child, had arrived at Porthos's thriving fencing school and asked to be taught— within a month or less—all there was to know about the art of sword fighting. Though Aramis had learned well enough and fought the duel, too, Porthos had never thought Aramis could kill a woman. In fact he'd never seen Aramis quite angry enough to even be rude to a woman.

From what Porthos had observed of his young friend's life, Aramis had no need at all to attack women. Women fell over themselves to please Aramis and never seemed to even exhibit much jealousy over his other sincere worshipers.

Confused and shocked at seeing his friend collapse forward, Porthos put out a huge hand upon Aramis's shoulder. "Aramis," he said.

But Aramis only made a sound, not quite a word. He'd been kneeling and sitting on his ankles, and upon collapsing, he'd collapsed forward, folding on himself. Porthos grasped his shoulder and pulled him upright by force of strength and determination. "Aramis, are you wounded? And who have you killed? And why?"

Aramis looked at Porthos, but his green eyes normally inclined to mirth and intent with observation looked unfocused. It was, Porthos thought, as though Aramis were very drunk or had suffered a blow to the head, as his eyes would not focus. "I didn't—" he said. "Violette." And then he slumped forward again, in silence.

Porthos noticed that d'Artagnan and Athos traded a look. Athos nodded, as though some conversation had passed between them. Porthos hated it when his friends did that, communicating without saying the words openly. It smacked, it seemed to him, of treachery and slyness.

"We'll get no sense out of him," d'Artagnan said. Then he lowered his voice. "And, besides, it is quite likely anything he might say could sound incriminating. We should get him away to his lodgings as soon as it may be."

Porthos nodded. "I'll take him," he said.

"Porthos," Athos said. "You cannot. You are on guard duty."

Porthos shrugged. "If anyone should check, tell them I am walking around, because I heard a suspicious sound. On a night such as this, no one will find it amiss."

"But—" Athos said.

Porthos reached down and clasped his hands just under Aramis's arms, hauling him up. The younger musketeer looked at him with nothing beyond mild surprise. "Can either of you hold him up, should he not find his feet?"

Both his friends shook their heads. Porthos nodded, as if his question had been perfectly answered. He was a simple man and unused to matters of philosophy and theology. When his friends discussed such issues and used words that seemed to Porthos much too long to have any real meaning, Porthos either got bored or amused himself with his own thoughts.

A tall, strong man, he's always been interested in the outdoors and physical sports. In fencing and riding and hunting. He thought with his hands as much as with his brain. This left him enough mind only to attempt to do what needed to be done and what needed to be done at that moment. It made him more practical and focused than any of his comrades and, in that, often the savior of them all.

And at this moment what needed to be done was getting Aramis back to his quarters with a minimum of notice. This—to Porthos—seemed to be most easily done by his supporting and half carrying Aramis.

The reputation of the musketeers was such that no one would notice if one of them were walking what seemed to be a very drunken comrade through the streets. Even if the comrade were barefoot. It wouldn't be the first time that a musketeer lost his boots at dice. "Let d'Artagnan take my place," he said. "While I walk Aramis back to his lodgings."

"You must be careful," Athos said. "There is every chance that his lodgings will be watched."

D'Artagnan, who had been looking for a while as though he'd like to speak, now said, "I shall go with you Porthos. If we have to fight back an attack, I can take care of them."

Porthos nodded. This seemed like a good idea to him. Besides, with two of them, one supporting Aramis on either side, it would look more natural. It was the classical way to help a drunken musketeer back to his abode.

"I'll leave Aramis in the care of Bazin," he said. Bazin was Aramis's servant, who had followed him from his ancestral estate and who stayed with Aramis in the blessed hope that one day Aramis would join a monastery and Bazin would be able to join also as a lay brother. "And tell Bazin not to allow anyone in the house. You know he's as capable as anyone of understanding that if Aramis is arrested for murder Bazin's dream of joining a monastery will never come true."

Athos nodded. He resumed his guard position, but his dour expression betrayed that he did not consider this a good arrangement.

Porthos worried about Athos. The man was, at the best of times, too hard drinking, too free with his gambling. At the worst times he became dour and inward looking, like a man meditating on some horrible memory.

That Athos had left behind some grand estate, some great position, was all too obvious. What would cause a great nobleman—a true nobleman and not like Porthos's family only one step removed from its farming neighbors—to leave estate and family? Porthos had thought this over many times, and so far he'd come up with no answer. Only he fancied there was unhappy love in it and that a woman had caused his friend great hurt.

Glancing at d'Artagnan, Porthos nodded towards Aramis. D"Artagnan, as always, understood the words that were not said, and, as Porthos put his arm around Aramis's waist, to support the younger man, he found d'Artagnan imitating the gesture from the other side.

They set out down the road towards the city of Paris proper. The palace the royal family was occupying just then sat on the outskirts of the city, in a sparsely populated suburb, bordering on woods. The road leading into town had been built by the Romans and assembled of stone blocks so finely fit together that not a blade could slide in between two of them. They'd been polished by centuries of use and till they'd become soft and slightly rounded under foot. Little stuck out that could cause Aramis to stumble, which was good because he seemed unsteady on his feet.

They walked for a while in silence, passing nothing but trees and gardens that, while not enclosed in the palace wall, yet were part of the palace, used for rousing hunts and chaperoned walks. Past that, the road changed to one flanked by large houses set back within well maintained gardens. Farther down, the houses got closer to the road, until finally the front walls of the houses themselves, standing next to each other and connecting, formed as though a wall on either side of the road. The facades, ornate stone and carved windowsills, denoted these townhouses as being still prestigious and expensive.

Above a door here, and a window there, lanterns glowed, lighting the street weakly. And though it wasn't very late at all, the streets were deserted. In this neighborhood, those who were still up and entertaining would be doing it within their houses, not outside.

Farther on, people walked along the street, in increasingly greater numbers as the roads grew narrower, the houses shabbier and covered in oft-crumbling plaster. Though the night had by then deepened to full dark, the only lanterns burned above tavern signs.

"Aramis," d'Artagnan whispered. "Aramis—was your . . . seamstress killed? Did you kill her? Why—?"

Aramis turned his head slowly, looking at d'Artagnan as though trying to determine who the young man was. Or perhaps the meaning of the words he said. He started and made a sound like a sob caught at the back of his throat. "Violette," he said, and his voice was high and complaining. "Violette," he said, again, and looking at Porthos, added, "She's dead, Porthos."

"Shhh," Porthos said. He glanced around. Only one or two people were looking in their direction and not at all curiously. After all they looked like three musketeers, two of them carrying a third, drunken comrade home. And such outbursts were not unusual from drunken musketeers.

However, and even though Porthos knew that Violette was not the woman's true name—not even close—wouldn't there be people who might remember later that the musketeers had spoken of this subject? And if they did, that, coupled with their description, would damn them, would it not?

"Shhh," Porthos repeated, and looked over Aramis's shoulder at d'Artagnan. "This is not the time to speak of these things."

D'Artagnan opened his mouth, as if to protest, but Porthos said, "There will be time. Now, someone might notice too much, or remember what they should not."

D'Artagnan looked dubious, but nodded and looked around with a most gratifying look of suspicion.

Porthos knew his friends weren't stupid men. In fact, he also knew that suspicion of stupidity tended to attach to him. At least, it attached to him from other people. None of his three friends seemed to take his sometimes odd or too-obvious seeming questions as a mark of a slow mind.

In return, he tried not to think of them as slow and strange. But he found himself oft marveling at how all of them—perhaps Aramis worst of all, but Athos and even d'Artagnan as well—could ignore the reality before their eyes for the fascinating thoughts inside their heads. It was Porthos's opinion that people with the turn of mind to get their ideas tangled in the words that formed them could act utterly senseless and get themselves in great danger thereby. He gave a sharp look at d'Artagnan. Good thing Porthos was here to keep his friends out of trouble.

They stumbled into the more crowded part of town where Aramis lived.

Porthos knocked at the door of Aramis's lodgings, causing the solid-looking oak to tremble, while his huge fist raised echoing booms.

Noise responded from within. Bangs and booms and the sound of ceramic dropping, followed by vigorous cursing in a male voice. Aramis rented his upstairs rooms from a family who occupied the bottom floor.

Presently Pierre, the son of the family, pulled the door open with the sort of gesture one makes when one wishes to intimidate the people knocking.

He was intimidating enough, being almost as large as Porthos, dark haired, dark visaged and with a villainous cast to his features that a gold hoop earring enhanced rather than diminished. The almost as large as Porthos was the deciding factor, though. Since he'd become an adult and grown to be considerably larger than normal men both in height and musculature, Porthos had seen many times the changes of expression that now played themselves across Pierre's face—cockiness, bewilderment, and, finally, obsequiousness.

Pierre bobbed something that might have passed for a bow in Porthos's direction, then looked over at Aramis and a slow smile spread his lips. "Got himself a bit too drunk, did he?" he said, and moved aside.

Porthos and d'Artagnan dragged the still-insensible Aramis into a small hall from which a narrow staircase led upwards, and a door opened to the left. The door led to the family's quarters. The staircase led to Aramis's lodging.

Porthos's bulk, by himself, took up the entire rung on the stairs. The stairs being open on the right side—with a mere railing dividing them from a fall onto the floor below, it was perilous to attempt to climb three abreast. But d'Artagnan managed to hold up Aramis all by himself all the way up. Though it slowed the young man down. By the time the two of them reached the top of the stairs, Porthos was already there, knocking at the door with what he hoped was a discreet and low-key knocking and was vaguely aware was only slightly less thunderous than the pounding he'd given the door downstairs.

He had a moment to be afraid that Bazin would not be at home. Most of their servants would be home if they were not out with their masters, but Bazin was an odd one and had interests and plots of his own. Truth be told he only followed Aramis because he hoped Aramis would still live up to the vocation the family had decided for him early on and become a priest or a monk.

But the worry passed as Bazin opened the door. He was a short man and almost as wide as he was tall. Nature had graced him with the round face of a medieval monk and a bald head that resembled a monk's tonsure. He looked at them out of little, surprisingly blue eyes.

His stare at Porthos conveyed displeasure, then a look at Aramis changed it to a half-open mouth and the appearance of shock. "My master," he said. "The Chevalier . . . Have you devils got him drunk again?"

Porthos always found it amusing that, as far as Bazin was concerned, Aramis was an angel of light and innocence forever led astray by the demon like musketeers and guard, his friends. Now he simply nodded and said, "Let us get him inside." He was not about to debate, here on the landing, how Aramis had got in his present incoherent condition.

He would bet Pierre or other members of his family were down there, ear glued to the door, listening for any stray word from up the stairs.

Bazin's expression betrayed that he'd very much like to pick a fight on this point, but in the end he didn't. Instead, he stepped back and back into the room, till he allowed Aramis and d'Artagnan, who was supporting him, to come in. Porthos followed into a little room outfitted much like a monk's cell. There was a narrow bed, a peg on the wall that held a change of clothes, and a massive wrought iron cross at the foot of which lay an oak-and-velvet kneeler much too ornate and elaborate to have belonged to a humble abode.

The candles burning at the foot of the cross cast a bright—if trembling—light upon the room. Enough light to allow Porthos to run the three security bolts on the door after he closed it behind them. Enough for Bazin to see his master's true state.

As d'Artagnan pulled the borrowed cloak off Aramis, more became apparent and Bazin covered his mouth with his pudgy hand. "My master . . ." he said again, but no more.

"Your master escaped the scene of a murder," Porthos said.

Bazin turned startled eyes to him. "My master murdered someone?"

"No. But he is suspected. Presently, there might be people along trying to arrest him."

"Arrest him?"

"That is what I said," Porthos answered. "Do not open the door to anyone but us. We'll be back to talk to your master. He's not coherent enough to answer questions just now."

"Will he . . . is he drunk?"

Porthos looked at Aramis who stood, where d'Artagnan had left him, near the cross and its complement of candles. Aramis swayed slightly on his feet and seemed dazed. But Porthos hadn't smelled any alcohol on his breath or his person in helping him here.

"Not noticeably. In fact, I doubt he has drunk at all. But put him to bed. He will be better in the morning."

"But—" Bazin started. He was pale, and his eyes wide.

"Don't ask questions," Porthos said. "We don't know how to answer them and it wouldn't do you any good to ask."

"And besides," d'Artagnan put in, his voice soothing and smooth. "The least said about these events, the better the chance you can find a religious house to take the two of you."

Bazin's eyes, still reflecting shock and surprise, now filled with the cunning of the desperate, and he closed his mouth and nodded.

When they left, Porthos heard the bolts slide home behind him. He had seen Bazin in a mood, and he did not fear that the rotund would-be monk would let intruders in. Aramis would sleep well tonight.

Which was more than Porthos could say for himself. He would lay awake and wonder at what trouble his friend had got into and how they were going to get him out of it.

The Inconvenience of a Murdered Noblewoman; Athos's Doubts; Aramis's Anger

Athos arrived at Aramis's lodgings the next day not sure how to face the coming trial, how to question Aramis, how to face Aramis's guilt, if it were such.

He'd awakened and dressed in silence, glad he'd trained his servant, Grimaud, to utter and silent obedience long ago. Oh, as a child Athos had been garrulous, talkative in the way of a smart boy. And as a teenager his overwrought emotions had flowed out in poetry and elegant prose.

But all had changed on the day that Athos had killed his wife and his innocence with her, and left his domains to escape condemnation and censure for what he then viewed as justice and had—in later years—started to fear had been murder.

The image of Charlotte pursued him still—her blond hair, her sweet features—and some days he would very much like to believe that the fleur-de-lis branded on her shoulder had been a mistake or an enemy's ploy. Even if that meant he was guilty of unjustly killing her.

And yet, his clear and uncluttered reason told him he'd never committed murder, or not unprovoked. He'd simply punished an escaped murderess, who'd wormed her way into his heart, his home, his family name.

Caught between guilt and grief, he'd stopped being able to speak. Or at least being able to enjoy speaking with any fluency at all. Instead, he hoarded silence like a treasure, and ordered Grimaud through a system of gestures and expressions.

He'd had few occasions to congratulate himself as much on this arrangement as he had this day. Because if he had needed to explain it all to Grimaud, he'd not have known how to, nor what to say. After all, what did he know about Aramis?

Later, yesterday, in the way of such news, rumors and hints had filtered down. After Porthos and d'Artagnan had returned to their guard post at the royal palace, they had heard through the servants of the duchess, that the murder weapon was missing. And everyone talked of her lover, that musketeer who pretended to be a priest—or perhaps that priest who pretended to be a musketeer—and who visited her in her room so many times. Who had been seen—the maid was sure—entering her room just that night.

It was no use at all for Athos to mention to Porthos that perhaps Aramis had killed his lover. Porthos's face just closed and his red eyebrows descended upon his eyes like storm clouds announcing a gale. Porthos said it was monstrous to even suspect Aramis of such a thing. That Aramis wouldn't do any such thing. Not ever.

But the truth was more complex than that. No one who knew Athos, before or after his wife's death, would suspect him of killing her, either. He had always struggled to be the embodiment of honor, the soul of probity. Striking an unarmed woman didn't seem to be within his abilities.

In fact, Athos himself would never have believed he could do it and only half understood it as he saw his own hands fashion a noose and hang Charlotte from a low-hanging branch.

In retrospect, it made all too much sense. Almost too much sense for his taste, as it could not in any way be called a crime of passion. He'd been revolted and shocked to see the fleur-de-lis on her shoulder when he'd opened her gown to give her air, after she'd fallen from her horse. The fleur-de-lis was the mark of an adulteress, a murderess headed for the gallows. She'd escaped somehow.

Oh, he could have denounced her to the local magistrates. But that would only ensure that his ancient family name of la Fere would be dragged through the mud along with her. So he'd killed her.

He'd killed her quickly and ruthlessly, before his brain had even had time to reason through all this.

What if Aramis had found the like treason and decided to take a similar solution?

With this in mind, Athos fetched up outside of Aramis's door just in time to meet Porthos and d'Artagnan coming from the other side of the street.

They both looked as ill as he felt. Well—Porthos had taken his usual care about his appearance, which was quite a bit more than other people took. For such a large man and one so sensible, Porthos had a broad streak of peacock. Right then that streak manifested itself in venetian breeches in velvet ornamented with Spanish lace, and an embroidered doublet whose sleeves showed a profusion of needless ribbons and buttons. All of this was topped off with a sky blue cloak and the hat of his musketeer's uniform, which—in Porthos's case—seemed to have been ornamented with a few more plumes than was normal. And d'Artagnan had dressed as he usually did, his wiry, muscular build lending elegance to the blue gray uniform of the guards of Monsieur des Essarts and the oval, olive-skinned face that showed between collar and plumed hat displaying well-trimmed facial hair and well cared for black hair pulled back with a leather tie.

But despite this superficial neatness, both of them looked exhausted. Porthos's eyes showed dark circles around them, marring his fair skin. And d'Artagnan's normally deep set eyes now seemed to be looking through a tunnel of shadows. And even d'Artagnan's youthful exuberance could not disguise the taut and worried line of his lips.

They nodded at each other and didn't speak, like strangers meeting for a difficult mission and unwilling to clutter it with unnecessary chatter.

Porthos raised his hand to knock at the door, but Athos grabbed at his wrist and firmly pulled the hand down, before knocking at the door himself. Porthos's knocking could, on a good day, eclipse the trumpet of the apocalypse.

Athos wondered if Porthos had knocked the night before and if so how many of the neighbors had looked around their shutters and behind their curtains to see who was trying to knock down the door. And how many had seen the state Aramis was in.

However, there was little for it. The time had passed to remedy that. Only thing he could do was not make it worse. Athos noticed Porthos's shuffle of impatience when their knocking wasn't immediately answered and raised his hand to knock again.

The door opened to show a young girl, the daughter of the family that rented lodgings to the musketeer.

Athos bowed to her and said, "We're here to see our friend," before pushing on, past her and up the stairs, to Aramis's lodgings.

There his knock went unanswered, but his whispered, "It is I, Bazin," at the crack of the door, brought a satisfying sliding of the bolts from the other side.

"My master is within," was all Bazin said, pointing at the door that led to the inner room of the lodging. Aramis's room.

"Is he awake?"

Bazin nodded. "He's washed and dressed, and now he waits you."

This was very much like Aramis. Like any of them, truth be told. Over the years of their friendship—which had enlarged a month ago to include the Gascon d'Artagnan— they had always dealt with private crisis by holding a war council and listening to the advice of their fellows. That Aramis treated this no differently might mean that he harbored no guilt.

Or it might mean that he trusted all of them to protect him despite what his private guilt might be.

And he was—as much as Athos hated to admit it— probably right. While Athos wasn't sure that Aramis hadn't committed murder, he was very sure that the murder—if such it had been—would have been justified.

He knocked at the door to the inner room and Aramis answered, "Come," in what could reasonably be described as his normal voice.

The room, twice as large as Bazin's pass-through room, still looked too Spartan for the Aramis that Athos had come to know. There was just a tall, dark, curtained bed that had probably come with Aramis from his estate, a tall wardrobe and, in a corner, a writing desk, with plain paper.

But Athos, who had known Aramis for very long, knew that the wardrobe concealed enough blue suits to outfit a whole regiment of the musketeers, and in silk and velvet enough to make even Porthos jealous. He'd seen those suits on Aramis often enough. He'd also wager that some false drawer on the desk, or some false bottom on the wardrobe concealed perfumed sheets of paper ornamented with a crest. Though Athos had to admit he'd never seen those, he could not imagine Aramis writing his duchesses, his countesses, his princesses, on plain and unmarked paper.

However that were, today Aramis was dressed in clerical black, as unadorned as Bazin's outfit. Still cut in the latest stare of fashion it consisted of venetians falling from waist to ankle, and a loose doublet with a ruffle that covered the hip. Both unadorned and plain for Aramis. A breviary, the daily readings recommended for priests, sat close to his hand. Despite this, his hair shone, newly brushed, and it was quite clear he'd shaved and trimmed his beard. Which must mean, Athos thought with some relief, that Aramis was close to his normal state.

As if to prove this, Aramis nodded to them as they came in and stood up—since there was no place for them to sit. "I want to thank you," he said. "All three of you, for lending me succor in my extremity yesterday. I shudder to think what would have happened to me without your help."

Porthos shrugged and shuffled uneasily. "You'd have done the same for us," he said.

"But we do wonder," d'Artagnan said. "What brought you to such need and what the circumstances were . . . why you fled the way you did, leaving even your uniform behind."

Even in his state of grave seriousness that implied, perhaps, true mourning, Aramis's lips quivered and his green eyes sparkled at d'Artagnan's tactful probing. "I did not have time to dress," he said. "Because the servants were knocking the door down. I'm afraid I screamed when I found . . ." He swallowed. "When I realized that Violette was truly dead and it was not a prank she was playing on me."

"You were surprised at finding her dead, then?" Athos asked.

"Of course he was, Athos, what a question," Porthos said. "Who would expect his lover to be killed?"

Athos didn't answer Porthos, but looked steadily at Aramis, whose gaze, meeting his, showed an understanding of Athos's question. Aramis, himself, clearly didn't think he was incapable of murder, no matter what Porthos thought.

"I was," he said. "Shocked. I'd only stepped to this little closet beside her room, in which she keeps—kept a chaise percée for . . . such needs as arose. Only a few minutes. And I came out to find Violette dead. I was quite shocked. Though . . ." Aramis's green eyes flickered with something, like a shadow passing over a sunlit landscape.

"Though?" Athos prompted.

Aramis sighed. "Though in the next few seconds, as I contemplated the locked door, the impossibility of a passage into the room, the inaccessibility of the balcony, I wondered if I . . ." Again he floundered, and he gestured, with his hands, as if expressing the inability of language to translate his meaning. Then he rubbed the tips of his fingers on his forehead, as if massaging fugitive memory. "I wondered if I could have committed the monstrous deed and forgotten all about it."

The Wisdom of the Tavern; A Musketeer's Regrets; An Unpleasant Decision

Aramis saw the look of disbelief in Porthos's eyes, before his friend said, "You did not kill her."

He wished he could be as certain as Porthos was. The truth of it was that his and Porthos's friendship had been founded on the fact that the two men were as different as two men could be. Aramis's mind ran on words and maxims, on remembered readings, on the wisdom of the ages, while he very often thought that if someone cut off Porthos's massive and skillful hands the man would become unable to think at all.

In Porthos's world the idea that one might not know whether he'd killed someone or not was preposterous, insane. If Porthos had taken the trouble to murder anyone, Porthos would very well remember it.

But Aramis knew his own mind and the perfidious way in which his thoughts could hide behind his words and his feelings behind his thoughts so that he could never be sure of himself until he'd acted. And sometimes not even then.

Take Violette, for instance. It had all started as a harmless flirtation on a summer night, when she'd been too bored to remain alone in her room and had sought him out, at his guard post, to talk.

And he had told himself it was just a silly romantic game, even as it progressed, from the guard post to her bedroom, from the bedroom to a thousand talks and discussions in her receiving room, until she knew all his thoughts and he knew all of hers. Until they were closer than most married people and, in fact, were married in all but law. That final union, her married state and his vocation forbade, as did the width of different classes that separated them.

But he had loved her. And what lunacy will love not induce? "I don't think," he started, and his voice cracked and wavered shamefully. He cleared his throat. "I don't think I killed her," he said. "Truly, I don't. But I cannot imagine how anyone else could have. The inaccessible room, the locked door..." He shrugged. "I tell you, for a moment I wasn't sure. I wasn't sure at all."

"If you'd killed her," Porthos said. "Why would you cry out when you found she was truly dead? Why would you think it was all a prank and a joke?"

And in this, Porthos was correct, would be correct. Aramis was grateful to his friend for bringing the witness of his own actions to his rescue. "Perhaps I wouldn't," he said.

But Athos cleared his throat. "You know how sometimes, when you drink too much you wake in the morning and have no memory at all of what you've done?" And to Porthos's nod, he added. "I've heard this happens sometimes, too, when you do something the mind finds too terrible to accept. There was . . ." He paused. "There was this wood-cutter in my father's estate, who one day cut up his entire family with an ax. People saw him do it." Athos shook his head, in wonderment. "And yet, he would swear by the Virgin and all the saints that he'd never done it, that his enemies must have gone in, behind him, and killed all his loved ones. And he wasn't lying. We are sure of it. He just couldn't remember it."

Aramis stared at Athos's stern features for a moment. Could Aramis have? Could he have killed Violette and forgotten all about it? He heard a low groan escape his throat and put his face down into his hands.

"Oh, nonsense," Porthos said. And added in a tone of someone making the final argument, "Aramis is not a woodcutter."

But Aramis wasn't sure at all that his social class protected him from suspicion. He wasn't a woodcutter. He was a musketeer. He had become used to killing people. It would be easier for him than for some peasant. He groaned again.

D'Artagnan drew in breath loudly, a sound that, in the otherwise still room, echoed like a shot. "Porthos makes a good argument," he said. "For a woodcutter, perhaps, killing someone would be something to forget forever. But Aramis . . . has killed people before. With no forgetfulness."

Aramis looked up at the youth with hope. D"Artagnan, he had suspected for some time, was the cleverest of them all. Oh, not the most cultured. That honor belonged to Athos. And not the most cunning. Modest though his beliefs and his future chosen profession obliged Aramis to be, they didn't force him into blatant lying. He was the most cunning and this he must admit. But d'Artagnan was the cleverest, capable of penetrating to the heart of a question or the main point of an event.

The heart of the matter here was that Aramis had no reason to forget, had he killed Violette. He blinked at the young guard.

D'Artagnan nodded, as though having read the desired response in Aramis's eyes. "Did you have any reason to wish her dead?" he asked. "Had she played you false or somehow betrayed you?"

Aramis took a deep breath and shook his head. "And even if she had," he said, then shrugged, unable to explain fully. "We were never . . . I was never for her nor she for me. She has a husband somewhere and I am bound for the church, eventually. If she had another lover or twenty, as long as she did not turn me away from her door . . ." He shrugged again.

"And that she clearly hadn't done," d'Artagnan said, and bit at the corner of his upper lip, a gesture he made when deep in thought.

Aramis shook his head.

"The problem is," d'Artagnan said, and his hand went to the pommel of his sword as though the very words required a defensive posture. "The problem is that not everyone in Paris knows you as we do, or can think through your actions as I can."

Aramis drew in breath. He understood the words d'Artagnan had not said. "I am suspected?" he asked.

D'Artagnan waved his hand in a way that reminded everyone forcefully that he came from Gascony, near the border with Spain. "It is only tavern rumor," he said unhappily. "But tavern rumor has it that you killed your . . . seamstress because she loved another better."

"It is hardly to be wondered at," Athos said. "When you left your uniform behind, and it is well known that you visited the lady at all hours."

"And stayed for hours too," Porthos said.

"I've often told you, Aramis, that associating with a woman in that way only gives her power—"

Aramis didn't think that he could listen to Athos's ideas on women and men's best way to interact with the female of the species. In the five years Aramis had known Athos, Athos had been involved with exactly one woman and that brief and disastrous[1]. "They say I killed Violette?" he asked d'Artagnan, unable to believe it. "Who says it?"

D'Artagnan shrugged. "It's the talk of every tavern," he said. "I went to a lot of them this morning, you know, to gather the talk, and it is the talk in every tavern."

"By name?" Aramis asked.

d'Artagnan nodded. "It is said everywhere that you stabbed her, and then jumped from her balcony and were brought to Paris by accomplices, just ahead of the pursuers."

"But it can't be very serious talk," Porthos said. "The guards of the Cardinal have not come by to arrest you, have they? And surely they would not fail to do it, and would rejoice in it, given the excuse? Besides the Cardinal thinks it is his duty to keep peace over all of Paris."

"This is true," Aramis said. He shrugged. "If it's just tavern gossip . . "

"I'm afraid it isn't," Athos said. "This morning, before coming here, I went to visit Monsieur de Treville, our captain, to set his mind at ease should he hear rumors . . ."

"And?" Aramis asked.

"The rumor mongers had been there ahead of me. He'd already heard of the events of the night, only—knowing us a little better than most people—he guessed we helped you escape."

Aramis felt a groan leave his throat, heard it echo in his ears with a sound of despair. "Monsieur de Treville believes me guilty then?"

Athos started to shake his head, then shrugged. "He did not weigh on his belief of your guilt. But he said the case looks bad for you, since the lady is well born and well above your station." Athos reached into his doublet and pulled out a filled leather pouch. "He sent this, which he says is an advance on your wages, which you can earn after you return when your name is cleared."

"Return?" Aramis asked.

Athos nodded. "Monsieur de Treville says he lacks the ability to protect you and, as such, must advise you to get out of Paris and stay out till your name should be cleared and you are no longer at risk for arrest."

Aramis took the pouch from Athos's hand and squeezed it in his right hand. The leather was soft and the heaviness of the parcel betrayed a quantity of money inside. "But how am I to be cleared if I leave town?"

"You leave us behind," d'Artagnan said. "And you must know we'll work to clear your name in any way possible."

Aramis nodded. He knew that, but it still seemed wrong for him to leave when he'd done nothing to deserve exile. And it seemed even worse for him to have to depend on others to clear his honor.

Athos had walked away from the group and was looking out the window, a frown on his face. "I think, Aramis, there is a patrol of guards up front even now. They haven't emboldened themselves to knock at the door, but I'd wager they're bold enough to arrest you if you should step outside. Is there another way out of this place?"

Aramis nodded. "There is the coal delivery trap," he said. "But—"

"Then I advise you head that way now. Fast. Before they can knock and question your landlord on your whereabouts." He paused for a moment and cleared his throat. "I know of a country estate where you can stay. It's near Ruan. I can give you a letter to my—To the steward there, who will—"

Oh, this was rich. Aramis was sure the estate that Athos spoke of was Athos's own. Some rural idyll where the servants would obey the lord's orders with no question. Even after the lord had been missing for years.

But if it came to that, Aramis also had an estate he could return to, and where the inhabitants would keep him in secrecy and protect him from the Cardinal's guards if it came to that. "I thank you," he said. "But I know of an estate where I might stay, with a widowed gentlewoman."

"Oh, not another of your women, Aramis," Porthos said impatiently. "They will say that you killed the other for this one, that you—"

Aramis felt a hint of his old accustomed smile come to his lips and twist them upwards ironically. "Oh, trust me, Porthos, no one will think I killed anyone for this lady."

He stood up, feeling more decision than he had in a long time, opened his wardrobe, and started stuffing suits into a leather bag, paying little attention to how he lay them in there. "Holla Bazin," he called, as he did it.

Bazin opened the door a crack and looked in, proving once more that he'd been listening—an abominable habit of which Aramis had tried to break him for years. Might as well try to break a cat of hunting mice.

Looking over his shoulder, Aramis saw Bazin looking at him, with every mark of anxiety stamped on his cherubic features. "Pack what you need to, Bazin," he said. "We are going to leave Paris for some days."

"Leave Paris?" Bazin asked. "But on what horses?"

"We'll hire some," Aramis said, feeling the weight of Monsieur de Treville's pouch within his sleeve. "Pack what you need. We're going out via the coal delivery door."

Bazin only nodded without asking why, because he probably knew very well why already. He scurried away.

Aramis, having finished throwing all his clothes into his leather saddle bag, in a way that would normally have horrified him, now assumed a sheepish look as he opened the compartment within the wardrobe which contained his crest-embossed stationary. He would not leave this behind, with such a blatant clue to his identity.

Throwing the few sheets into the bag, he backtracked to the table by the window where his silver hair brushes sat, with the initials R H on the handle. These, too, he threw into the bag, then turned with a smile he hoped was engaging. "And now, my friends, I'll leave everything that is of worth to me in your hands—my reputation, my honor and my ability to return to Paris and serve in the musketeers."

"You know you can trust us," Athos said.

"Indeed," Porthos said, with rather more enthusiasm. "We'll find the villain who killed your lady and we'll bring him to justice."

"Him or her," d'Artagnan said.

"I will trust you, then," Aramis said and, feeling self-conscious as he always did at these occasions, he put his arm forward, palm up. "One for all."

"And all for one," the other three responded, their hands, palm down, falling one after the other, atop of Aramis's.

And with this reaffirmation of brotherhood, Aramis slung his bag over his shoulder and headed for the door. In the little hall outside his lodgings, instead of heading for the stairs, he opened the smaller and inconspicuous door that led to the servants' stairs. These stairs, taken all the way down, led to the cellar and from hence to the coal delivery door and outside to the backstreet.

He hurried down the steps, hearing Bazin follow him.

Behind him and down the stairs to the other side, fierce pounding echoed. The guards had mustered their courage and were knocking on the door.

He wasn't afraid of getting caught. Even if they'd left one man at the coal door entrance, one man he could deal with. And if the guards went through the front door first— as they probably would—his friends would delay them long enough.

It was the prospect of going to his mother's house, now, that worried Aramis. How would he explain his predicament to Madame D'Herblay?

Oh, he wished he'd never met Violette, if he would now suffer this way for her death. He should have stayed in seminary and stayed away from all women.

Where Three Musketeers Can Slow Six Guards; The Fine Points of Gascon Honor

Aramis had barely vanished from the room, when d'Artagnan heard pounding at the door downstairs. He walked out, past Bazin's—now empty—monk like room, and opened the door to the hall, in time to see a confused half-dozen men, all attempting to climb the narrow stairs at the same time, in a flurry of angry faces, waving arms and the blood red tunics and hats that the guards of Cardinal Richelieu wore.

They were a lot more serious about it than the musketeers who, beyond the color, often allowed all manner of variation in what they called their uniforms. Those guards—the private army of the man who was, for all intents, the power behind the throne in France—were by nature and habit the enemies of the King's musketeers. In dozens of back alleys and up a hundred public staircases made slippery by the daily muck, musketeers and guards faced each other. At any time of the day the cries of "For the King" or "For the Cardinal," the rousing yells, "To me musketeers," or "To my aid, guards," could be heard throughout the city, where blue and red would meet in a clash of swords, a spark of conflict. And smart bystanders stood well away from the brawling factions.

It was therefore no wonder that the guards were the ones sent to arrest Aramis. His being one of the more prominent musketeers, who had so often bested them in fight and duel, would make them only too eager to accuse him of murder. That eagerness now carried the red-attired guards, stumbling and cursing, pressed together up the stairs, each unwilling to give the other the chance to reach Aramis first.

D'Artagnan backed into the room, but had no time to close the door before three guards—with a resounding thud—planted their feet on the tiny landing at the same time. He recognized them by sight and remembered them by name. The one in front was Bagot, a large, florid man with a bristling mustache. A good fighter if a little too prone to losing his concentration in a pinch. Pressed to his right side, his right arm swinging a sword, his left arm caught between his comrade's body and the wall, stood Dlancey, a stripling of a man, reedy and tall, with a straggle of long blond hair. He'd gone the interesting shade of red-purple that fair people went when vexed. To the left side of Bagot, his left hand holding a large sword, his right hand clenched onto a railing being all that prevented him from falling headlong onto the hall downstairs, stood Fasset, a small Gascon man whom d'Artagnan had never exchanged words with but who was reputed throughout Paris to be almost as sharp as d'Artagnan himself.

They were all talking at the same time. Shouting. Disconnected words, "murder, arrest, law" emerged from their screaming.

D'Artagnan took a farther step back and fetched up against the wall-like solidity of Porthos. A quick glance showed him the sword in Porthos's hand, and d'Artagnan, himself, swiftly pulled his sword out, and stood beside Porthos.

Bagot had managed to extricate himself from the press of his comrades, and stand slightly ahead of them on the narrow landing.

"Holla," he said, looking from d'Artagnan to Porthos. "You receive us armed, do you? Stand aside and let us arrest the criminal or it will go worse with you."

Without turning, d'Artagnan felt Porthos move. Then someone tapped d'Artagnan's shoulder lightly. D"Artagnan stood aside to let Athos through.

The older musketeer looked composed, his sword in its sheath, his hat on his head. He now removed the hat, and, as Porthos and d'Artagnan took a step back to allow the space, bowed civilly to the red-faced Bagot.

"I will greet you with all due courtesy," he said. "Though I should perhaps note that you were the first ones to unsheathe your swords." He looked markedly at Bagot's hand holding the sword.

Bagot followed his gaze and made a growl low in his throat. He punched his hat farther down on his head, didn't sheathe his sword, and glared at Athos, "We are keeping our swords out because we are here on a mission to arrest a foul murderer."

Athos threw his shoulders back. Even if he couldn't see Athos's face, d'Artagnan knew his aristocratic friend well enough to guess that Athos's face had acquired the proud, blind dignity of a marble statue, and that his eyebrow would have raised the slightest bit, to indicate his disdain for Bagot. Athos was the noblest of the musketeers and, with a step forward and the throwing back of his well-shaped head could make even a prince in silks and velvets look like rabble.

Bagot was no prince. His reaction to Athos's expression displayed itself clearly in a reddened face, eyes bulging out of their prominent sockets. "Mortdieu," he said.

And had no time to say more, because Athos, speaking with the icy calm of one who addresses an inferior so beneath him that it's hardly worth wasting words on him, said, "I know no murderers, nor do I associate with murderers. You are, perhaps, not apprised that this is the lodging of my good friend, Aramis?"

"Ah!" Bagot said. "Aramis is not even a proper name. It's a nom de guerre, a fake name. I wonder what hides beneath it, and how many women fell prey to the foul monster in the years—"

Slowly, in controlled movements, Athos's hand went to his sword. "Sir," he said. "I can't believe you know what you are saying. I only hope that, wandering in your mind in some distress, you have confused my friend with someone else."

"Aramis!" Bagot sneered. His hand, clasped on his own sword hilt, was so tightly clenched that the knuckles appeared white. "Aramis indeed. It is he, whatever his true name is, who killed the Duchess de Dreux not a day ago, in the palace, after having wormed himself into her bed with who knows what threats and cunning."

"Are you certain I'm not misreading your meaning?" Athos asked. "You do indeed mean to insult Aramis, my friend? Aramis who has served as my second in countless duels and, likewise, asked me to be his second in countless more?"

"Dueling is against all the edicts," Bagot said, his face now so red that it shaded to purple in places. "And you're confessing to it so calmly."

"Indeed," Athos said.

"Then I'll have no choice but arrest you."

Athos threw his head back, a gesture that made his long, blue black hair—tied back with a simple ribbon—flick upon his faded musketeer's uniform. He removed his hat and bowed slightly.

D'Artagnan didn't need to see his friend's face to know the mad rictus of a smile that distorted Athos's features and made mockery of its own frozen politeness. In this mood, Athos scared even his friends.

Bagot, though he didn't know Athos, must have been able to read expressions, because his eyes widened and for a moment shock replaced anger in his expression, as he took a step backwards.

"My dear sir," Athos said, still bowing, his voice icily polite and echoing with accents such that had, doubtlessly, been learned at the knee of the sort of tutor that only ancient and cultured nobility would think to hire. "You leave me no choice but to charge."

Athos rammed the hat back on his head, and, in a movement so fast that the eye could not perceive it, pulled his sword out of its sheath. In that small landing, atop a very narrow staircase, there shouldn't have been space for such antics. But Athos had the well-trained grace of the dancer, the agility of a born athlete. And Bagot had, at the very least, healthy self-preservation instincts. As did his cohorts.

Athos's sword had no more than gleamed in the dim light, the dusty air, than there was a scurry and scuffle, and the noise of several men scrambling, prudently, down the stairs.

This gave Dlancey and Fasset the chance to take a step back, and Bagot the chance to stand, solidly facing Athos, even if from a lower rung on the stairs. To his credit, Bagot looked not scared but annoyed, as though he were an accountant whose sums refused to come quite right. "Ventre saint gris," he said. "You are a madman. You—"

Athos pounced forward. D"Artagnan had often seen him in this state. He knew that the urbane, learned man whom he called a friend was the outward manifestation of something else—something repressed and dark, deep and brutish—that peeked out of Athos's eyes only on two occasions: when the musketeer was deeply drunk, and when he felt the bloodlust of a duel.

Bagot pounced backwards and put up his sword.

Bagot was a better fighter than d'Artagnan expected. Perhaps not as good as Athos, but good enough to defend himself from Athos's blind fury. For a moment, the two advanced and retreated in the narrow distance of the first three rungs of staircase and the tiny landing. Back and forth, in a scuffle of boots, an echo of grunts and wordless exclamations, a flash of swords hitting each other and sliding, metallic, along each other's length.

For just a breath, Bagot pressed Athos backwards, onto the door of Aramis's lodgings, forcing Porthos to retreat, and d'Artagnan to glue himself to the wall to allow the combatants room.

But Athos recovered. A low growl making its way through his throat, he charged forward, forcing Bagot to retreat. With remarkable cunning and even more remarkable agility, Bagot stepped back and back and back, halfway down the stairs, keeping Athos at bay but managing to retreat, without ever turning his back to escape. Halfway down the staircase, he jumped over the railing and to the hall downstairs. But there he turned to face Athos, as if to show he wasn't running, just seeking more space for his sword arm.

Athos yelled something that was no word, just formless fury, and jumped after the man.

And now Dlancey stepped forward. "We must look in there," he said, looking past d'Artagnan, still plastered to his wall, and to Porthos. "For the murderer."

"Aramis never murdered anyone," Porthos said, surging forward. "Killed, sure, lots of people. But he never murdered anyone. If you call him a murderer again, I shall have to cut your tongue out and feed it to you."

Dlancey grinned, a grin that made his thin and worried face appear more like the devil-may-care expression of a seasoned man of war. He pulled his sword out. "I should like to see you try."

"Oh, that you shall," Porthos said, and in the next moment, the two of them were fighting on the staircase, step up and step down, calling boasts to each other and advertising to each other the horrible things they intended to do to the other.

"I don't suppose you'll be reasonable about this," Fasset asked. He looked at d'Artagnan calculatingly.

D'Artagnan grinned. He knew better than to argue with a stooge of the Cardinal. And besides, if he judged the game properly, Athos meant to delay these men as much as humanly possible, keeping them busy, to give Aramis a chance to get a horse and escape Paris. "I'm always reasonable," he said, and let his sword hand fall upon the pommel of his sword with accustomed ease. "And here is my reason."

Fasset had anticipated d'Artagnan's response. His sword was out, and as d'Artagnan lunged, he parried most ably.

They fought silently for a few minutes, d'Artagnan taking care to close the door of his friend's room behind him in the one moment he had a chance to. They fought up and down the staircase, d'Artagnan keeping the upper hand but never quite prevailing. In the hall beneath, Athos had a spot of blood on his right sleeve and had moved his sword to his left hand.

At the bottom of the staircase, Porthos and Dlancey fought, cursing and threatening each other, but neither looked the worse for the wear, save for sweat and reddened features.

"I don't suppose he's even in his lodgings," Fasset said, as he parried d'Artagnan's thrust. "He's probably at Monsieur de Treville's as we speak, looking for justification from that worthy gentleman."

D'Artagnan managed to smile and hoped his face betrayed the proper triumphant expression and then just as quickly erased it. If he was lucky, he thought, as he battled Fasset down the stairs, then Fasset would think that Aramis was within and d'Artagnan was glad at the thought he had escaped.

"Curse you," Fasset said. "To the deepest hell. He's within, is he not?" and, with redoubled fury, he started fighting d'Artagnan up the stairs. But d'Artagnan couldn't allow him to check Aramis's quarters just yet, and he fought vigorously downward.

Down in the hall, the more timorous guards of the Cardinal had regained their courage. Not enough of their courage to help Bagot with Athos. Even madmen would scruple to get in Athos's way when his dark blue eyes shone with that unholy light. They started up the stairs towards Porthos. Porthos fought four of them without breaking a sweat.

Two of them straggled past Porthos to challenge d'Artagnan. Without a word, Fasset turned and fought beside the young guard against his own comrades, his concentration intense, his swordplay deadly.

"Would you side with me?" d'Artagnan asked, puzzled.

"I would side with honor."

"Is it honor to come arrest a man early morning, on a mere rumor?" he asked.

Fasset snorted, even as his sword made short work of his stunned former comrades. "Rumor? Spare me. We found his uniform in the lady's room."

"Knowing Aramis," d'Artagnan said, as he fought an enemy three steps down, only slightly worried about having Fasset now behind him. "I'm only surprised you didn't find two uniforms more —a normal one, one for special days, and his lace and velvet outfit for the days when he didn't wear a uniform. He practically lived at the lady's."

Fasset laughed behind him, as d'Artagnan sent his opponent's sword flying over the stair railing and to the hall below. Then he resumed parrying the attacks of another two.

"But this uniform was the only one, and it was clear he'd run away naked."

"How could he run away naked? And make it through half of Paris on the way back home."

"Ah," Fasset said, as he fought his three opponents down the steps, till he was side-by-side with d'Artagnan. "Ah, that I cannot answer, but we've long since, all of us in his eminence's guards, lived in awe of those we call the four inseparables." He turned and gave d'Artagnan a tight smile, before resuming fighting shoulder to shoulder with him.

Porthos had dispatched his more recent opponent who fell to the steps, his whimper the only mark of life left in him. Porthos jumped over the man's body to resume his fight with Dlancey.

In the hall below a sound somewhere between a grunt and a scream was followed by Athos's suddenly civil-again voice, "If you give me your sword, I shall help you fashion a tourniquet."

As the sound of clashing metal had ceased down there, d'Artagnan assumed the suggestion had been followed.

He, himself, quickly made short work of his opponents by inflicting minor but disabling wounds through thigh and arm. Soon the two who had attacked Fasset and himself were lying against the walls or on the steps, groaning. And now Fasset turned to d'Artagnan and bowed. "Should we resume our fight?" he asked. Something like an ironic smile twisted his lips.

Without looking, d'Artagnan was aware of his friends coming up the stairs, aware of Porthos and Athos standing behind him. But neither of them made a move or said a word.

"Would you insist on entering Aramis's rooms?" he asked.

Fasset bowed slightly, "I'm afraid I must," he said. "How could I face the Cardinal without having fulfilled the mission he gave me?"

D'Artagnan looked back at his friends to judge their reaction. Porthos looked impassive, waiting. Athos, who was holding his right arm with his left hand just below a spreading red stain on his doublet, shrugged, as if to say that none of this made any difference to him.

D'Artagnan was not stupid. He could understand hints. The rooms that had been of such importance and must be defended at all costs were now of no importance at all. That meant—and d'Artagnan's own internal clock told him this—that at least an hour had gone by. And Aramis, if nothing had befallen him, was now well on his way to his hideout. And the guards of the Cardinal could never intercept him unless they knew his exact destination.

D'Artagnan nodded to Fasset. "You shall see the rooms, then," he said. "But with us present."

Fasset's turn to shrug, as if all this meant nothing.

D'Artagnan, followed closely by Porthos and Athos, escorted Fasset into the rooms.

"A large cross," Fasset said, pausing in front of the crucifix on the wall of the entrance room.

"You must know Aramis means to take orders someday," Porthos said.

Fasset was kind enough to make no comment at that. He looked at the interior room and opened the wardrobe, as though to register its emptiness. He flicked through the papers on the desk, but all without much interest.

"How long has he been gone?" he asked, putting his gloves on, gloves he must have taken off before reaching the house.

D'Artagnan smiled. "You don't expect me to tell you that?"

"I don't expect you to tell me anything at all," Fasset said, and something very much like a grudgingly admiring smile crossed his lips. "It is fortunate for Monsieur Aramis that he has such loyal friends." He adjusted his gloves in place and looked up to meet d'Artagnan's gaze with his own, acute, dark gaze. "I hope your confidence in him is not misplaced. I will now collect my comrades and go back to the Cardinal's. Good day, sir."

A Council of War; The Various Kinds of Seamstresses; The Memory of Husbands

The wound in Athos's arm was deeper than it looked and more painful. Bagot's sword had pierced all the way down to his bone, and slid along the bone, so that every movement of his right arm brought a painful shock down to his hand and up to his shoulder.

He thought he was bearing it tolerably well, but he should have remembered his friends knew him better than that. Before he could make an excuse and leave for his own lodgings, to nurse his own wound with the help of Grimaud's tight-lipped wrapping of ligatures and a fine bottle of wine that could make the devil himself forget his wickedness, Athos saw d'Artagnan looking sharply at him.

They had just left Aramis's house, trusting the wretched Fasset to deal with the remainder of his expeditionary force, most of whom were either too wounded or too weak to walk.

Athos, in his role as the oldest and almost as an adoptive father to his friends, had got a key to Aramis's lodgings from the landlord and locked the door behind himself. He'd instructed the landlord to give no one the key, though he didn't know if the man had heard or if he would obey. These days it didn't seem as though any landlords were honest, any merchants respectful, or any noblemen honorable. Indeed, in Athos's dimmed view, the whole world was sinking into a morass of disorder.

Which was why it didn't surprise him to see d'Artagnan, a seventeen-year-old youth, staring at him with the disapproval that Athos would have expected of his elders and betters. He straightened his spine, insensibly, under the scrutiny, and found his upper lip curling in disdain, ready to refuse the young man's pity or scorn at his wounding.

But d'Artagnan's dark eyes shifted, and his expression became one of frowning concern. "The salve . . ." he said, and paused, as if searching for words. "You remember the salve, the recipe of which my mother gave me before I left my father's house? Be the wound ever so grave, the injury so severe, as long as no vital organ is touched, it will cause it to heal three days. I have had the chance to make it useful to you in the past."

Athos remembered this same speech. "Yes. Last month, when we first met and I was nursing a shoulder wound."

"My lodging at the Rue des Fossoyers is nearby and I have a jar of salve ready."

"It is nothing," Athos said. He didn't even know why, except that he didn't like for anyone to see him weak or wounded. And in their brief acquaintance d'Artagnan had seen this all too often already. "It is a scratch."

Porthos, who had held silent through all this, cleared his throat as he looked meaningfully at Athos's sleeve, which was now so drenched in blood that a trickle of it was dripping below his wrist and down his hand.

Athos looked at Porthos, then rounded on d'Artagnan, expecting to read pity or annoyance in the young man's eyes. But d'Artagnan had turned away and, as they walked, was scanning the street ahead of him as though something vital held his interest in the midmorning sidewalks and their sparse foot traffic of shopping housewives and surly apprentices.

"We have to talk at any rate," the young man said, as he looked ahead. "Upon topics best not described on the street. Unlike Fasset I have no fear for our friend's culpability, but still we told him we would do our best to clear his name and his honor while he was gone . . ."

And on that he'd got Athos, because Athos could not deny that they should be investigating the murder, that they should be talking in private. And d'Artagnan's house was nearest. And—if he owned the truth to himself— Athos knew he could profit from the salve upon his arm. The pain was near unbearable, and all the nursing that Athos's servant, Grimaud, would give him would be the wrapping of a ligature to stop the bleeding. But that would do nothing for the pain or the possibility of fever.

D'Artagnan's salve, if it worked, might keep Athos's head clear enough to find the murderer of Aramis' lover. Not that there was a murderer to find. Or none other than Aramis. Because, how could there be another one? Aramis had been alone with the woman, locked in. And yet Athos refused to believe that Aramis would lie to them.

Could Aramis kill the woman he loved? Why not? Others before him had. Athos himself . . . Athos stopped the image of his dead wife from surfacing in his mind. And yet . . . and yet, though he could believe Aramis capable of murder, he couldn't believe him capable of deceiving his friends.

Oh, truth be told, Athos himself had never told his friends of his crime, his dark, secret remorse. But the crime had happened long before he met even Aramis or Porthos, much less d'Artagnan. And he'd asked for their help with neither cover-up nor expiation, both of which he was managing on his own, though perhaps not as well as he would like to.

But once they were friends and bonded as closely as brothers, Athos could not imagine any of them keeping a secret from the others. It was impossible. Aramis would have confessed to his transgression as he asked for help. He would have given his reason for the murder. And he would be sure as one could be sure of eventual death that his friends would stand by him no matter what his crime, as ready to save his neck in guilt as in innocence.

No, it was a puzzle without solution, Athos thought, as he followed the others—who'd taken his silence for acquiescence—along the narrow warren of roads that led to the working-class street in which d'Artagnan rented lodgings. And yet there was nothing for it but for the three of them—none of whom was particularly well suited to the solving of mysteries--to attempt to solve this one. How could they do it without Aramis? He was their man in the court, the one who knew duchesses and consorted with countesses.

How was Athos, who was all but a recluse, going to do such a thing? And what were the chances of d'Artagnan, still new in town and a guard of Monsieur des Essarts—not even a musketeer—gaining entrance to the court? As for Porthos . . . Athos looked towards his friend who appeared both intent and worried, as if trying to solve some difficult puzzle and sighed. Porthos had trouble enough imagining anyone could lie, much less unraveling a duplicitous plot. It was all hopeless.

But at that moment they reached d'Artagnan's home and d'Artagnan unlocked the door. "Planchet will be out," he said. "He said he needed to shop for food."

Planchet being d'Artagnan's only servant, Athos supposed his absence made their conversation perfectly private.

They climbed the staircase to d'Artagnan's apartment, which was more spacious than Aramis's, though in a less fashionable area of town. The entrance room sprawled large and was lit by two sunny windows that let the morning sun fall upon a broad table and a set of benches that d'Artagnan had got who knew where.

This was the accustomed council of war headquarters, where the musketeers and their friend discussed whatever occupied their minds at the moment. Porthos and Athos fell, wordlessly, into their accustomed seats, on either side of the table, while d'Artagnan went within for his ancestral salve.

While he was gone, Athos unlaced his doublet and pulled it off, then rolled his shirt sleeve up to reveal a jagged, deep wound on his forearm, just above his elbow.

"The devil," Porthos said. "That does not look like a scratch."

D'Artagnan, returning with salve and a roll of clean white linen said nothing. He merely set it on the table, beside Athos. "Do you wish to bandage it, or shall I?" he asked.

Athos shrugged. "I will need your help to tie the bandage," he said. Left unsaid, but implied, was that he would prefer not to have anyone touch him unless it were strictly needed. Much as he disliked to admit it, any touch, any human touch at all, made him think of betrayal and mockery. He'd learned to be contained within himself and, in himself, contain all his own needs. Without another word, he started slathering the salve on his wound. The yellow green paste smelled of herbs and felt curiously soothing to the skin. It stopped the bleeding on contact.

"One thing I don't understand," Porthos said, while Athos was occupied at this task. He took a deep breath, like a man venturing onto unfamiliar waters. "Are we sure that this duchess was the woman Aramis called his seamstress? How could she be a duchess when she's just the niece of his theology teacher?"

Athos looked up, startled, to meet Porthos's innocent stare. He made a sound in his throat that he hoped didn't seem like laughter and reached for the strips of linen that d'Artagnan had left at his hand.

D'Artagnan got up and stepped around to provide Athos with the extra hand needed for this task and said, as he was doing it, "The seamstress who writes to Aramis on lilac-perfumed paper?" he asked.

Porthos blinked.

"A seamstress who seals her letters with the imprint of a ducal crown," d'Artagnan said, meaningly.

"But . . . why?" Porthos asked. "Why did the niece of a theology professor become a duchess? And how?"

Athos could have told d'Artagnan that trying to insinuate things wouldn't work with Porthos. Porthos was not stupid, nor was he incapable of deception. In fact, Athos was privy to a deception that Porthos ran on his very own.

However, Porthos was abysmally bad at deception. So bad, in fact, that though Athos hadn't spoken, he very much doubted either of their two other friends believed Porthos's light of love to be the princess he said she was. Being naturally bad at deception, and abhorring confusing words and complex philosophies, Porthos naturally found it impossible to believe that Aramis, his closest friend, would run a more complex deception. He also would probably not understand at all why Aramis would call his duchess a seamstress while Porthos labored so hard to give the impression that he slept with crowned heads.

"There was never a niece of a theology professor," he said, as Porthos looked at him. "Aramis has always been involved with a duchess."

"A Spanish duchess?" Porthos asked, in tones of great amazement. "The maid yesterday called her by a string of . . ."

Athos shrugged and was rewarded with a firm pull on the ligature that d'Artagnan was attempting to tie. "She was Spanish by birth," he said. "I believe she grew up with Anne of Austria, as one of the young noble ladies chosen to be her playfellows and friends from a tender age. And when the Queen married our King, Aramis's seamstress, too, was sent to France as part of her escort, and her marriage to a French nobleman was arranged, at the same time as the royal marriage. Her title is Duchess de Dreux, an old duchy in Brittany."

"She is . . . married then?" Porthos said, slowly. "Her husband is still living?

And for just a moment Athos thought that Porthos was going to express or fake moral outrage at the woman's liaison with Aramis while she was married. Which would be strange from Porthos, whose own lover was the wife of an accountant. And Porthos normally was not hypocritical. His very own lack of ability to explain away things with words made him unable to explain or excuse himself to himself.

But, instead, Porthos said, "Where is her husband. Is he at court?"

"No," Athos said. And thought of her husband who had been his playfellow, or what passed for such in their class, with each family living in its own isolated estate and rarely meeting the others. Raoul de Dreux's father and Athos's father had been best friends and, as such, once or twice a year one of them undertook the journey to visit the other and then stayed several weeks at the other's house, hunting through the fine mornings, discussing poetry or history or philosophy through the heat of the day. Both men had lost their wives at their sons' births and, both fathers being unusually devoted to their offspring, the sons and their complement of maids and nurses traveled with the fathers when they went anywhere. Which was how Athos had come to share a nursery with Raoul from earliest infancy for some weeks every year. And a school room with him later on. They'd learned fencing and reading together and later—as they grew to adulthood—they had developed a friendship as strong as that of their fathers.

They had married very different women with results that, while not similar, were equally disastrous for each of them. The dissolution of Athos's own marital bonds by means of a rope around his Countess's neck had made Athos leave behind his most ancient friendship, as he had left His estate and land and proud heritage.

He was surprised to find tears in his eyes and realize he was thinking with longing of the simple, uncomplicated friendship of childhood. As much as he liked and trusted his present friends, it was strange to have no one around who truly knew him, who'd seen him grow up, who remembered the garrulous young man as well as the silent musketeer.

"No," he said. "Raoul . . . Monsieur de Dreux has no taste for the court. Truth be told, I never thought he had much taste for his wife. She was not . . . his kind. He is a quiet man, much fond of his books and his horses. She was bright and noisy and . . ." Athos realized he was relaying information from private letters and stopped. "The thing is that the marriage was arranged by his father, a glittering affair that meant not much. And then de Dreux returned to his domains, and his wife stayed in town." He felt his lips twist into a wry smile, an expression that he knew well betrayed more bitterness than humor. "And found her own amusements."

D'Artagnan had finished tying the bandage in place. "Could he have been jealous of her? Could he have found a way to murder her?"

"How?" Athos said. "By hiding under her bed while she entertained her lover?" He tried to imagine that situation and shook his head. "d'Artagnan, I don't believe he cared enough for her to come to town and visit her, much less to kill her in a jealous fit."

"You speak as though you know him?" Porthos said, as always cutting to the heart of the argument.

"I did," Athos said. "Before I became a musketeer."

Porthos nodded. "And you don't think he could be a murderer?"

Athos pulled down his sleeve. D"Artagnan had turned his back and was rummaging in a trunk by the window where he kept his glasses and his wine. He came back with them and poured wine for both his friends, while Athos put his doublet back on and laced it tight. The doublet gave him a feel of protection, of covering up his thoughts as well as his body. It was part of his musketeer's uniform, a penitent's clothing he had assumed as eagerly as other men assumed sackcloth and ashes.

"I'm not saying he couldn't murder," he said. "You must know, Porthos, for I've said it before and you've told me I was speaking nonsense, that I believe every man can be a murderer, given enough temptation and enough provocation. But Porthos, I don't believe he is a murderer in this case. Not the murderer of his wife. If he loved her . . . Then I could believe he would turn on her." He took a sip of his wine, which tasted sour and acid. He really must send some wine to d'Artagnan to keep for these occasions. Monsieur Des Essarts barely paid His guards enough to keep them from begging on the streets. No wonder all the boy could afford for wine was barrel dregs.

"You believe if he loved her he would have killed her?" Porthos said. "That makes no sense at all, Athos. By that reasoning the most logical suspect would be—" Porthos stopped, as if his own horror had stayed his tongue.

"Aramis," d'Artagnan said what Porthos could not say. He sat next to Porthos, facing Athos. The seat beside Athos, normally Aramis's, was left vacant. "You suspect Aramis, do you not, Athos?"

"I don't know. Do I suspect him of the crime?" Athos lifted his glass of red wine to the light and looked through it. "Perhaps. I can't say I didn't think of it and you must admit it is the most logical solution. Aramis was alone with her, behind a closed door. Who else could have killed her?"

"But," d'Artagnan said in the tone of one who prompts.

"I cannot believe you are saying this," Porthos said, still looking shocked. "How can you think that of a friend."

"What makes you sure that there is a but?" Athos asked d'Artagnan, ignoring Porthos's outrage.

"There has to be a but, otherwise you'd have demanded Aramis tell you why he had killed her. And you wouldn't have told him to leave town till we could clear his name. You'd have told him to leave town and pledge himself to some remote monastery, some out of the way retreat, where he could disappear forever."

Athos nodded. "There is indeed a but, and that is that I can't believe Aramis would lie to us. And there you have it, Porthos, I do not think that of my friend."

"Your reasoning seems flawed. Aramis lies all the time," d'Artagnan said, looking puzzled. "He's a courtier. He lies as he breathes."

"d'Artagnan. I cannot believe that both of you would so revile—" Loyal Porthos said.

"Peace, Porthos," d'Artagnan said. "I am not reviling anyone. But surely you know that Aramis lies to us all the time. He makes up stories to explain his presence where he shouldn't be. He talks of the duchess of this and what she said to the marquess of that, and all the time I'm sure he's just spreading rumors or passing them on, which is a lie after all. He lies to be diverting, he lies to protect others and he lies to hide the true cause of his actions. I've known this about him since we first met, notwithstanding which I consider him a true friend and one of the best men I've ever known." He looked across at Athos, a keen, examining look. "But his being the best of men, I still fail to understand why Athos thinks he wouldn't lie to us."

Athos smiled. "Oh, he'll lie to us well enough." He lifted his hand to still the protest he saw forming in Porthos's features. "He'll lie to us about where he ate dinner and where he slept, who gave him an embroidered handkerchief, and by what means he enters the palace late at night, but I submit to you that this he would not lie about. I've thought about it myself, because I, myself, suspected it, until I realized that if he had truly killed her, he would be putting us in danger by asking us to help him. And that, I don't believe Aramis would do. He would only put us in danger if he thought it needed to vindicate his innocence. If he knew himself to be innocent."

It was the longest speech he made in a long time, and it rendered both of his friends speechless. Porthos still looked upset at the implication that Aramis might be less than honest, but he had stopped his protests.

"But how could someone else have killed her if the room was locked and Aramis was there all the time, except when he went to . . . uh . . . relieve himself?" Porthos asked.

Secret Passages and Palace Maids; A Count's Connections and a Gascon's Loyalty

THAT was the question that d'Artagnan could never answer. Only Porthos would put it so clearly, because—in the month that d'Artagnan had known Porthos he'd come to know this—Porthos's mind was clear and direct and untroubled like a straight road.

He sighed, as he looked at his friend. "I don't know Porthos, and I don't understand it. But when Aramis took me to the palace with him, when we were investigating the death of . . . Of the lady we thought to be the Queen," d'Artagnan said. He didn't dare look towards Athos whose heart had gotten broken perhaps forever during that investigation. "I found that the palace is honeycombed with tunnels and passages. Is it possible that there is a passage into the lady's room?"

Athos shook his head. "Didn't Aramis say that there wasn't? That there was furniture against every wall?"

"Yes," d'Artagnan said. "But Aramis was scarcely thinking clearly then. And besides, I know from seeing it, some of the doors to these passages have furniture built onto them. Surely Aramis knows that too, since he was the one who showed me these passages. But he was not himself..."

"Are you saying that there could be a passage into the lady's room that Aramis didn't know about?" Athos asked.

D'Artagnan nodded. "I am saying that is the only way I can think of for someone to gain access to her apartments."

"How are we to gain access to the palace, though?" Athos said.

"I don't know. Surely you have some people you know within?" He wasn't so slow that he hadn't long ago realized that his friend, in his unassuming musketeer's uniform, with his small rented lodgings and one servant whom he had trained to obey signals and gestures, was really someone else—some Lord brought up in luxury and honor.

Athos shook his head. "Not . . . in my present station. Oh, they would know me, but not in my musketeer's uniform. I avoid the palace except for when I'm on guard or when Monsieur de Treville escorts us there."

"But surely the secrecy . . ." d'Artagnan started, meaning to ask if the secrecy was needed or if it could serve a purpose larger than clearing

Aramis's name. But he looked up at Athos's face and saw Athos's glance close as firmly as if doors had shut upon the dark blue eyes.

"Well, then, it leaves us with no means of investigating the secret passageways of the palace and no way to verify if there are any into that room," d'Artagnan said.

"It would be difficult, at any rate," Athos said. "From what I understand, in the palace, as in all old noble houses, sometimes even those who live there aren't sure where the passages are or if they exist."

"Is there . . . any other way we can start to investigate . . . ?"

"What about the maids?" Porthos asked.

D'Artagnan turned to look at Porthos. The big man was often cryptic, sometimes inscrutable, but his opinion could never be discounted as being of no importance. And yet, d'Artagnan could not have the slightest idea what he meant.

"The maids?" he asked, staring.

"The palace has maids," Porthos said, waving his hand as if this explained everything. And, as the other two stared at him in utter confusion, he sighed heavily. "Maids are easy to approach." He blushed slightly. "I find it easy to talk to maids and working women."

"Of course," Athos said. "You do have that gift, Porthos."

"And if anyone knows of secret passages," d'Artagnan said. "Maids would. They clean and maintain and . . ."

"Keep secrets from their masters," Athos said, his eyes shining with the ironical light they sometimes acquired.

D'Artagnan nodded.

"I can take care of that part then," Porthos said. "Getting maids to talk to me is easy."

D'Artagnan smiled, as he saw Athos give Porthos a shocked look.

"I enjoy their company," Porthos said. "And I believe they enjoy mine."

D'Artagnan could only imagine how this shocked the very aristocratic Athos. He, himself—brought up in a manor house so small and unimportant that it had exactly two servants, both treated as family—was not so much shocked as amused. It seemed to him the contrast between Porthos's desperate seeking for the appearance of high connections and his enjoyment of maids' company made the man more human and warm than either of his two other friends.

"So what am I to ask them?" Porthos said.

"If there are any passages into the room," Athos said.

"That is all? There is no part of this conversation that I failed to understand?" Porthos asked, standing up.

"There is no part you failed to understand," Athos said.

"Good, because I don't want to be told later that there was something else I was to ask."

Athos frowned thunderously in Porthos's direction.

"What have I done now?" Porthos asked. "Did I ask something I should not have asked?"

Athos blinked. It seemed to d'Artagnan that the musketeer had awakened from some deep thought. "No Porthos, I was just thinking." He looked at d'Artagnan, then back at Porthos. "Did Aramis, ever, in his gossip, tell you of anyone who might have hated Madame de Dreux?"

D'Artagnan, never having heard that name before this day shook his head and added, "No, and no one who hated his seamstress, either."

"I thought his seamstress—" Porthos started.

"Never mind, Porthos. Did he tell you of anyone who wished ill to either?"

"Aren't they the same person?" Porthos asked.

"Yes, but Aramis would have referred to them as being two different people."

"Oh. No, he never spoke of anyone bearing animosity to either."

Athos let out breath with every appearance of anger. "He didn't speak of anyone who hated her to me, either," he said. "Which is remarkable in itself. For someone living in the hothouse that is the court, the lady made few enemies. Perhaps because her interest was more in Aramis than in court intrigue."

"I know she supported the Queen," d'Artagnan said, recalling the events of a month ago. "And as such, perforce, the Cardinal must be her enemy."

Athos tilted his head. "So are we the Cardinal's enemies. Yet I don't see him going through any trouble to murder us by stealth. Those the Cardinal wants dead or vanished either are killed in open daylight or disappear during the night into the Bastille, never to be heard from again. Besides, Cardinal Richelieu is not a fool. He would not murder a duchess and expect it to go unnoticed."

He drummed his fingers, impatiently upon the table. "There is nothing for it," he said. "I must go as soon as possible and pay a visit to Raoul—Monsieur de Dreux."

It did not escape d'Artagnan's attention that Athos had first mentioned the man by his given name. Twice so far. There was also something to the way that Athos said the name that implied great affection or great familiarity— perhaps both. He wondered if Athos thought he needed to go see Monsieur de Dreux because he wished to see him or because he really wanted to assess his guilt. And he suspected the first more than the second. "Her husband?" he asked, drily. "But you said, only a few moments ago, that her husband could not possibly be the murderer. That he was not in love with her."

Athos looked at him, for a moment, blankly, then rubbed his forehead with the fingertips of his bloodied hand. Though the blood had dried, it nonetheless left little flakes upon the pale skin. "I did. And it is true I don't think he loved her, which means he had no reason to kill her in jealousy and rage. But there is another way he could have killed her, and I did not give it enough thought." He looked at d'Artagnan and said, slowly, as though the words pained him. "He might have killed her in cold blood and calculatingly. He might have fallen in love with someone else, and killed his wife to be rid of her."

"Do you think that's likely?" Porthos asked, resting one huge hand upon the table. "I presume you knew the man well enough to guess that."

Athos inclined his head. "It would not be possible for the man I knew, but some years have passed. People change."

"Indeed," d'Artagnan said thinking how much he, himself had changed since he'd come to Paris full of high flung hopes and his father's instructions to obey the Cardinal and the King equally.

"So," Athos said, and sighed. "I shall borrow horses from Monsieur de Treville. Having been wounded this morning, I think I'm justified in taking a few days for my recovery. I shall go and see Raoul and study how much he's changed. I'll be back in a week."

"You are not going alone," Porthos said.

"I believe I must," Athos said. "You must stay behind and get to know all the maids in the palace. Even for a man of your excellent talents, such a work should take at least a week."

"But—" Porthos said, "If by chance her husband did murder her, and if he perceives your intentions in visiting him, he might try to kill you also. You cannot go alone."

"I believe I must," Athos repeated.

And once more, as he had many times in the past month, d'Artagnan felt as though he were invisible, as if his friends could not see him and would not dream of taking him into account in their plans.

Oh, he did not hold it against them or not exactly. He knew that for years there had been three inseparables, in feasting and fighting, in duel and field of battle. The three leaned on each other without thinking, as a man leaned on his own legs and counted on them to support his weight. To add a fourth to that number must feel as strange as adding a third leg.

At least d'Artagnan hoped that was it. He was not so foolish that he hadn't perceived, in their investigation of the last murder, that there were secrets his friends kept from all—even each other. Perhaps Athos was afraid that by accompanying him d'Artagnan would penetrate the secret of Athos's identity? But surely, d'Artagnan had gone a long way towards that with the last murder they'd solved. And he had spoken to no one about it. Not even to Porthos or Aramis. Surely Athos remembered that act of loyalty?

At any rate, d'Artagnan felt he must speak. "Athos," he said, very quietly. "I am sure I can visit Monsieur des Essarts and let him know that I must accompany you on your trip for your health. Monsieur de Treville will vouch for all of us. Oh, he'll know we're all helping Aramis in some way, but he will not refuse us his help. You know he values Aramis."

Athos frowned at d'Artagnan through this speech. Almost before d'Artagnan was done speaking, Porthos thundered his fist down on the table, making table and floor shake. "Sangre Dieu," he said. "That's it. The boy must go with you. He's almost a child, still—" Porthos flashed d'Artagnan a smile, as though aware of the wound he was causing to the young guard. "But he's the devil himself with a sword and he's almost as devious as Aramis. With him by your side, I shall not worry."

"But that leaves you alone in town," Athos said.

"Oh, I know how to take care of myself," Porthos said, and twirled the end of his red moustache. He grinned, a devil-may-care grin. "Look, Athos, most of the court thinks me too thick and too slow of mind to pose any threat in this type of case. They will think that Aramis is plotting something, and that you and d'Artagnan have been called to him. Me? I shall pass unnoticed."

The idea that someone could not notice the redheaded giant struck d'Artagnan as laughable, and yet he knew exactly what Porthos meant. He had seen that attitude himself. People tittered behind their hands at Porthos, and laughed at his utterances as they would never dare do to either of the other musketeers. They didn't seem to realize that Porthos's lack of interest in discussions or philosophy, his inability or disinterest in complex plots, did not mean he lacked wit or sense.

"Well," Athos said. He looked d'Artagnan over, appraisingly. "Certainly you've given proof of your trustworthiness in the last month." He extended his hand to the young man. "I shall be pleased with your company. Meet me at Monsieur de Treville's this evening, after you make your arrangements. I shall borrow horses for us and for Grimaud and Planchet. They must all be swift horses, for our servants must keep up with us."

D'Artagnan shook Athos's hand. The left one, he noted. And thought perhaps Athos was at least half-serious at going away to recover. D'Artagnan didn't think his friend could easily fight another duel like today's. "We shall meet here tonight, then," he said.

The Prodigal Musketeer; French Manners and Spanish Mourning; Regrets of Exile

The sun was setting when Aramis reached his ancestral domains. The D'Herblay lands were neither very extensive nor very prosperous, but rather in both struck that happy medium that Greek philosophers held to be the mark of all virtue.

Aramis approached it from the North, coming in past vast fields and farms that other families tenanted for the D'Herblays. The age of the houses, all stone and some covered in ivy, attested to the age of the domain which, Aramis's mother said, had been in the family since the time of Charlemagne. The first D'Herblay had been a companion of that great king.

Aramis wondered if it was all now to end with the scion of the house being executed as a murderer, and he had to avert his eyes and keep them upon the road. He didn't see, nor want to see whether the workers on the fields recognized or noticed his passing.

He rode along the beaten-dirt road until he found himself riding through his mother's extensive orchards, wreathed in bloom and leaf for the beginning of spring. After the effluvium of Paris, the smell of ripening fruit and flowers hit Aramis like a return to childhood. As a boy, he'd run through these orchards and hid in the branches from Bazin's searching eyes. Even back then Bazin, a good ten years older than Aramis, had fixed on Aramis as his pass into a monastery. And that, perforce, meant he must wish upon the child a virtue that Aramis was little inclined to take upon himself.

A memory of the last tree Aramis had climbed, or rather descended, intruded and he rubbed at his arms, where the scratches were still visible, and sighed. Perhaps it would have been better for him if he'd listened to Bazin in those early, apple-stealing days.

He walked his horse, apace, between the trees. Here and there he caught glimpses of men and women among the trees. They all stopped and watched him pass. Was this, then how the prodigal came home? Wasn't he supposed to be in tatters? And yet wasn't his heart, even now, metaphorically in tatters?

Bazin caught up with him. Though—speed being needed—Aramis had made sure that Bazin had his own horse, as fast as Aramis's own, Bazin always fell behind. Truth was, with his rotund build, the man was made to ride a mule and made the nervous Arabian buckle. Or perhaps the servant felt that it was not proper to ride side by side with his master.

In either case, he now dragged alongside Aramis and said, "I never expected to see this again."

And Aramis, his eyes filled with beauty, his mind streaming with thoughts of his happy childhood said, "You didn't?" in some surprise.

Bazin shook his head. His thin lips were set in disapproval, his eyes half closed in disdain. "I thought we'd be in a monastery by now, happy in the service of the Lord," Bazin said.

"And you never thought to visit the domains again?" Aramis asked.

Bazin shook his head, while his closed-tight mouth mirrored his disapproval of what he would no doubt call the allure of the world.

Aramis shook his head in turn, not understanding Bazin. Bazin was the son of prosperous tenants on the D'Herblay lands, and his father had sometimes served as the elder Monsieur D'Herblay's valet. Aramis, himself, as a child, had often visited the home of Bazin's parents, where he'd been feted and petted by Bazin's mother. He couldn't imagine what complaints could have made Bazin not wish to see the domain again.

They'd left the orchards behind and rode into what his mother pleased to call the park, but which was really only expansive gardens, set with some old statues and a few stones disposed such as made them suitable to sit upon. The abundance of prey for hunting and the ornamental fountains of other, more prosperous parks quite eluded the D'Herblays. There was a fountain, in truth, but too old and blunted by time to look in any way ornamental.

And yet, the park, such as it was, held a thousand tumultuous memories for Aramis. There, behind that rock, he had stolen his first kiss—from a giggling, fresh-faced farmer's girl. And there, where the oak tree spread its branches, sheltering the clearing around it from prying eyes which might peer from the upper stories of the house, he'd beheld his first naked . . . Well, girl. No one could call Yvette a woman, considering that at the time neither she nor Aramis had passed the magical age of ten. She was the daughter of one of his mother's friends and, truth be told, he'd found the whole experience rather unexciting. Her body, naked, looked just like his—skinny and muscular, the legs scratched by tree climbing and the mishaps of childhood. She'd looked at his naked body—his undressing, too, being the payment she'd demanded for her lack of modesty—and made a rude comment about that part of his anatomy which differed from hers. And Aramis had been so shocked and offended that he'd taken off running, out of the clearing, quite forgetting he was in fact naked. Which transgression had earned him his mother's disapproval and, at her order, a thrashing from Bazin.

Aramis smiled at the memory and at the one that came on the heels of it. The same Yvette, five years later, when her body had been not at all like his own and when she hadn't found so much to laugh at in his anatomy.

"Rene!" said a person that had been bent over in a clump of flowers and grass to the left of the road—while Aramis's fond memories held his gaze pinned to the right.

"Maman," Rene D'Herblay said. Indeed it was the only word that would come to his lips. The Chevalier's mother, Madame D'Herblay, was still a beautiful woman. She'd been born in Spain and from hence came her obsessive religion and her taste for ornate crucifixes.

However, her hair was that gold that was known to fascinate painters and she'd been brought up in France, having early on been summoned by the D'Herblay family, so she could be brought up by her prospective mother-in-law in all the habits of the house. As such, her voice betrayed no taint of a Spanish accent as she said, "Rene, here? Without warning?"

"Maman," D'Herblay said again, his mouth going dry. His mother had always dressed with severe modesty. At least since Rene could remember. Of course, since D'Herblay's father had died when the Chevalier was still a toddler, that meant he didn't remember his mother in anything but the severest black.

In the five years he'd been away, he'd expected some change. He wasn't sure he expected it in this direction, though. Madame D'Herblay had augmented her normal mourning by adopting all but a nun's habit. And not the habit of those nuns that lived near enough the court for their convents to hold soirees and salons.

No. Madame D'Herblay would not cater to such fripperies. Instead, she'd enveloped her head in a voluminous black cloth, from beneath which only a few straggles of reddish blond hair peeked. And her figure, which had still been quite youthful enough five years ago, had been wrapped in a formless black dress. The only jewelry she wore was a silver cross, the smaller replica of the one that D'Herblay had left behind at his lodgings.

She'd been bent, and weeding amid her roses—a pastime of which she'd always been fond. She stood, a bunch of weeds in each hand, their roots thick and tangled with dirt. "Rene," she said again, and this time D'Herblay managed not to answer. She took a deep breath. "We thought you dead."

To this, the Chevalier could only shake his head, because how could it be true? His mother had surely received the twice annual letters he sent her. He knew that sometimes she sent money, though she sent it to Bazin to dispense as needed and only to those needs she'd recognize—food, not wine, plain shirts, not embroidered ones, rosaries, not jewelry.

But he could not protest. Madame D'Herblay wiped her hands on her black dress, leaving streaks of brown across the black surface. "But no matter. You're here now and we shall rejoice."

She came near his horse, and waited while he dismounted, and offered her cheek to his kissing lips. Her cheek felt dry and powdery, not like human flesh at all, but more like the relic of some saint. The Chevalier felt the reverence he always did near his mother and, as always, was surprised anew that she was shorter than himself by a good head. In his memory she always grew to towering proportions and stood there, majestic and impassive, disapproving of all his choices and decisions.

As soon as he had kissed her, Madame D'Herblay turned and headed towards the house. Aramis followed, leading his horse, and heard the huffing and puffing behind himself that denoted that Bazin too had dismounted and was leading his horse.

At the end of the path it opened and widened to a cobbled patio. The house itself was severe, almost plain—if anything five stories high, a hundred feet wide, and built of dark gray stone could ever be considered plain. But it lacked all the carving and other fripperies that other noble houses sported. The only carving, the only ornamentation, were monumental gargoyles sitting on each corner of the roof. Aramis remembered their spouting water in storms, and the music of the resulting waterfall near his window.

There, without the lady his mother saying anything or having to raise her voice to call them, two stable boys materialized, one on each side, and took the leads of Aramis's and Bazin's horses. Madame herself led them all the way up the curving steps to the house door. At the top, Aramis realized that Bazin had left—presumably to enter the house through some other doorway reserved for servants. That he felt Bazin's absence as a loss and wished his servant would come back surprised him.

But the feeling as he went into the front hall didn't surprise him at all. The hall of the D'Herblay house was tall and narrow, tiled in black and white. The walls, covered in dark red velvet, were hung with the portraits of great and noble ancestors, glaring down, in their warrior poses— swords strapped at waist—with a look of disapproval at his wasted life, his plebeian disguise.

The Chevalier felt an all too familiar sense of having entered a prison. A quiet prison, where only virtuous thoughts would be allowed.

To the left of the hall, a locked door, heavily paneled in oak, led to what had been Aramis's father's study.

That room he'd never entered. On two signal occasions, at his insistence, his mother had opened the door and shown him a small room with a desk, a chair and a shelf filled with red-leather bound volumes, all of it covered in dust. Apparently Madame D'Herblay, shocked at her husband's sudden death, had decreed that this room never again be used nor, indeed, touched.

"Rejoice," Madame D'Herblay said to the empty hall, or perhaps to the servants who, if they were wise, were lurking in the shadows waiting for her slightest command. "For this son of mine was dead and now he's alive, he was lost but now he's found."

Aramis swallowed hard and reached for what remained of his wit within the terrified mind of the Chevalier D'Herblay. He chuckled, a sound that echoed hollow in the immense hall. "You mean to tell me you shall kill the fatted calf, madame?" he asked.

But Madame D'Herblay only turned around to fix her errant son with a withering glare. "A calf? On a Friday? I wouldn't dream of it."

The Chevalier D'Herblay sighed. He had come back home.

Kitchen Wenches and Maids; Food for Thought; A Musketeer's Loyalty

Porthos had never gone to the palace kitchens by himself. Oh, sometimes when it was cold and he'd stood guard too long, he'd sent his servant, Mousqueton, there, for a bit of wine, a bite of meat.

After all, Porthos was a musketeer, a gentleman of the sword. He had been received by his majesty himself, and he was often chosen to guard the royal family. He should not be seen consorting with mere servants.

Besides which, Porthos had long run a deception on all his comrades as well as his closest friends. Proud of his clothes, his weapons, his noble ancestors, Porthos knew he cut a fine figure of a man. He knew he should be consorting with princesses, reading poetry to duchesses and, generally, holding up his place within the nobility. It was neither his fault nor his intention to admit that noblewomen bored him to tears. They talked of lace and silk, of who had danced with whom at the last royal ball—but, most of what they talked about was gossip. The not so subtly disguised venom in their descriptions of their fellow courtiers made Porthos feel queasy and, quickly, tired of their company.

Give him peasant girls anytime, with their clean laughter, their simple jokes and their wish to make the giant feel happier by feeding him and cosseting him.

He blamed it all on his childhood in his parents' abode, when he'd consorted mostly with the farmers, who admired him for his strength and size. From there to falling in love with their daughters had been a step. In fact it had been such an unequal romance that had caused his father to send Porthos to Paris, in search of fortune—and away from an impudent, doe-eyed farmer's daughter who had dared dream of becoming Lady du Vallon.

But now Porthos had a legitimate reason to haunt the palace kitchens. He'd promised his friends he'd find out about passages. He took a deep breath, and twisted his moustache. He'd dressed as if he were about to pay a visit to a duchess, in the finest silk shirt, an embroidered velvet doublet and over breeches ornamented in a matching pattern of gilded flowers. In this garb, he'd stood guard, getting very odd looks from people who went in and out of the palace. Granted, the uniform of musketeer wasn't mandatory, yet most people wore it, or at least wore the tunic and the hat. And very few of them stood guard in clothing more appropriate to a royal soirée.

"Come, Mousqueton," Porthos said when he'd been relieved by another musketeer, a young man by the name of D'Evreux.

Mousqueton, who had been amusing himself nearby, playing dice with the other servants in the shadow of the walls, approached.

"Come," Porthos said, heading into the palace—which in this part meant heading into a narrow courtyard that looked much like the paved courtyard of a farmhouse, the place where hay would be baled and horses groomed. "Show me the way to the kitchens."

"The kitchens?" Mousqueton asked, catching up with his master. "Can we not go to a tavern? I have some money I won at the dice and I—"

Porthos shook his head, impatient. "This is not about food, Mousqueton. In a tavern I'm not likely to know what I need to find out about the palace."

"About the palace?" Mousqueton asked.

"Have you become like the Greek nymph that was transformed into an echo, Mousqueton?" Porthos asked, impatient and not a little happy to have remembered the legend which Athos had expounded upon the last time that Porthos had taken it into his head to repeat the ending of every sentence Athos said.

"But . . ." Mousqueton said, then, with a quick look around, as if to verify they were alone—which they were, in the middle of a deserted and dark courtyard—"Would this have to do with Monsieur Aramis?"

Porthos nodded. "We must know certain details about the layout of the palace, details that not even its inhabitants are likely to know. To be honest, it is something I need to ask the servants about."

Mousqueton moaned like a soul in eternal punishment. "And you think I can . . . help you in this? Because of all the times I got you wine and bread from the kitchen? You think I know the maids?"

"Well," Porthos said. "I don't expect you to know them by name, no. But I do expect that you'll have some acquaintance with them and that by having you with me, you can provide me with that modicum of introduction that a man needs before getting down to talking to maids and cooks."

Mousqueton only moaned again, while fixing his master with a look of such terror that if Porthos hadn't known the wretch he would think him in danger of being sent to the gallows. "Come, Mousqueton, what is the problem?" Porthos asked, as an idea occurred to him. "Have you romanced one of the wenches and are you afraid she might catch you in the bonds of matrimony?"

Mousqueton shook his head. "Would that it were," he said. "But the truth is . . ." He took a deep breath. "Look, the palace kitchens are haunted by the servants of musketeers. Servants, and sometimes their masters cluster around the maids and cooks begging for this, asking for that. So do the servants of all the noblemen and women who live in the palace. Hundreds of them. Cooks and maids and wenches have become hardened to pleas."

"But you bring me wine and bread and meat when I ask."

At this, Mousqueton shrugged shoulders that were almost as massive as those of his master, as though to signify that he couldn't help himself. The gesture took Porthos back to the day he had met his servant—then graced with the incongruously peaceful name of Boniface.

Porthos himself was then a young rural nobleman newly arrived in Paris, still dazzled by the wonders of the city. He'd just received his first pay, after having worked for a week teaching fencing in the school of a well-known master. He was headed, he remembered, towards a tailor shop, whose velvets and silks he'd coveted every day when he passed its door.

And suddenly, in what was a very modest street, he'd felt a hand snake into his doublet, making unerring way to the coin pouch tucked within.

Porthos was, after all, a fencing master. He'd grabbed at the wrist before the miscreant had a chance to withdraw it.

And found himself holding on to the skinny arm of a street rat, a child living by his wits in the rough and tumble poor streets of Paris. Boniface. Who, upon confessing that he hadn't eaten in some days and that he didn't have either father or mother, nor even a brother to look after him, had got rechristened Mousqueton and enlisted in Porthos's service.

That first fistful of coin that was supposed to buy Porthos the first fashionable clothing of his life had gone to feed the yawning chasm of Mousqueton's hunger. But Porthos had got more money—and clothing—along the way, and Mousqueton himself had grown to be almost as tall and strong as his master.

And yet that helpless shrug was so much like the one Porthos had seen in the erstwhile street waif that it must perforce have the same meaning. "Mousqueton," Porthos hissed it as a stage whisper. "Have you been stealing?"

Mousqueton didn't say a word, but his head hung down in guilt.

"How can you? And at the royal palace yet?"

"Oh, as to that, Monsieur, it's what every servant does who wants to get something extra for his master. I've even seen the king's valet himself filch a bit of meat while the maids' backs are turned. Otherwise, there is endless application and begging at various self-proclaimed authorities, before one is allowed a morsel of bread."

"Has anyone seen you?"

Mousqueton shrugged. "Since I still have my head on my shoulders, and my neck hasn't been broken by a rope, you can assume I was not seen. On the other hand you could say that the maids . . . suspect."

"I see," Porthos said. Internally he reasoned that although it was theft, it was no more than the kitchen staff deserved, for making it difficult for servants to get food for their masters. "Very well. Then you must tell me how to go to the kitchens from here and I shall attempt to find my way myself. Since what I'm looking for is not food . . ."

Mousqueton pointed to the left, "As to that, you take that corridor there, and push the door at the end. You'll come out at the top of the stairs, looking down on the kitchen. It is the best way to go in, at least when I go to filch something, as that door is rarely used and is in a dark area of the kitchen."

"The devil. How big are these kitchens, then?"

Mousqueton only grinned, a sly grin. "You'll see," he said.

Porthos followed the servant's directions, his mind mulling over how big the kitchen could be. The royal palace was huge, this Porthos knew, housing more people than lived in his own native town. And even if some of those noblemen came with retinues, including servants and cooks, very few were assigned the sort of space in which they could afford to cook more than the occasional egg over a spirit lamp.

Still nothing prepared him for what he saw at the end of his journey down a tangle of corridors, each darker than the other, ending in an unpromising hallway with no windows and only one door. The walls of the hallway were brick and had some sort of fungus growing on them, the gray black type that grows in dark, humid places. The area smelled musty and slightly as though gentlemen had relieved themselves there after giving up on finding their way out in time.

Thinking that Mousqueton had played a mean joke on him, Porthos grasped the handle of the door—a solid and well fitted oak affair—turned it, and . . .

His senses were assaulted from every direction. He stood at the top of a short flight of stairs, in the darker area of the kitchen, facing . . . Pandemonium.

Smells of roasts of all sorts, a medley of spices greater than any he'd ever experienced, assaulted Porthos's nose, mingled—alas—with the smell of sweat, of unwashed clothing, of spoiled vegetables. His gaze meanwhile took in a profusion of hearths, each blazing at a different intensity and upon which a different variety of beast was roasting. Though it was Friday, there were all manner of fowl and deer and pigs. Porthos thought that churchmen must have pronounced a dispensation on abstinence for the court, as they routinely did.

Between heat and cold, the smell of food, and the smell—and vision—of all the sweaty, crowded people laboring over hearths and tables, Porthos did not know if he was in heaven or in hell.

Before he could reason it out, though, a very fat cook, her sleeves rolled up to display capaciously muscled arms, looked up from her turning of the spit to see him on his step. "You," she said. "Monsieur Musketeer. What do you mean by sneaking into my kitchen?"

A Musketeer's Misgivings; Where Memory Intrudes Upon Life; d'Artagnan's Innocence

"**I**'m not sure I agree with your need to go on this journey." Monsieur de Treville told Athos and d'Artagnan, who stood before his desk. A small man, with the olive complexion, dark hair and dark eyes that matched d'Artagnan's, he had closed the door when Athos and d'Artagnan had come in, and now looked gravely at both of them, in their traveling clothes.

Had anyone else questioned his decision, Athos would have thrown his head back and said that he made his own choices. However, this was the captain, Monsieur de Treville, the man that Athos reverenced the most in the whole world. And besides, Athos and d'Artagnan needed to borrow Monsieur de Treville's horses for the job, something that entitled the captain to some explanation at least. "I understand that you think it is unlikely that the duke de Dreux is to blame for his wife's death. I confess that I find it unlikely too. However, I must eliminate the possibility before we look at other, even more far-fetched possibilities."

"Athos," Monsieur de Treville said.

He became uncomfortably aware that Monsieur de Treville's gaze was fixed evaluatingly on his own eyes.

"Athos, you can't mean to say you don't know who killed the Duchess de Dreux. Much as I prize Aramis as a fighter and I—"

"Monsieur," Athos said, snapping to attention though the movement hurt him. "Please don't say it. You can't mean it."

Monsieur de Treville looked up at Athos, who was taller than him by a good head. "I can't?" he asked, faltering.

"No, Monsieur. Because you sent a purse of money, an advance on Aramis's wages as a musketeer, and if you thought he was a murderer, you'd never have provided it and certainly never have expected him to come back to your service and earn those wages."

"But . . ." Monsieur de Treville sighed. "The money I sent was my own, though I said it was an advance so that Aramis would accept it. My good Athos, I understand your loyalty and your care for your friend. I understand, even, that you might not wish to find him guilty. I would not want to think that, either, at least if I had any choice but to think that. But Athos . . . He was alone with the woman, in her room. The door was locked. As far as anyone can tell—and you might know more about it than I—he escaped sure capture by jumping from the balcony onto a nearby tree, then scaling an almost smooth wall. How could anyone else have gone the reverse way, Athos? And all in a way that Aramis didn't notice? No, my good friend. We must face it that Aramis killed his lover."

Athos was speechless. He had, it is true, entertained such suspicions himself from the beginning. But hearing them voiced back at him, in his captain's sensible tones, made everything that was noble and loyal in him rebel at the thought. "And thinking this . . ." He said slowly. "You'd still send Aramis out of town to safety."

Monsieur de Treville shrugged. "Why should the corps be tainted or suffer by having one of its members executed as a murderer?" he asked. "Besides, this much I know. If Aramis chose to murder the woman, he must have had some great reason. He wouldn't do it in a mere moment of passion." Monsieur de Treville was looking intently at Athos.

Since the captain was one of the very few people in the world who knew Athos's true history, it made the musketeer wish to squirm. But Athos was nothing if not self-disciplined. He managed to nod. "No," he said. "If Aramis had killed the woman it would have been for some reason having to do with court and intrigue. The only reason I can think of is that perhaps because he had found her guilty of conspiracy."

"See?" Monsieur de Treville said, and smiled a tight smile that nonetheless managed to convey the pleasure of a teacher whose favorite pupil has just made a brilliant deduction. "And if Aramis killed the woman for a reason, there will be a proof of it and, in time, a rehabilitation. If Aramis is out of town, perhaps doing his novitiate in some isolated monastery, he can always leave it and come back to the corps when his vindication occurs. While if he had been beheaded or hung by the neck till dead, it would be impossible to give him back what had been taken."

Athos nodded, managing to keep his face impassive. Monsieur de Treville wouldn't be rebuking Athos. Though he was an intelligent and even cunning man, his beliefs and morals had been informed by a strict and rule-bound upbringing. It would never occur to him that Athos—or, as he was then, the Count de la Fere might not have the right to execute a wife who had lied to him about her past. Much less that the Count might not have the right to execute a woman branded with the fleur-de-lis. It wasn't for him to know Athos's doubtful, sleepless nights when only the bottle could make him forget Charlotte, make him stop seeing her specter by his bed, looking at him with those soft and sweet blue eyes.

"But, captain," Athos said. "What if Aramis isn't guilty? Yes, I know the circumstance seems to speak against him, but let's suppose that a subtle and cunning enemy, or the woman's long suffering husband, even, arranged her demise? Then proof of her involvement in intrigues will never come out because there aren't any intrigues. And Aramis will never be justified."

Monsieur de Treville stared at Athos. "But this is highly unlikely," he said.

"Yes, and how many times has the unlikely happened? In this kingdom, as it is, with that man that is almost a dark sorcerer behind the throne . . ." He stopped.

Monsieur de Treville nodded. He retreated behind his desk, as though talk of that powerful personage brought about a need to interpose a solid object between himself and the world. His desk was, was a broad, huge table, at which—so far as Athos knew—he never did any writing beyond the occasional order and the even more occasional safe conduct. The unblemished reddish leather surface had a stack of paper to the right and a pen and ink well to the left. And nothing else. But Monsieur de Treville stood behind his desk, and put his hands on it as if it were the physical center of his power.

"Still, I am loath to part with you for what . . . a week?"

Athos nodded.

"With Aramis already gone, if you leave, our guard rosters at the palace will be sorely depleted. Besides, if you must know, two of our musketeers have suffered grievous wounds in duels defending Aramis's honor. I don't know how to make up their numbers enough for a guard rotation. You," he looked at d'Artagnan. "Has my brother-in-law, des Essarts, consented to part with you with no complaint?"

D'Artagnan shrugged. "He said he would let me go, Monsieur, if you let Athos go."

Athos could see the captain's mouth shaping itself to say no, could tell by the glint of his eyes, by the frown that brought his eyebrows low , that Monsieur de Treville had already made up his mind that Aramis was guilty and, as such, found the idea of trying to save Aramis ridiculous.

Much as Athos despised the idea of admitting weakness, there was but one gambit for him to play now. Not that he, himself, was convinced of Aramis's innocence. But he was sure that Aramis, one of his oldest friends who had seen him through countless scrapes, deserved, at the very least, the benefit of the doubt. "There is something else," he said, just as Monsieur de Treville opened his mouth to deny them their leave.

And, as the captain turned to look on him, Athos sighed, still despising himself for what he had to say. "I received a wound on my arm, in duel over access to Aramis's lodgings. If I should stay in town, others will challenge me. I doubt I can fend off the next one, in this condition. A week from now, though, I should be able to fight again."

Monsieur de Treville's eyes widened. "Wounded?" he said. "May I see the wound?"

Athos recoiled, feeling his heart contract and blood flee his head, as if he'd been slapped. "Do you doubt me, sir?" he asked, his hand going to his sword immediately.

Monsieur de Treville might be the captain, and in this office Athos had heard lectures and rebukes that could skin an elephant without making any move to avenge his injured honor. But this was too much. To doubt Athos when he'd gone so far as to admit to a weakness . . .

But Monsieur de Treville shook his head. "My dear Athos, it would never cross my mind to doubt you on anything you stated. But if you're admitting to the wound, it must be grievous indeed, and I'm not sure I should let you leave without the services of my surgeon."

Athos relaxed, letting his hand fall from the sword, as though it had never been there. "There is no need," he said, drawing himself up. "I was seriously wounded and lost a great deal of blood. But d'Artagnan has the recipe for a miraculous salve, which he consented to let me use. He tells me it shall be healed in three days. I'm not sure it will be that fast, as it had reached bone. But I do believe it will heal by the time we return."

Monsieur de Treville evaluated both men with a wary eye, then sighed. "I see I cannot dissuade you from this travel into Dreux. Very well." He sat down, reached for his pile of papers and wrote rapidly, "This is in case anyone tries to stop you. Let it be known you're on a mission for the King's musketeers."

"It is hardly likely someone will try to stop us," Athos said.

But Monsieur de Treville only cocked his head to one side. "Only if Aramis is truly guilty and there is no conspiracy to account for it. Otherwise, Athos, the murderer will know that his friends will try to clear his name. And he will try to stop the friends." He shrugged. "Since we don't know who the murderer is, we will not know what lengths he'll go to just to put a stop to yours and d'Artagnan's journey. And we have to fear that he has great means indeed and will go to great lengths."

Athos considered this a moment and realized he could not argue with Monsieur de Treville's words. If it was true that someone had been so powerful as to strike Madame de Dreux through such underhanded means, surely he would be able to dispose of a musketeer and a guard traveling with their servants along country roads. He bowed to Monsieur de Treville's superior wisdom and took the proffered leather purse as well. His funds were low, since he'd had a run of damnable luck at cards. "I will pay it back," he said.

Monsieur de Treville allowed a smile to slide across his lips. "Athos, I would never doubt it."

They bowed to their captain, and left, to the stables at the back where Grimaud and Planchet already waited with four horses.

No more than a breath later, they were crossing Paris, on horseback. Newly awakened to the dangers of their journey, to the fact that if Aramis was innocent, then perforce someone else must be guilty, someone capable of great cunning and greater ruthlessness, Athos scanned the road and the upper stories.

And bridled, reigning in his horse as he noticed a knot of people ahead of him. There was a great press of apprentices and women, and others who could either legitimately be idle at this time of day or else who could legitimately be outdoors, pretending to be busy. At the edges of the crowd, at the back, street urchins pushed and shoved trying to get in.

One of those urchins noticed the two men on horseback, and came running back, to Athos's horse. "I'll show you a way around through the backstreets Monsieur."

"Thanks," Athos said. "But I know my way around Paris." And, seeing the urchin's great disappointment, he fished for a small coin from his sleeve pouch, and threw it at the boy. "What is the disturbance?"

The boy caught it midair, and looked at it, glinting in his palm, then flashed Athos a brief, feral grin. "It's the acrobats," he said. "Somersault artists and jugglers and tightrope walkers."

Athos blinked. Such troupes were a nuisance. They came from who knew where and they left without warning. And their acrobatic abilities were often put to use in cunning thefts. But people liked them.

He could see, ahead, the briefest glimmer of cloth, the slightest shimmer of silk. They dressed like kings and queens, too, these street performers, though often their clothes were threadbare and the supposed gold only so much painted glitter.

"Come d'Artagnan," he told his friend. "I know a way around."

D'Artagnan shook himself, as though waking. He'd been staring mesmerized into the crowd and Athos wondered if the young man wanted to watch the performers. D"Artagnan was, after all, little more than a boy and had come from some miserably forsaken village in Gascony. For him this poor show might be as entrancing as a royal ball.

But Athos could not find a way to ask his friend if he wanted to stay and watch without insulting the youth. So, he made sure that d'Artagnan was following, and then rode his horse apace through a maze of narrow streets, until they'd done a full circle and emerged again on the relatively large main street which had the width to allow two carriages to pass one by the other.

There, Athos spurred his horse to a trot and heard d'Artagnan catch up. Planchet and Grimaud's horses' hooves echoed still farther behind.

Cooks and Maids and the Secrets of the Fire; The Distinct Advantages of an Abundant Moustache and an Appreciation for Simple Pleasures

Porthos startled at the cook's yell at him, blinked at her, surprised, not used to being addressed by women in anything but an endearing tone. "I came," he said, as the lie occurred to him almost without his thinking. "In search of my servant, a thieving scoundrel, about this size." He pantomimed with his hand. "And about this wide, with abundant mustaches and a talent for the fast hand swipe."

"Ah," the cook said. "Mousqueton. He's a scoundrel that one. Faster than a cat and twice as sneaky, for all his size. Why, just last week he made off with a whole chicken, freshly roasted."

There was something Porthos—who had enjoyed the chicken quite well and thought of it with only the slightest hint of remorse—knew well enough from observing those around him. And that was that two people with a common grievance about the same person would soon find themselves on the way to friendship. And from what he could see, from the way the kitchen noises seemed to have hushed up at the woman's speaking, this was the person in whose graces to be. Either she was the head cook or the one who had seized the authority in the absence of any other contender. In either case, it mattered not. In this kind of environment she would be the sole authority and appeased as such.

He removed his hat and bowed to her, trying to look meek and yet roguish for it was his experience that meek men never interested women very much, while roguish ones never had their full confidence. Trying to strike a happy medium, he held his plumed hat to his chest and bowed. "Ah, madame," he said. "You have my condolences, for it's not the first time the rascal has made away with my own belongings. Surely you noted how he wore gold buttons and lace. Well, such disappear from my chests all the time."

The cook nodded. "And how come you tolerate the rascal?"

"Ah," he lied happily. "It was a promise I made his mother who was my mother's favorite maid. I told her I would look after Mousqueton and keep him from the gallows." He sighed, one of his big, contrite sighs.

The woman's eyes softened. "I have a brother," she said. "Who is exactly like that. And I wish I could find him as kind a master."

"So my rascal comes here often?" Porthos said.

"Often and often." The woman nodded. "He always says he needs the food for his master." She ran her gaze appreciatively across the breadth of Porthos gold-cloak bedecked shoulders and down his silk-bedecked muscular chest. "As if you'd need it."

Porthos shook his head in empathy.

"Come on down," the cook said. "Sit down with me, and we'll talk about it."

Porthos walked down the stairs, and, with the cook, sat at a broad table far from the fire and near the door. The cook twitched and made minimal gestures and in no time at all a fresh-faced country wench deposited two mugs of red wine in front of them.

It occurred to Porthos that this cook, like Athos, had worked out a system of signals by which means she commanded her subordinates. But then, he thought, listening to the din of knives and spits, of roaring fire and screaming women, how else was she to command them, but with gestures?

He sipped the wine, as the cook spoke again. "I don't suppose you have a friend looking for a servant? One who would use the same consideration to my brother that you use for your Mousqueton? My brother he's not bad you see . . . he's only . . . well, he doesn't understand why he shouldn't have the finer things of life that others have, and it upsets him. He's a good boy, but weak."

Porthos nodded and sighed. "So is Mousqueton," he said. Though his conscience reproached him for telling a falsehood. Truth be told, with his servant it was always more a matter of seeing what he could possibly get away with, what he could abscond with right from beneath observer's noses. Meanwhile Porthos, taking a sip of the wine and finding it of better quality than he expected, was trying to frame a way to ask the woman about secret passages in the palace.

His instinct was to come right out and blurt it, of course, ask her about the famed secret passages of the palace. But even Porthos was not so direct or so trusting in the simplicity of life as to plunge headlong into that subject.

Instead, he chose to take a detour and approach it by degrees. "Unfortunately," he said. "My friend who is best connected and who knows his way around every great house in Paris . . ." He stopped and sighed and drank his wine. He could feel the cook's beady eyes fixed on him. "Well, his name is Aramis and—"

The cook gasped and took her large capable hand to her mouth. "Not that Aramis. Not the blond musketeer who was the lover of Madame Ysabella de Yabarra y Navarro de Dreux?"

Porthos sighed and did his utmost to look grieved at having to mention this sad fact. Truth was, he knew people well enough. A friend who might be a murderer was even better than a thieving servant to buy him time and the attention of the cook.

"Aramis loved her well, it's true," he said. "He told us she was a seamstress, the niece of his theology professor . . . He called her Violette."

The cook smiled at the idea of the duchess being the niece of a theology professor. "He seemed so nice," she said. "The musketeer, not the theology professor. Always talking about doctrinal stuff and theology. He said he meant to be a priest one day." She sighed. "But I guess that is all over now."

Here Porthos stirred. "Why?"

"Well, having killed the Duchess de Dreux." The cook shrugged her capable shoulders, muscular from years of lifting pans and turning spits loaded with game. Her gesture, with no words, seemed to imply that Aramis's life was as good as over.

Porthos frowned. Part of the frown was automatic. He'd known Aramis since Aramis was little more than an apprentice priestling, his words all rounded, his manner all meek and mild. He still could not imagine Aramis killing a woman, particularly not that woman on whom so much of Aramis's heart and soul hung.

The other part of the frown was calculated, a deliberate move to draw in the attention of the woman.

It worked. The cook, her eyes on him, frowned, slowly. "You know something, don't you? You don't think he killed her."

"Oh, it is not that," Porthos said, and, because he was not used to deceiving anyone, he felt an odd excitement, his heart beating in his throat. He felt prouder than he ever did of his wins on the battlefield, and he wished that Aramis, who always said that Porthos couldn't deceive a child, would see him now. "It's just that Aramis loved the woman so much."

"Well, it is often the greatest lovers who kill their beloved, isn't it?" the cook asked, raising her thick eyebrows while a no less thick finger beat a delicate tattoo on the handle of her mug. "Passion is fickle, is it not? They discover that she has another on the side, or that she is intending on replacing them and . . . well . . . there it is."

"But . . ." Porthos felt his heart shrink within his chest. Perhaps there was something here that the entire palace knew, something that Aramis had kept from even his closest friends. As Porthos had told Athos, the servants always knew about everyone's lives.

"But was there such a one? One that she loved more, or that she intended to replace Aramis with?" He asked, and watched while the woman bit her lower lip, as though in deep thought.

Was that possible? While Porthos could not imagine Aramis killing the woman he loved even then, well . . . In Porthos's knowledge, Aramis just moved from girl to girl, from flower to flower hardly giving them time to realize they'd been loved, much less to experience the disappointment of losing him. But Aramis hadn't been quite normal about Violette. He'd stayed with her for years now, and he talked of her as other men talked about their wives. He trusted her with everything, even—Porthos suspected—his true identity.

But the cook shook her head, slowly. "No . . ." she conceded at last. "No . . . I can't imagine . . ." She shrugged. "Well, to tell you the truth, Monsieur, before the musketeer came to her bed, she dallied with many. Sometimes we took bets as to whether a valet sent to her room with hot water or a tisane would return quickly enough and unmolested. But then all of a sudden there was the blond musketeer--Aramis, as he's called. And all the kitchen wenches," she made a dismissive gesture towards the various girls and women laboring at the various fireplaces, chopping foodstuffs, kneading bread, throughout the expansive area. "All the kitchen wenches made jokes about how he must be endowed that he could make Madame de Dreux want no one else. And also . . ." She grinned. "About how long before she gave the Duke de Dreux a blond heir." She nodded as if to herself. "The woman was that smitten that she might have lost all sense of propriety."

Porthos took a deep breath in relief. If Violette didn't have a lover, then Aramis hadn't killed her. The whole case was that simple to Porthos who was not willing to entertain a moment of doubt on the subject of his friend's morals.

Aramis dallied with women—as, who didn't? Well, perhaps Athos whose taste in women was so wretched that it was safer for everyone, and himself too, if he didn't dally with anyone—and sometimes the women were married. It was just the way musketeers lived. What single woman would want to attach herself to a man with few prospects except those of living in the army forever, going here and there at the command of his king and risking his life on battlefields?

But Porthos couldn't imagine Aramis maltreating a woman for the fun of it. As far as that went, he was a good man. He fought in duels, with those who insulted or challenged him, and he dallied with the occasional married woman, but in neither case did he overrun his bounds. He didn't kill for fun.

He sighed, a sigh of deep frustration.

"I'd swear my friend didn't do it."

"And yet," the cook said. "He was alone with her, in a locked room. He jumped from the balcony so fast that he left his clothes behind."

It all came back to that again. That damned locked room. How could a murderer have got in it without Aramis's noticing? "Perhaps . . ." Porthos said. "Well, palaces are notorious for having . . . I mean, kings get jealous. And kings like to have a secret way to get at their mistresses. I mean . . . Passages and corridors and things with eyes in pictures."

He thought he'd made rather a bad jumble of it, but the cook's eyes widened. "Secret passages." She smacked her thick lips together. "Oh

. . . I hadn't thought of that. Mind you, I don't think there are any passages, but then I'm not the one who cleans or supplies the nobles up there . . ." She grinned, displaying crooked teeth. "Oh, I shall ask around, Monsieur. Thank you so much for giving me such an idea. Perhaps I can discover something . . ."

And while Porthos was thinking that there must be some way he could ask about what she found, without being too conspicuous, he looked up and found her staring at him with an expression akin to hunger.

"I don't suppose, Monsieur," she said. "Musketeers have to eat too. I don't suppose you would stay till dinner and then . . . perhaps . . ." She did her best at a coquettish expression. "I have my own room, you know, behind the kitchens."

Porthos blinked. He had never thought the woman would think of him in that way. Not that he, in the way of such things, disdained working women. On the contrary. He'd been aware for some time that he preferred hardworking women with callused hands. But this woman, though in a certain light she could be considered appetizing if not pretty—in a very dim light—simply could not have Porthos.

Porthos shifted uncomfortably in his seat. Truth be told, he was as attached to a woman as Aramis had been to his duchess. Perhaps more so. Madame Athenais Coquenard, an accountant's wife, might not be pretty. She was certainly no longer young. And nothing in her wardrobe compared to the clothes a duchess commanded. As for the largess she could bestow upon the musketeer that held her heart . . . well, that, too, was little and measured out, as her husband kept control of the household finances.

However, since he'd first climbed to her window, Porthos found that all other women had lost their allure. Oh, he could admire them, and he knew the turn of a full bosom or an elegant ankle would always catch his eye.

But when it came to it, and strange as it might seem, he would feel as guilty for sleeping with another woman as if he were committing adultery—oh, not the pleasing kind he committed with Athenais. Rather, as if he were betraying her. And his own heart. And that he could not do.

And yet, he needed to get this woman to tell him what she found.

Porthos managed to plaster a look of regret on his face—it was half felt. He could have used the dinner—and he bowed to the woman. "Madame. I would love to accept your very generous invitation, but I have business tonight." And seeing her face fall, he hastened. "Important business. For . . . Monsieur de Treville himself." He got up from the bench, and bent over the woman's hand, lightly kissing the fingers which were pleasantly perfumed of roast. "I shall return tomorrow, though, if I should be so favored."

"Oh, do," the woman said. "Do return tomorrow. Perhaps I'll have some gossip about secret passages for you."

Porthos hoped so. He also hoped that he would find some way to evade spending the night. In fact, he thought he'd best prearrange it.

He bowed again, and left the kitchen, thinking.

The Prodigal's Awakening; Brushes and Mirrors; Monkish Disciplines

Aramis turned in bed and woke up with the sun in his eyes. For a moment he was confused. His room in Paris didn't have a window directly facing the bed through which daylight could arrive and intrude upon his sleeping hours.

He blinked disconsolately in the light, while his mind caught up with the location of his body. His nose filled with a smell he hadn't smelled in a long time, a clean smell of . . . grass? Flowers? His eyes, wide open, gave him an impression of overwhelming light and whiteness. And his ears filled with the noise of birds and, distantly, the just-tuneless song of women in the repetitive, monotonous tune of a folk work song.

All of this worked in his memory to one thing. His childhood home.

He reached beneath himself to feel his narrow bed with its scrupulously clean sheets and looked around his small, clean room. No, not clean, bare. White walls. A wooden cross on the wall, watching over his bed, his every move, his very thoughts. A peg on the far wall was supposed to hold all his suits—all it held at the moment was the two black suits—velvet, but still black—that he'd been allowed all the time he was growing up. They consisted of knee breeches and tightly laced doublets in the fashion of twenty years ago, the fashion that Athos favored. Where his trunk with the clothes he'd bought in Paris had gone, was anybody's guess. No, not guess. His mother would have seen to it that it was . . . disposed of.

Aramis's head ached, and the previous day ran through it like a series of scenes, a series of shadows on the blankness that had invaded his brain. As if they'd happened to someone else, he saw his escape from Paris, his gallop across the late-spring countryside, his arrival here, his mother.

His mother had led him inside and to Mass, as if whatever had driven him from Paris had necessitated immediate shriving. She hadn't even asked what had happened.

He rubbed his fingertips upon the center of his forehead, as though trying to unknot the pain there. His mother had never asked. She'd never shown the slightest surprise that her only and prodigal son should show up like this, upon a fine spring afternoon.

She'd treated Aramis exactly as if he'd been fourteen and home from seminary on vacation. A Mass of thanks-giving for his safe arrival—said by his mother's tottering priest, who must be over a hundred, or at least looked it. And then dinner. Thin soup, bread and some boiled vegetables, because it was Friday and therefore a day of abstinence and mortification.

All through the meal one of the servants—or possibly one of his mother's hired companions—had stood and read passages from the lives of saints.

And at the end of the meal, at a movement or a gesture from Aramis's mother, Bazin had emerged from the shadows and escorted Aramis here.

And now . . . And now, Aramis became aware of heavy breathing from near the foot of his bed, by the window. He realized the heavy shutters on the window had just been pulled open to let daylight in.

Aramis sat up. Bazin, dressed in his clerical black, stood by the window. "Blessed be our Lord Jesus Christ," Bazin said, in the tone he had said it throughout all of Aramis's childhood, to wake him up.

"Oh, leave off, Bazin," Aramis said.

"Blessed be our Lord Jesus Christ," Bazin repeated, frowning.

"Bazin, I am warning you. I am not in the mood for this." Aramis pawed at his hair which, during the night, had lost the bit of ribbon with which he normally bound it. It had knotted upon itself and stood in clumps and whirls around his face, obscuring his vision.

"Blessed be—"

Aramis picked up his pillow and threw it at Bazin's pious face, before resuming combing through the tangled mess of his hair with his fingers.

"Monsieur, the lady your mother told me I was to wake you as I always did. She said that the rules of the house were to be followed, and Chevalier, this is her house."

"Don't. Call. Me. That." Aramis pawed through his hair and bit his lip at the sudden pain as he tugged on a knot. "And where are my hairbrushes?"

"What else am I to call you, Chevalier?" Bazin said. "We are at your mother's house and you—"

And he had foolishly come back into prison for asylum. Oh, he needed to be safe and he was safe enough. No one could penetrate this house and wrest Aramis from his loving mother's arms. But then, neither could Aramis escape. The first time, he'd managed it by going to Paris to study theology. And then by killing a man, by disappearing, by . . .

And he'd come back because Violette was dead. And in his heart of hearts he wasn't even sure he hadn't killed Violette. Oh, he didn't think he had, but . . .

He groaned aloud, let go of his hair and covered his face.

"Blessed be our Lord Jesus Christ," Bazin said, again.

"And forever blessed his mother, the Virgin Mary," Aramis moaned from behind the hands clasped on his face. The hands that, somehow, could not block the recalled image of Violette. Cold, waxen Violette with blood—

"As it was in the beginning," Bazin prompted.

"Be it now and forever."

"Secolum secolorum."

"Amen."

Aramis realized he was rocking back and forth, sitting on his childhood bed, with Bazin standing at the foot and, from the sound of his breathing, fairly alarmed.

He removed his hands from his face with an effort. Violette was dead. Nothing could be done about that. Aramis was sure he hadn't killed her. He couldn't have killed her. If he had killed her he would remember, wouldn't he?

And at any rate, what could be gained by coming back to his mother's house? Was safety worth this? "Where are my hairbrushes, Bazin?"

"Your mother said I was not to give you anything that reminded you of your intemperate life in Paris, nor of your vanity, nor—"

"Bazin!"

"Chevalier, you know better."

"My hairbrushes, now, Bazin. Or I shall run through the house in my small clothes, looking for them."

The servant huffed. He left the room at what tried to be a stately pace but bore the hallmarks of a hurried retreat.

Aramis waited, counting till a hundred, then started to get out of the bed. He was sure his mother would be shocked—perhaps halfway to her death—if he did run through the house in his small clothes. He was also sure he could never dress until he tamed his hair. His hair was blond and fine, abundant, and possessed of just enough curl to become a hopelessly knotted mass if not kept brushed. And his mother had never denied him his hairbrushes, not even when he was a child. He had no intention to put up with what he was sure was Bazin's tyranny.

He had set his feet on the scrubbed oak floor, and stood, when the door opened.

Reluctantly Bazin proffered two silver-handled brushes. "You may have these," he said. "But your mother said no mirror."

Aramis thought of what he would like to reply to that edict, as he plied his brushes with the well-accustomed ease of a man who had lived without a proper valet for far too long. Bazin had never been a valet in the sense of caring for Aramis's appearance, and Aramis had long ago given up on trying to get Bazin to help him dress or comb since Bazin disapproved of vanity.

He combed himself by touch, rescued his black silk ribbon from the bedclothes and tied his hair back with it.

When he looked up from this task, Bazin had filled the small ceramic basin on its bare metal stand with water from a pitcher.

The water was cold, but Aramis expected no more. He washed hands and face, quickly and found Bazin extending a rough linen towel, which Aramis used.

Then he slipped into his white linen shirt, and then into the very plain black breeches and doublet that Bazin had got from the peg on the wall. They were uncomfortable, confining and prickly, compared to his normal outfits.

Once fully attired, he put on his boots. But even with the boots—the same he'd worn with his musketeers uniform and which bore too military a cut to fit with this outfit—he was aware that he looked like the seminarian he'd once been.

He felt curiously naked and vulnerable as he walked downstairs to be greeted by his mother, who waited him at the bottom of the stairs. Madame D'Herblay was dressed in all black silk, a columnar dress that made her seem at once frailer and more unassailable. She was putting on her black lace gloves, and looked at him reproachfully. "Rene," she said. "You are late for Matins."

"Madame," Aramis said, rebelling at his mother, at the use of his true given name, and at the idea of starting the day with a religious celebration.

Truth was, while in Paris, in his musketeer's uniform, even with Violette's sweet caresses, even with all the pleasures of Paris, Aramis often felt like a displaced seminarian.

But now, here, in the wilderness of his native domain, in his mother's house with its monk-like discipline, wearing the same black suit he had worn as a seminarian, the Chevalier Rene D'Herblay had never felt quite so much like Aramis, the musketeer.

Where Old Friends Meet; The Count and the Duke; A Country Gentleman's Estate

"Count!"

This was the greeting addressed to Athos as he and d'Artagnan were admitted into the gated manor house of what looked like an enormous domain.

They'd ridden through the day yesterday, and then rested at an inn before riding again. Most of the morning they'd been crossing a verdant, well cared for land that had the look and feel of belonging all to the same domain and the same Lord. Serfs and farmers, in the fields, wore similar outfits. And were, d'Artagnan noted, well dressed and better fed than most peasants in France.

"This is all Raoul's land—the Duke de Dreux's," Athos had said, at a time when they were walking the horses apace. "Oh, he has other lands, in his vassalage. But these are under his care, proper."

And d'Artagnan's, whose hereditary domain was smaller than the cemetery Des Innocents in Paris, had looked around, openmouthed, at villages and hunting lodges, at palaces and chapels and churches. So this was the domain of Athos's friend? And the domain that Aramis's lover had disdained? If d'Artagnan had the like, this kind of property to retire to, he doubted he would have any interest at all in Paris. And had Athos left a similar property behind?

D'Artagnan didn't know, didn't want to think about it. But even he couldn't miss the respect in the voice of the servant that opened to them the ornate gates set in ten-foot-tall stone walls.

"Count," the man said. He was an old man, with an unruly crown of white hair, and the sort of manner old retainers acquired. And he was looking up at Athos as if he'd seen a ghost.

Athos, atop his horse, not bothering to dismount, looked proud and magnificent, like the statue of some ancient king. He inclined his head, giving the impression of great condescension.

Behind them, Planchet and Grimaud caught up.

"We thought you dead," the man said.

Athos sighed. "I am not, as you see."

"The master will be pleased," the servant said.

"He is here, then? Raoul?"

"The Duke is within," the servant said and gestured vaguely towards the inner part of what looked to d'Artagnan like an immense garden. He noted the old retainer's gaze examining him. Athos did not introduce d'Artagnan and d'Artagnan knew well that these old servants were by far more snobbish than their masters. Doubtless the old man was adding up the cost of d'Artagnan's clothing and his all too common visage and coming up with a low total for d'Artagnan's worth.

But Athos was spurring his horse ahead and there was nothing to do but to follow him down a lane bordered by trees. Which ended in a vast garden full of roses and bushes trimmed in amusing shapes, and interspersed by statues and fountains, all seemingly carved of white marble.

At the end of the garden was a vast space paved in a mosaic of white and black stones, the black stones forming the shape of a fantastical tree amid the white.

At the end of this space, two staircases with carved stone balusters climbed curving, to meet in the middle, on a vast balcony that led to an ornately carved door.

At the door stood a shorter man than Athos, wearing what looked—from this distance—like a plain russet suit, faded with age.

A servant, d'Artagnan thought, and had no more than thought it when the man started, raised his hand and shouted, "Alexandre," in the way of a youth greeting a schoolfellow.

To d'Artagnan's surprise, Athos, too, raised his hand and shouted, "Raoul."

The man who must—d'Artagnan deduced—be the Duke de Dreux himself, came rushing indecorously down the stairs. Even up close, he was as unimpressive as Athos was impressive, and looked as little like a nobleman as it was possible to look.

A short man, shorter than d'Artagnan, he had hair of an indeterminate brown and features that could only be described as apelike—a flattened nose, a mobile mouth and deep-set eyes. Only those eyes, dark brown and lively, were in any way extraordinary. That, and, d'Artagnan thought as the man smiled, his look of intentness and welcome.

He ran all the way to Athos's horse, and offered his friend his hand, to help him dismount. "Alexandre," he said. "We thought you dead."

"So your good Jacques has informed me," Athos said. "And yet, you see, I am alive. And Jacques, too, which surprised me a little, considering he was an old man when we were young."

"He wasn't old," Raoul said, and grinned. "He was only thirty. Younger than we are now. It was only that we were children and he was in charge of us and therefore seemed to us ancient."

Athos dismounted and Raoul clasped Athos's hand in one of his, while grasping Athos's other shoulder, in something not quite an embrace and yet betraying more emotion and more relief and happiness to see his friend still alive than an embrace could have.

"You must tell me how you've been and where," Raoul de Dreux said. "And why you disappeared in such a manner."

Athos shrugged. "There isn't much to tell," he said. "I made a mistake, and I've been paying for it."

De Dreux's intelligent gaze searched Athos, and seemed to accept that this was all the explanation likely to come in the near future. He nodded. "I see," he said, though it was clear he didn't. "Well, you must come and wash yourself and rest. I'm sure you've had a long journey, from the looks of you." He looked back at where Grimaud and Planchet had come to a stop, just behind d'Artagnan. "Your servant can take the horses to the stable and—"

"Raoul," Athos said. "This is my fault, I should have introduced you." He turned to d'Artagnan who, bewildered, remained on horseback.

D'Artagnan scrambled, hurriedly to dismount, while Athos said, "This is Monsieur Henri d'Artagnan, a guard in the regiment of Monsieur des Essarts, as well as a gentleman from Gascony." One of Athos's elusive smiles fled across the musketeer's lips. "And the most trustworthy friend you'd want at your back in times of danger or doubt."

"I see," Raoul de Dreux said. "I see." He bowed to d'Artagnan. "Monsieur, I beg your forgiveness, but you must know that it is not normal for the Count to travel without more than two servants. In fact, usually, he's accompanied by more than three. I did not mean to be insulting." He extended his hand to d'Artagnan, and clasped d'Artagnan's for the briefest of moments. "You must come. I'll order two guest rooms set up. I don't know to what I owe this visit, but you can have no idea how welcome you are. I have missed Alexandre very much and any friend who accompanies him on a visit is welcome."

It seemed very strange to d'Artagnan hearing Athos called Alexandre. Truth be told, he would have found it easier had de Dreux just called Athos "count." With his noble countenance, his fine figure, Athos always impressed anyone as a nobleman anyway. Count was no less than his due. Alexandre, on the other hand was a given name, the stuff of family and friendship dating back to the nursery. Both of which were hard to reconcile with Athos's severe countenance, his aloof bearing. Which he retained even as the two of them followed Raoul de Dreux down echoing corridors ornamented with paintings and tapestries and roofed over with carved ceilings gilded and painted and ornamented with figures from mythology.

"This wing is all new since you last visited," de Dreux said. "With your wife, right after your wedding."

Was it d'Artagnan's imagination or did Athos's bearing become more military and more rigid at those words and his expression more determinedly aloof?

D'Artagnan remembered the story that had come out of Athos's mouth almost a month ago, the story that Athos had told of the Count who'd killed his wife. Even back then he had had the feeling the Count was Athos. Now he was almost sure of it, even if he couldn't imagine Athos killing any woman.

"I had this whole area rebuilt after my wedding," Raoul went on oblivious. "While it might not be good for anything else, my marriage brought me money in the form of my wife's dowry, and that I used to make sure that this part was renovated as it should be. You probably don't remember, but in my father's day it was all but roofless."

"Ah, Montagne," the Duke said, at a servant who appeared at the end of the corridor and bowed to them. "Do we have guest rooms in some semblance of order, that my friend the Count and his friend, Monsieur d'Artagnan, can occupy?"

The young man in livery bowed. "Certainly, sir. The rooms by the library have just recently been cleaned, and I believe the beds are made."

"It is our policy," de Dreux said, walking past the servant who—d'Artagnan noted—was dressed more richly than him. "To keep a few guestrooms ready in case of a surprise visitor, just as it was in my father's day, though you must know I don't get nearly as many visitors. My father was a far more gregarious being than I am."

He led them down another corridor, which ended in two doors. The doors, once opened, revealed two splendid rooms with curtained beds piled high with pillows and cushions, with carved trunks waiting to receive a copious wardrobe that d'Artagnan did not possess, and with glazed double doors which opened on a spacious balcony.

In his room, d'Artagnan was almost immediately provided with warm water for washing. A servant stood by to help him dress, until d'Artagnan, embarrassed by the paltry simplicity of his wardrobe and by his own ability to dress and undress without help, sent him away.

Then d'Artagnan washed and changed into fresh clothes. He'd just finished lacing his doublet, when someone knocked at the door. "It is I, Athos," Athos said, before d'Artagnan had time to answer.

D'Artagnan opened the door a sliver, and found his friend looking at him, his face attentive and stern. D"Artagnan opened the door all the way to let him in.

Like d'Artagnan, Athos had washed the travel dust and changed into fresh clothes. But he looked even more browbeaten than d'Artagnan, whether by the decadent surroundings or by meeting his childhood friend, d'Artagnan could not say.

D'Artagnan backed into his own room, ahead of Athos, who closed and locked the door behind himself, then stalked around the room, straightening a picture and looking behind a tapestry. "d'Artagnan, I trust your silence on anything you see or hear here that relates . . . That has to do with my true identity."

"Athos," d'Artagnan said. "You know you can trust me."

Athos nodded. "I have in the past, and you have not failed," he said, and looked around once more, then lowered his voice. "I don't think Raoul knows his wife is dead."

"How can he not?" d'Artagnan asked. "Surely there's been time enough for a messenger—"

"I don't think anyone has thought to send a messenger. They lived such separate lives." Athos shrugged. "You noticed he said 'my wife' not my late wife?"

"But if he doesn't know she's dead, he can't have killed her," d'Artagnan said. He felt greatly relieved at this, not only because he sensed how much the possibility of his friend's guilt worried Athos, but also because he thought that since de Dreux wasn't guilt they would now be able to leave and go back to Paris and resume the true investigation there.

Athos shook his head. "Or he knows only too well and chooses to hide it. Don't be mistaken, Raoul can play the fool or the simpleton, if he so wishes, but he is neither. We must stay here till we find where he was two days ago or if he could have hired anyone to do away with his wife, in Paris."

D'Artagnan sighed and nodded. He hadn't been cut out for opulence, he thought. This ducal residence made him long for his small rented rooms.

And if the Duke was the murderer, in this vast domain who would prevent him from doing away with an inconvenient guard of a minor nobleman?

Cooks and Maids; Holes and Tunnels; Food and Love

Porthos returned to the palace promptly before dinnertime, counting on the cook's getting busy with dinner and making it easier for him to escape without paying her what she would no doubt consider her due. In the same way, he made sure that Mousqueton would come and call him with an important message from—he didn't know whom, nor did he particularly care. The King or Monsieur de Treville, either of them would do, so long as it called Porthos away from the cook.

However, for all his wish to avoid the woman's amorous intentions, Porthos had dressed himself carefully in his gold-embroidered doublet and his best dark blue velvet cloak, he had Mousqueton polish his boots till they shone, and he had combed not only his hair but his luxurious beard and moustache.

It pleased him that passersby—particularly women— stopped to look at his magnificence as he passed. In fact, the entire palace kitchen fell silent as he opened the back door and walked in.

Almost at once the head cook with whom he'd spoken the day before was standing before him, smiling. "Ah, Monsieur," she said. "I was afraid you didn't mean to come at all."

"Of course I meant to come," Porthos said. He ran down the steps, all seeming eagerness, and bowed deeply while kissing her hand. This brought a giggle—from a woman who was certainly as old as Porthos and who probably weighed almost as much.

"Oh, Monsieur," she said, blushing. Then she grabbed him by the arm. Her hands were hot. She smelled of cinnamon and ginger. "Come, come, I have news," she said. And, thus speaking, pulled him—he hadn't counted on that—to a small room at the back. Her room, judging by its narrow, sagging mattress, propped atop a pallet in a corner.

The devil! Porthos thought. Even if I meant to do the deed, her bed would prove as narrow and uncomfortable as Athenais's. Athenais bed, not the one she—rarely—shared with her aged husband, but her own, was a single bed that creaked alarmingly under Porthos's capacious weight.

The cook pushed Porthos in and crowded close. Truth be told, in that room, there wasn't that much space to contain both of them. And in the same way, the cook looked almost beautiful, her black eyes shining, her lips full and poised at the edge of a smile. But by the light of the single candle on a wall niche near the bed, almost all women who had only one head and all their limbs would look good.

Uncomfortably, more than a little scared by her proximity, more than a little determined not to betray his lovely Athenais, Porthos allowed himself to be pushed into a corner. "You said you had news?" Porthos asked. And hoped Aramis would appreciate Porthos's efforts and the peril Porthos was enduring for his sake.

"Oh, Monsieur, I've talked to all the maids," as she spoke, the cook brought her head close. "And none of them, not one," her hands moved upon Porthos's garments, to his waist, his breeches, the lacings.

"Madame!" Porthos said.

But she only giggled and left her hands where they rested, warm and inquisitive against Porthos's flesh, separated only by the insufficient—or so it felt—material of his breeches and his embroidered over breeches. Her face leaned close, the smell of cinnamon and ginger overpowering.

Porthos tried to back up against the wall, but his back was already against the wall and all he managed was to squeeze himself against it farther, feeling, even to himself, like a shy maiden trying to avoid a musketeer's advances.

The cook's face leered, close to him, and he tilted his hat desperately, trying to avoid eye contact with her. Stories crossed his mind—he could tell her he was injured. A knife fight, a duel. Something that made it impossible . . .

But, no. Even as he thought of it, her hands, moving softly, trying to figure the way to untie his breeches, had probably felt enough to give such stories the lie.

"The maids, madame, the maids," he said, desperately, his voice higher and far more nervous than normal. "You said you'd spoken to them. What did they say?"

"Oh, that there was no passage," the cook said. "So I guess your friend was guilty. This is what comes, you see, from getting involved with these high ladies with their fine manners." She grinned close to him, then planted a soft kiss upon his cheek. "You see, they're all strumpets who'll betray you and—"

"Madame," Porthos said, and slid against the wall, feeling the age-roughened plaster drag at his fine cloak, and not caring so long as he avoided the worst for just a moment. "It is impossible that Aramis is guilty." He turned slightly, trying to avoid her hands, which were making it hard enough for him to think, much less to think coherently. He invoked the memory of Athenais, bringing to mind her sharp eyes, her smiling lips, her sweet voice, as a way of avoiding responding too much to the present danger. "It is impossible, I tell you. Your investigation was incomplete."

"How could my investigation be incomplete?" the woman protested. Her hands found him again, and didn't relent, though in the insufficient light neither could she seem to see enough to determine how to untie his breeches. "I asked every maid, I tell you, every one of them."

Porthos slid farther and realized he'd wedged himself behind her bed. The only way to escape her hands—and her—now was to vault over her bed. He pictured himself jumping over the bed, pushing the woman aside . . . No. It was ridiculous. He couldn't do it. Not without hurting her. Not without raising alarm.

"Madame, I can't—" he said.

But she giggled. "Oh, I think you can." She gave him an emphatic squeeze. "In fact, I'm sure you can."

Porthos could tell her that he was not interested in women. But—curse it all—though several members of the royal family were just that way, for a mere musketeer to confess to such would bring the law on him.

A fleeting thought of discovering a sudden vocation crossed his mind, but how could he, when the whole city knew that Porthos was not even interested in Aramis's sporadic preaching.

He looked at her, so near, leering triumphantly. He felt that her fingers had finally figured the lacing in his over breeches and undone them. The breeches fell around his knees, revealing his under breeches. She made a sound of annoyance.

But the lacing for the under breeches was the same, and her fingers had the way of it, pulling the under breeches loose.

A knock at the door made them both jump.

"What is it?" the cook asked, ill-humoredly, her hands stopping at their task.

The door opened. A young woman, probably not much older than seventeen, stood in the opening. She had a sweet oval face and large blue eyes. A straggle of blond hair escaped from beneath her cap. "If you pardon me, madame, only they told me you wanted to know as soon as possible—" She curtseyed.

The cook let go of Porthos's breeches and turned around. Porthos's breeches fell, and he bent to grab them, and pull them up quickly, all too conscious of the maid's giggle.

But as he tied his breeches and over breeches back in place, he still paid attention to what the maid was saying.

"They told me you were looking for a passage into the room of the murdered Duchess."

The cook put her hands on either side of her thick waist. "I was, and there isn't one."

The little maid curtseyed again. "Begging your pardon, madame, but there is. Or if not that, then close."

"Close?

"There is a passage that ends behind a picture and through the eyes of the picture you can see the whole room," the maid said.

"Only see?" Porthos said. Having fastened his breeches, he now gently pushed the cook aside and managed to step out from behind the bed.

"Yes, Monsieur," the maid said, and curtseyed again, though the hint of a devilish grin still remained in her eyes and lips. "Only look. There is no opening, you see, that will allow the watcher into the room."

"Why did you interrupt us, then?" the cook asked. "This means nothing and it changes nothing."

"Begging your pardon," Porthos said. "As someone who knows a little more about such things—as someone who knows that his friend, Aramis couldn't possibly be guilty—I beg to disagree. I'm sure there is a way into the room that you've somehow missed." He was well past the cook, and face-to-face with the young maid. And . . . had she winked at him? "Please show me this passage and this picture. Perhaps you're only missing the spring that opens it."

"I don't think so, Monsieur," the maid said, looking dubious.

"Please," Porthos said, and, in turn, not sure what he was doing would be taken in the right spirit, he winked at her. "Please show me the place. I will not rest unless I am sure there is no way into the room. I can't believe my friend is a murderer."

"Well," the cook said from behind. "Your loyalty does you credit, but I would still say that he is guilty and that this is all foolishness. Do take him to the room quickly, Hermengarde, but bring him back right away once he's verified there is no way into the room from the passage. I have business with the gentleman."

The blond maid curtseyed once more, then turned. Porthos followed her out of the room, and up three flights of stairs from the kitchen with some relief.

The stairs were narrow, stone, unadorned, clearly servant stairs and probably not very popular servant stairs at that, since they didn't meet anyone while the maid scampered up the stairs ahead of Porthos and Porthos himself followed with much more lightness of step than was his usual.

Even then, Porthos waited till they were three floors up before he asked, "Mademoiselle, did you wink at me down there?"

The girl turned around and smiled, a devilish smile. "Indeed, I did, Monsieur. Mousqueton sent me to rescue you from the dragon. I told him she was a man-eater and there was no point at all his waiting the time you told him. By that time, you'd likely be squashed on that bed of hers."

Porthos swallowed. "Mousqueton?"

The maid had the grace to blush but she answered eagerly enough. "Mousqueton and I are great friends," she said. "I'm a maid on the third floor, you see, and we maids have our own little parlor there. He often comes and warms himself at my brazier, on a cold winter night."

Porthos would just bet he did. Oh, he was aware that his servant, no longer the little street rat that Porthos had rescued so many years ago, attracted women and, perforce, must have his share of love affairs. But till now the rascal had kept it all quiet enough.

"Well, well," Porthos said, smiling beneath his moustache and thinking he would have to tease the younger man about it. But then a horrible thought occurred to him, which removed all his joy in the revelation. "You were lying, then?" he asked. "About the passage."

Hermengarde blinked, shook her head. "Oh, no, Monsieur. I wouldn't lie about that. There really is a passage that runs behind the room, and which allows one to spy from the little holes at a portrait's eyes. It's very well done. Little bits of glass mask the eye holes, but . . ."

"And are you sure it doesn't open into the room as well?" Porthos asked.

"Hard to do. It's right behind a massive wardrobe. The portrait hangs above it, which is why it's never been changed and never moved since the room was the Queen's own. She only gave it to the Duchess two winters ago, you know? It used to be the Queen's own closet."

"Perhaps," Porthos said, chewing on the corner of his moustache, as he did when he was agitated or puzzled. "Perhaps there is a secret door that opens into the wardrobe itself."

The maid frowned. "I don't think so," she said.

"Please, Mademoiselle," he said. "Aramis is a dear friend and I cannot renounce all hope for his innocence without verifying."

The girl went very serious, and nodded. "That I understand," she said. "It's no use, but follow me then. I wish the blond musketeer no harm myself. I've often told the other maids he's the best looking man who's ever come into this palace. My Mousqueton excepted, of course."

Thus speaking, she led him down several corridors, softly lit by candles on holders upon the wall, till they came to a small hallway, whose wall was filled wholly by a large mirror set in an ornate golden frame.

Hermengarde pushed this and pulled that within the frame, pressing a rosette and twirling an ornamental nail till the whole glass creaked and moved inward, opening.

It revealed a narrow little space, dark and smelling of sawdust and disuse.

"You go first," she told him. "Otherwise you'll not get near enough the wall to push any part of it and make sure there is or isn't a door. You won't, for that matter, be able to look through the eye openings. Why, often my friends and I, when we come here, have to cram past each other to get a look, and we're much smaller than you."

Porthos wondered if they often came to watch Aramis and his lady at their sport, but it wasn't the sort of thing he could ask with impunity of a near stranger, even of a near stranger who appeared to be very well known of Mousqueton.

Instead, he walked briskly down the twisting tunnel, which ended in what looked like a little window ornamented by little shutters. The maid had got a candle along the way and was now holding it aloft. "You may open the screen," she said. "There's no one in that room so there's no risk they'll see even a spark of light from my candle. The Cardinal himself has taken a great interest in that room, and after the door they forced down was repaired, he had had it locked and kept under watch with the musketeer's uniform still in it, so that he can bring witnesses to see the musketeer's guilt."

"He's so sure he's guilty," Porthos said, and sighed. The maid didn't answer.

Porthos opened the little shutter and looked through. The room was dark, the only light coming through the door to the balcony, the same door that Aramis had used to escape.

By that meager light, Porthos could see that the room was full of furniture, and that the massive oak bed appeared to have been stripped of all its coverings. But Aramis's uniform was still where the musketeer had left it, flung across one of the arm chairs.

Porthos backed away a little and turned his attention to the wall around the little shuttered window.

It was smooth plaster, and he couldn't see any part that might be hinged or even any part that was different from the rest. But then again, in this palace, smooth walls often weren't and mirrors and portraits could swing unexpectedly to reveal passages and byways.

He felt the wall all over, methodically, from top to bottom, his massive but sensitive hands feeling for any irregularity, any soft spot, anything that might trigger a hidden spring.

"See, I told you there was no way."

"No," Porthos said. And since the little shuttered space covered by the portrait was no more than a handbreadth wide and a hand span tall, Porthos couldn't imagine any human so small as to be able to crawl through it.

He sighed, as Hermengarde led him out of the narrow corridor and back in the hall. As she opened the mirror and looked out, she said, "Mousqueton!"

Porthos looked over his shoulder to see his servant standing in the hall. It was at least a quarter of an hour early. Porthos would like to imagine Mousqueton's eagerness was due to the servant's wish to see Hermengarde. But he knew it couldn't be true. Because if he'd rushed to see his lady love, Mousqueton would have changed from his not-so-impressive day clothes—a much worn old suit of Porthos's. No, Mousqueton was disheveled, and hatless and looked red in the face as if he'd run the whole way.

Hermengarde must have sensed that something was wrong too, because she stepped aside, allowing Porthos to pass. "Mousqueton," Porthos said. "What is wrong?"

Mousqueton reached up, as if to remove the hat he wasn't wearing. Finding nothing, his hand dropped disconsolately. "It's the Cardinal, Monsieur."

"Oh, not that," Porthos said. "I said Monsieur de Treville or even the King. No one is going to believe the Cardinal wants to see me."

"But . . . Monsieur," Mousqueton said. "He does."

Where Families Are Proven to Share More than Coats of Arms; A Musketeer's Capitulation

The sun was setting and Aramis sat by the window of his room. He was all too aware that he should be at Vespers—having heard the bells of the private chapel on the grounds ring, then ring again as if his mother had ordered the bell ringer to remind Aramis of his duties.

But he sat by the window instead and reread, one by one the letters from the thick sheaf of letters that Violette had sent him. He'd kept them all, from the slightly formal ones at the beginning of their acquaintance, to the later ones, full of poems and stories of her daily life. He'd tied them together with a ribbon, and he kept them at his hand. Now, as he opened them, the faint fragrance of the paper reminded him of her.

The thing about Violette was that she was such a lousy writer. The beautifully shaped handwriting of the convent girl that Violette had once been was formed into words that were sometimes Spanish and sometimes French and sometimes some odd amalgam of the two which Aramis could only decipher thanks to his knowledge of Latin.

So many times he'd scolded her for her incapacity to write in one language only. But now he read her silly confusion through tears in his eyes and wished he could have her back—that he could spend one more night with her, receive one more letter from her. And he wouldn't complain, not even if it was all in Spanish.

He put his hands on the stone parapet of his window, and rested his chin on them, looking out onto the fields gilded by the setting sun. They were empty now, the farmers having gone to their homes for dinner.

If he squinted in the direction of the nearby hamlet of Trois Mages, from which most of his domain's peasants came, he could see faint traces of grey smoke climbing up against the blue sky. Suppers being cooked, he wagered.

And he wished—with all his heart and soul—that he and Violette could have been two of those peasants and able to marry and live together. He would leave every morning to work in the fields—his attempts at picturing this failed because though he'd lived in the country for most of his life, he'd never spent much time observing what farmers did all day. No matter. He was sure it was tiring and full of effort, but what did it matter? He'd come home every night to their hovel, to find his Violette and their children.

He pictured the children they would have had—blond as they were, with Violette's expressive blue eyes. The girls would all be beauties and the boys all tall and strong, like their father.

He sighed, a sigh to burst his chest. Then he got up and turned around, clasping Violette's letters, in their silk ribbon, to his chest. Sighing, he consigned them to a hiding place between a pile of books on his table.

He felt restless and small.

For years now, he'd been a musketeer, his own man, living in Paris as he pleased. And he'd had Violette.

But now Violette was gone and Aramis felt like he was a young man once more—helpless, bound to his formidable mother's will.

It was as though his mother had preserved Aramis's childhood, his youthful place in his home, just as she had preserved his father's study.

And now his father's study came to Aramis's mind as an excellent place to hide in from his mother's enforced devotions. His mother might keep it as a shrine, but he'd never seen her enter it.

It was locked, but as a musketeer in Paris—or even as a seminarian in his early years there—before Violette, Aramis had learned the fine art of picking locks and developed it into such a science that he could open almost any lock with a simple knife.

He found such a knife amid his youthful treasures, beneath a loose floorboard.

From there to running down the stairs to the entrance hall and his father's locked room, was a moment.

Picking the lock took no time at all.

The study remained as he remembered from childhood—all was covered in dust save for a path from door to desk, crisscrossed by small, feminine footprints.

His mother's, Aramis thought, as no one else had a key.

He followed the footprints to the chair behind a desk. The desk was a model that Aramis had often seen among courtiers in Paris. A series of little drawers and doors encircled a round writing surface, supported by spindly legs. A place for everything and, usually, one or two secret compartments in the bargain.

The desk was as dusty as everything else, but here and there, throughout, was the mark of Aramis's mother's hands as though she'd caressed it.

Suddenly the idea of hiding here was not so pleasing. He retraced his steps to the door.

Just in front of it there was an area where his mother's footprints took a semicircular detour as if around an invisible obstacle.

Curious, Aramis scuffed the dust there, with a foot. The floor beneath was black.

Paint or rot?

The noise of a key turning in the lock made him look up to see the door open and the disapproving expression on his mother's face.

For someone who'd once been beautiful and soft; for someone who couldn't be much more than minor Spanish nobility, his mother managed to look remote as a goddess and disapproving as a queen.

"Maman," Aramis said. He felt red climb his cheeks. "I just thought. . ." He said and stopped. He couldn't tell her he'd thought of hiding out from her.

"Rene," she said, and her face became a mask of deep sorrow. "You know you could have asked me for the keys, if you wanted to see your father's study. There was—" She looked jealously towards the desk. "No reason for you to violate this space."

Not sure what to say, Aramis nodded.

Suddenly there wasn't much place to hide in this room.

His mother sighed.

"You know your father and I married in the spring. In fact, next week is the anniversary of the day we married." Madame D'Herblay's eyes were full of distant longing, like a child who looks upon a dream. "It seems so long ago now. He died, you know, only two years after your birth. Sometimes I wonder what would have become of him, what kind of man he would be now, had he lived long enough."

Aramis said nothing. His mother rarely spoke of his father. In childhood, Aramis had formed a theory that his mother was a nun who'd escaped from a convent and his father an itinerant ribbon seller. It all seemed very logical to him, considering that no one ever mentioned his father, that his mother seemed to live at her devotions, and that the most dashing strangers to ever come to the manor were ribbon sellers. It wasn't till he was five or so that the whole had stopped seeming the most plausible explanation. And even then it had taken his nursemaid's shock at his theory to show him that it couldn't possibly be true.

He had to repress an urge to smile, thinking of the young peasant's look at her charge's telling her that he was the illegitimate son of an escaped nun. She'd wasted no time in setting him to rights. And then his mother had made him write, several times, the verses of the bible that pertained to marriage. Aramis lost all interest in smiling.

And realized his mother was staring attentively at him.

"You probably think it very odd that I've always wanted you to go into the church," she said, looking at him.

This was strange indeed. Madame D'Herblay had never cared what her son thought odd or not. "No, Maman," he said. "I know you discerned in me some vocation, some hope that I—"

She clucked her tongue on the top of her mouth and sighed. "I thought it was for the best, Rene, I really did. But I don't know how to explain it to you."

"You are my mother. What do you need to explain? I'm only—"

Madame D'Herblay moved away from the window, and walked past her son. "Come with me, Rene," she said. "To the cemetery."

"The cemetery?" Aramis asked, shaking. He had some strange idea that his mother meant to open one of the family tombs and make him jump within. But the idea was monstrous. His mother had never sought to kill him. Only to bury him, living, in a monastery.

Into Aramis's mind the suspicion that his mother had hated his father and now sought to avenge herself upon his son crept and grew. But he couldn't believe it. He couldn't countenance it. How could a son have such thoughts about his mother? Oh, he was the worst of sinners.

He walked after her, all the more determinedly because he was so sure he was sinning against her in his mind.

She locked the door again, then hurried out of the house, keeping two steps ahead of him, despite his walking fast on his long legs that often allowed him to keep up with Porthos effortlessly and made d'Artagnan, and even Athos, run to catch up. But then he thought he'd probably inherited his legs from his mother, as he had inherited her blond hair, her blue eyes, and her ability to seem innocent and in-approachable even while ruling the house with an iron fist. At least, he could rule everyone but her.

"Maman, wait," he said. But she didn't stop and he had to run down the front steps to catch up with her . . . at least only two steps behind.

He remained two steps behind her as they reached the family cemetery north of the park. This was not a place that the little Rene D'Herblay had visited often. Oh, he was brought here for Masses on the anniversary of his father's death, and for certain solemn occasions in which the life of the departed Chevalier D'Herblay was celebrated. But he had never had that morbid turn of mind that brought some adolescent boys to brood upon family cemetery stones.

And, of course, it had been many years since he passed through the ivy-choked gate in the half-ruined stone walls surmounted by rusty ironwork.

Within the cemetery, Madame D'Herblay stopped so suddenly that Aramis almost collided with her. He managed to arrest his movement just short of it, and go around to stand beside her.

She was looking around at a panorama of headstones and statues. The statues were few. The estate while wealthy when compared to the surrounding countryside, was, after all not a ducal estate, not even a count's portion. Most of the statues were very old, their features erased by sun and rain, by succeeding winter and summers till you could not tell if it was an angel's face or an old Roman goddess at which you were staring. In fact Aramis had often suspected that some of his ancestors had stolen the statues from nearby pagan temples.

Needless to say this was not an opinion that could be shared with his mother, who was looking around, her blue eyes lightly covered in trembling tears.

"So many graves," she said. "Your family has been here since the time of Charlemagne, you know?"

Aramis knew. Or at least he'd been told so. If he were asked his true, honest opinion he'd have said his family or someone else who'd succeeded to the same name had been here a long time and left it at that. But now he contented himself with nodding.

"Do you know what I think when I come here?" his mother asked.

Did she come here often? Aramis had left the maternal abode for seminary in Paris when he was just fifteen. He'd been away, now, almost ten years. His mother looked very different to this older Aramis than she had looked to the dutiful and shy seminarian. Did his mother walk the cemetery at night? Or during the day for her afternoon stroll? And why?

He realized she was waiting for an answer from him. "What do you think of, Maman?" he asked, though fairly sure he didn't want to know.

"I think that families share a lot more than coats of arms," she said and nodded, sadly. "Yes."

Aramis looked upward at the darkening sky and wondered what in heaven's name that meant.

"A lot more," Madame D'Herblay said, as if speaking out of her own thoughts. Then she looked back over her shoulder, her countenance suddenly animated. "Rene, do you know where your father lies?"

"Maman?"

"Oh, come, surely you know where your father's tomb is."

Aramis did. He thought. "Down this lane," he said, pointing. "And around that cluster of cypresses." He called to mind the memory of the last time he'd come into the cemetery, at his mother's instigation, to lay flowers on the paternal tomb before leaving for the seminary. "It is a white marble tomb, I think."

His mother nodded and led him the right way through it. "Here," she said, stopping in front of the tomb he'd described. "Can you read to me what the words say, Rene?"

"Maman, I've known how to read since the age of three. And Latin since the age of five."

His mother only shook her head. "Read the words to me, Rene, please."

Aramis sighed and nodded. "It says 'Here Lies Rene D'Herblay, gone to his rest at the age of twenty-five, October 1598.' " He paused, shocked, because every time he'd come to the cemetery before, he'd somehow had the impression his father was older. Not an old man, exactly, but older, more seasoned. "Twenty-five, Maman?"

She only nodded. "There, Rene, your grandfather lies. Can you read his headstone?"

As though in a dream, Aramis went from headstone to headstone. The headstones of his female relatives ran the gamut from those who'd died very young—including Aramis' own sister, dead just a year after his birth, at less than a month of age—to the very old. But all his male ancestors seemed to have died in their early to mid-twenties. All of them. Had the D'Herblays, then, always been raised by fearsome women like his maman?

"What do you see, Rene?"

"I see that most of my ancestors were raised by their mothers alone."

"And why do you think that is?" his mother asked.

Aramis shrugged. "I suppose illness and war did for their husbands?"

"For some," his mother said. "Come with me Rene."

And, giving him no time to protest, staying just ahead of him as before, she took him into the house again and down a long unused corridor to the portrait gallery. On the way she received a lit candle from one of her seemingly invisible, invisibly controlled servants. It had grown dark, and the portrait gallery was a long room immersed in the evening gloom.

As his mother passed, with the pool of light thrown by her candle, Aramis was aware of the ancestors peering down at him, many—so it seemed to him—disapprovingly.

Most of them were, he noted, as fair as he. He also didn't remember this from his younger visits to the place and he'd always assumed he'd got his coloration from his mother. Most of his ancestors, too, male and female alike, seemed to prefer the type of clothes that his mother believed brought with them the deadly contagion of sin.

Oh, there were portraits, here and there, of men in the somber attire of the church, or even in all black suits. But most of the men seemed to favor brightly colored silks and velvets in whatever the state of fashion was for their day. And they'd ornamented ears and fingers, hats and even their sword belts, with enough sparkling jewels to blind a passer-by.

"Here," his mother said, stopping. "What do you see?"

Aramis, not sure what the joke might be, looked up at a vast portrait that showed . . . himself. It couldn't be himself. He was fairly sure he hadn't sat for any portraits. And besides, this was a portrait of himself as he was now, wearing somehow oddly old-fashioned clothes. The collar was too narrow and the doublet in the old-fashioned, restrictive Spanish style that Athos was so fond of.

"It's remarkable," he said, forgetting all his annoyance at his mother. "How did you have this portrait of me made? And why? How could you have got an artist to Paris to take my likeness without my knowing? And why am I wearing clothes I've never owned?"

Madame D'Herblay sighed. "Rene, this was your father," she said, very softly.

"My father?"

"Your father, painted just days before he died. Rene, those men in the cemetery, most of them died in a duel over an affair of honor. As did your father. I never wanted to tell you because, after all, it doesn't edify a young boy to know that his father didn't take his vows of marriage seriously. Your father was courting . . . or paying attention to a young lady. The same young lady was being courted by a young man named Armand Jean de Plessis, who later would become Cardinal Richelieu They clashed, and de Plessis challenged your father for a duel. Upon which your father lost his life, when he was just a few years younger than you are now."

Aramis was speechless.

"This, Aramis, is why I tried to bend your steps towards the church, your mind to holiness. I would rather you are the last of your name and do not leave descendants behind, than you die young, as your father did. Do not let me have that pain, of seeing you dead before your time, son."

Aramis swallowed. "De Richelieu? The Cardinal?"

Madame D'Herblay nodded slowly. "Indeed. He lived to go into the church and to attain the highest honor of the kingdom. Unlike your poor father."

"The Cardinal killed my father?" Aramis said, and ran his hand down in front of his face, as though this would clear his vision and somehow show him something else than his look-alike father smiling down at him with his own sparkling green eyes and impudent mouth. "No wonder he hates me. No wonder he seeks my life when he can . . ."

"And am I right," his mother asked. "To think that you have given him some way to press his animus against you?"

Aramis thought of Violette, dead in her room, seemingly without anyone else's having a chance to murder her. If Aramis hadn't been very lucky and very quick that night, he would have been caught and probably summarily executed upon the moment.

But . . . No one could have got into the room to kill Violette. And yet, someone must have, or else Aramis was the one who had done it. And Aramis was sure he hadn't.

The agents of the Cardinal were everywhere. They often accomplished what seemed impossible.

"Wouldn't it be better, Rene, to stay here, this time? There is a nearby Dominican order that has offered to send over one of their confessors to examine your conscience and your learning and determine whether you might not be ready to profess."

"I always thought to join the Jesuits," Aramis said, without thinking. "They have no set habits, so I could dress almost as I pleased." He became aware of what he had said and of his mother's reproachful gaze upon him.

"As you say, Maman," he thought. Could he go to Paris? Would he dare go to Paris? If the Cardinal had murdered Violette solely to destroy the last descendant of his enemy, his friends would not find any proof of Aramis's innocence. He would look guiltier than sin. And if he ever set foot in Paris again, he would surely be immediately ensnared. "As you say, Maman," he said. "Send for the confessor."

Where Dead Wives Mean Nothing Near Horses and Vineyards; The Happiness of a Rural Estate

Athos didn't know whether to be amused or flattered that—while Grimaud tended to the horses—Raoul was kind enough to send a valet in to help Athos dress.

He settled on amused. It probably never occurred to Raoul—considering how both of them had been brought up—that Athos might have got used to dressing and undressing without the constant presence of a valet.

Not that Grimaud couldn't serve his turn, and quite honorably too, as a gentleman's valet when the need arose. The excellent Grimaud was most accomplished in all domestic arts, having been trained in the domains of la Fere and brought up to do all the jobs in turn, as he aged. However, since Athos was asking him to be housekeeper, cook and whatever else chanced to need doing in the house, including running messages when Athos required it, Athos did not think it was fair to also ask him to be his valet.

And so, for the last five years, Athos had dressed himself. But he could not turn away the valet Raoul had sent, a shy young man probably just recently trained. If he had, Raoul might take it amiss, or think that he had, somehow, offended Athos.

So Athos endured the young man's presence and his help as he washed and changed into the slightly less wrinkled clothing he had packed.

He was glad that Raoul's personal quirks meant the servants were used to noblemen who went about dressed like farmers. For the first time ever, in these surroundings which were close to the surroundings in which he'd grown up, Athos was aware of how shabby he'd allowed his wardrobe and his appearance to become.

The valet did not sneer at his mended clothes, nor at the worn through velvet of his old-fashioned doublet, but Athos still felt as if he had. And so, as soon as his doublet was laced, he thanked the young man and hurried out of the room and next door, to d'Artagnan's.

A knock on the door brought d'Artagnan's invitation to enter.

Athos opened the door. D"Artagnan also had changed, this time into his guard's uniform, probably because it was the newest clothing he owned.

Athos impressed upon him the reasons and need for secrecy and then why he thought that Raoul hadn't heard of his Duchess's death.

The young man stood by the window, with his back turned, and did not turn around to greet Athos. Instead he motioned for Athos to approach.

"There is a rider come," d'Artagnan said. "Express. He came down the lane, horse flying, both of them, horse and rider, foaming—I swear. Now the servants are taking the horse away, see there . . ." d'Artagnan pointed at two liveried servants leading away a horse that had doubtlessly started his journey black but was now grayish red with dust.

"I think," d'Artagnan said. "That our host has received news of his wife's death."

Athos nodded. "Perhaps, my friend," he said. "We should go downstairs and see how Raoul takes the revelation. A lot more can be discovered from a word or a look in a moment when one believes himself unobserved. Or at least not looked upon suspiciously."

D'Artagnan nodded. Together they left the room and hurried down the stairs. Athos imagined that his friend must already have read the missive or had the message relayed to him.

From his memory of the house and of Raoul's habits, Athos reasoned that at this time of day his friend would either be at the entrance hall—to receive the visitor—or else in the study at the back of the house, where he worked on the papers and bills for the estate. It was only when the heat of the day abated that Raoul would ride through the vineyards and fields to inspect the day's work.

But straight down the flight of stairs, they came upon Raoul, standing in the hall. He held a crumpled paper in his hand, and his mouth had dropped open in wonder.

As he heard Athos and d'Artagnan's steps, he turned to look up the stairs. "Alexandre. I've just had the most extraordinary news." He shook the paper. "It says my wife died in Paris. Did you come from Paris? Have you heard anything about it?"

Athos nodded, but said nothing, trying to spur his old friend into continuing. Well did he remember from childhood Raoul's voluble speech, his easy, flowing talk. If that had changed, then Athos would know that Raoul too, like him, had found reasons to change his soul and his inner self.

"How did she die?" he asked. "This tells me nothing save that she was found dead in her room and that they are even now trying to find the culprit." He paused, and his eyes widened, as though a monstrous thought, creeping through his mind, caused them to widen in shock.

"The culprit? It must have been an accident. They can't mean that she was murdered?"

If Raoul was pretending, Athos thought, then he was a better actor than those that graced the Paris stage. He found himself speechless, as the battered letter was waved in his face. "What is this, Alexandre? What happened?"

Athos shrugged. "I know no more than that," he said. It wasn't strictly true, but it was true in a way. He knew they were trying to apprehend Aramis and punish him, and since Aramis was the person, whoever had written that letter—the Cardinal?—meant by culprit, then Athos knew exactly what they knew and no more.

Raoul stared at him a while, and Athos was not sure if he read disapproval or suspicion in his old friend's eyes. Then suddenly Raoul's gaze changed. It softened, it . . . lit up, with gratitude or kindness or whatever other soft feelings made a man's eyes become suddenly gentle and lively with emotion.

Blinking, the duke thrust the letter at the hand of the courier who'd been standing by, waiting, watching. He turned to Athos, both hands extended. "My friend," he said. "You came to visit me because you knew. I wondered why you'd come after so many years and after all had reported you dead. Now I know. You thought I would feel pain and you came to soften it for me." He grasped Athos's cold hands in his and squeezed them.

It had been a long time since any man had greeted Athos with such effusiveness, such lack of reserve. Raoul's clear gratitude reproached his old friend who'd come to see if Raoul had murder on his mind and guilt on his conscience.

"You didn't need to worry, Alexandre," Raoul said. He squeezed Athos hands hard, again. "You see, my marriage was no marriage. Only my father's negotiations, the King's plans. It meant nothing, save that I got her dowry to spend and she came to France with her best friend." He shook his head. "I didn't wish the silly thing ill, mind you. I haven't seen her since we were both barely more than children, pronouncing our vows amid the pomp attending the royal wedding, so much more important than ours. She seemed a nice enough creature, at least for men who like them garrulous and ever ready with wit or dance or some other distraction. But I didn't love her." He squeezed Athos hands a final time and then let go. "So you see, you must not waste your sympathy on me, old friend." Suddenly he smiled. "Though for all that, I am glad you came to visit me. I've missed you terribly, Alexandre. You were my only childhood friend."

With that he turned to the messenger. "You must go to the kitchen. They will give you food and wine, and tell them I instructed them to arrange for lodging for you. They are to attend to you and make you comfortable, and you must rest with us a couple of days before you head back to the capital."

The man bowed and murmured, "Your grace," before— obeying the Duke's gesture—heading down the cool corridor that led to the back of the house. Then he turned to them again. "You must come with me, Alexandre, and your friend too. I have some new irrigation systems I would love to show you. I think the afternoon is cool enough now."

Speaking like that, he led Athos and d'Artagnan out and to the stables at the back. As Athos remembered from the time of Raoul's father, the stables were clean, spacious and stocked with some of the best animals in France. Perhaps the best animals in Europe.

A sleek black animal with a white star upon the forehead was presented for Athos inspection. "I think you'll like this one," Raoul said. "He is the grandson of your Samson. Do you still have Samson, Alexandre?"

Athos shook his head, as his heart tightened in his chest. He'd left his favorite horse—so distinctively his—behind, knowing that his lodgings and arrangements in Paris wouldn't be conducive to keeping Samson in the style to which the horse was accustomed. Athos knew—he kept in touch with his domain enough to know—that his manager, a distant second cousin, treated the horse well. But not a day went by that Athos didn't miss his four-hoofed friend.

He ran his head down the sleek flank of the black horse, aware that Raoul was looking curiously at him, waiting for an explanation. But Athos could not explain.

"Do you remember the area at the back, near the forest," Raoul asked. "Where the crops always failed and which my father just kept as grass and where rabbits multiplied? We channeled water from the lake through a system of baffles, to move it uphill. Quite ingenious and very much like something you and I discussed on the last letter we exchanged. Let me show it to you. I think it would work quite well for the fallow area in La Fere, at the farm."

They mounted and Raoul led them to see the drains, which were, indeed, a miracle of ingenuity and engineering which, in its scale, rivaled the pyramids.

And while Raoul extolled the virtues of this land, now planted with wheat, and talked to Athos of all the improvements he'd done on his land, and how he'd changed the arrangement of his vineyards so that they now were less likely to get the blight or the rust, Athos wondered if Raoul had even cared about his wife enough to have her killed.

Impossible, he thought. Worse than impossible.

Of Sons and Heirs; Where Love Is Not Guilt; An Inconclusive Leave Taking

"**I**S he your son?" Raoul asked, jerking his head towards d'Artagnan who had fallen asleep slumped on an arm chair, the book he'd been holding fallen from his fingers onto the floor.

Athos, sitting in front of the fireplace, across a table set up with a chessboard, started and looked at his friend on the other side with utter surprise, before he managed to discipline himself.

Raoul grinned. "Come, come, Alexandre. Did I penetrate your secret? Did you abandon your domain, your family, your honor to live with some Spanish beauty who gave you this fine son?"

His surprise past, Athos smiled. "No, Raoul. Though I wish it were true. D"Artagnan is a son I could be proud of. A fine sword hand, an honorable youth who will, I think, grow to be an admirable and honorable man."

"What—Is it too much if I ask where you've been and in what circumstances that you arrive here with such a companion?" Raoul looked over at d'Artagnan and smiled. "I believe the young man is all you say. You call him a friend, and I've never heard you misuse that term nor can I imagine Alexandre, Count de la Fere, bestowing his esteem on anyone less than admirable. But he's obviously a Gascon and, if you pardon me saying so, as far from you in class as he is in age. How can you have met him? How can such a friendship be forged that you asked him to come with you on an arduous journey?"

Athos evaluated his options, telling the truth or not, the same way he evaluated the game upon the board. He could lie to Raoul, but what did it matter? No nobleman—not unless he hated the other or worked directly for the Cardinal— would denounce another nobleman. And Raoul, whatever Raoul might have done to his wife, would never betray his oldest friend. Athos felt sure of it, just as he felt sure that even were he to prove that Raoul was a murderer he wouldn't denounce him. Give him the warning and tell him to flee, maybe. Turn him to the King's justice, never.

Athos moved his pawn, slowly. "I have . . . For the last five years, I've been living as a King's musketeer under the command of Monsieur de Treville."

"Have you really?" Raoul stopped, his hand upon the bishop. "But why, man? What is the sense in it? If you were that desperate to take arms for—"

"I've been hiding," Athos said, deliberately. "Under the name of Athos. Only Monsieur de Treville knows my name and the reason I'm hiding, though I suspect my closest friends have reason to guess it."

"Your friends? The boy?"

"Is one of them. The most recent one, though already he has proven his loyalty and his perfect ability to keep secrets and to discover them. The other two hide their identities under the names Aramis and Porthos—though they are all noblemen."

Raoul looked baffled, as if he suspected Athos of a sudden brain fever. The flames from the fireplace cast reddish and gold shadows upon his face. "All of you hiding under assumed names? Why?"

"Aramis was studying to become a seminarian," Athos said. "Until a gentleman found Aramis reading the lives of saints to his sister. At least that's what Aramis has sworn to us he was doing. Whether he thought it necessary to illustrate those readings with a demonstration of the attempts against the female saints' chastity, I hesitate to say." He let a smile curl across his lips. "But the brother challenged Aramis for a duel and Aramis went to the most accomplished fencing master in Paris for help. When Aramis then killed the man in duel, he realized only a time of hiding and expiating his sin would allow his name to be cleared enough to join a monastery. And since Porthos was the fencing master, and his second in the duel . . . He too had to hide. From their accounts this happened ten years ago, but they keep dueling enough to keep in trouble."

"I see," Raoul said. He moved the bishop, but not in any way that would further his game. "And yourself?"

Athos sighed. He threw back his head, to clear his face of a stray strand of hair that gotten loose from his ponytail. "I," he said. "Have never read the lives of saints to anyone."

Raoul grinned. He got up and went to a cabinet in the corner. This study was clearly Raoul's private domain, filled with books, with ancestral, carved cabinets, with swords and daggers and other things that had belonged to the de Dreux men for generations on end. Atop the fireplace, on the wall, hung the portrait of a man whose mobile face looked enough like Raoul's to be the face of a father or brother. But the attire was that of a gentleman of the time of Francis I.

Raoul came back with a bottle of wine, two glasses, and a corkscrew. He proceeded to uncork the wine, and pour some for Athos, then some for himself. The wine fell into the glass, red and sparkling like a ruby.

"It's from the new vineyards I've had put in, since Father died. Taste it and tell me what you think."

Athos leaned back and took a sip. Unlike the wine in Paris where the harsh, brass scents of the containers it had been too long kept in

THE MUSKETEER'S SEAMSTRESS

shouted at his consciousness like a blaring of discordant voices, this wine fell upon the tongue like a caress. Athos noted flavors of rosemary, a hint of clover, and the unmistakable sweetness of a wine grown on a sunny slope. He rolled the wine upon his tongue, savoring it, then swallowed, feeling as if he'd swallowed a mouthful of sun and summer and the unfettered freedom of his younger days. "Do I detect rosemary and clover?"

"Yes. I detect them too, at least. And there's plenty of those about . . ." Raoul took a slow sip. "Don't you find the body somewhat lacking though?"

Athos considered. He found himself smiling, one of his rare, fully open smiles. "Raoul, do you know what grade of wine a musketeer normally drinks?"

Raoul looked at him and arched his eyebrows. "My friend, you never told me how you ended up being a musketeer. You said your friends were lying low till the duels they'd taken part in were forgotten. Did you too fight a duel?"

Athos shook his head. His pain, his guilt, his remorse, all flooded over him. He needed to talk to someone. He needed to talk to Raoul who'd known him all his life.

And then, his mind whispered, if Raoul suffered from the like guilt, he would be more likely to speak to Athos about it.

Still, he hadn't spoken about it in a long time. And he wasn't sure he could. He tossed back the rest of his wine and extended his empty glass to Raoul, who filled it, but looked gravely at Athos. "It's not like you to drink a lot."

Athos made a face. "It wasn't like me," he said, and cast a look at d'Artagnan, to make sure the young man was still asleep. After they'd solved that murder mystery together, if d'Artagnan didn't know of Athos's past, he was a fool.

But then he didn't know the details, and it was the details that tortured Athos. "You remember my wife, Charlotte," he told Raoul.

Raoul nodded. "I remember being wildly envious of you," he said. "Not jealous, since I didn't know the lady, before you married her, nor did I have any interest in her once I met her. But envious, because I had to marry a Spanish noblewoman I'd never seen, while you got to marry your true love. You told me, if I remember, that she was the sister of the priest in your parish? Beautiful and kind like an angel?"

Athos inhaled sharply, as the memory of those words, the memory of Charlotte's beautiful face and open, kind eyes came back to him. He didn't know if it had all been a lie, but he hoped it had. He hoped so, because otherwise he was a true murderer. And now, looking back, he already couldn't recapture the complacency and certainty with which he had killed her.

"Yes," he said, instead. "I thought so at the time." He looked away from Raoul's inquisitive gaze, and took a deep draught from his glass.

"And then, about three months after my last letter to you, I was out hunting with Charlotte, which, if I remember well, was merely a pretext for our going out into the fields and spending a lot of time alone. Not that she wasn't a good huntress. She was. Like the goddess Diana herself." He shook his head. "But we were racing through the fields, and she was turned back, laughing at me. Her horse went under a lower-hanging bow. It caught her, and she was thrown and fell on the ground, insensible. You can imagine my distress."

"She died then?" Raoul asked.

Athos shook his head and swallowed. His voice sounded strangled to his own ears. "Wish that she had."

"Alexandre!"

"No, listen. I jumped from my horse and ran to her. She was breathing, but very shallowly, and she looked pale and I, fool that I was, thought she needed air. So I cut her dress with my hunting knife. And there, upon her white shoulder . . ." He closed his eyes, as if it would help block the sight he still saw every night in his dreams. "Was a fleur-de-lis."

"Sangre Dieu!" Raoul said.

With his eyes closed, Athos heard his friend jump up, heard him open the bottle once more, and opened his eyes just in time to see Raoul refill Athos's glass, before falling back on his own chair, staring horrified at Athos. "Sangre Dieu," he said again, this time softly. "You married a criminal."

"I thought so," Athos said, and took a draught of the wine, which was starting to make his head swim. He was used to drinking a lot more, but not this good a quality of wine. "I thought so, and I thought I could not turn her to the local court. At any rate, I was the local court, the judge instituted by God and the unbroken line of my ancestors, to adjudicate all local crimes and claims. I know, I know, even so, I should have brought it out in public, flung the case down before the lawyers in my domain, and then got her to tell her story, get her tried—" He took another sip of wine and a deep breath, which came out ragged and fluttering. "The shame to my domain, the shame to my name . . . Forever, I would be known as the Count who married the branded criminal. Myself, and my sons, should I ever have any, would be laughed at. We'd never dare declare what has, until now, been a proud name." He looked at the flames in the fireplace licking at the dark shadows of the logs, and dancing, like a prefiguration of the hell that waited him after this life was done. His reasoning had seemed so good at the time. "The tree against which she'd crashed was still nearby. I dragged her to it. I had rope in my saddle bag. I . . . I hanged her from an overhanging branch." The image of Charlotte swinging from the branch, her long blond hair waving like a flag in the wind, made him close his eyes again. The silence went on. So even Raoul disapproved of him.

When Athos opened his eyes again, though, he found Raoul looking at him, pale and shocked. But the expression in Raoul's eyes was all sympathy, all concern. "By the Mass," he said. "Sangre Dieu, man, how that must work at you. I've known you too long not to know you have the sort of conscience that wouldn't let you sleep at night, after that."

"Should I be able to sleep at night after that?" Athos asked, and immediately, without giving Raoul time to answer, he continued. "I didn't even return to my house for a change of clothes. I didn't want to be there when they found her. Oh, when they found her, they would find the mark on her shoulder too, and they would know that I had reason to kill her. As the local Lord I had the right to kill her for that—"

"You had the right to kill her for lying to you, for luring you into a shameful marriage," Raoul said heatedly.

"You don't really believe that, Raoul," Athos said, softly. All his thought of trapping his friend was gone, and he knew, knew with the certainty of an old friend that Raoul for all his heated words would never kill a woman merely for lying to him.

Raoul shook his head. "Perhaps I don't, but Alexandre, how can you expect your oldest friend to forgive a woman who has done this to you? Who has destroyed your life? You were the noblest and most accomplished man I've ever known. I expected—we all expected—great things of you."

"By the next day, I sent a message back to Grimaud, who had been my valet," Athos said. "And told him to join me in Paris and what to bring with him. When he joined me, they hadn't found her, yet, but I presume it can't have taken much longer.

"I made use of my father's friendship with Monsieur de Treville to get a post in the musketeers, under the name Athos."

There was a silence, then Raoul wrinkled his forehead. "Isn't that the name of a mountain?"

"In Armenia," Athos said. "The site of a famous monastery."

"Oh, Alexandre," Raoul said, half exasperated, half amused. "How your mind is still what it was as a child. A monastery, of course. Expiating your sin. Alexandre, you are a fool."

"I realize that," Athos said. "Only a fool would have married her."

"No," Raoul said. "Only a fool would indulge in such browbeating recrimination over executing a criminal. Because that's all you've done. You administered the justice she had too long evaded."

"But . . . what if the brand wasn't real? What if it had been set there by an enemy? What if—"

"A fleur-de-lis brand? By an enemy? Do you have any other fairy tales you wish to tell yourself, my friend? You executed a criminal. You've punished yourself enough. We heard you and your wife had both disappeared and, when you weren't found, were presumed abducted and dead. Since there is some doubt, your cousin, de Falonage, has been administering La Fere from a distance. But you should go back. Go back, marry again, marry a worthy woman, sire half a dozen sons. All this guilt, all this—" Raoul waved his hand as if to do way with the musketeers, Paris, with Athos's obsessive recrimination. "Drama will disappear. Like a bad dream. Which is all it is."

Athos shook his head. It wasn't that easy. He had always known that he and Raoul were made of different stuff, hewn of different material. He couldn't explain to Raoul that his guilt felt real, that his doubt about Charlotte was real. Nor that he loved her still. Instead, he forced a smile on his lips. "Is that what you intend to do, now, then? Sire half a dozen sons?"

Raoul smiled in turn and finished his own wine in the glass he'd been holding, seemingly forgotten, between his fingers. "The good Lord willing," he said. "You know, the funny thing is that my envy for what I thought was your love match inspired me. When it became obvious to me that madame my wife and I had nothing in common, I let her stay in Paris and I came here, to my vineyards, to the fields I love.

"Please don't think me bitter. There was nothing in it one way or another. Ysabella and I were two very different people, and she was no more than a stranger to me. My father had let our estate get to such a ruinous degree of downfall—between his bookish obsessions and his ignorance of all land management—that for me to go on living in it and raise a family in it, in estate, was impossible. My two choices were to run away from the debtors and do something like what you've done." He smiled at Athos, and waved his hand vaguely again. "The musketeer uniform, the . . . All that. Or I could find someone to marry who brought a large enough dowry to cover the expenses of restoring the estate. My father's distant cousin, his majesty, himself, wanted me to marry Ysabella and she certainly fit the bill."

He got up and threw one more trunk into the fireplace, then turned to smile at Athos. "Would you believe I was relieved she didn't actually wish to live with me? She had no interest in living in Dreux, or in being mother to my children." He nodded, possibly at something he saw in Athos's expression. "Believe me, I was. After all, if she didn't want to live with me, I had the time, the possibility, the ability to fall in love. And I could find someone who—like me— could never marry, but who would be happy with just our love."

"You took a mistress."

Raoul nodded. "Are you that surprised? Didn't Ysabella have her lover?" He paused and looked shocked. "Good Lord, his name was Aramis, wasn't it? He's your friend whom you mentioned."

Athos shrugged, as if this were of little importance. "How do you know his name?"

Raoul smiled. "There were always helpful people in Paris. My friends, or those who would have me believe them my friends. All too eager to send me information about what Ysabella was doing. I couldn't get any of them to understand I didn't care. And I didn't. Ysabella and I had a bargain, and she fulfilled it. Her part of the bargain was that she could do whatever she pleased, provided she didn't overspend her allowance, and she didn't . . . get herself with child. As far as I know, she kept both ends of it. Oh, the Queen often gave her jewels and money, so the first one wasn't difficult. And if she ever violated the second, she hid the pregnancy and got rid of the child, so I was not saddled with a bastard."

"And you?" Athos asked.

Raoul de Dreux shrugged. "I found myself a friend, first. She is one of my tenants. Widowed, with a large farm to her care. Common, with common ancestry. But I started dropping by her farm, and we started talking, and after a while, insensibly, I realized I was in love with her. She's a sensible woman, whose ancestors have been in this region as long as mine, and who loves the land as much as I do. The implementing of that irrigation project was as much her brainchild as mine."

"And do you have . . . bastards?" Athos asked. His friend's flinch at the word did not escape him.

Raoul took a deep breath. Athos guessed that if they were not such close friends, and if it weren't, in point of fact, the absolute, legal truth, Raoul would have challenged Athos to a duel then and there.

Instead, he shrugged and in a voice that sounded more brittle than indifferent, he said, "As a point of fact, though we've been very careful all these years, just these last two months, Aliberta has found herself . . . embarrassed."

Athos's turn to flinch, inwardly, because this provided Raoul with the best motive for killing his absent wife. How could this family-proud, upright man not want his son or daughter to be legitimate? How could he not wish to have for his children the benefit of that established solidity that had graced his own birth and childhood.

"What do you plan to do?" Athos asked.

"What I planned to do," Raoul said. "Was acknowledge the child, of course. Most of the people in my domain know that Aliberta and I are lovers. Not to acknowledge the child as mine would be churlish. And then I thought, particularly if it were a boy, I would apply to Rome, through the hierarchy of the church, and have him legitimized. Make him my heir."

"You said it's what you planned to do?"

"Well, by God, Ysabella set me free at a most convenient time," Raoul grinned, a wide grin. "I can now marry Aliberta. Oh, there will be talk because she is not noble, but my father is dead, the king has problems of his own, and I'm, fortunately, my own man, free to choose as I please. I'll marry her, and if the child is two months too early and seems a little well developed, who's to talk?" He turned his smile on Athos, then his smile froze and he chuckled. "Alexandre, did you come all this way to see whether I might have murdered my wife? Only you look as though someone plunged a dagger into your heart. Was my wife murdered? Do you suspect me, my friend?"

And Athos, who had indeed been suspecting his old friend and whose breath was frozen mid-drawing, now realized that were Raoul truly guilty he would never have come out and said that. He would certainly never have used the image of a dagger plunged in one's heart. And he wouldn't be smiling at Athos like a fool. Raoul was different from Athos, but that difference hinged on a more open nature, on a milder outlook on life. Not on his ability for consummate acting.

Athos took a breath, another and glared at his friend. "No, I do not suspect you."

"But you did? Did you think I actually traveled to Paris to kill her? I didn't, I assure you. You can ask any of my servants and verify——" He looked at Athos and guffawed, delightedly. "You did, you fool. You did already."

"I did," Athos confirmed, refusing to laugh with his friend. "But a man of your position, of your income, does not need to kill his wife himself."

"What, and subject myself to never ending blackmail? Or did you think me so lost to all proper feeling that I'd then kill the wretch who killed her?"

Athos shook his head. "I confess I can't imagine you doing either."

"Oh, good, that means you're just a fool and not a half-wit," Raoul said. He seemed greatly pleased with the idea that Athos had suspected him at any time. "And what did you mean to do if I had been guilty? Have me turned in and killed?" He shook his head. "No. I can't believe that of you. So it would have been the old, 'fly, all is discovered.' "

It took quite a while and much laughing before Raoul would let the subject rest. Then he extracted from Athos a full account of all that had happened and why Athos felt it necessary to investigate the crime. He sympathized with Aramis, though he couldn't fathom the mind of a man who would fall for his late wife.

By the time the two friends retired—without ever finishing their chess game—Athos was as sure as a human can be of anything that Raoul hadn't killed his wayward Duchess.

D'Artagnan hadn't awakened and Athos picked up the book the young man had let fall—Systems of Irrigation and the Building of Ditches with Diagrams. No wonder the youth had fallen asleep—before waking him and sending him to bed.

"I shall leave tomorrow," Athos told Raoul.

"Yes," Raoul said. They stood at the foot of the stairs, which Athos would have to climb to his room. Raoul's bedroom was in quite a different part of the house. "I understand why you must. Till your friend is proven innocent, you must investigate. But after he's proven innocent, come and see me again, Alexandre. I want you to stand godfather to my son."

The Best Intentions of a Novice; Dark Eyes and Dark Thoughts; A Message from the Cardinal

"**I** dreamed of her again, last night," Aramis said. He sat in his room, on a chair and had, unconsciously, adopted a pose that had been common to him in early adolescence— his body slumped down on the seat and his arms hanging over the arms of the chair.

The black suits his maman left out for him were linen mixed in with wool and itched like the fires of hell.

Which the man standing at the foot of the bed, in the black habit of the Dominican was about to remind Aramis of, if Aramis was any judge of the expression in his eyes.

"I despair of you, Chevalier," the Dominican presently said. He looked over at Aramis with an expression of the deepest despair and betrayal. "Indeed, I do. You are so gifted, in your preaching and your thought, so capable, so clearly . . . called to the life of the church and to convert others to the wonders of the faith—and yet . . ." The Dominican opened his hands, as if to signify that he couldn't possibly help Aramis if Aramis didn't reform his ways. "Don't you understand," he asked, leaning close. "Don't you understand that the woman is dead? She's even now suffering the pains of hell that her sin with you earned her. And yet you . . ." The monk looked like he would presently make a very uncharitable comment about Aramis, and Aramis looked away before the poor brother disgraced himself by stomping his feet or growling or something equally undignified.

He looked towards the window of his room, which was open to the still afternoon air, warm and suffocating with a foretaste of summer in its stultifying heat.

Oh, he'd entered this of his own volition. Or at least, he supposed it had been his own volition, though when his mother was around, when she was concerned in anything at all, it became hard for Aramis to tell which was his decision and which his mother's gentle manipulation. Though she was his mother, Aramis wasn't blind to the reality that he'd got his guile and his ability to manipulate others from her. Nor that the master remained superior to her pupil.

After she'd taken him to the cemetery and the gallery; after he'd seen where the enmity of the Cardinal had got his father, Aramis could only think to avoid the like fate. And avoiding the like fate—his mother had assured him— meant taking the habit as soon as possible.

But now Aramis had started thinking that it made no sense. After all, being a musketeer had helped him avoid his father's early death so far. Aramis had simply learned to use the sword better than anyone who wished to kill him.

And the more he thought about it, the less he could believe that the Cardinal would have killed Violette because he meant to entrap Aramis. She was too close to the Queen, too high of rank, too connected in the court for the Cardinal to kill her as a mere pawn to his purposes. No.

Violette had been killed for other reasons. And Aramis was here, hiding, while he left his friends to figure out the crime. He chewed, thoughtfully, on his lower lip. The idea that his safety, his ability to return to Paris as a free man depended on the cunning of Porthos made him sigh. Porthos, after all, had many admirable qualities.

Porthos's loyalty Aramis would vouch for; his strength could not be impeached, and even where his intelligence was concerned, Aramis didn't think it was quite so dim as many in the musketeers would avow.

In fact, having known Porthos for these many years, Aramis was sure that Porthos was, if not brilliant, of more than average intelligence. Even if his was a peculiar form of intelligence that often had trouble translating itself to words. But Porthos's cunning—well, Porthos's cunning could only be considered at the same level as Porthos' sense of fashion, which often made Aramis cringe and caused sensible people to shield their eyes.

Then there was Athos. Athos was, of course, very intelligent. Or at least, he'd read a lot of books. And been given as good an education as an old, well-grounded noble family could afford. Ask Athos about philosophy, about the virtues of the ancients, about that corruption which had caused the fall of the mighty Roman Empire and you'd get well reasoned explanations, concise and set into words so carefully picked that even a school master could take no exception to them.

Athos, when he was thus inclined—often after he'd drunk far more than anyone should drink—would debate even theology with Aramis himself, and could make his points over Aramis's even on those things in which Aramis was well schooled. But Athos's practical intelligence, his knowledge of people and people's motives ...well . . .

Like most misanthropes, Athos tended to assume the worst of humankind. While this was better than assuming the best, it was just as fallible. Athos saw every man as a mirror of himself and himself as composed of the worst qualities he'd not even observed but read about. Aramis was not so dense that he hadn't gathered that in Athos's past there was something he viewed as a crime and for which he blamed himself. He would bet—from knowing Athos—that it was something no other human being would feel guilty about. Or at least, no other sane human being. Athos's long silences, his brooding, his imbibing,

his reckless and always unlucky gambling all seemed to bespeak a great
love with ruin and death.

How could Aramis trust Athos to save Aramis from ruin and death,
when those seemed to be the older man's true lovers?

Then there was d'Artagnan. D"Artagnan was cunning. Aramis would
give him that. In fact, when he'd first met d'Artagnan, Aramis thought
he might very well have met his match and watched the young man
in careful, if horrified, attention, to make sure that d'Artagnan did not
mean to maneuver behind Aramis's back.

He'd come to be satisfied of the young man's loyalty and probity.
None of which meant he didn't think that d'Artagnan wasn't cunning.

But part of what made d'Artagnan's cunning not so threatening was
the fact that the young man was young yet. Just seventeen and newly
arrived in Paris, d'Artagnan wouldn't be able to penetrate the secret
places of the court, nor to ask questions of those who knew Violette
best. And even if he did, their motives might be opaque to him, who
had never been a courtier.

Oh, with the four of them together it was true that the whole often
seemed far more than the sum of its parts, and yet . . .

Aramis became aware that he had been quiet for a long while. And
his quietness was echoed in the thunderous frown on the Dominican's
face.

"You were thinking of her again," the man said. He was middle-aged.
Though, to be honest, he was probably no older than Athos's thirty-five
years of age. But he was grayer, what remained of his hair around the
monk's tonsure, an iron grey and faded. And his face too had a curious
faded look, the skin seeming almost colorless and wrinkled, around
mouth and eyes, as if he'd frowned disconsolately once too many.

"Tell me at least," he said, with a beseeching tone. "That you were
thinking of her in sorrow. That you were sorry for the torments she
must be suffering for those delights you shared with her."

"I wasn't thinking of—" Aramis said.

The Dominican smirked. "No, I imagine you weren't. You were thinking of her luscious thighs, her soft breasts. This is what you dream
about, is it not?"

"Her breasts were not so much soft as firm," Aramis said, and then
realized what he had said, as the Dominican stared at him in horror.

"I cannot save you, Chevalier. I cannot save you," he said. "You are
headed for the fiery pit headlong, and I can't save you. As much as I
respect your honorable mother, as much as I would like to help her
convert her son, I don't think I can do it." He opened his arms in a show
of helplessness and, instead of resuming his ranting as Aramis hoped,
he opened the door and headed out, slamming it behind himself.

Aramis took a couple of breaths, contemplating the closed door.
Truth be told, he was growing bored with the sermons and tired of

the narrow view of a man who had entered a monastery as a child and clearly knew nothing about the world he railed against.

On the other hand, the Dominican was his mother's spiritual counselor and had great influence over Madame D'Herblay. If Aramis's mother heard about how he had offended the priest . . .

In Aramis's mind a horrible panorama arose. Things that had happened when he was very young and had, somehow—most often without knowing how—aroused his mother's ire.

There would be pilgrimages. There would be attendance at the sermons of nearby preachers whose words were reputed to hold some great sin-fighting virtue. There would be shrines. And relics.

The horror of it made him spring to his feet, and race out the door at a most undignified pace, slamming the door behind himself in turn.

In the corridor, outside his room, he saw the Dominican some steps away. Walking with the necessary tactful pace of a holy man, he'd gone a much smaller distance than Aramis had just covered in a rush.

"Stop," Aramis said, running to catch up. "Stop, you must forgive me if I love the world. Did not God so love the world that He gave the world His only son?"

The Dominican turned around and looked at Aramis with the expression that would make perfect sense if Aramis had been something smelly and repulsive found at the bottom of the monk's sandal. "The Lord does not love the world," he said, and, turning, started to descend the stairs, his dignified pace only slightly pressed by Aramis's hurry to catch up with him.

"But listen, it's in the Bible, that God so loved the world He sent it His only son," Aramis protested.

"God did not love the world," the Dominican insisted, hurrying down. "He sent our Lord Jesus Christ to redeem those in the world who were willing to be children of God. He sent Him to pull us above the world, to take us out of the world."

"Uh . . ." Aramis said, and sped up his pace of descending the stairs to keep up with the Dominican whose sandals were now slapping the steps with a rapid fire force. "Uh, but . . . But . . . Even Augustine said that—"

He couldn't find his breath, much less his mind to complete the thought, and they'd reached the last flight of stairs before the lowest landing—the entrance hall to the house.

Aramis stopped talking because his mother was in the hall, and looking over her shoulder at him and the Dominican with an expression of mingled incredulity and horror.

"Maman," Aramis said, but it came out as a squeak.

The Dominican started more coherently, "Madame, I believe you might be deluded as to your son's vocation, because—"

Madame D'Herblay waved them both into silence, and Aramis realized that there were sounds coming from the wide open front door.

Sounds of people walking, sounds of talking, and a dulcet female voice as though the angels themselves were singing in his ears.

Through the door, in order, came several servants, carrying trunks, an old priest who looked like a much older and blander version of the Dominican and a couple of older women. All of them were dressed in the Spanish manner, the women in vast skirts and high-necked gowns, the men in dark clothes with much embroidery. They all looked grim as Spaniards, too, their features set in that harsh disapproval of the world and everyone in it that was bound to make the Dominican brother happy. But at the end of the crowd, a woman entered. She was slim, dark haired, her black hair, with just the slightest hint of curl confined by a coif at the front, but falling free in the back, past her waist and, it looked like, past her buttocks. She would be able to sit on it . . . Though she wore Spanish-fashion clothes, which meant the neckline was high and the bodice constructed so that her chest appeared flat, there was something to her graceful walk and the narrow confines of her waist that told Aramis she probably hid a beautiful figure.

He imagined her naked, cloaked only in her luminous dark hair and he was sure an "oh" escaped his lips. At least the Dominican brother gave him a most venomous look.

But then she raised her eyes and looked directly at Aramis. Her eyes were large and the normal way to describe them would be to say they were light brown. To Aramis, though, they weren't so much light brown as distilled sunlight, collected, amassed in amber and shining forth with the luminosity of a thousand childhood afternoons.

All purity, all beauty was there, captured in those eyes. Looking into her eyes, Aramis was a boy again, the same boy who, still innocent of that world that the Dominican disapproved of, had run wild and free through the summer afternoons amid ripening wheat stalks.

"Rene," his mother said, sharply. "This is my sister's goddaughter, Leda D'Armato. She's come from Spain as the intended of the Count de Bassompierre, whom she is to marry in two weeks. Until then she'll stay with us, under my careful supervision."

Aramis nodded to his mother's words, even to her stern warning pronounced last. But in his mind—he couldn't help it—he was imagining the beautiful Leda naked. He was kissing her lips that so resembled a newly opened red rose. He was . . .

"In fact, quite mistaken about his having any vocation," the Dominican said. And, with one last look of reproach, he headed out the door.

"Rene," his mother said. "You will explain to me the meaning of this. I thought you—"

From outside, through the open door, came the sound of hooves, then the smart sound of a man dismounting. A few of Leda's servants—and a few of his mother's own, who'd come to watch her arrival—jumped forward to look out the door and see the commotion.

Words pronounced now by one, now by the other servant, reached Aramis's ears.

"A fancy livery."

"The red of the Cardinal."

"Carrying something."

"Looks like a letter."

And then a servant in the red livery of the Cardinal stepped into the front hall. He bowed at Madame D'Herblay—who for some reason paled—and must quite have missed seeing Aramis who had, without anyone noticing, drifted behind a couple of servants holding a trunk made of that painted leather that was the specialty of the Spanish city of Cordoba.

"Madame D'Herblay," the messenger said. "I've been sent to bring a letter to the man they call Aramis."

"Aramis?" Madame D'Herblay said. "I'm sure there's no one here by that name. It doesn't sound like a real name."

If there was one thing that Aramis knew, it was that one didn't trifle with the Cardinal or his messengers. Fool them, sure. Duel with them, whenever needed. But in this case, if he held himself in secret, it would only mean the messenger would tell his mother it was him—and then proceed to explain, probably in front of the beauteous Leda, why he was seeking Aramis, and all of Aramis's nefarious nature.

So Aramis stepped forward, and bowed to the messenger. "I have on occasion called myself that," he said.

"Rene!" his mother said.

The messenger smiled. "Very well, Chevalier. His eminence has asked me to give you this. It outlines your possible choices. I hope you choose well."

And with those words, the messenger turned and walked out of the house and down the steps, back to his waiting horse.

How had they found Aramis? And what choices could the Cardinal be speaking of?

Cardinals and Passageways; The Slowness of the Quick; Porthos's Wisdom

"**S**o there is no passage into the room?" Athos asked.

Porthos shrugged. "It is not as simple as that," he said. He'd come with his friends, reluctantly, having been pulled from watching street acrobats. Athos had said that the street was no place to discuss such secret matters. This seemed to Porthos very foolish indeed. If he watched people and saw them going into a house together to talk, he would be far more likely to think they were talking of forbidden matters than if they stood around, on a street corner, watching acrobats and jugglers and discussing the matter.

Besides, Porthos liked acrobats and jugglers and since they had taken the trouble to perform on the street outside Athos's home, all of them somersaulting and walking on wires and who knew what else, he felt the least he could do was watch them.

But no, they must go within to the dark and dreary interior of Athos's home and there—with serious eyes and serious voices—discuss the matter while a serious Grimaud circled around filling their cups with wine.

At least the wine was the best Athos—who usually served the best wine of them all—had ever served. Two bottles, he said, given to him by his friend Raoul. Porthos was grateful that Athos shared the wine—too good for one of Athos's solitary drunks. But he was less amused at Athos's words, Athos's implication that Porthos had found nothing.

"It's not that simple," he said, and, searching his mind for the right word, the kind of word Aramis might well have used, he added, "There are . . . implications to what I discovered that you're not taking into account. Mousqueton tells me that Hermengarde, the palace maid, says that the Cardinal himself wanted Aramis's Violette placed in that room. Because he was afraid she conspired with Anne of Austria in favor of Spain. And she said that the Cardinal often stood in that secret hallway and listened to them."

"And what would you have that mean?" Athos asked. "That the Cardinal actually saw our friend murder his lover?"

Porthos shook his head. Sometimes Athos could be exasperating. Porthos was as appreciative as anyone else of Athos's admirable qualities—his noble looks which in truth translated a matching nobility of mind, one that few people could match. But with it all came the conviction that his true superiority to the mass of men meant that his thought was always, perforce, correct.

It seemed to Porthos as though Athos had early on decided that Aramis must be guilty of the murder and, once having decided it, kept right on repeating it, unable to change his mind. Or if he hadn't he still reverted to this point of view when the investigation didn't go as he expected. "Athos," he said. "Aramis didn't kill anyone."

Athos waved his hand exasperatedly, as if to sweep the comment away. "No, Porthos, I believe he might not have, but don't you see those would be the only circumstances in which the hole in the wall would be relevant? Because it can't possibly be that Violette was killed through that hole. So it must . . ."

Porthos shook his head. "You're missing the larger picture. The Cardinal spied on the woman, the Cardinal is so involved in this that he sent someone to my lodgings, wanting to know where I was, what I was doing. He seems afraid I know something about Aramis, or about this whole affair. Doubtless he's sent someone to your lodgings, and even d'Artagnan's too, but I was the only one in town. Athos—it is stupid to try to find out who would have wanted to kill Aramis's lover."

Athos raised his dark eyebrows upon his broad pale forehead, then brought them down over his eyes in a frown. He took a deep draught out of the wine cup in his hand and glared at Porthos. "I don't have the privilege of following your meaning, Porthos. What can you possibly mean by that? Why is it stupid to try to find out who might want to murder a woman who was murdered?"

"Because too many people might well have wanted to," Porthos said.

"I don't follow you," Athos repeated, his expression even more annoyed.

"I suppose," d'Artagnan put in from the side, in the conciliatory tone of voice he often used when his friends disputed. "That Porthos means that at any time many people might want to kill many other people and that, thus to find who might want to murder the seamstress is a lost cause."

Porthos nodded. "You have it. By the blood, the Gascon has it. Think Athos, how many people would not want you dead, starting with his eminence and ending with the men you've bested in duels. Yet, none of them has murdered you."

Athos shifted in his seat. "No one has murdered me, Porthos. While someone has murdered Violette, something that puts the whole case in a different complexion. We have to find who had cause to murder her, and then whether they could have executed it."

"But that's the most important part of it," Porthos said, setting his wine down and pounding so hard on the arm of his chair that the wood resounded with a loud boom and Grimaud, quietly approaching them with another bottle of wine, jumped into the air and paled.

"What is the important part of it, Porthos?" Athos asked impatiently. He'd been rather impatient since his return from his friend's house. As though he'd seen or heard something that hurt him or worried him. "Would you do me the courtesy of speaking a language the others of us understand? French by preference, though Latin and Greek will serve in a pinch."

Athos was insufferable in this mood, Porthos thought. If he didn't remember his friend's many kindnesses to him and services to the king over the last years, he'd challenge Athos to a duel. He hated it when Athos went all grand seigneur, and rubbed it in that Porthos hadn't had Athos's superior education.

And of a sudden Porthos realized what was wrong. Aramis wasn't here. Aramis, though not quite as noble—or at least not of such a prestigious family as Athos—had the same excellent education and a background at which Athos himself couldn't possibly sneer. So when Athos started getting above himself and disdaining his company, Aramis could bring him to ground with a resounding thud—or more likely with a joke and a quotation. The problem, Porthos thought, was that they were incomplete without Aramis. Aramis was necessary to the proper functioning of their group.

But Aramis wasn't here, Aramis couldn't be here, unless they found out who had killed Aramis's seamstress. And the only way to do that was for Porthos to explain to his friends just how foolish their present course of action was.

He took a deep breath and prepared to do battle with the language, which he always found a harder and more slippery foe than any enemy he'd taken on the field of battle or the field of honor. "Athos, listen," he said. "I did not mean to call you stupid and there was no offense there. We've all been equally stupid, as we wonder who could have killed Violette and not how." He lifted his hand to ward off Athos's interruption, as he saw his friend open his mouth. "No, listen. In other murders, it might very well be an important matter to find out who wishes to murder the victim. If the victim is fortunate enough to have few enemies, or few powerful enemies, then motive is all. But this is not the case here. Here . . . Look, how was the Duchess killed?"

"She was stabbed through the heart," Athos said, frowning. "I fail to understand what you mean."

"No. She was stabbed through the heart while in a third floor room whose only door of easy access was locked. If we assume—and I am assuming, no matter what you think—that the only person locked in the room with her did not kill her, what is the greatest indicator of who might have committed the murder?" He looked at Athos's eyes and found total incomprehension. Again, he lifted his hand, but this time looked at Grimaud and stopped himself before pounding the arm of the chair. Instead, he brought his hand down, open, and rested it upon the wood, flexing the fingers against the carving. "The greatest indicator is the ability to do so. By what means could someone gain access to the room? Who could have come up and killed her, in the space of time it took Aramis to answer a call of nature? Find that, and the means they used to get there will tell us who it might be. And then it will all be easy." He smiled at Athos's frowning countenance, and extended his cup to Grimaud for a refill.

He'd refrained from pounding the arm of the chair, and he felt he was owed something in return. Grimaud obligingly refilled the cup.

All this while, Athos continued to frown. "But . . ." he said. "If that's true, then it's impossible. No one could have got to the balcony, three floors off the ground and far enough away from a tree that the tree presented no means of climbing there. The tree was just near enough to break Aramis's fall, but it was not near enough, could not be near enough to allow anyone to get into the room. If we're going with the means to commit the murder, then Aramis would be guilty. Is that what you're trying to suggest?"

"No," Porthos said. "I merely think you are ignoring other means by which someone could have got into the room." He waved towards the window, through which, faintly, could be heard the sounds of cheering and a faint off-key music. "Look outside, for instance, and you'll see men and women performing feats of agility and strength that most of us would consider impractical if not impossible. Walking on a rope suspended between two buildings, jumping up to impossible lengths, walking on stilts."

Athos's eyes widened. "Are you trying to tell me, Porthos, that you believe an acrobat, who cannot possibly even have met the Duchess de Dreux wished her dead? Or that she was killed by a stilt-walking villain who traipsed around the gardens of the palace on his walking stilts, in his gypsy motley?"

Porthos shrugged. "I'm not suggesting either, Athos, only that you are ignoring other possibilities like that."

"Someone could have come in through the ceiling," d'Artagnan said. "Or have you looked into that?"

"No," Porthos said. And frowned in turn. "But the ceiling is not the most common means of entry into a room, and I'm sure if there were something unusual there Hermengarde or one of her friends would have told me."

D'Artagnan shrugged. "It might be under a bed, or a chest, and it might have been forgotten. After all, in my own room, there is a place on the floor where the floorboard lifts and, with care, I can get a good view and listen to the people below."

Athos looked shocked. "You spy on the people below you? Surely even in Gascony they know this is dishonorable."

I' faith, if Aramis didn't come back soon, either Porthos or d'Artagnan would murder Athos, Porthos thought.

But d'Artagnan answered patiently enough. "No. I do not spy. But I tripped on the board by accident and it came loose and I realized I could see and hear my landlord with perfect ease. And I'm sure he doesn't even know it's there. Look, Athos." He waved his hands excitedly as he spoke. "Look, I can see what Porthos is saying. If there were such an opening in the room above, concealed by a chest or a bed, or even a chair, and we found it and determined, by scuff marks or signs of recent use that this is how the murderer got in and out, we'd have a perfect clue of how the murder was committed. Because only someone who knew the palace in and out would know of that particular quirk. Do you understand?"

"I suppose I do," Athos said, rubbing his forehead, as Porthos had observed him to do when he was nervous or worried. "But it seems like a foolish endeavor."

"No more than what we've been doing," d'Artagnan said. "Trying to find out motives for someone to want to kill the Duchess de Dreux. To some extent her husband was the logical suspect and it made sense to at least eliminate him first. But you seem convinced that he's not the one."

Athos looked very tired, and somehow aged, all of a sudden. "If he is, he's a better actor than the devil, himself," he said. "And it is a talent I never suspected in him."

"So we'll assume that is not it. And other than him, what obvious suspects do we have? Half the court? If she was conspiring with the Queen and the enemies of France, we need to count upon that number, the King and possibly the Cardinal too. And if she'd given away some of the Queen's secrets, then the Queen too would fit that number. Surely you see the problem."

Athos looked tired but nodded. "I suppose I do," he said. He looked at Porthos and sighed. "And I apologize for losing my temper with you, Porthos. I know your problems with explaining your often brilliant ideas. But, Porthos, you must understand that this too seems like a dead end. However, I suppose we'll go back to the palace and look at the room and the room above it, if we may."

Porthos nodded. "That," he said, "is one of the things we should do."

"I don't suppose it would be possible," d'Artagnan asked, "for someone to throw a knife through that hole in the wall?"

"It wouldn't be impossible," Porthos said. "But it would necessitate moving the picture aside to throw the knife. I don't know how it would look from the room or how visible the picture is from the bed." He frowned. "You are right, I suppose we'll have to go back to the palace." Then he sighed, thinking of his last visit there. "Only you must promise me I don't need to go near the kitchen."

And because he'd told his friends all about the cook, this brought an amused grin to d'Artagnan's face and an empathetic nod from Athos.

"I can promise you," Athos said. "We shall not inflict the cook on you."

A Letter from the Cardinal; Choices and Conflicts; The Inadvisability of Leaving the Mouse Near the Cat

Aramis waited till he was in his room to read the letter. It was short and written in his eminence's characteristic, decisive handwriting, in black ink which gave the impression that he had slashed angrily at the paper with the pen.

"Dear Chevalier D'Herblay," the letter began primly. "When living as a musketeer under an assumed identity, it is, you should know, a good idea to refrain from sending one's lover letters headed by our true crest."

Which the Cardinal would know having been acquainted with Aramis's father. For that matter, Aramis thought that considering his resemblance to his sire, doubtlessly the Cardinal had long had some inkling of who the young man was but had not spoken because he could not without calling attention to his own illegal duel. "It took some trouble to find you, though, amid all the minor noblemen in France," the letter continued with withering disdain. "Now that I trust I have accomplished it, I must give you my orders and they are these: I have proof you killed your lover. Your uniform and sword left behind in her room are proof enough, as is the certainty—my having examined all the other possibilities. That no one else could have come into the room. As such, I must therefore lay orders—and yes I mean orders, for one can always give orders to a murderer. My orders are simple—do not come back to Paris. Gratify your desire to take orders, or else find a likely provincial lass and marry her and devote yourself to your crops and your fields, your tenants and your servants. Do not come into Paris though, for if you do, I shall find it necessary to have you taken into the Bastille where, under the usual persuasion, you'll doubtless tell us all we might want to know about how you committed the crime and why."

Aramis read the letter twice through and then twirled the paper about in his hands, unsure about what it all meant and even more unsure about what to do. As a strange missive, it was exemplary of its kind.

The Cardinal said that he knew that Aramis had committed the murder. But if that were true, if he were indeed sure of that fact, why would he not want Aramis to return to Paris? Surely the Cardinal didn't have any tender feelings that prevented his clapping Aramis in irons or sending him to the gallows. No. There must be more here. What it was, Aramis couldn't begin to guess.

He turned the letter over and over in his hand. Take orders or marry some likely provincial lass.

Everything in him rebelled at the thought. The Musketeer in him, that Aramis who, for the last five years, through scuffle and duel, through conspiracy and peril, had fought the Cardinal at every turn and opposed him at every chance, now wanted to go back to Paris. Go back to Paris as soon as possible. Go back to Paris and find out what the Cardinal was up to and why he didn't want Aramis to return.

There were other reasons. His mother had consented to give Aramis back his mirrors upon his agreeing to talk to the Dominican, but now that the Dominican was gone, this privilege would probably also be retracted. And Aramis's hair remained too intractable for him to give up on brushes and mirrors. Besides, there was always the possibility his mother would take him on a never ending round of pilgrimages to expunge his supposed sin and to make it more likely he'd choose to go into the church.

A light sound from the window—laughter and a woman's voice—called Aramis. But the pilgrimages and the visits to saints and their holy relics, would be unlikely to start while Leda lived with them.

Aramis crept close to the window and looked down. Somehow, somewhere, a kind soul had found Leda a gown cut in the French fashion. It was a frothy thing, all intense pink and lace, and low cut like the gowns that Violette used to wear. In this attire, it could be seen that Leda had, in fact, an abundance of female charms. Oh, not disproportionate to her light and pleasing figure, but abundant enough when pushed up by her tight-waisted gown, and displayed by the low cut of silk and velvet.

Aramis's hands gripped the parapet, as he looked down on the girl, who appeared to be running and dancing amid the trees in the garden for no other reason than to enjoy her own running and playing. With two of her older, ponderous companions following, she sang out in Spanish accented French, "How freeing this gown is," and laughed.

The two gorgons, still attired in Spanish style and in black, to boot, followed close. They had, Aramis supposed, instructions from his mother. But Aramis had spent most of his adolescence at home out-witting his mother on just this kind of instructions. His mother should know, he thought, that there were ways to get around the tightest of vigilances. After all, when he was only fourteen Aramis had introduced one of his mother's companions to the lives of the saints with such thoroughness that the much older girl had been married off in some haste to an elderly and probably confused nobleman.

He looked at Leda and licked his lips. He would go out the side door, the servant's entrance, and cut around behind the cover of trees to that dense place over there, where Leda danced closer and closer. With a little luck, he could give her a note without the two chaperons even knowing he was near.

With care, he wrote in a small piece of paper, "Dear Madame, if you wish for some diversion before your inevitable marriage, be kind enough to tell your companions that you wish to pray in solitude and then retire yourself to the small chapel on the left side of the house between the hours of four and five o'clock, when the local chaplain is busy with my mother at her devotions." He signed it RH and it never occurred to him it wouldn't be accepted or that Leda would prove incorruptible.

Any woman who delighted so in a low cut gown longed for corruption. And Aramis, with his bright green eyes, his more than pleasing features, his muscular body and his noble bearing, had always been found enticing by the ladies—long before he'd fallen to Violette's charms. Leda would prove no exception.

He smiled lightly, a smile only a little tinged by thoughts of Violette. The lady his mother should know it was not wise to put the cheese next to the mouse, nor the mouse near the cat.

Floors and Ceilings; A Secret Panel and a Masked Stranger

"**I am** sure that there is no way to get into this room through the room above," Hermengarde said. She had procured them the key to the room from the Cardinal's staff— at great peril, she said while looking at Mousqueton with the expression of one who expects a reward for her troubles.

They'd come in, in a group, and ambled around the tight, confined space.

To d'Artagnan it seemed like luxury beyond all possible dreaming. Each of these furnishings was better than the best furniture that Madame d'Artagnan could command in her spacious house in Gascony. In fact, d'Artagnan was sure that there were more furnishings in this one room than there were in all of his mother's house.

Massive wardrobes stood next to vast arm chairs, which in turn stood next to tables, and trunks and more arcane cabinets like something that Athos, casually, identified as an incense cabinet and a largish trunk that Athos had said looked like a jewelry box. In fact, opening it, d'Artagnan found that it was filled with bracelets and rings, with beaded necklaces and necklaces made of pearls, the valuable tossed in with the puerile, all of it without rhyme or reason, as though the owner had tossed things in at random and without caring how they fell.

He was tempted, for a moment, to say that someone must have rummaged through the trunk. But he didn't. After all, Athos glanced over at the open jewelry box and made no comment. Which meant that, probably, this was how high-born ladies kept their jewelry.

By all piling on the side of the door and looking over towards the portrait hanging over the heavy wardrobe, they agreed it was just possible to throw a knife from there onto the bed, and that it wasn't likely—and certainly not probable—that the Duchess de Dreux would have noticed the portrait moving.

Particularly not if she was looking towards the little room next to her bedroom where the chaise percée was kept, and anticipating Aramis's return.

"And are you sure?" Athos asked again of the pleasing-faced blonde that Porthos had introduced as the maid Hermengarde, Mousqueton's good friend. "There is no way through the ceiling?"

The girl curtseyed, as she seemed to do whenever Athos spoke to her at all. "I am sure, Monsieur. I attend on the Countess upstairs, and she has nothing on the floor in the middle of her room, which compasses all of this room. I can see clearly that there are no breaks, no cuts in the floorboards. Not even well disguised ones. As to that, I can respond that it's impossible to come to this room from the room above. And look you, above," she pointed at the ceiling. "See you a joining, any place where the ceiling would open?"

Athos looked up, and reluctantly had to admit that the ceiling was smooth plaster, virgin and innocent even of scratches much less of any point at which it could open or cut, or in otherwise allow anyone to come through.

"And besides," Hermengarde said. "The Countess was in her room at the time, playing cards with friends, all of a certain age and all as respectable and religious as possible. In fact, she was one of the first to give the alarm when she heard the murd—The musketeer's scream. So, you see, it is impossible."

"Can we go to the passage then?" he asked, gesturing with his head towards the portrait over the wardrobe. "So we can see from there how easy it is to move the portrait aside?"

Hermengarde curtseyed, seemingly automatically, but she looked at all of them with a half-amused expression. "It will be a tough fit, getting all of you in there," she said. "I will open the passage for you, and you may go in, and I'll stand guard to make sure his eminence doesn't come near. He's been like a hornet whose nest has been disturbed, about this whole affair."

She fished for the key, which she had hung on a loop inside the waistband of her skirt, and then she led them out of the room and locked the door. To d'Artagnan it was all like being led down the palace corridors and secret passages by Aramis and his lover, less than a month ago.

Hermengarde opened a mirror in the wall, after touching certain points in the gilded frame. D"Artagnan wondered if there were any mirrors in this palace that were perfectly normal and didn't open. Somehow he doubted it.

Past the mirror was a narrow passage and Porthos led the way into it with the look of a man who leads his friends on a path he knows well. Athos went second and d'Artagnan was third.

This meant that, being the shortest, he couldn't really see more than a brief glimpse of the little shutter in the wall, as Porthos slid it aside.

"Impossible," Athos hissed, as he prodded with his fingers. "You can see, Porthos, the portrait is fixed in place and there is no way to move it." The back is a wooden panel and it is either nailed or glued in place."

"I bet you I could move it nonetheless," Porthos said in what he seemed to think was a whisper, but which was actually a suppressed boom, like a cannon firing under water.

"Porthos," Athos whispered back. "You could move most things. That doesn't prove that it is not fixed in place or that anyone else could move it."

Porthos inclined his head, and seemed about to answer, but never uttered. And from Athos's lips, something like a gasp emerged.

D'Artagnan, at the back, saw that each of his friends was looking through one of the eyes of the portrait the shutter allowed access to.

He might be the shortest. He might be the youngest. He might, in point of fact, know nothing about Paris and the court and its intrigues. And he certainly lacked the culture of Athos, the strength of Porthos or Aramis's ability to understand what other people might be planning.

However, he was a Gascon. And this was a breed not known for letting itself be kept quiet, or silent, or pushed to the back of what was happening.

And so, with more force than strength, d'Artagnan pushed his shoulder forward, and stood on tiptoes, managing to squeeze his shoulder and upper body past Athos and, with Athos, look over Porthos's shoulder and into one of the eyes of the painting.

Through this incomplete, narrow opening, he could see the room, bathed in the sunset light. And he could see the balcony door shaking, then opening inward.

Next to him, he felt more than saw as Porthos crossed himself.

A Musketeer's Scruples; Between Girdle and Garter; A Decision Made

Truth be told, Aramis began to feel regret before he put his hand within the warm, tight confines of Mademoiselle Leda's girdle.

Oh, it was not that she was not all that was pleasing, or that she didn't look very pleased in him. In fact, her reaction to his extending her the note was all that he could hope. Her eyes had widened and her dark red lips had opened in a smile.

And she'd played it like a woman used to these intrigues, so it wasn't as if Aramis could feel guilty of despoiling an innocent. When receiving his note, she'd done no more than slide it into her décolletage and flit away, as if nothing special had happened.

But he'd waited no more than a few breaths in the cool, dim chapel before she entered, demure looking, wearing a small hat from which a veil hung that hid her face. Such his state of mind from the few days he'd been here, and subjected to his mother's vigilance and chastising that for a moment, on seeing the veil, Aramis was reminded of the story of Leah and Rachel and wondered who his mother had sent in, instead of the fair Leda.

But almost immediately, the temptress pulled the veil back to reveal her fine-featured olive-skinned face, with its mobile mouth, its large dark eyes. Her hair was modestly bound at the back, but he could still see it peeking, arranged in delicate ringlets, beneath the hat.

On seeing him, she rushed the four steps that separated them, crossing the chapel in the movement, because the chapel was almost no length at all, being a narrow space with three chairs and five kneelers and designed for the private devotions of Madame D'Herblay and the Chevalier's family.

The family church proper, on the other side of the house, was much larger, more ornate, and contained pews at which the servants and the more important farmers of the domain would sit at Mass.

This small chapel contained only—over the altar—a painting of a nursing Madonna, at which Aramis could not glance without blushing because it had been painted in the image of his mother when she was very young. It figured Madame D'Herblay as the virgin Mary, arrayed in much richer attire than ever the poor Galilean could have mustered—rich cloth of gold veil, and ornate brocade dress, from which a pert, white, round breast showed, offered to the mouth of the babe. The fact that Aramis knew the babe to be himself and not the holy infant did not in fact make things any better. He'd been pictured at six months or so of age, a plump, handsome little boy, attired in a frilly satin dress and reaching longingly towards the maternal breast.

He knew breasts well enough to know the one portrayed in that painting had never nursed. In fact, not only couldn't he imagine his mother doing something as uncouth as nursing her own child, as he had quite fond memories of his peasant nurse with her large breasts, her smell of milk and warmth. She had nursed him until he was three and a half and quite capable of speaking, so it was not extraordinary he should remember it.

All the same, knowing he'd never sucked his mother's breast didn't make the picture any easier, and looking up at it, as he crossed himself hastily, Aramis wondered if he should have found another place for the rendezvous.

But as Leda rushed towards him, she glanced at the figure over the altar, and smiled, a sweet smile, and coming closer, she asked him, "The woman is clearly the lady your mother—is the infant yourself as a babe?"

He swallowed and nodded and felt his cheeks color.

"Oh, he's so sweet," she said, and, standing on tiptoes, she planted a kiss on Aramis's cheek. "And you've grown up to look just as sweet, if a lot more manly."

She spoke perfect French with just the slightest trace of a Spanish accent and, as she stood on tiptoe to kiss him, he caught a fragrance of roses from her, as if she had bathed in macerated flower petals. It reminded him very strongly of Violette, and of Violette's smell, and for just a second, he hesitated.

But then Leda threw her arms around his neck and, standing on tip-toe, covered his lips with hers, and pushed her tongue, boldly, between his lips.

Her passion inflamed him. His hands reached to encircle her, then, as though of their own accord, up towards her hair, which he loosed down her back.

His fingers entwined in her hair, so soft, so silky as to seem a substance that had been sent down from heaven. Like wisps of dream. Like bits of cloud. Her mouth tasted sweet and, faintly, of strawberries.

As she pulled away, at last, to draw a deep breath, she said, "Oh, when I saw you at the entrance, I think I fell in love with you at first sight. I wanted so badly that you would be my intended husband, instead of some dry, old count whom I've never met and with whom my father wishes to curry favor." She kissed him again, and pushed herself against him.

Aramis was only human. She felt warm and delightful in his arms. It had been too long and he had endured great trials. And she was bold and capable—much too capable if truth be told. She pushed him down onto one of the chairs and sat on his lap, and toyed with his blond hair.

"You look so severe," she said. "In your dark clothes. And your mother says you have a vocation for the church."

Aramis said nothing. He allowed her to press herself against him and to caress him. It seemed to him he had been cold for a long, long time, and her warmth against his flesh was a welcome comfort.

And then he found his hand beneath her skirt and searching around for the girdle which cinched her undergarments.

Her thigh, between girdle and the beginning of her stocking proper, was warm and soft. He moved his fingers upon it, feeling skin like velvet.

Violette had felt so. And Violette had smelled like this. Of a sudden, it was all too much for him. He put his head on her shoulder and moaned, a soft moan of loss and regret, as his hand retracted, to rest upon his own thigh.

"What is wrong?" Leda asked, alarmed. "What is wrong?"

Aramis realized he was shaking. The overwhelming grief of losing Violette hit him suddenly and without reprieve. He thought of Violette's soft skin, her luscious body. And he thought of other things . . . The way she played with him, the way she teased him. Her words, her letters where she pretended to be a mere seamstress. The way she understood him. The way their souls resounded together like goblets cut from the same crystal. He didn't even know why or in what way.

Before her there had been many, and perhaps there would be more after her, but not yet, not . . .

He realized he was crying on Leda's shoulder, his tears soaking the velvet of her dress. She pulled him to her, called by some ancient maternal instinct, resting his face upon her softly rising and falling bosom.

This reminded him even more of his Violette, and it brought out his tears yet more abundantly, till he was sobbing openly, like a child.

"You poor man," Leda said. "You cry for fear of sinning, do you?" And, with gentle hand, she pulled back the hair that had got stuck to his moist face. "Don't be," she said. "You could marry me. I could break my engagement to the horrid old Count, and you could marry me. Then you could do as you please to me, and not feel guilty."

Slowly, slowly, Aramis brought himself under control.

"Mademoiselle," Aramis said. "If you must know . . ." He swallowed hard. "I had a lover. As close a lover as one can have without actually being married. I was with her for years, forsaking all others. And she got murdered, just a few days ago, while—"

"While you were in her room," Leda said. "I know. I thought you might feel guilty over that, and that's why I say you could marry me."

Aramis stared into the dark, dark eyes and wondered if the girl was telling him she was sure he had killed his previous lover and then could marry her.

"How do you know about my mistress?" he asked.

"Your servant told your mother who told me, by way of warning me." She smiled reassuringly at him. "I don't know why your mother wished to warn me. The lady was not a lowly woman or a peasant," Leda said. "Clearly your tastes are to the highest nobility. And if she had the misfortune of being already married when you met her, I do not have that misfortune. I find that your being so in love with Ysabella de Navarro de Dreux that you feel guilty about having an affair without marrying her is quite romantic. One of the tenderest things I've ever heard."

Aramis shook his head. How could he explain tender to her? And how could he explain love? He didn't think any less of her because she didn't understand the depths of his feeling. He, himself, wouldn't have understood anyone's feelings on the matter. Hadn't understood anyone's feelings on the matter. He'd comprehended marriage only within the bounds of arranged unions. That someone could marry for love, marry by their own free will, contrive to live with one person his entire life was alien to him, and strange.

Leda's words poured into his ears, inconsequential and meaningless, like the pleasing babble of a brook, "You know, they were from our area of the country and they had only two girls—those two. To preserve the dowry of this one, her twin was consigned to a convent before the age of ten. They say she's very holy and has visions. Strange, isn't it? Perhaps she expiated the guilt of her sister, and perhaps Ysabella is in a better place." Leda patted Aramis on the shoulder. "Yes, I'm sure that must have happened. So, you see, Chevalier, there's really nothing to fear of guilt or sin, because Ysabella's holy twin, the nun, will have expiated sins for both of them. And doubtless, even now, your lost lover is in heaven praying for you. And as for you, you don't need to commit any more sin. You can marry me, as I'm yet maid, and then you can do as you please." She smiled wide at him. "Your estate is not nearly as grand as that of the tiresome Count I was to marry, but you know, you are younger and more pleasing to the sight, and I don't mind. I'm sure I can learn to be pleased with your small estate."

Leda poured into his ears assurances that he could marry her and that once they'd engaged in conjugal bliss all would be well. He wished he could believe her. He wished life were that simple. In his heart, in his mind, he now realized he'd never forget Violette. When she'd died she'd taken a piece of him to the tomb.

And he, wretch that he was, had accepted his friends' offer of investigating for him. He, wretch that he was, had come all this way, had hid behind his mother's skirts, had spent all this time thinking he could forget her. Had thought, even, that he could replace her. Or at least forget her beloved touch in the touch of another. But life would not permit it.

Slowly, he edged himself out from beneath Leda till at last he moved her to the chair, and he stood beside her.

She blinked her lovely eyes at him, in confusion. "Chevalier?" she asked.

"I'm sorry, mademoiselle," he said. "I am so sorry."

"But..." She blinked. "You have done nothing wrong. You have done nothing to me."

"No," he said. And because, in looking at her, he felt guilty for bringing her all the way out here and then crying on her. In his long and abundant experience with women Aramis could safely say this was the first time he had cried on a woman's shoulder.

He left Leda sitting in the shadows of the chapel, and went in search of Bazin.

Bazin was in the garden, sitting by the fountain, looking as though he were in deepest contemplation or perhaps in prayer.

"Bazin," he said. "I am not fooling. Get me my luggage and the horses. We're going back to Paris."

Bazin looked at him, and his mouth dropped open. "Chevalier."

"Do. Not. Call. Me. That. Again. Go and get the luggage. We're going to Paris. Now."

Bazin looked miserable. He blinked at Aramis, but he didn't—as Aramis half expected—say anything about Madame D'Herblay or her expected wrath. Instead, he got up and left.

"Meet me at the stable," Aramis said to his retreating back.

And though he half expected Bazin to come back with Aramis's mother or some other way to restrain Aramis. But Bazin came back alone, carrying Aramis's bag. A glance inside showed that both his brushes and the mirror were in there.

Bazin's strange acquiescence puzzled him, but he didn't dare ask anything, lest his words broke it. It wasn't until they stopped at tavern for some food that Aramis asked Bazin, "You've decided to throw your fate along with mine?"

Bazin sighed, pushing is plate away. "Your mother... She said you'd never be a satisfactory monk and that she would find you someone to marry." He looked up at Aramis. "Do you still intend to take orders?"

"Of course," Aramis said. "In due time."

A Masked Ghost; Dead Woman's Jewelry; The Immovable Porthos

Porthos held his breath as the balcony door of the dead woman's room shook. It shook. It shuddered. The glass rattled in the frame.

Visible through the small square panes was someone— or rather the shadow of someone. But even size and shape were a guess, at this distance and looking through a narrow hole in the wall.

But the door shuddered open and was pushed inward with force. A small hand. That was Porthos first impression of the intruder. A small hand attached to a small arm in a black sleeve.

"Someone is breaking in," d'Artagnan whispered.

Porthos said nothing. First, he was well aware that his voice boomed when he meant it to hiss. Second, the fact seemed well established and hardly warranted words.

Then the intruder stepped into the room, and looked around—as though he suspected someone of watching him. As though he knew about them in their hideaway.

The intruder was—Porthos thought—a boy, barely out of childhood. Small, slim and slight, he dressed in black— stockings, breeches, tunic and hat.

The shapeless hat looked like something a farmer's boy might wear, or a fisherman's son. It was a round thing, of some undefined black material looking spotty and faded in places.

But the strangest thing was the face, which was covered in a hard, glittering white mask which looked like the shape of a face made out of porcelain and with holes cut out for the eyes and mouth.

Porthos felt his heart beat faster, and—as though in response to it, the person's head turned, fully, to look in their direction. Or so it seemed. But even as Porthos felt d'Artagnan shuffle a little backwards, as though afraid his eye would be discerned, the figure crossed the room, quickly.

There was something about the movement of the creature in the room that made Porthos uncomfortable and worried. It was as though the . . . person weren't quite human. It moved like a cat, or as people did sometimes in dreams, when they floated past the dreamer, as if in another reality.

Now it floated this way, then that, tiptoeing around the room and, silently, opening trunks. Porthos expected it to turn at any moment and hold a finger to its lips as though to impress an invisible audience with the need for secrecy.

But it didn't. It just went on, opening trunks and boxes, then closing them again rapidly, till it came to the ornate jewelry box, which it opened.

It rummaged wildly through the jewelry throwing it here and there, like a cat or a small child. Porthos felt as though he were watching an act of madness or perhaps truly dreaming. Were it not for the presence of his friends, equally silent, equally immersed in what was happening, if it weren't clear that they too were watching the figure, he would think he was dreaming it all.

And then, the figure made a sound, for the first time. It was an exclamation of surprise and delight. A skinny, black clad arm plunged into the jewelry trunk, and out of it emerged, holding a gold chain from which depended a simple cross with no ornament.

The arm, with the hand, moving while the rest of the body remained immobile, lifted the cross up by its chain. It shone in the light from the open door to the balcony, throwing sparkles of gold everywhere.

With exaggerated motions, still, as if on the stage, the figure kissed the cross. And then . . .

Porthos blinked. Before his amazed eyes, the dark-clad apparition took a caper, a bow, back flipped towards the door and then out the door to—

Porthos realized that the person, whoever it was—and if it was indeed made of flesh—was about to jump from the balcony, just as Aramis had done.

Porthos's body was always one step ahead of his mind. In fact, Aramis, in his more sarcastic moments, would say it was Porthos's mind. Now his body, whose quick reflexes served him so well in duel and dance floor realized he should intercept the creature, man or phantom, who'd been in the room. Porthos leapt towards the door of the passage, half shoving d'Artagnan ahead of him.

D'Artagnan, not prepared for the sudden move, perhaps because he could not see into the room as well as Porthos could, fell headlong under Porthos push. Or rather, seemed to twirl upon one leg, then fall crosswise in the passageway.

Porthos could not stop in time and tripped on the boy, falling with his legs half entangled in d'Artagnan's. His body, not fully understanding what had happened, kicked and squirmed by reflex, trying to push out, trying to get to the door, trying to intercept the phantom.

And he realized he had caught Athos a smart kick to the knee that caused the older musketeer to roar and fall, in turn, upon them, in an entanglement of swords and limbs, of shoving, impatient feet and rushing, impatient minds.

"Porthos," Athos said, in his most polite voice. "If you should only stop kicking me, I believe I'll have a chance to help you up, and then d'Artagnan should be able to get up also."

A polite voice in Athos—or that polite a voice in Athos, was always dangerous after one had just tried to break the older musketeer's kneecap.

Porthos was hurried and hassled. He could see in his mind's eye the figure all in black standing poised at the edge of the balcony. He could imagine it escaping, out of their range forever.

It wasn't only that they couldn't catch it, but that it, having made its way up here, should have a form of making its way down. And that even if this were not the murderer, it could give them an idea of how the murderer had got in.

However Porthos's self-preservation instinct knew that one did not trifle with Athos in this mood. By a supreme effort of will, Porthos managed to stand still, while Athos disentangled himself and stood.

Athos waved a hand in front of Porthos eyes. "Here, Porthos, take my hand. I believe I can help you stand up."

Porthos obeyed, taking Athos's hand. Despite his being almost twice the other man's bulk, and all of it lean muscle, it did not surprise him that Athos could pull him upright with little effort. After all, he'd had other occasions to meet with Athos's wiry strength and besides the older musketeer had that type of will power that often made up for physical prowess.

Upright, holding onto the wall, Porthos felt relieved to see d'Artagnan get up. "You did not twist a leg?" he asked the young man, who had fallen in a most unnatural position.

But d'Artagnan only shook his head. "No. It's no worse than what I did to myself every day when practicing sword fights with my father in the fields behind our house."

"I'm very glad not to have caused you injury," Porthos said.

But Athos nudged him on the shoulder. "If the two of you gentlemen could manage to make it down the passage without tripping over your own feet or each other's feet, we might yet see how the creature got into the room."

"We never will make it in time," d'Artagnan said. "I know that we'll never catch him."

"It wasn't a him," Athos said, laconically behind Porthos. "It was a her."

"Indeed," d'Artagnan asked, as he started walking down the passage towards the door hidden by the mirror. Porthos followed as close as he could without risking tripping over the young man. "I would have sworn it was a young man."

"No," Athos said. "It did not move as a young man. The . . . Steps were wrong."

"Perhaps it was a ghost," Porthos said. Here, in this passage, walking in the half darkness, it seemed wholly possible. "Perhaps it was the ghost of the young woman who died here coming back to reclaim her lost faith. Did you notice that it was a cross she retrieved from the trunk cluttered with much more expensive baubles?"

"Porthos," Athos said, as they came to the mirror door and d'Artagnan opened it slowly, looking out. "Just because Aramis isn't here, there is no reason at all for you to start thinking like him. It was not a ghost. That is the worst of metaphysical nonsense."

Just then the door opened fully. They rushed out. Hermengarde, in the hallway, looked at them, her eyes widening slightly, probably at their disheveled condition.

"There was a ghost in the room," Porthos said. It was the first thing that came to his mind and he flinched as he said it, even as Athos turned around to glare at him.

"There was an intruder in the room," Athos said.

Now Hermengarde looked at all of them as though they had taken leave of their senses. "There can't be an intruder in the room," she said. "I was here. I can see the door," she pointed down the hallway. "No one came or went."

"She came through the balcony door," Athos said.

Hermengarde's blond eyebrows shot up towards her hairline, as she stared at Athos. If Porthos had made such a statement, he thought, the girl would have laughed at him.

But this was Athos, and it was Athos with his head thrown back, his lips tightly compressed and a look of utter disdain on his face.

Hermengarde tilted her head sideways. "It's impossible," she said.

Athos only stared.

Hermengarde reached under her waistband for the loop of keys. From it, she pulled the key to the room. One step into the room was enough to confirm for Porthos that they hadn't been dreaming. The room was deserted, but the door to the balcony stood wide open and the jewelry box too was open, with handfuls of jewels strewn about.

D'Artagnan ran to the balcony. "Nothing," came his voice. "Not a ladder, not . . . Nothing."

Athos cast a look at the jewelry trunk, managing to convey the impression that it had personally offended him, then he stalked out to the balcony, himself.

Their voices came to Porthos, slightly distant but completely understandable.

"A rope ladder," Athos said. "Whoever it was could easily have used a rope ladder."

"Easily?" d'Artagnan asked. "But how? It couldn't have been thrown with hooks up here. What are the chances it would reach? And then, after the person left, who would loosen the ladder and remove it? No one could have entered this room while we were gone."

It wasn't strictly true, Porthos thought. Hermengarde could have. He looked at the little blond maid, though, and failed to believe she had. Or that she was, even now, hiding a rope ladder somewhere about her person.

"It was a ghost," Porthos said. His voice echoed strange even to himself. And he normally didn't really believe in ghosts and spirits, or to be honest, anything he couldn't touch, feel and bite. "It must have been a ghost."

Athos came back into the room. "Porthos, don't speak nonsense. Why would a ghost wear a mask? Why would a ghost wear male attire? And why would a ghost come in from the balcony, and open the door rather than just walk through it?" He looked down. "Besides, look here. Footprints."

As he spoke, Athos pointed down, at a row of footprints from the balcony door. They'd been made in reddish dirt, and they faded progressively more till they ended a few steps from the jewelry trunk. "Only a corporeal entity could leave these," Athos said.

Porthos felt better. He didn't really want to believe in ghosts, anyway.

"Perhaps the dirt can tell us something," Athos said. "Perhaps it will tell us where she came from."

Porthos sighed. This was another of those instances of his friends getting lost in their own thoughts. "Athos," he said. "The entire garden has that same fine reddish dust. It won't tell us anything but that she stepped in the dirt of the garden, beneath the balcony, before she came here."

Athos straightened up, from where he'd knelt, examining the foot prints, and looked up at Porthos and sighed. "Perhaps," he said. "But if so, how did she get up here? She can't have flown."

The Prodigal Musketeer, Revisited; The Sins of Musketeers; Nowhere to Hide

Aramis made it to Paris as night was falling. He hurried, with the natural impatience of one who'd been too long away from his home, and who feels as though everything must have changed in his absence.

He dismounted as he came to the city, and told Bazin to take the horses back to the rental stable from which they'd acquired them.

"And then?" Bazin asked. "What am I to do?"

Aramis had given the matter some thought, just as he had given thought to the attire he was wearing. He'd changed in the inn, last night, into one of the suits his mother had wished on him—black linen and wool mixture. Scratchy against the skin and, truly, a garment of mortification.

Oh, Aramis was well aware that not everyone could wear silk and that many, many people went through their lives wearing wool, even in summer. He was duly grateful that he didn't often have to submit himself to such penance. But the truth was that in this undistinguished suit, the equally black hat pulled low over his eyes, no one would know him. To ensure this, he'd taken the care of tying his hair firmly and tucking all of it under his hat. Even people who didn't know Aramis called him "the blond musketeer." His curtain of golden blond hair would make it impossible for him to hide.

This way—at least from what he remembered, having surveyed himself in the full length mirror the night before— he looked like a servant or a common apprentice. At least in nighttime and with the hat pulled down to hide his features.

Because of the disguise, he could not wear his sword, which was in the luggage he surrendered to Bazin. He could, however, and did wear his dagger, concealed under the hem of the longer than normal tunic.

In this attire, he gave Bazin the rein of his horse, and leaned close. "Go to the monastery on the Rue des Jardins. Do not tell them where I am, only that you need asylum for this time, while your master is unjustly pursued for a murder he didn't commit."

"What if they don't believe me?" Bazin said. "About your not committing the murder?"

Something to Bazin's beady eyes gave Aramis the impression that Bazin, himself, was none too sure Aramis hadn't committed the murder. Aramis wouldn't argue the point with him. In fact, he did not wish to argue anything with Bazin. Instead, he shrugged. "Ask for brother Jerome. No one will question you further. If they ask anything, you tell them you don't know, which is near enough."

"And you," Bazin asked, staring up at Aramis. "What about you?"

Aramis waved a hand, airily. "I know . . . people. I'll go and find lodging, and I'll clear my name, and then I will come for you."

"When?" Bazin asked.

"As soon as possible," Aramis said, and, with that, let Bazin go away.

Watching his servant's retreating back, he realized that while it was true that he knew . . . people—in fact, his three friends had the disquieting habit of grinning every time they found themselves in a tight situation and Aramis uttered the words "I know a man"—he didn't, in this particular situation, know anyone who could avail him.

Oh, he knew monks and crafters, merchants and apprentices. But anyone he went to now was likely to already have heard rumors about the murdered Duchess and the blond musketeer's guilt. And if his own servant didn't believe him . . .

No. There was no chance of his finding asylum with his casual friends, or even with those for whom he'd done favors, and who owed him favors in return. They would be likely to turn him in, if they thought him guilty of murder. They would not wish themselves tarred with the murderer's guilt. No.

His own lodgings were out of the question. Looking at his servant's back, now a rapidly retreating point in the Paris throng, Aramis scratched his forehead and, just in time remembered not to dislodge his hat.

After all, though most people in Paris didn't know him, all it would take was one who did and who would see him and denounce him. He couldn't go to his friends' lodgings either. Someone would be watching those.

His best hope was to go to Monsieur de Treville. Go in through the back at the headquarters of the musketeers— enter through the stables.

Oh, they might be watched too. In fact, they almost certainly were watched and not just for Aramis's sake, but around the clock, by the Cardinal, who liked to be aware of what Monsieur de Treville was likely to do, and how he was likely to play the game of one-upmanship that constituted politics and vying for royal favor between the two men. Beyond that, Aramis, who was no fool, would wager that there were spies in both men's organizations. There would be guards in the Cardinal's pay who reported to Monsieur de Treville. And though he shuddered to think it, there might very well be musketeers who ate the Cardinal's bread. In fact, Aramis, if pressed, could name two or three that would easily and gladly do that.

But the Treville house was such a bee hive of coming and going musketeers, servants, petitioners, old friends, family of musketeers and whoever else could claim any connection at all with Monsieur de Treville that one more servant coming in at the back, without fanfare, likely wouldn't be noticed. And Monsieur de Treville could help Aramis hide—could find him a more permanent hiding place. As well as, possibly, point him to ways of rehabilitating himself.

Even then Aramis was careful. He walked to Treville house via a criss-crossing network of streets, where he wasn't likely to be recognized, and if he were recognized his objective wouldn't be guessed.

He looked behind him, often, and around him too, to make sure no one was following him—that no face remained constant among the crowd near him.

And then, near Treville house, he waited, at the rear, by the great, always-open iron gates, through which servants and horses came and went. He waited till a large, noisy group of servants headed for them, talking and laughing and, clearly, returning from some tavern dinner or some gathering.

Aramis slipped in at the back of the group, not so close that they would think he was trying to mingle with them, but close enough that anyone watching the group would think he just straggled a little behind.

And then . . . Well, and then he needed to find a way to see when Monsieur de Treville's office was deserted. Or rather, when Monsieur de Treville was alone.

The great man was alone sometimes for quite a few minutes together, while he signed some order, or read some paper. Every day a few of these happened, though more commonly his door was wide open and so called private interviews were conducted within the hearing and attention of the whole crowd in his antechamber.

And Aramis could not afford to have his interview seen or heard. All his care, his avoidance of being recognized all the way here, all that would be wasted if he now allowed himself to be recognized talking to the captain.

So . . . he couldn't go in through the normal route.

It was well known—at least it was well known to musketeers—that the captain never closed his window. Certainly not unless the wind were blowing snow onto his desk. Through that window, on the first day he'd arrived in Paris, d'Artagnan said he had glimpsed Rochefort. Which had caused him to run the other way, out through the antechamber, colliding with Athos and courting a duel with the one of the three musketeers he had not yet offended.

But the captain's window did not face the street—or not directly. It was on the second floor of the house—a staircase, at which the musketeers often played a dangerous game of king of the mountain involving swords, led the way up to it from the first entrance room. And up there, it overlooked a wall. It was only by looking at a certain angle, above that wall that encircled the property, that it was possible to see the street.

In normal times, and before his harrowing escape from Violette's room, it would never have occurred to Aramis to try to climb into the captain's room through the window. But these were not normal times, and his normal risk, of being challenged or embarrassed by the Cardinal's guards, had now become a risk of being legally condemned for a crime he'd not committed.

He edged around the property, till he was directly below Monsieur de Treville's window. From there he studied his way to it. Fortunately for him, it was not nearly as impossible as his descent from Violette's room. Around the captain's property, a tall wall ran, and up against that wall, an additional protection of trees grew. Tall, sturdy trees. The branches of one of which extended almost to touching the window.

In his childhood in Herblay, Aramis had often—to escape his mother's attention as much as for fun—climbed trees or made his way through the orchard from one tree to the other.

His present size and body were not as small or flexible as the ones he'd possessed in childhood. But he was still flexible enough. It wasn't as though he'd never needed to climb anything either in his time as a musketeer or in his more personal adventures between coming to Paris and meeting Violette.

He found the boots he'd adopted as part of his disguise sturdy enough to allow him a toe hold on the bark of the tree and thin enough that he could feel the irregularities in the tree trunk as he climbed. He shimmied up the trunk to a likely branch, then, lying flat, edged along it, till he could almost touch the window.

He was lucky in that as the office came into view, he saw the captain say goodbye to a musketeer—one of the newer arrivals in town whose name Aramis wasn't yet sure of—and then sit down again to write something.

Monsieur de Treville's servant opened the door from the antechamber and said something, from which Aramis caught the words: petitioner, request and now.

Monsieur de Treville shook his head. His more resounding voice carried louder and more clearly as he said, "No, Batiste, no. Give me a few minutes leave. There is something I must write. I shall tell you when I'm ready for another audience."

With that the servant was dismissed, and Aramis spied his opportunity.

Actually getting into the office was the difficult part, since the branch thinned, where it almost touched the window, making it if not impossible very difficult for Aramis to support himself on it.

So Aramis chose the reckless route, which he would have disdained just a week ago. He stood totteringly on the thickest portion of the branch from which he still had a hope of reaching the window. And then he launched himself, head first through the opening, managing, just in time, to get hold of the window frame as he swung himself in, so that he landed feet first, behind the captain, rather than hitting his superior with his head.

At the sound of feet falling behind him, Monsieur de Treville got up and spun around. Proving that there was a reason he was the captain of musketeers and not the abbot of a religious house, he pulled out his sword, even as he stood, and faced Aramis with sword in hand.

"What is the meaning of this?" he asked. "Who are you?"

"I am unarmed," Aramis said, as loudly as he dared, without calling attention from the antechamber. "I am unarmed. " And to emphasize how inoffensive and peaceful he was, he lifted both arms, showing his open hands to Monsieur de Treville.

When the captain made no movement to actually attack, Aramis dared take his hand to his head and, with a sweeping gesture, remove the hat that hid his face and hair. His hair tumbled down his back, and he lifted his head to face the captain.

"Aramis," Monsieur de Treville said, but did not let go of his sword. "Aramis."

"Monsieur," Aramis said and bowed slightly, not sure how to read his captain's expression. Monsieur de Treville looked both guarded and pale. "Monsieur. I am back in Paris."

Monsieur de Treville backed to his desk. Without turning, he spun his chair around with a foot, and he fell to sitting. His sword remained in his hand. "Why?" he asked.

Aramis gulped for air. There were many things he could say. One of them, and entirely truthful was that his mother could scare the bravest of men and tempt the calmest of saints to a fury. Another, and just as important consideration was that Aramis had found himself, amid the fields and the silence, thinking more of Violette than he could in the confusion and crowd of the city. And his mourning for Violette seemed to have just begun and to make him into a very different—and much weaker—man.

But neither of these reasons were of the sort he could, gladly, confess to his captain. And so, instead, Aramis bowed and said, "I could not allow my honor to be besmirched. I could not allow my friends to have the charge of clearing it, while I sat, unmolested, so far from them."

Monsieur de Treville stared at Aramis. He stared at Aramis so long that Aramis started to feel uncomfortable. He stared at Aramis so long that it seemed to Aramis as though the captain could have memorized his features, or else seen in them the shape of some great and future portent.

"By the Mass, D'Herblay," Monsieur de Treville said, using Aramis's true name. A rare occurrence. "Are you insane? Have you taken leave of your senses?" He stood up and sheathed his sword, but stood a few steps from Aramis. And his hand rested upon the sword hilt. "Why would you come back? We sent you out of town, your friends and I, who have your best interests at heart. We sent you out of town and asked you that you remain there. You always say you want to be a priest or a monk—well, you could have taken holy orders in any of a hundred monasteries between here and your native domains. Why didn't you?"

Aramis blinked. "Monsieur de Treville, I never thought this would cause a permanent interruption in my service." This was not the reception he expected, and receiving it shocked him to the core, and made him shake. "I never intended to leave forever. Only till my innocence was proven, and then—"

"Innocence!" Monsieur de Treville said, making the word echo of blasphemy and lie. "Innocence." His stare at Aramis became more suspicious and he frowned hard at the young man. "Did you come back because you were afraid that your guilt would be discovered and even your friends would turn against you? Did you come back because there was some evidence you must destroy?"

Aramis felt blood leave his face. He bowed, more to keep himself from saying anything he would regret, and to keep his expression from being seen, than to show respect. When he looked up again, he felt he had his expression under control, except for a nervous tic he could feel pulling at the corner of his mouth in rhythm with the pounding of blood through the veins at his temples.

His voice sounded slightly strangled, as he said, "Monsieur de Treville, it is neither fair nor honorable to insult an unarmed man and one, besides, who has sworn to defend you with his life and who, therefore, is barred from challenging you to a duel."

Monsieur de Treville smirked, which was not—Aramis thought—a reasonable response to his words. He shook his head, and, bringing his hands up, clapped them together, slowly, in mock applause. "I must compliment you, Chevalier, on a performance worthy of the stage."

"Monsieur," Aramis said, feeling his blood vessels constrict. "Monsieur, there are things I cannot tolerate. Not of you, not of the King himself, not of the devil, if the devil should be so bold. Either tell me why you are so sure of my guilt or lend me a sword that I can defend my honor right now and right here."

Monsieur de Treville said nothing. He stepped towards the desk, pulled up a letter, and handed it to the musketeer, who received it without comment. And then felt his vision dim and his knees buckle, as he recognized his Violette's handwriting. A faint scent rose from the paper, and if he squinted he could almost imagine her standing beside him.

"Rene," the letter started. "I am writing to let you know the most alarming news. For two months now I have found myself lacking that course of blood which all women got from the sin of Eve. Yesterday I consulted a woman who is experienced in these things, and she has confirmed that I am expecting a child." Aramis blinked. The paper was Violette's, and the handwriting hers, but the words seemed strange, alien. They were shaped as though Violette had been writing very slowly, immersed in thought. The pen bit more deeply into the paper than usual. Had Violette truly penned this, or was it a clever forgery. And if she had penned this . . . He swallowed hard.

"Hiding my state is not that difficult," the letter continued. "There are gowns aplenty and frills of which I can make use to pretend I'm as svelte as ever, even as the time draws near. Disposing of the child is also not difficult. There are many ways ranging from anonymously leaving him or her on the doorstep of a holy house to delivering him or her to some place a little better where they will be cared for on a stipend we provide. However, considering your future intent of joining the church—an intent that even this will, I know, not damage—and that you are the last of your line, I thought you might want to make arrangements for his upbringing yourself. Particularly if it is indeed a boy. Then, in the fullness of time, the child can be called upon to inherit and no one the wiser." The letter finished with, "Yours and only yours," and the complex crisscrossing of lines that represented Violette's many, crisscrossing names, and which was Violette's official signature.

Aramis looked at the letter and swallowed. Looking up, he found Monsieur de Treville looking at him, attentively, examining Aramis for . . . signs of surprise? Signs of guilt?

Aramis shook his head. There were tears in his eyes, and he felt them fly, as he shook his head. "I never saw this," he said. Then, "How odd that she would write to me, like this, when she saw me that very afternoon. How did you . . . How did you come by the letter?"

"De Bonne," Monsieur de Treville said, gesturing with his head towards the door. "The musketeer who was leaving before you made your entrance. He stole this letter from his eminence's desk. He thought I should see it."

"Any chance the Cardinal forged it?" Aramis asked.

"Not a one," Monsieur de Treville said. "But it was this letter that absolutely sealed his belief in your culpability." He took the letter from Aramis's unresisting fingers and slapped the open sheet with the tips of the fingers of his other hand. "You must admit, Aramis, it is a damning letter."

"I never saw it." Aramis felt cold and distant. Had anyone told him, this morning, that his spirits could fall lower or that he could feel worse than he already did over Violette's death, he would have dismissed them for fools. But . . . But now he felt as if a piece of his heart had been torn, bleeding, from his chest, and was now being burnt before his very eyes. "I never saw it."

Violette had been pregnant. There had been a child growing within her, a babe with Aramis's blood, Aramis's inheritance. There had perhaps been a boy, who would have had Violette's features, Aramis's blond hair. A child he could—easily enough—have commended to his mother's good care, never telling her who the mother was. A child who would have grown up climbing trees in the orchard of D'Herblay house, as his father had.

Oh, he could imagine why Violette hadn't told him. She'd probably feared his reaction. Feared he'd say he had no interest in the child—women in such situations could be fools. He turned the letter and saw the date was the day before Violette's last. The Cardinal had intercepted the letter. Sequestered it. Doubtless that last afternoon together Violette had been dismayed when Aramis made no mention of it.

Monsieur de Treville must have seen Aramis grow paler. For the first time in their interview, he reached over, and got hold of Aramis's arm. He guided him to Monsieur de Treville's own chair.

"Do you swear," he asked, "on your hope of salvation that you didn't kill the woman?"

Aramis nodded, but his sight had gone unaccountably dim and he felt as if his legs would never support him. Leaning forward, he put his head in his hands. He felt as though he were wounded, mortally wounded.

He'd sustained wounds, in combat and duel, and bled from them, without ever feeling as he did now, as if his heart were open and pouring out blood.

"Dents Dieu," Monsieur de Treville whispered. He stepped across the room and, for a moment, Aramis thought the captain was going to open the door to the antechamber and call on his valet and tell him to call the guard, because from Aramis's reaction he could easily tell the musketeer was guilty.

But instead, he heard the clinking of glass on glass, and then the captain was standing by him, touching him on the shoulder.

Aramis looked up to see a glass held before his eyes. He took it, had time to smell the harsh edge of alcohol, and then opened his mouth and drank it all in a single gulp. It was brandy and tasted like liquid fire.

Setting the glass on the captain's desk, Aramis wiped his mouth on the back of his hand, and looked up at Monsieur de Treville, who was looking down at him, with a mix of horror and pity.

"D'Herblay," Monsieur de Treville said. And then, tilting his head, as though he'd reached an internal point of decision. "Aramis. What am I going to do with you? Do you have any idea what the devil of a danger you've put both of us in? And your friends too?"

Where Locked Doors Aren't Always Impassible; Secret Passages and the Jealousy of Kings

Athos and d'Artagnan walked away from the palace alone. Porthos, who seemed to have some sort of a bee in his bonnet, had parted from them, mumbling something about street performers. What that might be, Athos didn't know nor did he care to inquire.

After all, Porthos now seemed prepared to act as both Aramis and Porthos. And though Athos missed Aramis and thought their group was not the same without the young theologian and philosopher, he was not yet prepared for nonsense about ghosts and repentance to come flying out of the lips of his sensible, down-to-earth friend.

A while out of the palace, walking towards Paris, d'Artagnan said. "Perhaps Porthos craved a rematch with the cook?"

Athos allowed himself a slight smile. "I' faith, he didn't sound interested when he told us the story. But Porthos's taste in women has always been unfathomable to me."

As he said it, he remembered that his own taste in women could be said to be less than exemplary. And on the heels of that, Raoul's words, his teasing on the subjects of what he called Athos's drama, flew through Athos's mind, and Athos sighed.

By the corner of his eye, he saw d'Artagnan give him a sharp, evaluating look, and half dreaded what the young man would say.

They were halfway between the palace and the city, in that portion where noblemen had built well-spaced houses, to bask near the glow of royalty. There was no one on the street, in these early evening hours, not even a servant. And Athos stared at d'Artagnan. He shook his head. "Do you know where the girl got the key?"

"Porthos said she told Mousqueton that she got it from one of his eminence's maids, by special arrangement, and that it will have to be returned to him by nighttime. Now, I'd suppose."

Athos swallowed. "His eminence. Why would he have the key?"

"Because he took it after the door was broken down," d'Artagnan said.

"I've wondered . . ." Athos said. "Why did he want the room sealed with Aramis's uniform in it? He seems to have altogether a too active interest in this case. And if he wanted a door opened, somehow, wouldn't the Cardinal be able to have it open? But he can't be the killer. Surely you see that, d'Artagnan. As with the body of the murdered woman we found before, if he wanted the Duchess de Dreux killed or taken out of the way, he could have paid any of a thousand minions to do it. He wouldn't need . . ."

D'Artagnan took a deep breath. "No," he said. "And you are right. He would have no need of it. But think, Athos. You are not thinking. Beyond the death of the Duchess, what else happened?"

Athos stared at d'Artagnan. "Raoul is free, but I really can't believe—"

"No, Athos, no. Please. Think of the other person most affected by the news."

"Aramis."

"Exactly. And if he wanted Aramis killed, taken out of the way, how easy was that?"

Athos shook his head. A smile crossed his lips despite himself. "He would need to go through us. He would need to go through Monsieur de Treville. He might have had to set himself against the King himself, if Monsieur de Treville got to him first. His only other hope was to kill Aramis in an arranged duel, in a dark alley, by an assassin with a dagger."

"And it's not as if he's not tried that, dozens of times already," d'Artagnan said. "Only, it's never worked."

"While by making it seem as if Aramis was guilty of murder, he managed to get Aramis out of Paris easily enough," Athos said.

"Not only that," d'Artagnan said. "But you see . . . by having it look as if he'd killed his lover, he had Aramis leave Paris in disgrace. That means, as you saw by our interview with Monsieur de Treville, that even Monsieur de Treville, who would normally defend our friend, now thinks that our friend is guilty."

"But why would he want to get rid of Aramis?" Athos asked.

D'Artagnan shrugged. "I'm sure there is a reason," d'Artagnan said. "If only we look for it."

Athos nodded. They walked for a while in silence.

"But if it is his eminence," Athos said, at last. "If he's guilty, how do we prove it? For we must prove it, else we're but the small wave breaking against the shore."

D'Artagnan nodded, frowning. "That dagger. The dagger Aramis handed you . . . I presume the dagger that killed the Duchess. Do you still have it, Athos?"

Athos nodded. "Yes," he said, and could not believe he had forgotten it so long. He had put it in his sheath, alongside his sword and then, afraid to leave it in his lodgings, he'd transferred it to its own sheath, one he often added to his sword belt, to carry a dagger.

"Is there anything unusual about it?"

Athos shrugged. He'd taken the dagger from Aramis in the dark of night, and then later he'd transferred it to the sheath without thinking anything but that it belonged to Aramis and was Aramis's business. And then, all these days, he'd removed his belt at night and put it back on in the morning, without giving the dagger in its sheath any thought. "I assumed it was Aramis's. Though I didn't know it, unless it was his I could not imagine why he'd brought it with him," he said, but as he spoke, he drew the weapon from his belt. He had a dim memory that the first glimpse of it had startled him, that it didn't look like something that Aramis had ever owned.

Now he lifted it into the light of the moon. And d'Artagnan whistled softly.

"Seems like someone took a lot of trouble over that handle."

Athos focused on the handle, and blushed. He'd never remembered to clean it, so there was still blood in the crevices, highlighting the carving on the pale ivory. And the carving was . . . A couple, entwined in lovemaking. Man and woman were amazingly detailed and well done for such small figures. Her breasts were visible, and the tiny, pointed nipples. At least the right nipple, the other one being hid by his back. And his buttocks and waist, and each individual leg. Even their faces, united in a kiss were visible, and Athos would swear he could almost recognize them.

He turned the object in his hand.

"Does it belong to Aramis?" d'Artagnan asked.

"I don't know. I mean . . . I couldn't swear to it, but I would doubt it." Athos frowned down at the knife. "If it did, I think I would have seen it before. Each of us brought very few objects . . . very few comforts that are worth anything from our former lives. And those, the others have seen, at our homes, or on our person, or else, at campaign or in duel. I've never seen this."

"Would you have remembered it?" d'Artagnan asked.

Athos permitted himself a smile. "My dear friend. While I may look ancient to you, I'm not quite at the age where I'll lose my memory and go tottering into the dark of not remembering something like this."

D'Artagnan blushed, his olive skin showing a dark red flush on his high-cheek-boned face. "I didn't mean that," he said. "I never thought you'd . . . At any rate you're younger than my father, who would beat me black and blue if I told him he was getting too old to remember things." He looked away, clearly embarrassed. "It's just that . . . Could Aramis have won it at a game, or have been given it as a gift? Recently?"

"Only if it was the day of the murder," Athos said. "Because if it were given to him as a gift, Aramis would have shown it to us. Or if he had won it at a game. Something like this, he wouldn't have resisted showing off, particularly—" He stopped himself, afraid he was going to say something indelicate and sound as if he were making fun of his friend.

"Particularly?" d'Artagnan asked.

Athos sighed. There was nothing for it. "Look, I'm not saying that Aramis is envious or that . . ." He gave up explaining. "It's just that as long as I've known them, Porthos and Aramis have envied the sword I brought with me from my domain."

"The one you keep on your wall, beneath the portrait," d'Artagnan said.

"The very same. It was my great great great grandfather's sword, and every heir in my house has inherited it. Mind you, I no longer use it in duel or combat. It needs certain material repairs which, at this moment, I lack the money to achieve. And without them, there is too great a chance it will break on clashing it, ruining it and possibly costing me my life besides. But . . ."

"But?" d'Artagnan prompted.

The boy was relentless. Athos smiled, thinking that Raoul would doubtlessly tell him this was good, that d'Artagnan drew Athos out of his long, self-imposed silences. "But both Aramis and Porthos envy it. Porthos for the way it looks and Aramis, I think—though I wouldn't want you to tell him I said so—because it is an inheritance come to me from my male ancestors, which signifies I'm the adult man in my family, the heir."

"I have gathered," d'Artagnan said. "Though not through anything he said, that Aramis too is the heir, and I think the only son."

Athos sighed. "Yes, but . . . I . . . Aramis has a mother. At least I've heard references to his mother a few times."

D'Artagnan nodded, as though he understood, though Athos very much doubted he did. Judging from d'Artagnan's personality d'Artagnan was very much the only son and heir. And though he had once jokingly commented that all of his father's domain would fit in the little cemetery des Innocents in Paris, yet however much he stood to inherit, his position as heir would never have been disputed.

And though Aramis never spoke of his home life—not to Athos—Athos had caught references over the years, mostly in what Porthos said. Porthos was Aramis's oldest friend and, for all the two men's differences, the one in whom Aramis confided unstintingly. Athos gathered that Porthos thought that Aramis would be much happier if he were an orphan. And for all his plainspoken, down-to-earth approach to life, Porthos could be a shrewd observer of such things.

"At any rate," Athos hurried on. "And for whatever reason, he admires my sword. He wouldn't resist showing me a piece such as this. It would, you know, in his mind, somehow, even the score. Show me that he too had a piece worthy of being coveted. And it would make Porthos green with envy."

D'Artagnan didn't dispute this. He had got in a duel with Porthos—that very first day in Paris—by showing that the inside of Porthos's cloak was not quite so magnificent as the exterior. And that had been enough to excite Porthos's murderous ire. Impossible, after that not to know that Porthos liked showing off and expensive things.

Athos turned the dagger again in his hand. It was well balanced, exquisitely so for something whose carving meant it had been intended for a bauble, more than for serious grappling. In fact, Athos thought, taking it in his hand, though he often liked fighting—at least in battle— with a sword in one hand and a dagger in the other, he couldn't imagine grasping this dagger for very long. Though it was finely polished, after a while the crevices and curves of the two lovers would indent themselves upon the palm. He frowned at it.

"Is there any way of finding to whom it belongs?" d'Artagnan asked. "Or belonged?"

Athos shrugged. "Perhaps," he said. "Perhaps. Depends on how old it is, and through the blood it is impossible to tell how pale the ivory, and whether the slight tinge on it is aging or blood." He looked at d'Artagnan and caught a look of total incomprehension and cursed himself for a snobbish fool who assumed that everyone had been raised in the same circumstances he'd been. "Ivory yellows as it ages. If this was carved much longer ago than my father's time, then it will be visibly yellow." He returned the dagger to its sheath with some care. "But if it was made in this generation, then someone will likely know who made it. There is a distinctive style to these pieces and usually only a few people in the world at any time can carve this finely. This was an expensive piece. If I take it down to the jewelers' streets and ask around, someone will tell me where it came from, which will be a step to telling me who owned it last."

He paused in his long speech and thought it over. "Of course, they might also have bought it and sold it recently, even if it is old. A lot of old families at court buy and sell their finest belongings as the occasion offers or the need arises. Sometimes I think the jewels of most noble families spend more time at the jewelers than in the family home."

"Not an armorers?" d'Artagnan asked. "A jeweler?"

"I think so," Athos said. "No serious armorer, nor anyone who intends this as a combat weapon would carve the handle in such a way. Judging from the theme of the carving, and the way it's executed, I'd guess it to have been an engagement gift," he said. "From some great lady to her betrothed."

While speaking, they had reached Paris proper and were now in the thickly populated streets, bumping elbows with groups of jovial men out for a night of drinking, and with laughing couples on their way who knew from or to where.

Night had become darker, or at least, the light of the occasional lantern suspended over a tavern doorway seemed to be brighter than the light of the moon above.

"Jewelers' street is just down here," Athos said, taking his bearings, even as he covered the dagger with the end of his cloak, to obscure it from potential thieves. "Shall we go there now?"

"I can't," d'Artagnan said. "I'm due at Monsieur des Essarts's, to stand guard from eight till midnight."

Athos felt he'd been remiss. This last month, they'd all been standing guard in a group, either at the royal palace, at the Treville house or at Monsieur des Essarts. There had been much joking that by acquiring a young guard, Monsieur des Essarts had also availed himself of the three best swords in the musketeers corps.

"I'm sorry," Athos said. "I had quite forgotten the schedule. This last week seems like a dream. Do you wish me to come and stand guard with you?"

D'Artagnan shook his head. "I feel it's important we discover the murderer as soon as possible, particularly if . . . Particularly if it's . . ." He cast a look around and didn't pronounce the recognizable name.

Which was just as well since Athos often believed that the Cardinal had spies everywhere. Even, he thought, the ravens and the doves spied for his eminence. "If it's someone important," he said, before d'Artagnan should recover his courage and actually pronounce the name aloud.

D'Artagnan nodded.

"Yes," Athos said. "I too feel it would be for the best if our friend's name was cleared as soon as possible. And if whatever the plot is to get him out of Paris and out of circulation were foiled."

D'Artagnan turned. "I wish you luck," he said. He bowed slightly and parted company with Athos, who went his way into the jewelers' street.

Footprints and Somersaults; Ghosts and Words; Monsieur Porthos's Very Deep Doubts

Porthos parted with his friends just outside the palace. He had taken care not to leave by the kitchen area, and he'd left Mousqueton deep in conversation with Hermengarde.

He rather doubted he would see the scoundrel tonight, and that was as well. Because Porthos was thinking.

It still seemed to him that his friends were approaching this in a completely wrong way. How the two of them could still maintain that it was impossible for anyone to come in through the balcony when they'd seen someone come in through the balcony baffled Porthos. He classed it under the stupidity of very smart people, with a few other examples he'd seen from his friends such as Athos's strange tendency to drink heavily and then gamble while drunk, as if wine made him more qualified to spot the marked card and the weighted dice.

He walked around the garden, fully absorbed in these thoughts, to stand under the balcony that gave onto the dead Duchess's room. Well, truth be told, he could not— anymore than his friends could—see how anyone could get in through the balcony. He looked up and up and up, at the little stone parapet, then turned around to look at the nearby tree. The tips of the branches there still showed the signs of Aramis's disastrous fall among them. But there were no fresh leaves on the ground. And no fresh leaves meant that no one had climbed up into—or out of—the tree recently.

Not that climbing up the window from the tree would be possible. At least, as Porthos measured the two or three body lengths of his body between the tree and the stone parapet, he couldn't imagine anyone even leaping that distance.

But of course, they might have left that way. They might. Except that here were no leaves.

He then looked at the ground and set about tracing the path of the footprints that were about the same size as the ones he'd seen upstairs in the bedroom.

Easier said than done, as the foot size had looked average for a woman or a young man. About the size of Porthos's extended palm, from tip to wrist. And a lot of women and young men lived in the palace or worked there, to judge from the maze of crisscrossing footprints upon the reddish dirt. To make it worse, there were areas of grass and areas in which the dirt was quite packed.

However, Porthos reasoned, to make the footprints that the intruder had made upon the bedroom floor, he or she (he was not yet convinced of Athos's determination of gender—after all, how much did Athos look at women?) would have needed to step on very loose red dirt.

The only place Porthos could find dirt loose enough was upon the flowerbed in which the tree was planted.

Experimentally, he put his foot in it, then on a grassy area nearby and the traces of dirt looked the same. In fact, he if looked at the tree bark closely, he could see, here and there, bits of the same dirt.

Someone had climbed the tree. But that made no sense. If there were signs that the person had come down via the tree, as Aramis had, that would at least make a little bit of sense. But no. You'd leave red dirt on the bark going up, not coming down.

Porthos stepped away from the tree and looked from it to the balcony and back again. Impossible. Also, insane.

Oh, he would readily admit that the tree went as high as the balcony, but at the very top, it was a mere wisp, a thin trunk, like that of a year-ling tree. And, yes, Porthos readily admitted that the masked person in the room had been smaller and lighter than him. Probably smaller and lighter than d'Artagnan, whom Porthos was fairly sure of being able to lift with one hand and without straining—despite the young man's muscular build.

But let's suppose the woman—or man, or the devil himself—was as light and lithe as a human could possibly be. Let's suppose that he or she had climbed all the way up to the top of the tree, and, from the top of the tree, eyed the distant balcony.

Could he or she have made it there? Porthos would be cursed if he could figure out how, barring growing wings.

And on this, it seemed to him, the whole thing hinged. Who could have got into the room, not who had a motive to kill Violette, or even who had a motive to kill Violette while Aramis was in her room.

Achieving the heights of that room was such an impossible, miracu-lous task that Porthos could not imagine its being simply an incidental step in murdering someone. No. He was sure of it. Whoever knew a method to scale those heights was the person who'd killed Violette.

Something else bothered him about the phantom who'd pranced into the room. The mask. If you were nobody, and nobody in the palace knew you, why would you care if someone saw you there? Why would you mind if you were recognized?

He was sure that if he solved those two puzzles—who might have gained access to the balcony, and why whoever had done it wore a mask, he would have the solution to the whole thing.

But right now it seemed a hopeless endeavor.

Meanwhile, it was getting dark. He felt his meager coin pouch. He couldn't wait for Mousqueton, nor send Mousqueton to get him food as he normally would. And he really couldn't hope that Mousqueton would steal something for him. For one, because he was afraid the cook would avenge herself on Mousqueton for her disappointment in Porthos.

He would, he thought, go to a nearby tavern and see if he could get some bread and cheese, and think over the whole puzzle of how a human being could grow wings.

In his mind, he could hear Aramis say that wings were the reward for a life well lived, for an attainment of sanctity.

Somehow, he didn't think the person who'd come into the room, for all his or her devotion to the little cross, was a saint. Or an angel.

Messengers and Queries; The Elusiveness of Musketeers; Where Aramis Gets Tired of Waiting

"Monsieur," Aramis said. "I never meant to cause you difficulties, or—"

Monsieur de Treville waved it all away and sighed. "Oh, it means nothing," he said. "I'm sure you didn't mean it, just as I know you did it. You musketeers are all the same. Sometimes I feel I would have fewer foolish actions and intemperate, unconsidered plots to contend with had the King put me in charge of the royal nursery at the palace."

Aramis said nothing. He said nothing because he couldn't feel offended by such a claim, which was one of Monsieur de Treville's favorite claims, an expression of his exasperation at his headstrong subordinates.

Monsieur de Treville drummed his fingers upon his desk. "The devil of it," he said, "is that I believe you're innocent."

Aramis nodded, slightly. He was still in shock over having found out how close he'd come to fatherhood. The whole thing was a nightmare. He'd thought he'd lost a lover, the other half of his soul. As it turned out, he might have lost much more than that.

He might have lost a chance at future generations of Herblays, at continuing his father's name. He might have lost a chance at uniting his blood with that of the highest families in Spain, even if his son would never have been able to claim the connection.

Had her husband known of the child? Could he have killed her for that?

Somehow Aramis doubted it. Violette spoke of her husband occasionally and from the sound of it what they possessed between them had all the warmth of a business arrangement. In the midst of the feasts for the King and Queen's marriage, they'd never even consummated their marriage.

Not that Violette had come to Aramis's bed a virgin. No. By the time she'd asked him to lay between her silk sheets that cold winter's night, Violette had already had several lovers, most of them more important personages than Aramis.

But she had loved him . . .

Lost again in his misery, he was looking at his boots and pondering the futility of life in general and the futility of his own life in particular.

Monsieur de Treville's closing the door between the office and the antechamber roused him. He looked up. The captain stood at the door, tapping the toe of his boot in an unconscious gesture of impatience. "None of your comrades are in the antechamber," he said. "Neither Porthos, nor Athos, nor even the young Gascon. I'd have sworn they, all three of them, live in the antechamber, hoping for an invitation to dinner or a duel, both of which they seem to consider essential for their lives, but now none is there."

Aramis made a gesture of dismissal, trying to remember the day of the week. Wrinkling his brow with the effort of thinking of anything but his sudden and cruel bereavement, he said, "I think d'Artagnan is standing guard at Monsieur des Essarts. And they're probably with him."

"I've thought of that," the captain said. "And I've sent three runners, one to each of their lodgings and one to my brother-in-law's palace. One or the other of them should be home, and I've asked that he come here right away."

Aramis didn't understand this at all. "Why?" he asked.

"Because one or the other of them should have some idea of where to hide you. I confess I don't. I could put you in one of several monasteries where I have acquaintances, but I think you're rather well known at all of them. You have, if you forgive me saying so, Aramis, a recognizable face. And everyone knows the story of the musketeer who quotes theology."

Aramis nodded. He supposed he'd made himself notorious. It was only one of his many sins. Woe to him who gives scandal.

He continued contemplating the sad state of his boots and the sorry state of his soul. He never quite felt as though he owed enough penance to go back to his mother's house and face the humorless Dominican again.

If he had to, at any rate, he'd profess here in town and with the Jesuits.

Of course, no order would take him. Not now, when half of Paris believed him guilty of murder, and the other half didn't only because they'd never heard of him or met him.

Monsieur de Treville brought him out of the reverie by closing his door to the antechamber again. The captain stood by the door, his hands open in a gesture of impotence in the face of the trials of life. "None of them are at their lodgings and the man sent to Monsieur des Essarts couldn't find the Gascon." Monsieur de Treville shrugged. "I truly don't know what to do with you, Aramis."

Aramis didn't quite know what to do with himself either. But he knew sitting in this chair, listening to the accustomed chatter from the antechamber was sheer torture. After all, the chatter was as distant from him just now, as barred to him, as if it had been the language of the angels or the musings of the gods. Aramis couldn't simply walk out there and meet his old comrades at arms and fall easily into the pattern of gossip and bragging, of friendship and rivalry that had been his life for these many years.

The corps of musketeers was not so different from a monastery, he thought. Both offered brotherhood. And he imagined that being defrocked hurt as much as having suspicion and doubt bar him from the musketeers.

He turned to Monsieur de Treville, "Let me go," he said. "I will find my own way."

As he spoke, he was gathering his own hair—the fine, soft mass of it, twisting and knotting it, till he could pile it at the top of his head and pull his black hat down over the whole.

"How are you going to leave?" Monsieur de Treville asked. "My plan was to get one of your friends here, or preferably all of them, and have you follow them, through the antechamber, play the part of one of their servants."

Which meant only that either it had been a very long time since Monsieur de Treville had engaged in any sort of covert intrigue, or that even their captain had no idea of how well the musketeers, as a body, knew each other.

They'd fought together, roomed together at the battle fronts, challenged each other on the stairs up to the antechamber, got drunk together and wenched together. There were very few men in the corps, and those new acquisitions only, that Aramis wouldn't know even with the degree of disguise he was wearing.

As for himself, as long as he'd been in the corps, as notorious as he was? A turn of the head, a step into that antechamber, and a dozen voices would call out "Aramis."

Which meant that Monsieur de Treville's plan had been useless all along.

"I will go out the same way I came," he told Monsieur de Treville.

And saying this, he perched on the parapet of the window and prepared to jump. The tree was a little ways away, but nothing like what it had been jumping from Violette's window. And what was more, he could—if he got to the tree—run along it right to the wall. Some of the branches seemed to overhang the wall or close enough. That meant he could leave here, and not go around to one of the entrances that were doubtless watched.

If he took minimal precautions, to jump when the street was not busy, no one would notice.

And then . . . And then he would make his way to Porthos's house—the one that offered the best view of its front door, being situated on an ample, broad street.

He'd hide on the other side of the street, in some doorway. And contrive to intercept Porthos or Mousqueton, before they got to the door.

Hopefully before they fell within observation of whoever had been set up to observe the door.

It wasn't a wonderful plan, but it would have to do.

Aramis jumped towards the thin limb of the tree.

The Drawback of Good Jewelry Stores; The Horrible Suspicion; Attacked in the Night

Athos had been to most of the jewelry stores, or at least to most of those that were still open at night and which either had some ivory piece in the window or had been recommended to him as being knowledgeable in ivory.

Before starting on his quest, he'd taken the trouble to stop at a public water fountain and wash from the dagger any vestige of blood. No reason to excite the curiosity of the jewelers about the use to which the dagger had been put.

A connoisseur of blades, or at least a frequent user of them, Athos felt somewhat guilty washing the fine metal in cold water. But there was no oil nor polishing compound on hand. So water would have to do for now. And water was, doubtless, better than blood on the blade and the handle.

Naked of its red patina, the dagger handle looked almost white, with only that slight tinge that ivory always had to it. Athos, examining it under the flickering light of a lantern over the nearest shop, had thought that it was new ivory.

The owner of the very first shop he visited, one of the better shops, with an actual display of jewelry up front, and a guard beside it, had agreed. He'd also looked from the dagger to Athos's worn musketeer's uniform and frowned.

"How did you come by this?" he asked. "Won it at the die?"

Athos had thrown back his head and assumed his most haughty expression. He'd been using it long enough and in enough varied circumstances to know that when he looked that regal it intimidated even the most hardened of noblemen, much less a lowly shopkeeper, not matter how grand he thought himself.

"It is hardly any business of yours to interrogate a King's musketeer," he said.

The man visibly shrunk from the words and, probably—if Athos knew himself—from the glimmer of anger in the musketeer's eyes. It was well known all over Paris that offending a musketeer could very well get your ears cut. Or—if you were so unlucky and a lot of them were nearby and drunk enough to react with furor at whatever trivial insult one of them had suffered—you might get your shop and house burned down.

The jeweler looked towards his guard, but he was not so foolish as to imagine that this down-at-heels man could hold his own against a musketeer. He polished the dagger handle on his sleeve and passed it to Athos, handle first. "It's fine work," he said. "But we don't do anything like it, and know next to nothing about it. If you want to talk to someone about ivory work, you should go down the street, to my brother-in-law at the sign of the Lit Candle. He is the man to talk to about ivory."

And so Athos had gone, from shop to shop, and from jeweler to jeweler, until the last of the shops sent him to a place that wasn't even on jewelers' row, but on a side alley.

The shop was clearly not very prosperous. Indeed, on first approach, Athos thought they were quite closed and no more than the door of yet another home.

The alley on which it was located reeked strongly of urine and vomit both, since it made a convenient pass-through between two streets where taverns abounded. And the only light there was the light that came from the lanterns of those distant taverns.

He looked at the dingy door that looked as though it were in the terminal stages of wood rot. Set in a wall that was probably stone but seemed like caked dirt, it looked unappetizing in the extreme. If you concentrated mind and eye both, and got very close, it was possible to see that the door was open a crack and that a wavering light shone from within. The type of light cast by homemade candles burning the fat that had been saved from the pot.

Athos almost turned around and left. He'd not been brought up even near extreme poverty. In his father's domain, the peasants tended to look clean and well fed. And even if Athos was not too sure that they ate well, or how they were provided candles, he would wager that none of them lived in a place as dirty or dismal as this one.

But the man at the last shop had told him. "Oh, but if you want to know who might have done work such as this, you must go and interview Pierre Michou."

That man, a voluble creature with rapid-flowing words and rapid-moving hands, and a suit that was more flashy than good, had told Athos all about how the brother of Pierre Michou, Antoine Michou, had been the best worker in ivory this side of the Indies. How commissions had come for him even from the kings of France and Spain and even, it was rumored, from England and Germany and, once, from Venice.

Unfortunately for the Michou family, the promising Antoine had died, leaving the business and the family fortunes in the hands of his brother Pierre, who had some problems. And here, the voluble jeweler had made the motion of someone tipping a glass onto his mouth. Besides, Pierre had never been as talented as Antoine, and now ran a little shop that specialized only in the buying and selling of jewelry and not always from the most legitimate sources, if Monsieur Musketeer quite understood the jeweler's meaning?

Monsieur Musketeer understood. And now, recollecting the conversation, he sighed. What could he expect from a shop where the owner traded in stolen goods, buying and selling as the opportunity offered? Of course he would not have a sign over his shop, or a lantern. And of course the door would be mostly closed. And of course he would take great care not to appear prosperous. After all, in this neighborhood, chances are if you looked prosperous you wouldn't remain prosperous for long.

On the other hand, the last jeweler had sworn that Pierre would know any ivory that had crossed the shop, or his brother's hands, during his brother's life. And he might very well know other ivory, if it had crossed his shop, in more or less illegal ways.

And so, Athos was here, and knocking at the door.

"Yes?" a man's wavering voice spoke from within.

"I have a question to ask you, Monsieur," Athos said.

"Come inside," the voice said.

Athos pushed the door open. Inside, the room was small and dark. An older man—or at least one that looked loose lipped and shivery—sat behind a table. Around the table, in piles and half-open boxes, jewelry glittered. Stones and gold and silver shimmered from the shadows.

And behind the older man, two young men stood who reminded Athos of no one so much as of the son of Aramis's landlord. They were broad of shoulder and brutish of feature. And both showed the same gratifying widening of eye and respectful expression upon noticing Athos's uniform, his musketeer's hat.

"You have something for me?" the jeweler asked.

"I have something to ask you," Athos said.

The jeweler pursed his lips. He evaluated Athos with a long up and down glance and did not seem as intimidated as his children or employees—whichever they turned out to be. "We buy and sell," he said. "We do not answer questions."

He was either a fool, near blind—enough not to recognize the musketeer's uniform, in which case his expertise on the ivory would be useless—or a fearsome man. Or perhaps near enough to his death that he didn't care if a musketeer hastened it.

Athos sighed and fished in his coin pouch for a pistole. He brought the glittering coin out and laid it on the table in front of the jeweler. "Will this be enough to buy an answer?" he asked.

At the back of his mind he was thinking that he, himself, would need to moderate his drinking. He could see himself in ten years, as loose lipped and shaky of hand as this man. And what would he do then? He didn't even have a seedy jewelry trade, nor an expertise in not quite legal ivories to trade upon.

When you were a musketeer—or a nobleman—you were a warrior, a man of the sword. Lose that, lose the ability to do that, and you were near useless.

The jeweler looked at the coin, then up at Athos. "Ask," he said.

Athos pulled the dagger out from within its sheath and laid it on the table. "I came by this. Never mind how. What I want to know is to whom it belonged last."

The jeweler's eyes lit up, animated by a sudden interest and, seemingly, focusing for the first time since Athos had come in.

"Antoine," he said. "Antoine's work." He picked up the dagger with hands that were suddenly firm and inquisitive, and ran loving fingers along the handle. "Antoine's work."

"Your brother?" Athos asked.

The jeweler nodded. "Antoine made this ten years ago," he said. "I remember because he was ever so pleased with himself at how much detail he put in. And also, it was his little joke, you know. It was for a wedding present, so he thought—"

"A wedding present for whom?" Athos asked.

"Why . . ." The man blinked at Athos, as though Athos were the one who was addled by wine or age. "Why . . . for his majesty, the King."

Athos would never be able to remember how he'd got out of the shop, nor how he'd got the dagger back from the jeweler's caressing hands. But he must have done both, because he found himself outside in the alley, taking lungfuls of air as though he would drown and sheathing the dagger.

The King. How could it be the King's dagger. Well, it could be said that the King was not, after all, the most brilliant of men. Athos was clear eyed and intelligent enough to respect royalty and the function of the king without respecting the man who, at present, fulfilled the responsibilities.

Oh, he'd allow himself to be cut into ribbons for Louis XIII, if it was needed. Such his oath, such his duty as a nobleman. But he would do it knowing that the King, at the present time, was little more than a figurehead and a hope of descendants for his royal line.

The man who held the reins of power, the man who made plans and executed them, the man who was responsible for the course of France at the moment, was Armand Jean de Plessis Cardinal Richelieu.

Which meant that the King could very well have thought that the Duchess had conspired with the queen or . . . anything. And have killed the Duchess. Or arranged to have her killed. Athos couldn't actually imagine the King, middle-aged and thick of waist, vaulting onto the balcony from an impossibly low perch, killing the Duchess and jumping down again. He couldn't even imagine the King unlocking the door, rushing across the room, killing the Duchess and then disappearing, all before Aramis returned to the room. No.

Besides, wouldn't the Duchess have tried to get up from the bed, if she'd seen the King?

And besides, it would have left unexplained exactly what or who the person who'd come in, dressed all in black and wearing a mask could be.

This, of course, left the Cardinal even more culpable in Athos's mind. Not having control of his own purse, and often not managing to commandeer for his expenses more than he won at cards or was given as gifts by courtiers, the King often gave objects to his favorites. The objects could be jewelry, or anything at all he had laying about.

Athos himself, after some successful duels, or some conspicuous acts of battlefield bravery, had received from the royal hand a ring or a trinket that the king found lying about.

Was it not possible, then, that the King had given the dagger to the Cardinal? And was it not possible that the Cardinal had decided to use the dagger in this manner, giving it to his minion to kill the Duchess, because he knew it would be traced back to his majesty?

Athos's head was swimming, as if he'd been drinking, though, as of yet, today, he'd had no more than a glass with his meager lunch. He stood in the alley very still, then thought he had to talk to his friends. He had need of d'Artagnan's cunning and Porthos's down-to-earth thinking.

He took a step northward, towards the larger road, lined with taverns. He might have need of a glass of wine, too, he thought, but then thought of the jeweler with his shaky hands.

No. Not now. Not yet. He took a step and then another.

Two dark clad figures detached themselves from the shadows and approached him, swords unsheathed.

Athos barely had the time to pull his own sword before the two were on him, swords raised, fighting for all they were worth, with no regard for honor, nor care for any rules of combat.

Athos met them bravely. He was tired from his travel from Raoul's domain, and the day had been a busy one, but he was up to fighting two men—two guards of the Cardinal, by their moves—easily enough.

And then he heard the running steps behind him. He managed a look over his shoulder, hoping wildly that they were his friends.

The men running were dressed in dark clothes. But they moved with the cocky sureness of the guards of Richelieu.

Athos turned and prepared to sell his life dearly.

Blood and Wine; Guards and Thieves; The Prey Turns Hunter

Athos woke up. There was mud beneath him and a horrible smell all around. He raised himself on his elbows, confused.

The first thing he saw was his sword, his good, serviceable musketeer's sword. It lay broken by his hand. The second thing he saw were two pairs of boots, in improbable positions, one by his head and one near his feet.

The boots puzzled him, in the same measure that the broken sword dismayed and angered him. It wasn't until he'd pulled himself up to sitting on the squishy mud of the alley, that he realized that the boots were attached to feet, the feet attached to legs, and the legs belonged to men who, judging by their positions, were definitely, unavoidably dead. And judging from the quantities of dark blood glistening on their clothes, and on the mud of the alley, they'd been killed by the sword.

Since Athos couldn't possibly imagine that two of his assailants had turned on the other two, he had to assume he had killed them. It only surprised him a little. He had a vague memory of thrusting and parrying, always with the certainty that he would die here, he would die from this.

That he was awake at all was the big surprise. Why would they leave him? And how, unless they thought he was dead.

His head felt confused and right at the back it hurt like the blazes. He was lying close enough to the wall to have hit it hard when he fell. He put a hand up, tentatively. It was hard to tell, for all the mud in his hair and on his face, but he thought he felt the peculiar consistency of blood.

So, he'd fallen, struck his head, bled, and they'd assumed he was dead. This made a certain sense. The edicts against dueling were still in place. So, of course, once they thought Athos was dead, they had left him and their dead comrades, and run.

But why had they wanted to kill him? Why was he so important that the Cardinal, himself, had sent his guards to kill him? Had the Cardinal sent them? Or was there another power play at work, perhaps within the guards corps, itself?

Athos couldn't think, and he certainly wasn't going to think lying down, like this in the mud of the alley. Instead, he reached for the wall to help himself up and managed to pull himself upright.

He was dizzy, which fit in with having hit his head, and possibly with the loss of blood. A veteran duelist, he knew as well as anyone else that head wounds bled profusely. And yet, if the way he'd evaluated this alley before still held, if he knocked at any doors here and asked for help, at best they would knock him on the head again and steal his boots and clothes. At worst, they would kill him, then steal his boots and clothes. He was sure he was not steady enough to intimidate anyone, not even in his uniform.

He tried to stand away from the wall. Blazing pain surged through his right leg, as it folded up under him. He reached for the wall again, to steady himself.

Sangre Dieu. He was wounded. Holding himself against the wall with his right hand, he used his left to feel his right thigh. He found his breeches, soaked in blood down to the beginning of his stocking.

In the dim lighting of the alley—now coming only from a distant moon that hardly penetrated the narrow space flanked by tall walls—he couldn't see his own thigh to evaluate the extent of the damage. He knew there were veins in the thigh that, if cut, would have a man dead in no time at all. He didn't think his had been cut, or he would not have awakened. But where was the wound and what was the extent of the damage? What were the chances that he, on his own and wounded like this could make it to place where he might get succor?

With impatient fingers, Athos tore at his breeches, and the small clothes beneath, for once glad that his clothes were so threadbare as to rip with very little effort.

He prodded at the flesh beneath, till he found the hole, doubtless made by a rapier thrust with force. From the location, it would have got only muscle. Or rather, skin, and a very thin sliver of muscle.

It was bad enough. He leaned against the wall, fully. Just trying to find the extent of his wound had tired him. How could he make it anywhere?

The nearest home of a friend was d'Artagnan's, and it was a good ten blocks northward. As for any other place where he might get help, he supposed he could always stick his head into a tavern and scream "To me musketeers."

The problem was getting to a tavern. Even the length of the alley seemed too long with this injury and with nothing to support himself upon.

He was leaning against the wall, taking deep breaths, when a voice said, "You're alive," in a tone of great surprise.

Athos tried to wheel around, and put his hand to the scabbard in which he'd kept the dagger. He found it empty.

He also found a strong hand under his elbow, before he could fall upon his right leg again.

"Easy, Monsieur, easy," a voice with a strong Gascon accent said. Not d'Artagnan's voice. Athos turned, to look into the thin, intent face of Fasset. Shorter than Athos by more than a head, the man stood at Athos's right shoulder and held Athos's elbow. "I believe, Monsieur, it might be easier if you throw your arm over my shoulder, as one does when one has drunk a little too much? Then it might be possible to walk."

Athos was too tired and in too much pain to fight it. Why a guard of the Cardinal would be helping him to walk made no sense at all. Unless Fasset meant to walk him right into the Bastille. But then Athos remembered what Porthos and d'Artagnan had told him of Fasset's behavior in the battle for Aramis's lodgings. The man seemed to be a conscientious man, even if he worked for the devil himself. And, Athos might allow, as there were some devils who worked for Monsieur de Treville, there must be saints who worked for the Cardinal.

He looked at the man's face and saw no harm there. At any rate, what else could he do? He didn't know how much blood he had already lost, but if he lost much more—and he would if he tried to walk on his own—the thing would be decided without any fighting and, if the Cardinal had meant to eliminate Aramis, he'd eliminate Athos too, with it.

He put his arm over Fasset's bony, wiry shoulders.

"Come," the man said, taking a step with the care that demonstrated that, for all Monsieur de Treville, when he wished to revile his men, upheld the guards as models of restraint and clean living, they too had plenty of experience in helping drunken comrades to walk.

After ten such steps, northward, out of the alley, Athos said, "Where are we going, Monsieur? Should I be concerned?"

"We're going to my lodgings," Fasset said. "It's just on that street," he pointed ahead. "Above a tavern. The sign of The Maiden's Head, in fact. As for whether you should be concerned, no, Monsieur Athos, you shouldn't. I intend no more than to bind your wound, perhaps in a way that will allow you to walk again, at least a little, so you can get to your own lodgings? If not, I will procure you a horse."

Athos took a deep breath. "Won't your comrades be upset that you are undoing their work today? They took a great deal of trouble to leave me in the mud of that alley."

He could not see Fasset's face, not in the way they were walking. But he felt Fasset's shoulders tighten beneath his arm and he heard a long, drawn-out hissing of breath from the man. It occurred to Athos, a little belatedly, that in his condition the last thing he should be doing was goading or baiting a man who had some reason to resent him.

But when words came out of Fasset, they didn't seem to bear any trace of resentment against Athos. "They said they left you. In the alley. Dead." Another of those long, hissed out breaths that sounded to Athos—an expert in the art himself—as an attempt at fighting extreme anger. "I came to verify that you were beyond help."

"And do they expect you to finish their work, then?" Athos asked.

"They expect me to do nothing, Monsieur. I resigned my commission in the guards before I came for you. It was not the cowardly way they set upon you. You and I, doubtless, have taken part in ambushes. We are soldiers, all. I disapprove of cowardice, but I could understand it if there were a reason for it. However there isn't. They tried to kill you without orders and just because they heard some words."

"How long . . . how long have I been . . . ?" Athos couldn't quite frame his question. Walking like this wasn't hard, as he didn't need to put any weight on his thigh. And he could tell—at least from the feel of dried blood on his skin—that his bleeding had stopped, save for a trickle instigated probably by his efforts at assessing the wound. But his mind was confused and he felt as if he'd just awakened and hadn't fully come to his senses yet.

"I don't know. More than an hour. They returned to the Cardinal's palace to report," he said. "Which is when I heard them, and I gave his eminence my commission back."

"And . . . ?"

"He seemed to be amused." This was said with some fury. "But I was not. And I got one of those two surviving wretches and pressed him to tell me exactly where they'd left you. I had to come and help you."

"How did you know I wouldn't be beyond all help? What did you intend to do, aid with my funeral?"

"Monsieur," Fasset said. "The only way I'd believe someone had killed you in a fight, no matter what the odds for or against you, was if I'd personally removed your head and carried it away with me. And even then . . ." He paused. "There is an anger in you, a determination, that might very well manage to survive the loss of a head."

"Is this a case of a man recognizing his own reflection in the mirror?" Athos asked.

A short bark of laughter escaped Fasset. "Perhaps. Ah, here we are. Let's turn. I live three doors down."

He looked at Athos, in the sudden light of the lanterns over the tavern doors. "I have unlimited water at my lodgings," he said. "Though not the means to heat it. I hope you will not mind cleaning up with cold water."

Athos nodded. At this moment he didn't mind cleaning up with much of anything. He was aware of mud in his hair and mud on his scalp—the later worrying him more, because his scalp was torn and had bled and the presence of mud brought the risk of infection and fever. As for the rest of him, he thought the uniform would be hopeless, as would, probably, his stockings.

But he would take advantage of Fasset's hospitality to clean as much as he could. And to find out why it was so important to kill him that the Cardinal was willing to resort to four of his men to achieve it.

Armand, Cardinal Richelieu was not so much a dishonorable man as a practical man. He would move heaven and Earth to achieve his goal and use whatever means he had to.

But why had he thought it a worthy goal to get rid of Aramis? And, by extension, of Athos?

A Gascon's Lodging; The Secrecy of Salves; Where Musketeers Must Walk Even Without Legs

Fasset's lodging was as small as Aramis's, as simple as d'Artagnan's. The man had no servant or else, if he did, the servant wasn't home and Fasset didn't call him.

They accessed the lodging via an external staircase with no rail on the open side, and climbing four flights to a landing outside Fasset's door had proven a trial for Athos. But Fasset, once more proving that a noble heart hid somewhere beneath the Cardinal's uniform <u>3</u>—which he still wore—and his brusque Gascon mannerisms, made sure to keep Athos on the inside, so that Athos's two or three uncertain lurches almost sent Fasset flying from the steps to dash brains on the ground below. But it kept Athos safe.

And up on the landing, Fasset threw his door open and ushered Athos in to a single room that comprised about as much space as Aramis's two rooms. The near part of it had been arranged with a small table and a single chair. Against the wall was a rack containing plates and cups and other oddments. Against the far wall, beneath the single window, was a single, rumpled bed, at the foot of which hung two uniforms. At the top of the bed hung a crucifix, a simple one, made of plain metal, without a figure or any unneeded ornament. It was much like what he expected to see in a monk's cell, and it made him look at Fasset again, curiously.

Oh, it wasn't so much surprise that Fasset was religious. Weren't they all, in their different ways? Aramis used his religion as a shield between himself and the human beings who often baffled him; Porthos seemed to think that his religion commanded him to love the world and those in it, and seemed to derive from it an ability to be charitable to children and women; d'Artagnan never said much about his religion, except to swear by the Mass or the divine blood. And no man could, ever, swear convincingly by religious symbols unless he loved those symbols in his deepest heart. As for Athos—he remembered the crystal clarity of his first communion, and the feeling of holiness, of sitting in church knowing he was in God's grace. It was like being in love. Since then, he'd done many things that made it unlikely he'd ever feel grace again. Since then he'd also learned the failings of human love. But grace and love, in memory, still held his loyalty as they'd once held his heart.

And yet, he couldn't imagine putting a cross above his bed. And though he'd never caught more than a glimpse of Porthos's bedroom, over the years, he was sure there had been no cross on the wall. There were no crucifix's in all of d'Artagnan's simple lodging. In fact, the only one of them to ornament his walls with religious symbols was Aramis. So . . . why did Fasset?

"Here, Monsieur," Fasset said, pulling the chair away from the table, and helping Athos sit in it.

Freed of the encumbrance of Athos's leaning on him, Fasset grabbed a small, cylindrical tinderbox from the rack with the plates. He brought it to the table. It was too dim in the room for Athos to see exactly what Fasset was doing, and other than catching the glimmer of the brass box and the striking of the flint, he noticed nothing much till the spill caught, blazing brightly in the room.

With a quick gesture, denoting much practice at doing this—which probably meant he didn't have a servant— he lit the two candles on the table and blew out the spill. He closed the tinderbox and took it back to the rack on the wall, but came back shortly, carrying an oil lamp, which he proceeded to light from the candle.

He left the lamp burning brightly by Athos's side, and walked away, to come back with a rolled strip of immaculate linen, a basin of water and a small bottle of brandy.

Then, beside all these supplies, he set another, a small jar which he opened to reveal grayish ointment. "This," he told Athos. "Is a salve whose recipe has been in my family for generations. Any wound, so long as it hit no vital organ, be it—"

Athos's loud laughter cut his explanation, and Fasset started, his eyes opening wide. Athos, taken by surprise by his own mirth—never a normal reaction these days, and totally unexpected after the torment the night had turned into—took a deep breath and managed to finish the rest of the explanation he'd already heard from d'Artagnan twice. "Be it ever so deep or so injurious, will be healed in three days and leave no scar."

Fasset raised his eyebrows and closed his mouth. "I see," he said. And gestured with the jar. "You have no need of this, then?"

"Oh, I do," Athos said. "I've used Monsieur d'Artagnan's to almost miraculous effect twice already."

Fasset set the jar on the table, next to Athos's elbow.

"I'm sorry," Athos said. "I do beg your pardon. My laughter surprised myself. I never knew . . ." He shook his head. "I never knew I was going to laugh till I did it. It's just . . . does every family in Gascony, then, have the recipe for this salve?"

Fasset frowned, then grinned. "Wouldn't surprise me if they did, Monsieur Musketeer. What, with the Gascon temper, it's quite possible that without this salve no Gascon would have ever survived to have children." As quick as the grin had appeared, it vanished. "Monsieur Athos, use the water as much as needed for your thigh. I shall go and get more for your head, from the well downstairs."

"It is not needed," Athos said. "The water will do."

"Monsieur, it will not do," Fasset said, going to the corner, and grabbing a couple of leather buckets. "Your hair is all over equal parts mud and blood, and mud that's mostly blood."

And with that, he left. While he was gone, Athos undid his breeches and then his under breeches. Both were ruined, and he saw not much reason to try to save them. They were both threadbare and worn to the last patch.

With his breeches removed, his shirt fell almost to his knees, the way he normally let it fall, at night, to sleep in. He sat back down and pulled up the white cloth to look at his thigh.

The wound was relatively clean, for which he was grateful—a simple thrust in and out. And it had caught no more than muscle and skin, and very little muscle and skin at that. He'd fought duels with greater injuries. It was only the dizziness of having hit his head combined with the pain from his thigh that had made it impossible to walk.

He ripped a bit of cloth from his breeches, dipped it in water and washed away the blood from the wound. Then he dried it, and proceeded to apply the salve. As d'Artagnan's salve—to which it smelled remarkably similar—it stung as it went on, causing him to grind his teeth. But almost immediately the pain receded, faded, and then all feeling faded from the affected area.

Following instructions he'd often heard from his Gascon friend, Athos pushed as much of the salve into the wound as he dared, without risking making it bleed again. Then he bandaged the wound with a couple of turns of the white linen strip.

He was just finishing as Fasset returned and it occurred to Athos that the former guard had waited just long enough to make sure Athos was decent—or close to it—again. As soon as Athos heard the door open, he pulled his shirt down, and looked no more indecent than he would have had he been awakened in the middle of the night, suddenly. He'd fought duels like this in the past . . .

Fasset set the buckets down, picked up the blood-tainted basin, emptied it out the window and set one of the buckets on the table.

"Monsieur Athos, this might sound strange, but it will save us both a lot of time if you just plunge your head into this bucket."

Athos blinked. It wouldn't be the first time. He had done something like it often when he'd been drunk, just to clear his head.

He stood tentatively, supporting himself on the edge of the table, and, reaching back, removed the now mud-encrusted tie that held his hair back. Then he plunged his head into the bucket. The cold water touching his wound both relieved it and made it hurt, in a way he couldn't quite describe.

As he pulled his head up, he had a glimpse of the water, turned grey and red, from mud and blood. Fasset pushed another bucket in front of Athos, "Again," he said.

And while Athos was obeying, he heard Fasset clatter out the door, throw away the water in the bucket, then— faster than would seem possible—return with another filled bucket.

"I have them outside the door," he explained in response to Athos's stare. "I filled half a dozen while you were tending to your thigh. I keep some of them on the landing, always."

How he could see Athos expression while Athos remained half bent over, his hair streaming water and filth back into the bucket, Athos would never know.

It took three more buckets of water, and then judicious and careful use of a comb and brush before Athos's hair streamed only clear water. At which time Fasset handed him a large square of cloth for drying his hair, and had Athos lean slightly upon the chair so that the lamp lit the wound on his scalp.

Fasset's fingers prodded at the wound, and Athos heard himself gasp, before he could even register the sharp stab of pain that seemed to paralyze his breathing.

"Easy, milord," Fasset said. "It is something you cannot do for yourself, this one. And I'm afraid I must sew." He went to the same cupboard from which he'd got his tinderbox and returned with a small cup, and a slightly larger, polished wood box. He set the box on the table, and poured brandy into the cup, which he proffered to Athos. "Drink, please," he said.

Athos took the cup and swallowed the brandy so fast he barely tasted it, save for the burning sensation at his throat. He coughed then looked at Fasset. "Milord?" he asked.

"Pardon?" Fasset said. He was rummaging in his wooden box, bringing out thread and needle.

"You called me milord . . ."

Fasset grinned, a grin that was more politeness than amusement and which flashed across his face and was gone. "I don't know your name," he said. "Your true name. But everyone in the Cardinal's guard says you're a nobleman of some sort, hiding from some heinous crime. I'm not going to guess as to the crime, but I'd wager my right hand that you are a nobleman."

He touched Athos's head, very lightly. "I'm going to sew the wound shut and it's going to hurt. It's not actually . . . It's just skin. But anything on the scalp hurts like all the devils. You might want to take another shot of brandy."

"No," Athos said. "I believe I can take it."

"As you please," Fasset said. His fingers went for the salve and the burning coolness of the potion touched Athos's scalp.

"Brace now, milord," Fasset said. This time his touch was firmer, holding Athos's scalp in place. Then came the pain.

It felt . . . like strings of liquid fire streaming across his head. Athos knew only two ways to deal with this kind of pain. One was to scream, the other to abstract his mind from the actual suffering. "You do this well," he said, choosing the second. His voice only trembled slightly.

"I learned it in seminary," Fasset said.

"Seminary?" Athos asked, his eyes going to the cross on the wall.

Fasset chuckled. "Here before you stands the younger son of a moderately wealthy family. Oh, not like yours. I don't think we were ever noble. Not as such. Just landowning. My parents had two sons, you see, and since both of us were rude enough to survive to adolescence, it was determined I was to be a monk. That way my brother could inherit the whole land, without throwing me out into the gutter, or suffering any dispute from me about the inheritance."

"I'm sorry," Athos said.

"Why? You didn't do it. And it's common enough. Done every day. I had loving parents. The only thing is, they didn't give me a choice between the military and the monastery. I entered the monastery as a novice at eleven and the closer I got to professing the more I found that I was a military man at heart." He pulled on the needle, bringing an especially sharp pain to Athos's scalp. "So I ran away before I professed. Took another name and came to Paris where his eminence was kind enough to employ me."

He picked up a dagger and cut the thread. He reached for his salve and slathered it along the suture.

A post which Fasset had now lost, Athos thought, but didn't say anything about it. He guessed at depths of pride and reserve in the man, and he didn't wish to prod them, any more than he would wish a stranger to question him. And besides, there were other things which Athos must know.

While Fasset rolled up his remaining thread and put it away with his needle, Athos said, "Why was I attacked? Do you know? Is it something you can talk about?"

Fasset took a deep breath, something between a sigh and a gasp, and didn't turn from where he was.

"You don't have to tell me," Athos said. "I realize while you may have resigned your commission, you still have a certain amount of loyalty and probably took oaths that—"

Fasset turned around. He shook his head. "No," he said. "The reason you were being followed—and all of you were being followed—is that your friend Aramis left his mother's estate sometime yesterday and the Cardinal was trying to intercept him and arrest him. Anyone could guess that the four inseparables would cleave together, so the fastest way to find him was to guard the three of you."

"Aramis left his mother's estate?" Athos asked, shocked. And, to Fasset's quick nod, he added, frowning. "But why try to kill me then? And you know that this was an attempt to kill me, nothing else. No one asked me where Aramis was. No one . . ."

Fasset was shaking his head violently. "No. I could understand their following you. I could understand their apprehending your friend Aramis. What I couldn't understand, nor could I accept or condone, was that they'd tried to kill you on such a slim excuse."

"Excuse?"

"The . . . there was an object."

"The dagger!" Athos said.

Fasset sighed. "Yes. The dagger. The one used to kill the woman. We'd been looking for it for some time, and today you were seen washing it in a fountain, presumably to rid it of blood. And then you went from shop to shop, to find out to whom it belonged."

"And it turned out it had been made for the King, for his wedding."

Fasset nodded. "The . . . man who was following you heard that conversation and thought you'd have to be killed."

"Why?"

"Why? Milord, surely you know better. What if you spoke to anyone of the King's dagger being used for the murder?"

Athos spread his hands, palm up, on his lap, as if to signify his helplessness in the face of oaths given and education received. "How could I?" he asked. "I am the King's musketeer. Even if I thought his majesty—"

"Of course," Fasset said. "And that's what I told them. But by the time I told them, the man who'd been following you had assembled a group, and they'd . . . You know how I found you. I only heard about it when I overheard them reporting to his eminence."

Athos got the impression that Fasset overheard a lot of things. Probably not all by accident. Not even most of them.

"And then you resigned," he said. "Seems excessive for the deeds of some guards."

"Oh," Fasset said. "I told you I overheard them reporting to his eminence. Well. I also heard his eminence's reply."

Athos felt as if his heart skipped a beat. There was an idea forming in his head, an idea that he really didn't want to condone nor think about. But it was growing. He wasn't quite sure what it was yet, except for a feeling of something looming over him, a feeling that he should be doing something. Aloud, he completed Fasset's reply. "The Cardinal approved."

Fasset shrugged. "I could not work for someone who accepted unjustifiable murder."

Murder. Was there more to it than that? What if the King had given the dagger to the Cardinal? What if the Cardinal had then used it, via a minion, to kill the Duchess? What if he was afraid they'd discover this through the knife?

If he hadn't stolen the knife, Athos would have been able to present it to the King as proof.

And then the idea, monstrous, immense, breathtaking, hit him like a clout to the head. "My friends," he said, his mouth hurrying ahead of his brain and trying to explain his fear to Fasset ahead of his mind's fully connecting the thoughts. "My friends. Does the Cardinal know . . . Does the Cardinal think they have seen the dagger and heard of it, they might find the same link to the dagger once I'm found dead?"

He stood, on trembling legs. His thigh didn't hurt nearly as badly. He could walk. He looked at Fasset who stood, eyes wide open, looking like he too had been hit hard, between the eyes.

"Hurry, man, lend me a sword," Athos said. "I must go help my friends."

Fasset shook his head. "Monsieur, you're in your shirt. You're not in the state to fight anyone, and you're surely not going to fight the guards of the Cardinal in your shirt and bare bottomed."

Athos looked down impatiently. His breeches, lying on the floor by his feet, were useless. But his over breeches . . . He reached for them.

"Catch," Fasset said. And Athos turned, to catch a pair of breeches thrown in his general direction. They were the blood red of the Cardinal's guards, and loose venetians, but that hardly signified at the time.

"They should fit you," Fasset said. "Though they'll be perhaps a tad short."

Before he'd stopped speaking, Athos had already fastened the breeches. His drying hair, he likewise tied back with a scrap of the same strip he'd used to bandage his thigh.

"A sword or a dagger?" he told Fasset.

"You cannot mean to go fight. You cannot get there in time. You cannot even walk the distance to the nearest of their houses, much less run it as you'd need to do if you wish to get there in time."

Athos ground his teeth. "Watch me," he said.

Fasset sighed. From a corner, he retrieved a sword, which he extended to Athos, pommel out, even as Athos finished fastening his sword belt. Athos sheathed the sword, then slipped his feet into boots. He pulled his doublet on, laced it tightly.

He was aware, if he allowed himself to think about it, that his thigh hurt like the blazes. But it was properly bandaged, it had been treated and he refused to give it more attention than it deserved. He would go to d'Artagnan's first. If he was careful he could follow an itinerary that hit each of his friends' houses in turn, in a minimum of time. That way he could aid whoever needed aid.

Opening the door, he rushed out. He was two flights down the rickety stairs, when he heard Fasset's door slam and a rush of feet.

Looking up, over his shoulder, he saw Fasset—fully attired and wearing his sword—following him.

At the look, Fasset called out, "I'm sure there is a commandment that forbids someone who almost became a monk from letting a madman go alone to seek his death."

Where Porthos Discovers the Virtues of Recessed Doorways; The Guards of the Cardinal Get a Surprise; And Aramis Comes Back Home

Aramis had stood in the recessed doorway so long that he must have dozed.

He was fairly sure he knew where his foe was. Or at least, he had some inkling of where the Cardinal's spy hid—in a doorway three doors down. He wondered if the spy had any idea he was there. He was fairly sure the man could have no idea of who Aramis actually was. If he did, he would long ago have walked down the street and arrested Aramis. No. His identity remained hidden. His presence might not, but then, the guard wouldn't know anything but that someone else was spying on the same door.

Aramis felt worn out. Exhausted by vigilance. He stared at Porthos's doorway so much his eyes hurt. He wished for a glimpse of his friend and realized, with an almost physical pain, that he missed Porthos.

Had anyone asked him before today, he would have said that of course, Porthos was one of his best friends. After all, he had allowed Aramis to escape sure death in that first duel. And he'd been so kind as to stand second in a duel to a seminarian who could have found no one else to stand with him. But he'd have said that he tolerated Porthos's company. Barely. He would say Porthos was too uncouth, his education too deficient. And while Porthos's mind left nothing to be desired, what came out of his mouth often bordered on incomprehensible gibberish.

All that he would have said before this week. Now he realized that he'd grown used to Porthos. Oh, perhaps it was only that. Or perhaps it was that he and Porthos had long grown used to functioning as a unit, a complete person. Aramis supplied the philosophy, the ease of expression, the fluency. And Porthos supplied the strength, the solidity, the unswerving loyalty.

Aramis would wager that of all the people in Paris and the many who called themselves his friends, Porthos was the only one who—not for a moment—would have never considered Aramis's guilt in this. And he would not talk about it, nor would he dissect it. The moment he saw Aramis, the only thing in Porthos's mind would be to make everything as it had been before these horrible events. And that was all Aramis wanted. All he could hope for.

So, where was Porthos? Why didn't he come home?

Aramis leaned against the door frame, and must have dozed. He must have dozed because he woke up to the sound of clashing swords, as well as the continuous stream of talk that was characteristic of Porthos when he dueled.

"Five of you, is it?" Porthos said. "Five of you to take the one man. Ah. Watch as I fight all of you. Cowards. Canaille."

The shadow three doorways down detached from the building and ran, to join the guards. Six. Six against Porthos.

Without thinking, Aramis's hand went to where his sword normally hung, and he cursed at finding the scabbard gone from his belt. Blindly, he grabbed for his other scabbard, and pulled out his dagger, as he ran forward, a formless scream tearing his throat.

At some level in his mind, he knew this was madness, he knew this was suicide. But he could say, with complete honesty, he'd have done the same had he seen any other single man being attacked by five armed men.

"Ah, Aramis," Porthos said, while he flashed and danced and parried the swords of all opponents, seeming to be in ten places at once, and to have eyes behind his back besides.

It was only when seeing him do something like this that one remembered that Porthos was a fencing and dancing master.

"Catch," Porthos yelled, and as he did, he brought his sword up from below, catching an opponent's sword at the tip, and sending it flying, in Aramis's general direction.

This was so much like a dozen duels they'd taken part in, that Aramis didn't even think. At any rate, the worst thing you can do is think while a sword is headed for you, turning end over end.

Instead, Aramis leapt forward and grabbed the sword handle, plucking the weapon out of midair as easily as if it had been handed to him. In the landing, he kicked his foot up, managing to hit the man who'd lost the sword just so, as he dove for it. The man went flying in turn, falling to the dirt, immobile.

Aramis called, "A moi canaille. See how you fight when the odds are more even."

Half of Porthos's opponents turned towards him.

Aramis had come home.

Evening the Odds; Two Gascons and a Musketeer

Each step Athos took, he thought might be the last. His leg hurt and threatened to buckle under him. But Athos had long experience in refusing to give in to his body.

He had fought drunk, he had fought wounded, he had fought after he had spent nights without sleeping and his dreams, like waking phantoms, plagued his daytime vision. It would not change now. He would not give in to his pain, or his weakness now. What he lacked in strength, he made up for in sheer determination.

He ran and every time he thought he would fall, he forced himself to run faster. Behind him, he could hear Fasset panting, trying to catch up.

His pain spurred Athos on, faster and faster, till he heard the sound of swords clashing on swords, nearby. And then he stopped for a moment, catching a breath, as the thought caught up with his panicked mind.

D'Artagnan. They'd already got to d'Artagnan. D"Artagnan was suffering through an onslaught like the one that Athos had endured.

Oh, d'Artagnan was the devil himself with a sword. Ventre saint gris, the King himself had called him. But even so, d'Artagnan was young. And for all his theory, he was short on practice.

And those men would be the Cardinal's best, most merciless killers.

If Athos had been running fast before, now he flew, his feet barely touching the ground, his borrowed sword somehow moving out of the scabbard and into his hand.

"Athos," d'Artagnan's voice yelled, as Athos rounded the corner.

Without ever slowing down, Athos took in the scene before him. There were five men fighting d'Artagnan. Only d'Artagnan was not on the same level with them, but was suspended from a trellis, heavily plaited with ivy, that ran up the side of d'Artagnan's building. In a position only possible to someone as young and agile as d'Artagnan, the young man was hanging from the trellis with one hand, and keeping the guards at bay with feet and sword.

At d'Artagnan's call, some of the men turned, all of them looked. D"Artagnan took the opportunity to jump down from the trellis and engage the guards fully. Athos registered, without giving it much thought, that the young man was wearing only his shirt—white and knee long.

"But it is impossible," one of the guards said, facing Athos fully. "You are dead."

"No," Athos said, jumping into the battle. "But you soon will be."

And then the battle plunged into what it always was for Athos—a red mist, and a craving for fight and death and blood. When he'd first come to Paris, when he'd first started his self-imposed exile, he was afraid he was possessed by some evil spirit. His dueling which, up till then, had been mannered and masterful but more art than anger, had become a screaming pit of rage after his wife's death.

He still wasn't sure he was not possessed. And he didn't care.

He fought in the red, hot mist of his own rage, from which only his friends—d'Artagnan to his right and Fasset to his left—were protected.

When the fury abated, and his heart, that had been threatening to break the bounds of his ribcage, slowed down enough for Athos to stop fighting, he found himself standing with his back against d'Artagnan's wall. D"Artagnan was still to his right, and still in his nightshirt. Fasset was still to his left, bent double, clutching his sword, while breathing so hard that Athos thought the man must be wounded.

But it didn't matter if he was, because they'd carried the day. In front of them, in various positions of death, lay six guards of the Cardinal.

"Are you wounded, Fasset?" Athos asked.

Fasset shook his head, while still drawing deep, chest-straining breaths. "No, curse you, but I'm also not a demon, like you."

Athos nodded. He might be a demon, for all he knew. "We must go to Porthos's place now," he said, as much to d'Artagnan as to Fasset. "I don't see any reason to go by Aramis's lodging because he wouldn't be so stupid as to go there and they must know it. But they'll be at Porthos's. Porthos will need our help." He thought of his capable, giant friend, who bragged of being able to take three duelers at once, and usually could.

But could he stand-alone against determined killers who didn't care for the rules of war?

"Will you come with me?" he asked both of them.

"Yes," d'Artagnan said.

"In your nightshirt?"

d'Artagnan grinned, and kicked up his foot. "It's warm and I have my boots on."

Athos nodded. "And you, Fasset?"

Fasset shook his head. "I don't think I could. The two of you aren't human."

"Better, perhaps," Athos said. "These six are dead, but we don't need the guards, as a whole to know you've betrayed them. Thank you, my friend. I owe you my life."

Without delaying, Athos took off running, following d'Artagnan who ran like a demon, taking every possible shortcut between his house and Porthos's.

What To Do with a Fugitive; Where the Cardinal's Guilt Is Agreed Upon, but Guilt of What Is Strenuously Argued

D'Artagnan arrived at Porthos's house before Athos, just in time to join the melee.

As he arrived, Porthos and Aramis were close to carrying the day, with three of their opponents lying dead. As d'Artagnan started fighting the fourth, he dropped his sword, turned and ran away.

He was shortly followed by number five, while the sixth fell to the ground, Porthos's sword having neatly speared him through the chest.

Athos arrived just in time to see the three friends standing there, looking at their dead foes. With immediate and complete composure, Athos stopped and slid his sword into its scabbard. He looked down at the foes, and crossed his arms on his chest, while he frowned at them, as though holding them responsible for cutting his fun short.

D'Artagnan became aware of being very informally attired. Even in the warm evening air, his legs felt naked and cold, as the breeze ruffled his nightshirt's hem.

And he became aware that Aramis was looking at him, and frowning vaguely in his direction.

"I was in bed," d'Artagnan said. "And I heard men talking, beneath my window. They were going to force the door open."

"So he jumped down from his window, scrambled down the trellis and gave battle," Athos said.

"And then Athos and . . . was that Fasset?" d'Artagnan asked, and Athos nodded. "Joined, and Athos killed three of them, I killed two, and Fasset killed one."

"But why?" Porthos asked. He cleaned his sword on the clothes of a fallen opponent, and slid it back into its scabbard. "Why were they trying to kill us? Because that was not a simple challenge for a duel. They wanted to kill us."

"They thought—" Athos started.

"No," d'Artagnan said. It occurred to him that in the dark, with darker doorways all around, there was a very good chance of being overheard if they stood here, in the middle of the street. And, d'Artagnan thought, looking at the corpses at their feet, if this was not secret matter, it should be. "Porthos, may we go inside?"

The redhead's face fell. He looked guilty, immediately, of lack of hospitality. "Of course, of course," he said. "Do come in. I'm a boar. I should have invited you in sooner." And, as he spoke, he started unlocking his door.

"Hardly," Aramis said, his voice dry and humorous. "If you had invited us inside sooner, we'd only have got blood all over your stairway."

Porthos's stairway was very grand, as was indeed, his entire lodging. The rooms had been subdivided from a much larger, much grander home, and the vestiges of it remained in marble panels on the walls, and in columns separating the entrance from the area where they gathered.

As in all their homes, in Porthos's home too they had a room, a particular place where they gathered for their war councils.2

Here it was a broad table, which Mousqueton kept polished to a high gloss. Around it, disposed, were four arm chairs.

D'Artagnan took his place beside Athos, facing Porthos, while Aramis sat next to Porthos. But Porthos sat for only a minute, before getting up, mumbling, "Mousqueton is not here tonight. I'll get some wine."

And d'Artagnan who remembered Mousqueton's pretty friend, smiled and thought that Mousqueton was luckier than all of them. And then thought of his own Planchet, the redheaded stripling, whom he'd cautioned against leaving the house under any conditions.

Fortunately, through their short time together, Planchet had learned that his master meant what he said when he made such conditions. D"Artagnan thought he would be safe, but wondered what Planchet thought had happened. And how much of a confusion would envelop the neighborhood when the bodies were found.

"Why are you back in Paris," Porthos asked Aramis, as he set a jug of wine and four cups on the table. "I thought you were safe in the countryside."

D'Artagnan couldn't read Aramis's expression at all. It wasn't dread and it wasn't boredom, but it was as though both of those and something else besides—something very akin to the terror a pious soul might display at the thought of hell—crossed Aramis's perfectly symmetrical features. He made a little gesture, as though tossing the idea out of his mind, and he said, "I couldn't. I couldn't stay in the country and know my friends were battling who knew what perils for my sake."

He said it prettily and bravely, and d'Artagnan would almost believe it. Except there was still that look of haunted terror in Aramis's face.

Porthos only nodded, though, and disappeared, to come back again with a pair of breeches in his hand. "Try these ones, d'Artagnan," he said.

D'Artagnan took them and pulled them on. They were much too large and since they were ankle length on Porthos, had to be rolled up, but he supposed that looking like he'd gone out wearing his father's clothes was better than looking half dressed. He tied them on, as tightly as he could.

They sat around the table, and sipped the wine for a long while. D"Artagnan could feel that Athos was working towards saying something. He'd only known the three musketeers for a month, and yet he knew Athos well enough to guess that everything the musketeer said emerged as if out of a deeper silence upon which it was no more than a frail bridge.

After a while, he found himself looking expectantly at Athos, waiting for Athos to speak.

"Aramis," Athos said, at last. "Do you know any reason why the Cardinal should hate you?"

Aramis frowned. "Not that I . . ." He paused, shrugged. Then sighed. "A week ago I would have told you no, no more cause than he has to hate any of you."

"And now?" Athos asked.

Porthos turned half around in his chair, as though waiting to hear the revelation.

"Well," Aramis said. He cupped his long, delicate hands around his wine cup. "I have only one reason, though I don't understand why it would make him hate me."

D'Artagnan found himself raising an eyebrow at Aramis, and Aramis's gaze met his. Only a month ago, those green eyes would have been full of suspicion. Now, when he looked at d'Artagnan, Aramis softened his look, as though in response to the young man's effort to understand. "You see," he said. "I found out that the Cardinal Richelieu, when he was young, killed my father in a duel over a girl whom they both loved."

"Your mother?" Porthos asked.

Aramis closed his eyes, as though fearing the onset of a headache. "Porthos, I'm not a posthumous son."

But Porthos only grinned. "I fail to see what that has to do with anything, Aramis. You were having an affair with a married woman. Surely you know . . ."

Aramis looked as though Porthos had waved a poisonous snake in front of his eyes. "Not Maman," he said, with a look of horror. "I'm sure Maman never had an unholy thought in her life. It's true that she . . . but . . . No!"

And there, d'Artagnan, though he was only seventeen, had to make an effort to remain impassive. The temptation to laugh was much too strong and at finding such a blind spot in such a worldly man as Aramis. D"Artagnan was aware of a smile quirking at the corner of Athos's lips and of Porthos's biting his lips together to prevent himself from laughing.

But Aramis, who surely was aware of the great amusement he'd caused all of them, said, looking determinedly ahead, at the face that d'Artagnan hoped was impassive, "Why do you think the Cardinal hates me though? More than he hates any other musketeer?"

D'Artagnan's Theory; Athos's Explanation; Porthos's Ghosts

"I don't understand," Aramis said, facing his friends. He'd drank a cup of wine, and he was almost feeling like himself. Here, in Porthos's lodgings, sitting across from Athos and d'Artagnan, it was possible to pretend that nothing out of the ordinary had ever happened. It was possible to while away the time as though Violette were still alive in her room at the palace.

"You," he pointed to d'Artagnan. "Think that the only purpose of this whole plot is for the Cardinal to get me out of the city and keep me out of the city. I have to tell you there is some—well, one piece—of corroborating evidence for this theory, in that the Cardinal has sent me a letter."

"A letter?" Athos asked, his eyebrows raising.

"A letter." Aramis fished in his sleeve, where he'd earlier put any documents that might be of importance, including Violette's letter, which he'd managed to retrieve from Monsieur de Treville's desk. He pushed the Cardinal's letter across at Athos and d'Artagnan. He did not inflict it on Porthos, who could read as well as any of them, but who had only learned to read after he'd come to Paris to live away from his father, who thought reading was an effeminate activity that should be kept away from boys at all costs. Having learned late, and having taught himself, Porthos often had trouble with the curlier of cursives, such as the one the Cardinal used. To save Porthos the humiliation of trying to peruse the letter, or of asking what the letter said, Aramis said, "As you see, he enjoins me to make a provincial marriage, or to join a monastery out in the country and not to attempt to return to Paris."

He could feel Porthos visibly relax at the explanation, while Athos nodded, pushing the letter towards Aramis again. "That much I see," he said. "And yes, it fits well with d'Artagnan's theory. For you must know, even though I've grown to be convinced of it, it was d'Artagnan who created this theory."

"The theory ignores one thing," Porthos said. He was bouncing around on his seat, as he did when he disagreed with something that was being said. "It ignores the ghost."

"There was no ghost," Athos said. "It was . . . a prank. Possibly engineered by Mousqueton's Hermengarde."

"She would never," Porthos said. "Not if I know Mousqueton. She would not dare. And at any rate, what kind of a prank was it, and how was it effected?"

"Oh, it would be very easy," d'Artagnan said. "You only had to have someone standing out in the balcony. A slim young girl, so she could crouch out of sight and cast no shadow upon the glass. Then when she got the signal that we were in position, she could pop up and open the door and do her little scene."

"That's it," Athos said. "All through it, I kept feeling as though the girl were performing on a stage. All of it. The mask, the suit, the careful steps, the caper and kiss upon finding the cross."

"The cross?" Aramis asked, now convinced that in his absence his friends had gone utterly insane. "I don't have the pleasure of understanding you."

Athos sighed, in turn. "When we went to the secret passage—"

"There is a secret passage?" Aramis asked.

"Behind the picture," Porthos said. "Atop the wardrobe, to the right side of the bed. There is a passage, and you can look through the picture's eyes. I heard that often the Cardinal—"

Aramis felt his eyes widen and his face blanch, and his expression must have stopped Porthos who suddenly looked horrified at what he had almost said. But Aramis could not let it lie. "The Cardinal spied on us? The Cardinal ? Why?"

"I don't know," Athos said. "What we heard is that he didn't trust the Duchess de Dreux because he feared she worked with the Queen for the Spanish. As such, he was prepared to spy on her."

"She did not work for Spain," Aramis said, indignant. "She never even mentioned Spain to me . . . Well, unless she was reminiscing about her childhood."

The silence around the table echoed back to him, and he waved all that away. "But let's suppose that this was the case and that . . . I imagine the Cardinal only spied when she was with the Queen, then?"

He did not like Athos's silence, or Porthos's fidgeting.

"d'Artagnan, my friend," Aramis asked, addressing himself to the boy and hoping that d'Artagnan's great cunning had kept his mind from the insanity that affected the others. "Why would his eminence spy on us?"

"I don't know," d'Artagnan said, looking uncomfortable.

"But you think he did?"

"I suspect he did. From the reactions of the servants and what they didn't say."

Aramis nodded. This was the type of reasoning that he could understand. "And if you had to hazard a guess as to motive?"

D'Artagnan sighed. "I would have to guess that he wanted to have material to force the Duchess to do something he wished to have her

THE MUSKETEER'S SEAMSTRESS

do. Or perhaps . . ." He looked towards Athos. "Your friend said he had news of his wife?"

Athos turned around to face d'Artagnan. "You think the Cardinal was sending Raoul news of his wife's exploits? The Cardinal? Why?"

"Athos," d'Artagnan said in that world weary voice that so often made him sound like the oldest—instead of the youngest—of them all. "The Duke came to his wedding and now doesn't live at court. Have you never thought that perhaps the Cardinal has a grudge against him?"

"The Cardinal has a grudge against all great nobles, and tries to keep the King as far from his extended family as possible," Aramis put in drily, then concentrated on the part of the conversation he found most fascinating. "You know Violette's husband?"

Athos sighed. "Raoul is an old childhood friend. I visited him."

"Did he kill her?" Aramis asked. Only that mattered.

Athos shook his head.

Aramis fished in his sleeve for Violette's letter announcing her pregnancy. "Not even in light of this?" he asked.

Athos looked over the letter and shook his hand. "No," he said. "I'm sorry, Aramis." He pushed the letter back. "I really am sorry, Aramis, for what you've lost. But no, not even that."

He shrugged. "Look, Aramis," he said, as Aramis took the letter and folded it and put it back in his sleeve. "I knew Raoul when we were both so young that neither of us knew the meaning of dissimulation. I knew Raoul before either of us understood the meaning of lie. I know when he's lying, and yes, he has lied to me in the past, particularly when we were both very young. He wasn't lying when he told me he hadn't killed his wife." Athos looked as if he was about to say something else, then shrugged again. "Please believe me. You know I'm rarely wrong on such things."

And it was true. Athos was rarely wrong on such things. Unless, of course, the liar were a certain kind of woman, in which case Athos's testimony should be taken in the reverse, because he was always wrong. But Aramis would not say that. He would not remind Athos of his luck with women. Instead he said, "I'll trust you, but it seems very odd to me. And I still don't understand why the Cardinal would want me to leave town or to stay out of town."

"Oh, by the Mass," Porthos, who had continued fidgeting all through the conversation, exploded. "Really, Athos, Aramis, d'Artagnan. The Cardinal has no special reason to want Aramis out of town, only the murder having happened and its looking like Aramis did it, it suits the Cardinal to think that it was Aramis. That way, particularly if Aramis either is arrested before he can disprove the charges, or never comes back to dispute them, the Cardinal, in his next tug of war with Monsieur de Treville can say that at least none of his guards ever killed a defenseless woman. That is all. You are making this into much more than it is."

"But why would he try to kill us, then?" d'Artagnan asked, baffled.

"I'm afraid that is my fault," Athos said. "Aramis, do you remember the dagger you gave me that night?"

Aramis had forgotten all about it. Now, as though it were happening all again, he felt the dagger in his hand, slippery with Violette's blood, and he shrunk from the idea of her corpse, the feel of her skin, the—He realized he had covered his mouth with both his hands, as though to stop a scream struggling to form somewhere deep within himself.

Athos was still waiting for an answer, and Aramis nodded.

"We forgot all about it, till last night," Athos said, and proceeded to detail how he'd gone from store to store in the jewelers' row, asking about the dagger and its exquisite ivory work, till he'd come to the shop of Pierre Michou.

"But . . . The King?" Aramis asked.

Athos shrugged. "It was given to the King, but you know his majesty's habit of giving away whatever he considers a trifle, and which he has lying on his table at the moment of the audience."

"But that would mean the murderer could be anyone," Aramis said.

"No, only the persons the Cardinal would be willing to commit murder to defend. Aramis, he's not as amoral as he seems. Think how many times he must have wished to do away with the three of us," he looked at d'Artagnan and smiled. "Even perhaps the four of us. But he has never truly tried it till tonight. So it must be to defend someone who is valuable to him, or on whom his good fortune depends."

"The King," Aramis said.

"Or the Cardinal himself," d'Artagnan said.

Porthos's Clarity; The Greatest Need; Porthos's Duchess

Porthos understood that Aramis knew of Porthos's impatience with the whole chain of reasoning. Alas, Porthos also knew that if he said anything about that, he would be silenced again, as he had been so many times before.

So Porthos kept silent, but fidgeted in his seat and—only catching himself as he was doing it—sometimes found himself rolling his eyes at Aramis's or Athos's comments.

As Athos and d'Artagnan seemed determined to draw the conclusion that the Cardinal himself was responsible for the murder of the Duchess, Porthos let them draw it. He had no doubt at all that Aramis agreed with them, either. It was all part, he thought, of how his three friends viewed themselves. They lived with their heads so firmly stuck in the world of duchesses and countesses, of mannerly households and court manners that they simply couldn't imagine how someone smaller, someone more at their own level or below could have a true influence in their destiny.

It was not their fault. They'd been raised in noble houses. At least Athos and Aramis had. Noble houses of the kind that had libraries, and which could enumerate their pedigree going back centuries uncounted. Porthos had no doubt that Athos's and Aramis's families had been around in some form since the Roman Empire.

Early on, the two of them had been broken on the wheel of how to behave and what people would think of them. In that, he thought, even d'Artagnan who was an outsider and from a relatively poor region, was more like them than like Porthos. His family—though d'Artagnan made fun of their wealth and his own prospects for inheritance—would be the most influential in their village, or even their hamlet. Everyone would have looked up to him as he grew up. He would have been important and regarded as special.

Porthos—ah, Porthos. Oh, theoretically his family was noble, that sort of undefined nobility that had no particular position at court and merely came from their having held power for so long in one particular region.

Porthos was not blind nor stupid, and had heard enough stories and learned enough history to think that his family must have come over with the Normans, the wild ones in their boats, ravaging and pillaging. There were times when Porthos felt he could have made a good go of ravaging and pillaging too. Particularly when faced with rules he didn't fully understand or intend to obey and with comrades who seemed so intent on blaming the most powerful man in the land for all their misfortunes.

Look at them, Porthos thought, as he tapped the heel of his left foot on the floor, gently causing his knee to fall and rise with the movement. Look at the lot of them.

"So, how can we determine if the Cardinal meant to entrap Aramis?" Athos was saying, leaning over the table, his dark blue eyes seeming more lit up with enthusiasm than normal. Like the night sky in August, instead of their normal blue: so dark that it passed for black in certain lights.

"We need to talk to the guards," d'Artagnan was saying. "And to Monsieur de Treville, and see what he knows, what he has heard."

"Yes," Athos said. "Surely Monsieur de Treville knows what is happening."

Porthos doubted it. From what he'd heard in the antechambers and the taverns, Monsieur de Treville actually believed that Aramis had done it.

And all the while, all the while they were talking, Porthos pushed his knee up and down and drummed his fingers on the table. It was like watching children discussing a play. What did the Cardinal matter to them, or they to the Cardinal? Unless they interfered directly in the Cardinal's plots as they had done before, the Cardinal tended to leave them quite alone and to their own devices.

He noticed Aramis's look at him out of the corner of his eye, and Aramis only frowned at Athos and d'Artagnan. "I can't go with you," Aramis said. "I can't . . . If they should see me in the city, the Cardinal will send someone to capture me."

"Or kill you," Athos said, his features all grave, and he nodded. "No. You are absolutely right. You cannot go."

"I should probably not stay here, either," Aramis said. "I mean, I don't know if they have watchers on this place already. Perhaps not, as I've heard no noise of anyone discovering the bodies outside. But whether the Cardinal takes it upon himself to revenge himself on each of us, whether he still finds it needed to kill us all, or whether he merely wants to capture me—we are all at risk and I'm the most endangered."

"Here's the plan," Porthos said. He had known all along it would come to this, and while they were all talking, he had made a plan to protect Aramis. Because the last thing he wanted was for Aramis to be convinced that he had to leave Paris again.

Porthos had felt like a man who has his left leg cut off at the knee, and wobbles around with a wooden leg. Only they'd all been such men. The truth was, whether they liked it or not, they were a quartet and they all balanced each other, their best qualities feeding the others', their worst qualities neutralizing each other. Without Aramis, Athos became too aristocratic and demanded too much of them all, himself included. Without Aramis, d'Artagnan patterned all his actions on Athos, and became unable to oppose the older musketeer's excesses or to cajole him out of his black moods with humor, as Aramis did and as d'Artagnan was learning to do. And Porthos? Without Aramis, Porthos felt even more inarticulate than he knew himself to be. Without Aramis, Porthos felt as though the language didn't obey him and as if he lacked the means to communicate with either Athos or d'Artagnan.

So, to prevent the chances of Aramis's disappearing into the void of the countryside again, where he would be inaccessible to Porthos, Porthos had decided to find him a safe place. Now, as he announced that he had a plan and all the others turned towards him, he said, "It's like this. I have a friend. D"Artagnan has met her, and been at her house. As has Athos."

"Your Duchess?" Aramis asked, suspiciously.

Porthos sighed. He didn't think that Aramis believed the lie that Porthos's lover was a duchess. At least he hoped that Aramis didn't believe it, because if he did, he would be forced to think far less of Aramis's intelligence. The lie had been started long ago, when they knew each other a lot worse and when Porthos felt frustrated by his own inability to be interested in anything like duchesses and princesses. It wasn't that he couldn't attract them. In fact, they tripped over themselves to admire the fine musketeer, whose uniform normally contained twice the lace and more golden embroidery than even the fine clothes of the fine noblemen around the court.

But their conversation—their conversation was all about whatever topic was fashionable at the moment, or else about themselves, their clothes, their carriages. Porthos had a very limited interest in those. Oh, he liked clothes. His clothes. But he ordered them made, and then he wore them. He didn't talk about them.

So when he'd found himself, happily and confusedly, falling in love with a woman of mind and sense, of understanding and a keen appreciation for the wonder that was Porthos, and had realized she was a mere accountant's wife, he'd made up the story of a princess in disguise to camouflage it.

But since then his friends had got to know him much better. And Athos and d'Artagnan had even met Athenais. For a moment, in fact, Porthos had been uneasy that Athos admired Athenais too much. He very much doubted that from the others' conversations, Aramis hadn't gleaned that Porthos mistress was no noblewoman. Or that Aramis, the consummate gossip and courtier hadn't realized that Porthos's lover did not, and could not, live at court.

So Porthos sighed and said, "Aramis, she's an accountant's wife. But here is the thing—you see, her husband takes on apprentices and clerks all the time, and really, her circles and ours do not mix, so no one will know you."

There was a wild snort from d'Artagnan and Porthos glared at him.

"Porthos," Athos said. "No one will see him. The husband of your excellent Athenais keeps his clerks in the cellar and feeds them on bread and water."

Aramis shrugged. "But I'll be here," he said. "I'll be in Paris. And Porthos can bring me news of anything that happens. I can . . . not be shut out of all your investigations, all your discoveries. I can be available, should you need me."

"Yes," Athos said, and twitched his lips upwards in a bitter expression that was not a smile, though it had the effect of a smile. "And if the Cardinal should decide to seek our lives, we can at least leave Paris all together."

D'Artagnan grinned. "Well, if we can leave together, it won't be so bad, will it."

"But I have to get Aramis to Athenais before full day-break, before the city awakes. And before they find the bodies on the sidewalk."

Athos nodded once. "How will you hide Aramis till you get to Athenais's?"

Aramis stood up. "I have my disguise," he said. And saying that, he rolled up his hair, and put it beneath his hat.

Porthos pursed his lips. Oh, he would still know Aramis on sight. He had known Aramis on sight. But he had been friends with Aramis for many years, and he'd taught Aramis how to use a sword, how to defend himself. In other words, he'd studied the way Aramis moved, and he'd sought to improve it.

This meant that he knew Aramis better than most people. He had to assume that in the sagging, threadbare black suit and with the hat hiding his hair and tilted to hide his face, Aramis could have been any of a hundred apprentices or clerks in Paris.

"It will do," he said. "However, an additional precaution for all of us. Do not leave by the front door, just in case the Cardinal has been alerted and has sent someone to ambush us."

Just because Porthos didn't believe the conspiracy had originated with the Cardinal, didn't mean he didn't believe that Richelieu, a man forever likely to confuse the best interests of France with his own, hadn't decided that France, and he, would be better off for the disappearance or death of three meddlesome musketeers and their equally meddlesome guard friend. And Richelieu would not be pleased with having lost a dozen or more guards tonight.

"Mousqueton has a way out of the house," Porthos said. "That he thinks I know nothing about. You leave by the window of his bedroom, jump on the roof of my landlord's henhouse, and from there to a low wall that runs around the property. From thence it is but a moment to find your way to the alley at the back of this house." As he spoke he noticed Athos flinch. "I can guarantee, Athos, that they are all small steps," he said.

Athos nodded. "I am sure I can manage," he said. "Fasset was most kind with bandages to bind my wound, and my thigh is not really painful anymore."

"Your wound?" Porthos asked. He'd seen Athos arrive, running. And d'Artagnan had spoken of Athos fighting with him against the guards of the Cardinal.

Athos shrugged. "I escaped the attack on me by being stabbed through the thigh—don't worry, just flesh and some skin—and falling against the wall, which not only rendered me momentarily insensible, but also caused me to lose a vast quantity of blood, which was taken as proof of my death."

Porthos was astonished. With any of the other of them, if they'd come to the aid of the others in a fight, and been severely wounded throughout, they would, at the very least tell the others as soon as possible. But not Athos. Sometimes Athos was unreadable and unfathomable. As though he believed his wounds made him weak or less admirable.

The three friends were already moving towards Mousqueton's room, and Porthos followed them into the narrow chamber with its single bed, and across it to the window, which opened noiselessly—part of Mousqueton's conviction that he was hiding his escapades from Porthos.

"I'll go first," d'Artagnan said.

Athos went after him, then Aramis and, finally, Porthos, who closed the window behind himself to give the impression the house was closed and to keep Mousqueton in his blissful innocence.

It had always been Porthos's opinion that he could not possibly keep his servant from disobeying him. He viewed it as much more reasonable to know the ways that his servant was likely to disobey him, and then attempt to control the consequences of such disobedience.

For instance, since Mousqueton always used that one window, and because Porthos knew that the window was a weak point in the defense of the house, he could lock it while Mousqueton was out and open it just before his errant servant was likely to return. And when they were both in the house, he could insist that Mousqueton keep a wooden shutter over the window.

He leapt from the roof of the chicken house to the wall, and thence down to the street. Where his three friends gathered talking.

"Porthos," Athos was saying. "We think even our houses might not be safe, not if the Cardinal hears that we dispatched over a dozen of his guards. You know him. Even if he hadn't been determined to murder us before, even if he'd only sought to scare us, he'd be determined to murder us now. He holds grudges and punishes all slights and all offenses."

"Where will you be staying?" Porthos asked.

"Probably at Monsieur de Treville's," Athos said. "Even if I have to sleep in a corner of the antechamber, though normally it is not that hard for the captain to find me a guest room. And d'Artagnan can share the room, as well. If you come later, you might as well share it too. Just come through the back entrance, so your arrival is not too obvious and you're not set upon on the street. But I think going through the antechamber should be no danger to us."

"No indeed," Porthos said. "I would say our best chance of survival is to always be surrounded by so many people that there's no chance to kill us quietly, in secret." He looked at Aramis, undistinguished in his black suit. "All of us except Aramis, of course. Because he can be caught and imprisoned in public, on presumption of murder."

The friends parted, Porthos and Aramis heading towards the middle class parts of Paris, where wealthy merchants and accountants lived, and d'Artagnan and Athos headed towards the Treville house.

Porthos's Theory; Families and Friends; The Accountant's Abode

Porthos and Aramis walked for a long while in silence. Aramis wondered if he should tell Porthos how much he'd missed all of them but Porthos in particular, and how he'd come to realize how important their support of each other was.

But he could not find the words. Or at least no words that wouldn't sound silly and affected, and Porthos was not the kind of person to understand metaphors and all the imagery that literature had created to express the sense of friendship, the sense of loyalty that didn't involve family or blood relations.

So, instead, walking besides Porthos through the still silent late night of Paris, Aramis said, "I felt as if you don't believe what Athos and d'Artagnan think. As if you don't think that the Cardinal truly engineered my lover's murder simply to see me out of Paris."

Porthos shrugged. "They are more learned than I," he said. "And Athos far more knowledgeable in the ways of the court and the high nobility."

Aramis grinned. "Porthos, I have known you a long time. Don't try to tell me that your brain is slow or that you do not understand what is happening. Your words might be—and often are—slow, but your brain is not."

Still Porthos didn't answer, and after a while, Aramis decided to be direct. "Tell me what you think. What do you think happened."

Porthos nodded. "I think someone—an acrobat, perhaps, a dancer, someone trained to perform feats that seem impossible to us—managed to climb to that balcony, go in and kill your . . ." he permitted himself a smile. "Seamstress. I don't know why. But I know that this same person returned, a few days later, wearing a boy's outfit, and a hard, glittering ceramic mask. She rummaged through the trunk where your mistress kept her jewelry and pulled out a golden chain from which a plain gold cross hung. She kissed the cross, and then she left the same way she had come. And no, Aramis, the woman was neither a product of our imagination, nor a prank played upon us by someone.

Only by the most fortunate coincidence were we there to see her, but . . ."

"Woman?" Aramis asked.

Porthos shrugged. "Athos says it was a woman, and though we can't trust Athos on the character of any woman, we can probably trust him on the appearance of femininity in a stranger. I'd say a woman or a very young man, and the gestures were not those of a young man, nor do I think a young man could do what the murderer did, get away undetected, come back, steal something and get away undetected again. That takes self-control and planning, neither of them natural qualities of young men."

Aramis nodded. "A plain cross and a chain?" He shook his head. "I think I remember what you are talking about. Violette never wore it, but once, when I was going through her trunk, looking for a jewel I might borrow, I came across it. She said it was given to her in her early childhood, in the convent."

"The convent?" Porthos asked. "Your mistress lived in a convent?"

Aramis shrugged. "I assume she was brought up in one." They'd left behind the narrower streets of the working class and had entered broader streets. The houses were bigger, though they still abutted directly to the sidewalk. And there were gardens behind each house, often vegetable plots too.

"What do you know about her?" Porthos asked. "Her family?"

Aramis shrugged again. "She was not from a family far above mine, but early on, her sister and she became play-mates to Anne of Austria. I believe the Princess chose them herself, and enjoyed their company above all other mates. So when it was decided that the Queen would marry the King, the Queen decided that a French marriage should be arranged for Violette, also, so that Violette could accompany her to France and be her companion in her new life. So the marriage with de Dreux was arranged. And the Queen supplied the dowry required by the Duke's family. I don't think they've ever even lived together."

Porthos nodded. "And her sister?" he asked.

"The Queen's sister?"

"No, you fool, not the Queen's. Your . . . Violette's."

"Oh, I don't know," he said and then, remembering the babble of Leda in the chapel at his mother's house. "Wait, I do. Her sister is a nun in some monastery near the border with Spain, and is developing a reputation for sanctity. At least that's what I heard from . . . one of my mother's protégées."

Porthos looked inquisitively at Aramis, but said only, "Did she have a miniature of her sister? Or a painting? Or some other means by which we might recognize her?"

Aramis shook his head. "No. In fact, she rarely spoke of her sister. Though I know she wrote to her, now and then."

He had no idea why Porthos would want to see a portrait of Violette's sister. Except that this was Porthos. He might very well have the idea that the quickest and most expedient way to cure Aramis's shock and grief over Violette was to find the convent where Violette's sister was professed and kidnap her for Aramis.

Aramis smiled, at the thought. And though it would be insane, he would likely still be grateful to Porthos. Oh, not for the woman, but for the thought, and the desire to make Aramis feel better. Right now Aramis wasn't sure he ever would.

Porthos stopped in front of a somber house, and lifted his hand to knock, but before knocking, he whispered to Aramis, "Remember, once anyone comes, that your last name is Coquenard, and that you're Monsieur Coquenard's distant cousin. Your poor old mother died, and you have come to Paris to apprentice as a clerk. You were brought up in a convent. That will account for—"

"Porthos, I could not have been brought up in a convent." And to Porthos's quizzical look. "I am still male, Porthos."

"Oh," Porthos said. "You were brought up in a monastery. We were speaking of convents and I got confused. The monastery will account for your fine hand and your knowledge of Latin. You do not know me and only asked me to escort you across town in the dark of night, because you were afraid of robbers or murderers."

"Then perhaps you should keep this," Aramis said, undoing his belt and handing it to Porthos. "Clerks rarely wear swords."

"An excellent point," Porthos said, buckling Aramis's sword belt alongside his own.

"Won't they be suspicious?"

"Of someone coming and offering excellent skills for low wage? Aramis, even if Monsieur Coquenard thought you were the devil himself, he would keep you as long as he could. As for Madame Coquenard, she will know better, but Athenais knows when not to speak. And she'll enjoy having someone in the house who understands her."

Aramis must have given Porthos an alarmed look. Because when Porthos said that, about understanding her, Aramis thought of all the women who, throughout the years, had thrown themselves at him and declared themselves madly in love with him. What if that happened to Madame Coquenard too?

But his look of panic was met with a genuine grin and a chuckle from Porthos. "Oh, Aramis," he said. "I don't fear your competition. You can dazzle your duchesses and enthrall your princesses, but I think that Athenais is just mine, and I wouldn't trade her for all the crowned heads in Europe."

Speaking that way, he lifted his hand and knocked hard on the door. When no one answered he repeated the action. After a long while, the door opened a sliver and a head appeared—a disheveled young male head, looking like it had just woken up.

"Good morning," Porthos said, all happy courtesy. "I have brought someone who wishes to speak to Monsieur or Madame Coquenard."

The young man gave them a weary eye. "It will have to be the mistress. If we wake the master like that, this early in the morning, it will kill him."

"Well, the mistress then," Porthos said, in the tone of one who thought this by far the worst alternative. "But make it quick. Tell her that Monsieur Porthos and Monsieur Francois Coquenard are waiting."

"Francois?" Aramis asked, as soon as the door closed, and the young man presumably retreated into the house to call his mistress.

"Would you prefer Rene?" Porthos asked.

Aramis could only shake his head.

Moments later, Madame Coquenard—wearing a cap, and a dressing gown, appeared at the door. When he first saw her, Aramis was shocked. Oh, Porthos might lack the sophistication of the court, but surely even he could attract a woman whose skin wasn't lined, whose eyes weren't sunk from worry, and whose hair didn't have many silver strands entwined in it.

And then, Athenais Coquenard raised her head. And Aramis found himself staring into the most intelligent eyes he'd ever seen in any woman. And realized that the woman had noticed and marked his look of distaste.

"Madame," Porthos said. "This gentleman who says his name is Francois Coquenarde, claims to be your husband's sixth cousin and has come from the provinces to seek a post as a clerk in your husband's firm. He says he had a letter of introduction from his unfortunately late mother, and that it was stolen from him when ruffians set upon him on the way."

Porthos's playacting wouldn't deceive a child. He recited the whole thing in a monotone, and Aramis was about to bristle with resentment at it, when he realized that, in fact, if Porthos were repeating what some new acquaintance had just told him, or someone he'd escorted across town out of charity, and whom he never intended to see again, he would not speak it with any more feeling than that.

Athenais looked Aramis over, then looked back at Porthos, her eyebrows raised. "Is this going to bring us any problems?" she asked.

"Harboring a distant relative who will help in the office?" Porthos asked. "I doubt it."

"If he can help in the office. Can you, Monsieur?"

"I was brought up by the church, madame," Aramis said, bowing. "And I write quite a convent hand." This with a teasing glance towards Porthos.

Madame Coquenard frowned at the word convent, but then she must have caught the flicker of amusement in Porthos's eyes and known this for a joke. She bowed slightly. "So long as he pulls his own weight and demands no privileges, nor complains of the food, I'll keep him here, then," she said. And, with a look at Porthos. "And safe."

The Matter of the Knife; A Dead End

Monsieur de Treville had offered them a room. Or rather, d'Artagnan thought—as the servant led him into the small but well-appointed room which actually had three narrow beds, a trunk for clothes, a washbasin, a pitcher of water and even towels—Monsieur de Treville had offered Athos a room for the night.

D'Artagnan was aware—and had no doubts—that no one would make such gestures to him. He didn't resent it, any more than he resented that, without Athos, he'd not have been able to stay at the home of the Duke de Dreux.

If people had made such gestures for Athos just because he was, presumably, a count in disguise, d'Artagnan might have felt the sting of envy. But he knew that with Athos, people reacted as much to his nobility of character as to his nobility of birth.

What he resented was that he'd been sent up, with the servant, ostensibly to look at the room, but in fact so that Athos could speak with Monsieur de Treville in relative privacy.

He ambled over to the bed on the right side of the room and sat down on it. Even though it was a narrow and clearly a collapsible bed of some sort, it felt softer and springier beneath him than his bed at home ever had.

He realized he'd only slept a few hours tonight even though night had almost fully become morning and a thin, grayish light was starting to shine through the window.

With a gesture, he sent the servant away, indicating that he found the room adequate enough. He didn't know if Athos would find it equally satisfactory, but then d'Artagnan was just a Gascon from a poor household. He could never and would never be able to understand the tastes of a French count.

Bending down he removed his boots, thinking that he would lie down and close his eyes and wait for Athos.

He woke with the bedroom door closing and with what sounded like stealthy footsteps. By instinct, he unsheathed his sword, and found himself, fully awake, sitting up, sword in hand ... looking at Athos, who stood in the middle of the room, managing to appear, at once, alarmed and amused.

"I beg your pardon," d'Artagnan said, sheathing his sword. He glanced towards the window, where the light was now full. In fact, from what d'Artagnan could determine, it was now possibly close to noon. With the light, noises filtered in through the window—vendors calling their wares, an insistent hammering, probably from some near-by workshop. Through the door came the incessant sea of noise from the antechamber. The yells of men, the confusion of brags and gossip, of jokes, the occasional sound of swords which meant that someone was playing king of the mountain on the staircase and defending it with his sword against all challengers.

Athos held a bundle of dark fabric in one hand and looked so tired he was swaying slightly on his feet. The middle bed, which d'Artagnan had mentally thought Porthos would occupy, was empty. "Porthos?" he asked Athos.

The older musketeer looked momentarily surprised, as though he'd forgotten all about Porthos or their agreement to meet here.

D'Artagnan rose, started looking for his boots. "He was waylaid," he said. "Someone found him and Aramis. They tried to kill them once again and were successful. They—"

Athos smiled. He made his way to the farthest bed, laid the bundle of cloth beside him and sat down, to remove his boots.

"Athos, you don't understand, they could even now, be preparing to sell their lives dearly."

Athos shook his head. "I've known Porthos for five years," he said. Having removed his boots, he looked down, with a dismayed expression, at his stockings which were a mass of holes, then shrugged. "I know something of the way he works. That expression he had, while we explained our theory to Aramis? Porthos has some theory of his own, or thinks we are fools for some reason, and he will not come back, he will not rest until he has either proven his theory or so totally disproved it that even he might give it up." Athos frowned at his breeches as he started unlacing them. "d'Artagnan, do you know what kind of abuse one receives when crossing the antechamber twice wearing what is clearly the breeches of the uniform for the Cardinal's guard?"

D'Artagnan blinked, realizing for the first time—so busy had they been—that Athos's breeches were not only clearly a great deal too small for the musketeer, straining at the seams and ending a couple of palms below his knees but we're also red. He remembered the story of how Fasset had helped Athos, and presumed the breeches were his. However, he must still have been staring in horror at Athos when Athos looked up.

"Mine were utterly ruined," he said. "Between the sword thrust and the mud, and my ripping them further, in the dark, to try to feel the wound and assess my odds of surviving it."

A shiver ran up d'Artagnan's back. It was so much like Athos, and not like anyone else at all, that clinical examination of a wound while he was alone, in the dark. D"Artagnan didn't doubt for a moment that, had the musketeer decided the wound was fatal and he could not survive it, he would have laid back down in the mud and patiently waited for death.

The idea was so disturbingly likely, and so inhuman, that d'Artagnan felt he had to banish it from his head. "So Porthos will come back to us when he has proven his theory wrong?" he asked.

"Or correct." Athos had removed his breeches and was pulling on linen under breeches and a pair of dark blue breeches, clothes that—clearly—Monsieur de Treville had loaned him. He met d'Artagnan's gaze, then looked down again, to tie his breeches together. "Porthos is not stupid, d'Artagnan, nor is he always wrong. You should not confuse facility with words with intelligence, though the two often work together. Look at Porthos, and the size of him. Can you not believe that everyone in his family, generation after generation, was trained as a warrior or a guardian? And that both they and those who employed them, found little use for a cultured mind in a body that was twice as large and strong as anyone else's?"

"I didn't think Porthos stupid," d'Artagnan said, then felt heat on his cheeks. "Well, at least not since I first met him. After I got to know the three of you a little better, I could not imagine either you or Aramis having a close friend who was impaired in judgment or thought."

He'd noted the bandage on Athos's thigh, stained with blood, and he wondered how Athos's judgment was, on the other hand. What kind of man runs and then fights duels while nursing a wound through the thigh?

D'Artagnan was starting to suspect that Athos was not fully human or more than human. He didn't know which, but whichever it was it gave the older musketeer a glittering hard edge that both made him capable of accomplishing the impossible and kept all people—even his closest friends—at a distance.

"But Porthos must be wrong," d'Artagnan said. "He has to be. Our theory is the only one that makes sense."

Athos inclined his head, and shrugged, as he finished tying his breeches and slipped on a clean doublet of the old-fashioned type he preferred.

The clothes seemed to fit perfectly, d'Artagnan noted, and wondered if Monsieur de Treville kept clothes in all sizes around, just in case one of his musketeers arrived without breeches. Having seen the unruly mob in the antechamber, he could well believe that they ruined several breeches and doublets, tunics and shirts per day.

"We might have been wrong about this, d'Artagnan. Or at least, I think we've hit a dead end," Athos said.

d'Artagnan said nothing, as he wasn't absolutely sure of what the older musketeer spoke of.

Athos sat on his bed. "I asked Monsieur de Treville about the knife. It occurred to me that he spends a lot more time with the King than we do, and he has known the King much longer. In fact, so far as the King has any friends and not merely courtiers, we'd have to admit that Monsieur de Treville is one of them. And the Cardinal, possibly, the other." Athos shrugged. "I apologize for sending you upstairs but I was afraid the captain wouldn't speak frankly with you there. He has at least as high a regard as the Cardinal for the King's reputation and for protecting it, even from his musketeers. Though I doubt," he said, and permitted one of his quick smiles. "That Monsieur de Treville intends to send men to kill us just to prevent us from talking."

"The men—" d'Artagnan started, as it occurred to him that the last time they'd killed a large number of guards it had occasioned an incident at the court.

"I've forewarned Monsieur de Treville. In fact, even now, he should be at the palace, complaining to the King about how the Cardinal sent a mob to kill his innocent musketeers."

"I hope he gets there before the Cardinal," d'Artagnan said.

"He will, or he'll find a way to get the King's ear and convince him. Trust the captain, d'Artagnan. He would not have kept his post all these years if he couldn't convince the King that we are not an undisciplined bunch of ruffians." This time the brief grin was far more than an elusive smile. "Which, at times, must take some skill and effort." Athos looked up, fully. "But the knife, d'Artagnan, and who might have owned it, will apparently lead us nowhere."

"Why?" d'Artagnan asked blinking. "Was it truly the King's and no one else's? Was it . . . Did . . ."

"You must banish the thought from your head," Athos said. "Even if he had, he would be our lord and liege." He shook his head. "But I doubt it. Our . . . His weakness is not of the sort that strikes out suddenly, with a knife. If he'd truly felt such a great animus against the woman, he would have exiled her or hounded the Cardinal to make her life miserable. He's done it often enough, before, to other friends of the Queen. No. The reason I say the knife is a dead end, is that I believe it was in possession of the Duchess herself."

"The Duchess?"

"Monsieur de Treville says he was with the King, when the King sent the knife, via a valet, to Madame de Dreux as a sign that her scandalous and immoral behavior had her walking on the thin edge of the King's good graces. This was the day before the murder."

"A knife? He sent an ivory knife of such manufacture as a warning?" d'Artagnan asked.

"You have to remember he pays very little attention to such things, which he considers mere trinkets. And sending a knife saved him the need to write a letter—a task to which he is at least as averse as our dear Porthos."

"But then . . ." d'Artagnan said. He couldn't imagine how Athos, wounded, tired, could still think clearly. Thoughts trickled through d'Artagnan's mind like bubbles in mud, each in complete isolation and seemingly invisible from the others. It was an effort to string them together. "But then the knife would be in the Duchess's room." He could imagine the object, tossed carelessly on one of the many ornate side tables, amid books and discarded jewelry and who knew what else. "And the murderer might simply have got hold of it as a convenience. You are right. We are indeed at a dead end."

Athos nodded. "Only perhaps," he said, as he lay back on the bed. "We'll be lucky and Porthos's investigations won't be as fruitless as ours. He was, perhaps, right and the intruder in the room was the murderer. Perhaps—"

But Athos stopped, and d'Artagnan realized that he, himself, had toppled onto his bed, and his eyes were closing of their own accord.

"Sleep, d'Artagnan," Athos said. "It's a been a long day and a longer night. I doubt the morning daylight will keep us awake."

D'Artagnan took the words with him into deep sleep. Sometime later, he thought he heard Porthos come in, open the door, close it. The shudder of the middle bed as Porthos collapsed on it made d'Artagnan smile in his sleep.

Sometime later, still in the depths of a dream, d'Artagnan was aware of one of his friends leaving the room.

Fire and Color; The Very Deep Reasoning of Porthos; Where Aramis Becomes Acquainted with a Different Side of Petticoats

Porthos came to Monsieur de Treville's house late. He'd been looking for acrobats, but found none, and finally exhaustion led him to Treville house, where he was directed to a room in which d'Artagnan and Athos lay asleep—Athos face up, arms at his side, looking like a marble statue upon a noble tomb; d'Artagnan sprawled, one arm above his head, a leg angled towards the floor.

Porthos looked at them and smiled. He couldn't understand these two and their conviction that the Cardinal was trying to . . . kill them, make them seem guilty of murder, and who knew what else they might have come up with to ascribe to His Eminence by now.

Shaking his head, he collapsed on the middle bed, and fell into a deep sleep. Only to wake with what seemed like the dim light of sunset coming through the window.

He started at the reddish light. He truly didn't want to stay till they woke and have to listen to them discuss the Cardinal's designs to their fate as though they were vitally important to the most powerful man in France. So important, in fact, that he would go to all this trouble just to do something to them. He didn't want to be told that the person on the balcony was a prank or a dream.

Fine, he was willing to concede it was probably not a ghost, since ghosts didn't need to disguise themselves and rarely wore masks. But in the same way, why should a prank or a dream disguise herself and wear a mask.

He got up quietly and got out of the room and out of Treville house through the back gate, unnoticed.

Last night he had been working towards something. There was, in his mind, as yet mostly hidden, a shape, a puzzle that was about to be completed. He felt as though he had all the pieces. Almost. But not quite yet.

In fact, the problem was that Porthos didn't seem to be filling in a puzzle but two, and he didn't know where, in the middle, the puzzles would converge. Or if they would.

On one hand, he still thought the right way to find out who had killed Aramis's Violette was to find out who could have done it. In the circumstances, this immediately limited the field. And Porthos had an idea as to that. It had started forming when he first saw the acrobats on the street, leaping about, walking on stilts.

Oh, he took Athos's opinion on that, that it was unlikely anyone would feel comfortable walking on stilts near the palace: That near the palace. Though Porthos didn't view it as impossible. That by itself was manageable. Put the stilts near the tree, totter across, remove them. Porthos knew enough of how these big houses worked to suspect that two boards leaning up against a balcony would not particularly call anyone's attention.

No, the problem there was that Porthos did not believe it was possible for anyone to walk on stilts tall enough to reach the balcony.

But there were other things. He had seen acrobats flip and dive midair, with every appearance of near flight. If they could do that, perhaps they could reach the balcony from the tree. After all, even Aramis had managed to survive going the other way.

As he thought this, he heard the noise of an acrobat troupe down the street. He let his feet walk that way, because he thought he should watch this. Acrobat troupes, who performed on the street and did everything from short burlesques to juggling, thronged to Paris in the spring and early summer. They came from as far away as Italy or Spain. And this fit, in Porthos's head with the image of the person in Violette's room. Perhaps she had looked as though she were performing because she was, in fact, used to performing. She was used to cavorting around on the street, for the entertainment of the crowds. Every gesture, every movement would have been honed to entertain, to please, to call attention. Hence, the exaggerated kissing of the cross.

But the cross was a problem. As was why the woman would cover her face. The only reason for her to cover her face would be if she was known at the palace. Or thought she would be known at the palace. Which was why Porthos had asked Aramis if Violette had a portrait of her sister.

Of course, the idea of a nun becoming an acrobat was insane. But then, hadn't Athos said that Fasset, the Gascon fighting demon, almost as lethal as d'Artagnan himself, had been brought up to be a monk? Why shouldn't an acrobat have been brought up to be a nun?

But alas, Violette didn't seem to have a picture of her sister.

What then? Was it possible that the acrobat was someone else? Someone from Violette's family? If it weren't that Athos was so sure it was a woman, Porthos would suspect an ex-lover of the Duchess.

He stopped, as he'd reached the edge of the street carnival, and he watched, with divided attention, his mind going through the steps of imagining who or what could have done it. Perhaps a minor noblewoman whose lover Violette had stolen? Perhaps that woman had become an acrobat and then . . .

His eyes, with very little attention from his brain, looked over fire-eaters and dancers, and a man who was making a bear do very amusing tricks.

Porthos wondered how to find out if there were any troupes from Spain in the capital, and then it came to him that, of course, the people most likely to know would be the acrobats themselves. He didn't quite know how it worked, but he imagined that living a vagabond life, and playing on the streets for coin, they'd all bump into each other a lot.

He plunged his fingers into his sleeve, looking for his small purse where he kept his ready money and change. If he meant to get answers out of these people, he would need to pay them.

Pushing through the crowd, with his huge frame, he made it to the edge, near the dancers. And when one of them twirled close, he asked, as close as he could come to a whisper, "Mademoiselle, pssst, mademoiselle?"

She looked at him, so startled that she missed her step. Her motley skirt, in sparkling colors and much too short— displaying her leg almost to the knee—fell.

Porthos whispered again, "Mademoiselle," and took care to make sure the coin pinched between his two fingers sparkled enough for her to see. Her eyes widened and she whispered something to the girl next to her, then she sidled up to Porthos.

"Can you wait?" she asked. "Till after the show? Then we can go to your room or—"

"Mademoiselle?" Porthos said, not sure what she was talking about and certain that she was confusing him with someone else. And then he realized that possibly these girls, who danced and twirled and performed acrobatics for the amusement of the crowds might also do other things, on the side, for the amusement of strangers. He shook his head, and held the coin just poised over her fingers. "I only want to ask you a question," he said.

She looked puzzled for a moment, then smiled. "Then I am at your disposal, gentleman, provided I know the answer."

"Well, the coin is yours whether you do or not. All I want to know is, are there any Spanish troupes in town? That you know about?" He saw her start to move her head and said, "Or any other troupes that might make to Spain in . . . other seasons."

The girl laughed, a pleasant, musical sound. "As to that, gentleman, all of us go into Spain when the weather turns cold in France. Sometimes as far as the South of Spain. And all of our troupes have members from Spain and France both—and sometimes from Italy for those troupes that go that far. Whoever runs away from home, or is sent away, or just wants to be a member. You understand?"

Porthos nodded. He understood. He started to hand off the coin, but then stopped. "I'll pay you in either case, but if you'd answer just one more question."

She said, "Well, that's far more than one, but—" She looked at the coin in his fingers. "You are being generous with your money, so ask."

"What other troupes are there in town, just now? How many? Where are they performing?"

She grinned. "Right now I know of six, and the nearest ones are performing there." She pointed. "At the Plaza de Saint Anne. "And one there—at where the street of Saint Antoine meets cobbler's street."

Porthos let the coin fall. "Thank you mademoiselle." And, with that, he stalked away, in the direction she'd pointed, still thinking.

He knew if he told his friends anything about his idea, that an acrobat had done it, they'd both laugh at him. Both being d'Artagnan and Athos, of course. He supposed Aramis might listen—Aramis seemed very subdued since all this had happened. None of which meant that Porthos thought that Aramis would believe him.

It would seem impossible to them—it seemed somewhat unlikely to him—that the lives of a duchess and an acrobat should intersect so much that one would wish to kill the other.

But the thing was, they were living in strange times. Porthos remembered the stories from his father and his grandfather. There was a time, and not so long ago, when noblemen were noblemen and peasants were nothing but dust under the noblemen's feet.

Porthos wasn't sure when it had all changed, but he suspected it was with commerce, and craftsmen, and, of course, accountants. Some of them had started making more money than the fixed incomes of the noblemen. And then there was the sad fact that no nobleman could keep serfs on his land, anymore. Or not without giving some real care and thought to keeping those serfs and tenants happy. Long gone were the days when a nobleman treated his serfs not much better than his oxen. If he did treat them better.

Nowadays, a serf, a craftsman, a tenant who was ill-treated could always leave the land and disappear into one of the big cities, where he could easily make money from learning a craft or becoming a servant to a wealthier man. Not a lot of money, and the life wouldn't be easy. But it would be easier than in most feudal domains.

And then, the sons of the lords, those who, left without serfs and servants, saw their rents diminish by the day, left their lands, too, and came to Paris. That was Porthos's story, and d'Artagnan's too. Athos's was, of course, different, as was Aramis's. But Porthos would wager that there were far more people like him in the city than people like Athos and Aramis.

In the city, as in a big pot, stirred by disruption and need, the more prosperous sons of the newly rich interacted with the sons of the poor old families. And sometimes, too, both of them fell a long deal lower than either of the classes would like to admit. Sometimes—Porthos smiled into his moustache—noblemen's sons became musketeers. And perhaps noblemen's daughters or repudiated wives became acrobats?

He stopped, short of the second troupe, and watched them perform. The stuff was much what he had seen the other troupe do. Only this troupe, instead of a trained bear, had a little troupe of trained dancing dogs, dressed in the fashion of the day, the bitches as court ladies, the male dogs as musketeers.

Porthos watched the performance and roared—as the crowd around him laughed too—as one of the dogs dressed as a musketeer tried to mount one of the bitches dressed as a court lady. An endeavor persisted upon until the trainer bodily dragged him, whining, away.

Walking away, Porthos found himself smiling still. Sometimes, he thought to himself, these shows had a way of showing truth that was more true than truth itself.

The thought crossed his mind that the dog dressed as a musketeer probably had another outfit that was a cassock, and that the trainer, clearly, was only waiting till the dog was ready to put the cassock on him. And the dog's name would be Aramis.

He was still amused as he approached the third group of acrobats. They had a larger attendance and, from a distance, Porthos heard a barker's voice. It wasn't until he got closer that he understood the words though.

"A daring, death defying feat," the barker was saying. "You will see Violeta walk on sheer air between these balconies."

Porthos looked up at the balconies. As far as he could tell, in the night air, and so far above the torches that lit the street level, there didn't seem to be anything between the balconies.

And then the girl appeared. And Porthos held his breath. She was as blond as Aramis, though her hair was caught up and tied with a giant bow. The rest of her attire was masculine, a bright, sparkling suit in red and purple, shimmering in the night air. She wore slippers. And she was walking, midair, between the two balconies.

Magic, Porthos thought. Only he didn't believe in magic. "There must be a way," he said.

The man next to him snorted. "Oh, there is. I saw them set it up just before nightfall. It's a very thin rope. In twilight, you cannot see it. To be honest, it's so fine you can't see it in daytime either, or not very well. It is made of silk and very strong. Some strange eastern art."

"She's walking on a rope?" Porthos asked. "That must be devilishly difficult."

The man shrugged. He was attired in peasant clothes, with an immense leather apron that meant he was probably a smith. "It's as with everything else," he said and shrugged. "You practice enough that you do it without thinking. Not that accidents don't happen. Last year a boy who did this, with this troupe, in fact, plunged to his death from the rope. We barely had the time to get the crowd out of the way. And even then, he fell so near my shoes, he splashed them with blood and brains." The man looked down at his boots, as if the splashes of blood and brains might still be visible, and he went on talking, in an animated voice.

But Porthos was no longer listening to him. He was looking up at the blond woman, who seemed eerily familiar. The strange thing was, though he'd only seen Aramis's lover once or twice and from a distance, she looked exactly like that.

But how could it be? Porthos had already decided that she couldn't possibly be a ghost. Ghosts didn't wear masks.

He remembered that d'Artagnan, and perhaps Athos had seen the woman up close. And then there was Aramis. It would be dangerous for Aramis to come out. These twilights in summer could last forever, and be bright enough to recognize anyone by. But Porthos would ask Athenais. Athenais would have some idea. Aramis was, of course, the ultimate authority. Plus, if this woman was his Violette— and hadn't the barker just called her Violeta—surely she would respond to him, and stop when she saw him. Perhaps it was all tied up with her being pregnant? Perhaps she'd had to escape to hide it.

Though looking up, at the slim figure in its male attire, Porthos could not discern any signs of her being pregnant. But then . . . you never knew.

He leaned close to the man who had stopped talking, but who was still watching the wire walker with a fascinated expression, as though sure that at any minute he would get more blood and brains on his shoes.

"How late do they perform," Porthos asked.

"Usually till full dark."

Porthos nodded and squinted at the East. He thought he had an hour, perhaps a little more. He didn't want to wait any longer, didn't want to put it off for another night because, with the troupes' itinerant habits, who knew where they would be tomorrow?

Quickly, he turned and almost ran all his way back home. There was no point inviting arrest by going through the front door, near which the bodies of the guards must already have been discovered. So he approached his house through the network of alleys, till he came to the alley that ran behind the property, where he jumped atop the low wall and . . .

And stared right up at Mousqueton, who was standing atop the henhouse—clearly, from his fresh clothes and bright look, on his way out—and looking puzzled.

"Monsieur," the servant said.

Porthos grinned at Mousqueton's discomfiture. Even if he had to figure out Mousqueton's next attempt at disobedience, for now it was

worth it just to see the self-assured Mousqueton look scared and confused.

"Good to meet you, Mousqueton," he said, without giving away that
he was in any way surprised, and without explaining why he, himself,
was standing atop the low wall. "I need you to run to the Treville house.
Go in through the back, as there might be people watching for us or our
servants. Once inside, ask Athos and d'Artagnan—who are probably in
one of the guest rooms—to meet me at the corner of Saint Antoine and
cobbler's street as soon as possible. There will be a show, and I'll be in
the crowd."

He jumped off the low wall, and started running again, this time
towards Athenais's house. If he ran all the way, he figured he could get
Aramis back in time. Or if Aramis could not for some reason come and
didn't trust his disguise in the twilight, then Porthos would at least
have the opinions of Athos and d'Artagnan on how much this Violeta
looked like Aramis's Violette.

Porthos was not even going to try to guess how all this fit into the
plot, or how Violette could really be alive. All he wanted to know was if
it was the same woman.

He arrived at the Coquenard home and walked around it, to the alley
at the back. This time, he didn't think it was the kind of visit he could
bluster with disguise, past the servants and the household watchers.

Instead, he went around the back. Long ago, Athenais and Porthos
had worked out a system whereby he pelted her window with pebbles,
and she let down a rope ladder. After Porthos climbed it, Athenais
locked her bedroom door, and the two of them could stay together till
dawn, uninterrupted.

Of course, sometimes Porthos erred and pelted with gravel the window next to Athenais—that of her husband, Monsieur Coquenard. This
always led to problems and delays, which he was not willing to countenance now. So he threw carefully.

It occurred to him belatedly that it was rather early and Athenais
might not be in her room yet. But then Athenais opened her window
almost immediately.

She leaned down and her eyes widened at seeing him standing in
the garden. "Porthos," she said, leaning down. "It is too early. I was
dressing for dinner."

Porthos shook his head. "I just need to speak to you," he said.

Athenais hesitated for a moment, then let the rope ladder down.
Porthos climbed it with the agility of long practice. But once at the top,
he didn't try to jump into the room.

Instead, with all speed—because while on the ladder he was, of
course, susceptible to discovery—he gave her an account of everything that had happened, from Violette's murder to the show he'd just
watched.

And Athenais, proving once more that there was a reason Porthos loved her, understood the account, though it was a garbled version of the events, even for Porthos.

She nodded once. "So you need Aramis, and Aramis cannot be seen abroad until full night, just in case someone recognizes him, since doubtless the Cardinal has a price on his head."

Porthos nodded. "But by that time the acrobats will be gone!"

Athenais twisted her lips to the side, something she did when in deep thought. "Very well, Porthos, but . . . I'll have to tell him it was your idea. I am guessing if I tell him it's mine, he will not cooperate."

"What was my idea?"

"Never mind, Porthos," she said. "Trust me. I'll open the front door in fifteen minutes, and send him out to you. Be waiting."

Puzzled, but trusting his mistress implicitly, Porthos nodded and held onto the window sill, ready to start his descent of the rope ladder.

Before he could step down, though, Athenais reached for him. She put her lips over his, and kissed him, ardently. Dazed, it was all Porthos could do to hold on.

As she pulled away, he was sure he still looked dazed, because she wiped his mouth with her palm, then giggled as she said, "You are a fool man who makes me get in adventures a woman should not have to engage in."

And with that dubious blessing, she sent him down the ladder and pulled the window closed.

He walked around the house, then paced up and down the street, attempting to look unremarkable, which he had some inkling was a lot like his trying to look like a bird or a frog.

At long last the front door of the Coquenard home opened, and Porthos hastened towards it. But the person who came out was not Aramis.

It was a tall woman, in a green velvet dress, ornamented at chest and waist, and hemline with a profusion of frills. Her waist was tiny, her bosom abundant, almost large enough to offset very capacious shoulders straining the seams of the tight dress. On her head was a matching hat, with a broad brim. A veil fell down to hide her face.

"Oh, pardon me, mademoiselle," Porthos said, removing his hat and stepping back. "I thought you were someone else."

"Porthos!" Aramis's voice spoke from beneath the veils.

Porthos looked again. Well, when he had said he'd know Aramis no matter in what disguise, he'd been lying. Although, now that he looked closer, he could see Aramis's long hair, tied with a series of bows at the back.

Having trouble keeping from laughing, Porthos lifted the veil and stared into Aramis's maddened green eyes. "Oh my," he said, in a tone of awe. "Athenais has a sense of humor."

"She said it was your idea," Aramis said, his voice low and vicious.

Porthos let the veil drop, and turned around, offering his arm to Aramis as he would to a lady. "Well, she is right that no one will ever recognize you in this attire." He bit his lips to keep back the guffaws and said, "The . . . uh . . . the . . . front of your dress . . . ?"

"Cushions," Aramis said, indignantly. "She stuffed cushions there."

He tried to keep his laughter silent, but Aramis's head was turned towards him, and he must have seen Porthos hide his mouth with his free hand, while his shoulders shook.

"I have a sword," Aramis said. "Underneath the skirt. I'm wearing a sword. I made her find me a sword."

"Indeed," Porthos said, and gave in to mirth. Aramis might be well disguised, but all the same Porthos was glad they didn't cross paths with anyone, because everyone would remember a musketeer laughing so hard that tears ran down his face.

Dancing on a Rope; Not Everything in a Dress Is a Lady; Ghosts

D'Artagnan and Athos, having received the message from Porthos, followed his instructions, though they debated the matter on the way to the rendezvous and neither of them could imagine why Porthos would want them. But, as confused as Porthos often was, he usually didn't summon the others unless he needed them.

Besides, as Athos said, "Our only hope is that whatever theory Porthos has been pursuing is right."

And d'Artagnan had to hope that with all his heart.

But he couldn't understand why or how this could be true. Particularly because the place they were told to meet Porthos was an intersection taken up by a troupe of traveling acrobats.

Athos seemed to understand it. At least, he said, "Ah!" as they arrived. And, "I see."

But before d'Artagnan could ask him what he saw Porthos arrived. Porthos, as usual, was as impossible to miss or ignore as a galleon at full sail upon a wheat field. He came cutting through the crowd of people, the tallest of whom reached no higher than his shoulder. On his arm, being dragged along was a . . . lady? d'Artagnan blinked, and looked up at Athos, to see if Athos understood this too. Athos had a most disquieting smile upon his lips. So disquieting, in fact that d'Artagnan didn't dare ask him what he saw nor why.

D'Artagnan removed his hat and made a bow in the lady's general direction, not sure why Athos kept his hands planted on either side of his waist. Normally—for all his dislike of females in general—he was the most courteous of men to any particular woman.

Porthos made straight for them. "You arrived," he said. "Good. Now, I want you to pay attention—"

"It is not needed, d'Artagnan," Aramis's voice said and d'Artagnan jumped back and half out of his skin, realizing it came from beneath the hat and the veil.

He stood, open mouthed, staring at Aramis. How? And why?

"It was Athenais's idea," Porthos said. His lips were shaking convulsively and he spoke in what, for him, was a low whisper. "She said it was the perfect disguise, and you must allow it is, but, my word, I wonder what she had against him."

"I have a sword," Aramis's sullen voice said, from beneath the wrappings.

And now Athos's lips too were shaking, and Athos was the closest to laughing that d'Artagnan had ever seen. D"Artagnan couldn't understand what was so funny about it all. The disguise seemed to him perfect and yet he could quite understand Aramis's annoyance at having to wear it. Of course, for him to stop wearing it they must—they truly must—find the murderer of the Duchess.

At any rate, if they didn't, soon Paris wouldn't be safe for any of them. And d'Artagnan still had hopes of being in the musketeers, someday.

He turned to Porthos, "Why did you ask us to meet you?"

"There is someone," Porthos said, "in the troupe, whom I want you to see."

He turned, as if to point someone out, but before he could, there was a noise from Aramis. It wasn't a scream and it wasn't a moan, nor a gasp, nor a sigh, but it had hints of them all and wavered on the spectrum between shock and grief.

D'Artagnan looked the way Aramis was turned and there, seemingly suspended upon the air between two balconies, was a young man. No. A woman. A woman who looked eerily familiar.

Before d'Artagnan could put a name to the look, Aramis sank to his knees. His voice, fortunately strangled by emotion, came out between a whisper and a moan. "Violette," he said. "Violette."

"It cannot be her," Athos snapped. "She's dead."

"Oh, but it is her," Aramis said. "See how she moves upon the air. It is her ghost."

"There are no ghosts," Athos said, his voice so loud that several people turned back to look at them. "There are no ghosts."

"It's a silk rope," Porthos said. "It's a silk rope stretched between the buildings."

But while Porthos and Athos spoke, Aramis had let go of Porthos's arm, and had pushed into the crowd, hurrying, tripping and tangling himself upon his unaccustomed petticoats, but recovering before fully falling, pushing people aside with unfeminine strength, rushing.

"Aramis," d'Artagnan said, and took off after the blond musketeer. He hoped Athos and Porthos would follow too. Aramis was not, d'Artagnan felt, in his right mind, and someone needed to protect him. But if it came to holding the musketeer down, d'Artagnan was not sure he could do it. Aramis was taller than d'Artagnan, and older, and had been a soldier much longer. And, as he was all too fond of reminding them, he had a sword beneath that dainty green skirt.

D'Artagnan couldn't understand it, either, how Aramis's duchess could be up there, dancing on the silk rope. He remembered Aramis's description of the blood and the cold skin, and he knew it couldn't be her. There had to be some other explanation. There just had to be.

Aramis was faster than d'Artagnan and d'Artagnan was still trailing several steps behind as the musketeer reached the building where the rope ended. There, the lithe figure jumped onto the balcony and then scurried down from the balcony on an inconsequential rope ladder.

And Aramis was there, his arms open to receive her, the masculine voice emerging, thick with emotion, from beneath the female attire, "God's blood, Violette, God's blood. I thought you were dead, I thought . . ."

She hesitated upon the rope ladder, a good jump from the ground, frowning down at this strange apparition.

D'Artagnan wasn't sure what was happening, but they'd seen a woman who looked like the Queen before and who yet, clearly, wasn't the Queen. What if this was a stranger? What if she—?

He rushed forward, running.

Aramis removed his hat.

And the woman jumped from the ladder. "Fornicator," she screamed. And, "Corrupción."

She flew at Aramis like a wild cat, tearing at his hair, his face, raining punches upon him.

Aramis stayed very still underneath the assault, looking shocked and never even attempting to make use of his sword.

Porthos and Athos ran by, one on either side of d'Artagnan and rushed to restrain the woman.

Restraining the woman was like trying to hold an eel. At least the thing it brought most to mind was Porthos's experience fishing with his father's steward in the river near their property and coming up with a fresh water eel that writhed and twisted in his ten-year-old hands until Porthos let go of it and it plunged back into the river.

Now there were Athos and Porthos, both, each holding her on one side. And yet she twisted, she flexed, she wrenched her spine this way and that and, as she did it, she rained blows and kicks on Aramis.

All this while the crowd laughed, probably thinking this was part of the act, and Aramis stood there, stricken, staring, his feminine hat in his hand, his face almost utterly devoid of expression.

D'Artagnan, catching up with them, touched Aramis's elbow. Aramis blinked, as though awakening, and turned to stare at d'Artagnan. "It's not her," he said. His voice sounded very young, like the voice of a lost child. "It is not Violette."

D'Artagnan only shook his head.

Porthos had managed to get a firm hold on the girl's arms, and pulled both her wrists together behind her back.

Just then, two large men approached. "It doesn't look as if Violeta wants to go with you," one of them said.

Athos spun around, unsheathing his sword. "Your friend has committed a murder," he said. And while Porthos wondered if this was true, Athos interposed himself between the two men and Porthos, Aramis, d'Artagnan and their prisoner. "We're the King's musketeers," he said.

He saw the two men look at his uniform, then at Porthos's. They cast a dubious look at d'Artagnan's and they stared in wonder at Aramis. But the uniforms and the name of the musketeers had an effect on street performers who lived at the mercy of the local authorities. They stepped back.

One of them asked, "What murder? What has she done?"

But Porthos held the woman and d'Artagnan followed with Aramis, while Athos, with sword unsheathed and his feral face on guarded their retreat. It would take one more foolhardy or braver than could be found in that crowd to oppose them. And besides, the crowd had seen her attack on Aramis.

They retreated into an alley, then along it. "Where are we going?" Athos asked.

"Damned if I know," Porthos said. "We must go somewhere to question this lady."

The "lady" had gone limp in his arms and was muttering in Latin at a speed too high for Porthos to follow, though it sounded to him like Ave Marias.

"I know a man," Aramis said. And as Aramis said it, Porthos felt as if his soul had been set free above human problems and soared towards the heavens. Because it was the characteristic of Aramis that he always knew a man. If you needed a strange garment, a rare vintage of wine or a piece of jewelry unlike any other to be found even in Paris, that capital of the civilized world, Aramis knew a man who could supply it. If you needed a favor, a theological opinion, a dispensation for some act that fell outside church law, Aramis knew a man.

Since the murder of his lover, Aramis hadn't uttered that phrase, and after he'd gone all pale and still back there while the woman attacked him, Porthos had thought never to hear those words again.

But Aramis cleared his throat and said, in a stronger voice. "I know a man, at the sign of The Fighting Saint, up at the next road, to your right. I'll go in. He'll let us have a room at the back, to question her."

Porthos looked dubiously at his friend, who carried the hat in his hand and walked in a thoroughly masculine stride that made mockery of his velvet skirts. If none of the others would remind Aramis that he wore a dress and that this might look funny, then neither would he. He had that feeling from Aramis now that he often got from Athos. That Aramis was poised on the thin edge between madness and sanity and that any push could send him careening into irrationality.

So Aramis took the lead. For reasons known only to him, he slammed the hat down on his head, adjusted the veil around his face and walked into the tavern above whose door hung a sign of a man with a halo holding a bloodied sword.

By the time Porthos got in, holding the woman firmly still, Aramis was leaning on the counter at the back speaking to the host.

Porthos got closer, conscious of the stare of the three or four customers who yet had not the courage to say anything to a giant in a musketeer's uniform or his two equally intimidating friends. Close enough, Porthos realized that Aramis had pulled up his face veil to show himself to the host, and that the host wasn't laughing.

Aramis pulled the veil down, as the host gave him a key. Turning, he led the group down a dark corridor to the side of the counter. The host nodded to them as they went and none of the customers made a sound.

And Porthos realized that Aramis was a genius. If he'd walked in there with his face uncovered and everyone able to see he was male, some would-be hero or other would have got up and objected to four men taking a woman into a backroom—visibly against her will.

But the fact that there was, seemingly, another woman in the mix stopped any acts of would-be heroism in the bud. And they got unmolested to a door that Aramis unlocked to lead them into a small room with no windows and no other door.

Its only furniture was a small table and assorted chairs, which led Porthos to think it was normally rented out to gambling parties.

Aramis locked the door behind them, slid the key into his sleeve, flung his hat into a corner of the room. Turning around, he said. "Let her go, Porthos."

Porthos obeyed, but stood by to hold the woman should she become a snarling fury again. Instead, she fell to her knees, as though she'd lost all strength, and muttered something in Spanish.

Aramis rounded on her, "You're Violette's twin, aren't you? Why did you kill her?"

The woman looked up at Aramis and blinked. For a while it looked like no answer would come, then she said, as if speaking from a great distance, "She was sinning. She had taken her first vows and she was sinning." She blinked at Aramis. "With you. And she told me all about it in her letters, when she deigned to write. Page after page of filthy details of your . . . fornication."

She spoke French well, with a slight accent, and her words seemed to make some sense to Aramis, who bit his lower lip and looked moist eyed. But they made no sense at all to Porthos. "Her first vows?" he boomed.

"When we were children," the woman said, looking now at Porthos with the sort of resignation the musketeer had only seen before in a deer at bay and surrounded by dogs. "Our parents decided that one of us would have a dowry and a marriage. While the other would be a nun. I was the older, so the dowry was mine. But Violeta didn't have a vocation. She was bored in the convent." The woman was crying now, with tears running down her face. "I got to visit her. Sometimes for weeks at a time. Our parents would let me spend time with her." She blinked at Porthos. "When she was ten Violeta took her first vows. But she really didn't want to stay. And I did. I'd listened to the sermons, and I'd listened to the nuns. I wanted to be a nun. Not her. We'd . . . Our parents couldn't tell us apart. We changed. We switched. I stayed in the convent, she went back. Then she got married."

"I thought it would be fine. I thought marriage was a holy vocation too. But as I became more . . . holy, and I thought about it, it didn't seem acceptable. She had taken her first vows. She had promised chastity. And she kept sending me these letters telling of her . . . fornication."

The woman looked towards Aramis. "So I ran away from the convent. I ran away with an acrobat troupe. I practiced . . . Walking on rope. And I ran away. I thought I'd come here to France, and I'd preach to Violeta and she'd either go back to her husband and live as a holy married woman should, or she would give up her . . ." She looked at Aramis again. "Fancy man." She shook her head and two tears ran down her face. "I tried. She wouldn't. She told me to go back to the convent. She told me I was crazy. She told me she didn't believe. What was I supposed to do?" She shrugged and opened her hands, in front of her thighs, as though to signify her inability to control the situation. "What could I do? She wouldn't listen, but she was my sister. So I came back. Many times I came back. And then I thought if I caught her in the act, and preached to her, and exorcized her, the evil spirits would come out."

She looked at each of them in turn. "But then, I used my little rope. It's weighted and you can throw it in such a way that little hooks fasten on the balcony railing. We've done that when we're not given permission to enter the house to hook the rope. And I used my little rope from the tree to the balcony, and walked across it, and looked at the window. Many times. Finally I caught her in bed with him." She pointed at Aramis who blushed. "Then he went away and I went in, and I tried to exorcize her." The beautiful face showed total disbelief. "She laughed at me. She . . . laughed. At me. I couldn't let her go on mocking and sinning. There was a very sinful knife on a nearby table. It had a woman and man, fornicating. I . . . I stabbed her with it." Her jaw went slack. "So much blood. I must confess. I shall never be cleansed."

"And the cross?" Porthos asked.

The woman shrugged. "I thought if I got the little cross she'd received when she took her first vows, it would be as if I'd taken my first vows. And then everything would be well again. It would be as if we were the same person, then."

Having finished speaking she knelt there, looking at all of them, and seeming regretful and sad, but not in the way of a murderess. Rather in the way of a child who has committed a minor offense.

Silence reigned for a while. Athos was looking at his hands, and d'Artagnan had removed his hat, as if he were at a funeral.

"Her name really was Violette?" Aramis asked. "She said her legal name was Ysabella."

The woman on the floor shook her head. "I am Ysabella. She was Violeta. We changed names when we changed places. We went by the other's name. But my true name is Ysabella."

"She told me her true name," Aramis said.

It sounded like an epitaph, Porthos thought. And then realized his friends would go on sitting here, forever, looking at the woman, unless he made a decision.

"I told you it was all a matter of finding who could have got in that way," he said. And then, "Now we must take her to Richelieu. He can talk to her and she can confess. And then he can stop trying to capture Aramis and trying to kill us. And it all can be as it was."

"No,"Aramis yelled. "No."

"No?" Porthos said.

"Please don't deliver her to the Cardinal," Aramis said. "He will kill her."

He realized how odd that sounded when all their eyes turned to him. He opened his own hands, by the side of his body. "Please, understand. She looks like Violette. If she were executed, it would be like watching Violette be killed all over again."

They all looked at him as if he were insane, except Athos, who nodded. "But how can we be sure she won't kill again?" he asked.

Aramis sank to his knees in front of the woman, and delicately tilted her head upwards. "Listen, Ysabella, for that is your name, that you will be called by at the final trumpet. Your only hope is to go back to your convent and live a holy life and expiate your sin, do you understand?"

She moaned in his direction. "I am damned," she said. "I have killed my sister. The sin of Cain is upon me."

"No, not damned. Look, didn't the Lord say those who repent will be saved? Trust me, he did. I studied to be a priest. If you confess your sin." He looked over his shoulder. "d'Artagnan, get paper and ink from the hosteler." Then he turned back to the woman. "If you confess your sin, and you live a holy life, you will yet be redeemed. But you must never leave your convent, you understand. Because if you do, then we'll find out. And if we find out, we'll kill you, and then you'll die unshriven and unprepared with your sins upon you. Do you understand?"

She nodded, with tears in her eyes.

D'Artagnan came back in and set the ink and the paper on the table.

"Now, get up and write your confession and everything will be forgiven. When I am a priest—for you must know I intend to become a priest—I'll read it and I'll give you absolution."

She got up, very composed and sat on the chair and wrote, rapidly, in excellent French. She seemed not to trust Aramis to read Spanish. D"Artagnan read over her shoulder and the confession seemed complete. At the end she signed with both names, Ysabella and Violeta and a string of names, and she handed the paper to Aramis.

"You will become a priest, then?" she asked him.

"Yes," Aramis said. "I promise you."

He unlocked the door and let her go then.

He found his mind turning to Violette's blood, soaking, black, onto the floorboards. When Ysabella talked of the blood it had made Aramis think of his father's study, of the black stain on the floor. Could it be blood? His father's blood? But how?

Porthos's Doubts; Aramis's Appeasement

"**W**hat if she doesn't return to the convent?" Porthos asked. The idea of letting a murderess go seemed insane to him.

Aramis smiled, a sweet smile all the more unnerving for his still wearing a dress. "She will. She is a little crazy. It's a type of madness I understand. She will go to the convent. She will live out her penance. She would be too afraid not to."

It seemed to Porthos that the woman was more than a little crazy. But then, now that he thought of it, so was Aramis. He nodded. "But Aramis, what if the Cardinal doesn't believe that paper. For he's not likely to."

"We'll leave Paris together," Athos said. "My friend Raoul might have need of a small band of armed men. We can—"

Aramis shook his head. He looked . . . like a man who has had a revelation that has turned his world upside down. He retrieved his hat, put it back on his head and pulled the veil down, daintily. "I have a plan," he said.

"You know a man?" Porthos asked, smiling a little.

"No, Porthos. I know a woman."

Sins and Atonement; Where Aramis Refuses to Bend

Aramis hadn't brought Bazin. Until he was sure the Cardinal was not searching for him anymore, he saw no reason to get his servant from his safe place.

As for his friends, he'd left them all lodging together at Treville house, as safe a place as they could find.

And Aramis, having shed his green dress, had donned again the black suit, and the black hat that hid his hair. And he'd ridden a fast horse through most of the day without incident, till, after nightfall, he fetched up at the D'Herblay estate.

Dismounting in front of the main door, he tied his horse to a pillar, and he ran up the stairs, two steps at a time.

A satisfying few minutes of pounding on the door brought three alarmed maids and a footman holding a very thick walking stick. Which was dropped when Aramis removed his hat and was recognized.

"Chevalier!" the footman said, while the women curtseyed.

"Get me Madame D'Herblay," Aramis said, walking past them, hat in hand. "Tell her I will be in the study and I must see her right away."

The footman stared at him. "She won't like being awakened in the middle of the night."

Aramis smiled, conscious that it was not a pleasant smile. "And I won't like to be kept waiting. Kindly remember I've attained my majority, and I'm my father's heir. This is my house. Now get the lady my mother and tell her to hurry."

He walked past them to the study that had been his father's and that his mother kept locked. He took his dagger out and forced the lock.

He then took the candle and candlestick that one of the maids was holding, opened the door wide and entered.

There . . . Right where he stood, on the floor he kicked dust around, to reveal a stain much larger than he'd guessed it to be before. Blood. He had been in enough duels to know a place where a man's blood had flooded out taking his life with it.

When his mother arrived—and she did make him wait a little, though not as much as he'd expected—he was sitting behind the desk.

He had done a cursory search of the drawers, which confirmed what he expected.

"Rene," his mother said from the doorway. "You should have told us you were coming. I would have had your room prepared. I—"

He smiled, his not-nice smile. "Don't trouble yourself, madame. I won't stay long. I just came for your confession. Now sit down and write it." He extended to her a piece of paper, a quill and an inkwell.

"My confession?" Madame D'Herblay asked, taking her still beautiful hand to her still beautiful breast.

"About my father's death."

"I did not kill your father."

"No, madame, you did not. Your lover did," he spoke calmly, factually. "That spot where you stand is soaked with my father's blood. Because I look like him, I am going to assume I am truly his son, but the only way the duel over the woman both he and Richelieu loved would have been fought in this room is if my father came home and interrupted you and your lover. They fought their way down the stairs, and my father backed in here, perhaps because it was his room and therefore he felt safe here. But it didn't protect him, and here your lover stabbed him through the heart, judging by the profusion of blood on the floor."

"How dare you?" Madame D'Herblay said. "How dare you accuse me of adultery?"

"Very easily, madame," Aramis said. "In your husband's desk, in a secret compartment I suspect you knew existed but couldn't figure out how to open, I found a packet of letters I'd wager he removed from your room. The letters are addressed to you. Signed by your Armand. With a note from my father about how he'd removed them from your room and if he should be found dead . . ." Aramis grinned. "I'd guess this is why you kept this room locked and everyone out of it. Because you didn't know where those letters were. These desks are a common design. It is a common secret, madame, with a common spring. If you'd lived more in the world, you'd have found the letters."

Madame D'Herblay was trembling now. She sat in a chair, trembling, and turned her tear-filled eyes to her son. "Don't judge me so harshly. I was so young. All my life, I'd been brought up here. All the life I remembered. I thought of your father more as a brother than as a husband. Armand was . . . exciting. And he told me he loved me." She swallowed, then rallied a little. "And, you must know, it wasn't a murder. It was a duel. Your father was killed in a clean duel. If you ask me to say he was murdered, I can't for that will be a lie."

"Oh, no, you can say it was a duel. You should write it exactly as it happened. You see, it will embarrass your lover that much more, to have his youthful indiscretions revealed and to have it known he was once a lethal duelist." He glared at her. "Now sit down and write, madame, or by the blood, I shall take these letters to the local magistrate and tell him I suspect you of having killed my father. By the time you're proven innocent—and that's if anyone subsists in the house who's willing to testify against your former lover, now the most powerful man in France—everyone will know what is behind your facade of piety."

Madame D'Herblay sat down and wrote.

When she was done, Aramis took the packet of letters and her confession, and slipped them into his doublet, near his heart. At the door, he turned back and said, "You weren't sure I was my father's, were you? That's why you determined that I should join the church, both to expiate your sin and to make sure I didn't inherit property I might not be entitled to."

His mother shrugged. "You didn't look so much like your father as a child. I . . ."

"You've said quite enough," Aramis said. "It might please you to know that I have decided I will enter the church, anyway. When it pleases me."

He left the house behind and rode away, thinking that it was probably a sin to enjoy inflicting suffering on one's mother. But his heart felt light and sunny as a summer's day.

Cardinal Doubts; Cardinal Sins; The Importance of Church Latin

"**A**nd why should I believe this letter," the Cardinal asked, dropping the nun's confession onto the table. "And who else will believe it? It seems all insane. Twins and switched identities, and vows." He flicked the confession with the tip of his finger. "I don't know this girl, if she exists. And she sounds more than a little mad, at any rate. Who will believe this, gentlemen?"

He looked up at them and stopped on Aramis. Aramis smiled. He knew he had the way to make the tiger obey him, even if the tiger didn't yet see the whip. It was there, hidden, and ready to be used when needed. And he'd told his friends they would be safe, arranging an audience with the Cardinal. His friends hadn't believed him. They still didn't believe him, judging by the looks they were giving him.

The Cardinal got up, put his hands behind his back and paced. "Frankly, gentlemen, the Queen wants an execution to avenge the murder of her childhood friend and right now, at this moment, only you"—he looked at Aramis— "look good for it. I would, though you'll never believe me on this, prefer not to have to do it. This is why I told you to stay in the country. But you wouldn't listen."

Aramis smiled. "I completely understand, Your Eminence, and yet, I have some papers I think will make you change your mind."

"Papers?" the Cardinal asked.

"Yes. I'll show them to you if my friends would be so kind as to wait outside."

"Outside?" the Cardinal asked.

"Certainly," Aramis said. "We wouldn't want certain . . . facts to be common knowledge. I do not even wish to divulge them to my nearest friends. So if they leave, I'll let you read . . . a document." He gestured for his friends to leave.

After the door closed behind them, Aramis pulled a letter from his sleeve, and set it in front of the Cardinal.

The Cardinal read it, and color fled his cheeks. Still, he looked up and snarled, "What is this? This is not Juana's handwriting."

"Ah, no, it isn't," Aramis said. "Though it is her phrasing. The real letter, as well as the letters you wrote to her and which my father intercepted have been placed with someone whom you'll never guess.

In the unfortunate event that something should happen to me . . ." He shrugged.

The Cardinal looked at him, stricken. "She didn't burn the letters," he said. "Women. They never burn the letters." Then he raised his eyebrows. "You know, for a long while I thought you might be mine. Till you started looking like D'Herblay." He tapped his fingers on the desk. "Perhaps you have something of me all the same. You have a deal Chevalier."

Aramis nodded. "And Fasset, your ex-guard, he is not to be harmed in any way."

"Fasset?" the Cardinal asked. "It would never occur to me to harm Fasset. His conscience is perhaps more delicate than it should be. So he's not suitable to serve me."

"Which is just as well, since Monsieur des Essarts has offered him a post in his guard," Aramis said.

"I see," the Cardinal said. "So it all falls into place, does it? I hope he does well."

OUTSIDE, Aramis found his three friends waiting. He smiled reassuringly at them. "All is well," he said.

"How?" Porthos asked.

Aramis smiled. "Ah, Porthos, the Cardinal and I are men of the world. All you have to know is how to speak his language."

"Well," Porthos said. "That can't be French, because I'm sure people have tried. Is it church Latin?"

Aramis smiled. It was good to have his friends back, but he was as lost as ever when it came to deciding whether Porthos knew he was making a joke or not. Was he teasing Aramis? Or was he really that literal minded? He looked at the giant. It was impossible to tell.

"Jesuit," d'Artagnan said, with a hint of irony in his voice. "I think Aramis spoke Jesuit to him."

"Ah," Porthos said. "That, I never tried."
****

In the street outside, the servants were waiting, with the horses. "There is a letter here for you, Monsieur," Bazin said, bowing to Aramis and extending a letter printed on fine rose paper, which exuded, even from a distance, a smell of roses.

Aramis took it and broke the seal, which, he saw, was a count's insignia. The writing inside was feminine and beautiful, though utterly unknown to him. It informed her dear Chevalier that Leda had decided to marry the boring old Count, after all. And since both of them would be living in Paris now, would the musketeer Aramis condescend to coming and seeing her now and then?

Aramis had to give her credit for having gone to the trouble of finding his assumed name.

"It came by courier to the Treville house, and they sent him on here," Bazin said.

Aramis folded the letter carefully, smiling, and put it in his sleeve.

"Aramis has another seamstress," Athos said, with a hint of mockery in his voice.

Aramis looked at his friend and smiled. "Not yet, Athos. Not yet."

Footnotes

1 *Death of a Musketeer.*

2 *Here it must be allowed that Monsieur Dumas twisted truth, for he claimed that the musketeers had never seen the inside of Porthos's home. This falsehood—fabricated to emphasize Porthos's vanity and entertain Monsieur Dumas's contemporaries—must be forgiven. Monsieur Dumas's main purpose was, after all, to entertain. Now the d'Artagnan Diaries have given it the lie. It is noteworthy that even Dumas slipped, for on the occasion of the famous tennis match, he says the musketeers met at Porthos's.*

3 *Though there was no real uniform for either corps—or at least none was strictly enforced, the musketeers generally wore blue tunics and hats, while the guards of His Eminence wore red ones.*